Murder
at the
Seaview
Hotel

GLENDA YOUNG

Murder at the Seaview Hotel

HEADLINE

First published in 2021 by
HEADLINE PUBLISHING GROUP

1

Cataloguing in Publication Data is available from the British Library

ISBN 978 1 4722 8564 5

Typeset in Adobe Garamond by Palimpsest Book Production Limited, Falkirk, Stirlingshire

Printed and bound in Great Britain by Clays Ltd, Elcograf S.p.A.

HEADLINE PUBLISHING GROUP
An Hachette UK Company
Carmelite House
50 Victoria Embankment
London EC4Y 0DZ

www.headline.co.uk
www.hachette.co.uk

For Grace and Alfie
May you always know the joy of a family
holiday in Scarborough

Acknowledgements

The Seaview Hotel, the Glendale Hotel and the Vista del Mar in this story are fictional hotels and are not based on any hotels in Scarborough. Likewise, Windsor Terrace and King's Parade are fictional streets.

My thanks go to Scarborough's Elvis tribute singer, Tony Skingle, whose invaluable help enabled me to make up my fictional troupe – visit his website at tonyskingleiselvis.me.uk; to Lynn Jackson, VP of Scarborough Hospitality Association; to Angie Pearsall for her help in bringing Suki the greyhound to life; to Jamie, Elaine and Tony of La Baia Hotel in Scarborough; to Norman Kirtlan, Joe Parkinson, Gillian Galway, Iain Rowan of Holmeside Writers, Sunderland, and my little brother Chris Young. To my husband Barry for his love, support and all the frothy coffees that kept me fuelled while writing this book. To my wonderful agent Caroline Sheldon and my editor Kate Byrne at Headline for always pointing me in the right direction. And last but by no means least, to Scarborough, my happy place, always.

Thank you, everyone. I couldn't have done it without you.

Chapter 1

Helen Dexter was sitting on the window seat at the Seaview Hotel, looking out over the sea. The Seaview was her home, a three-storey, ten-room hotel on Scarborough's North Bay. She'd been sitting there all night, gazing out of the window, a bottle of whisky by her side.

It wasn't something she made a habit of, sitting up all night drinking. But then it wasn't every day that she held a memorial service for her late husband, who'd been the love of her life. Helen and Tom had known each other for over thirty years: attended the same schools, gone to the same youth clubs, hung around with the same friends. But it wasn't until their late teens that they finally started dating and became inseparable. Everyone said they were made for each other. They married on a warm July day when she was twenty-one and Tom twenty-three. On their wedding day, Helen pledged her love for Tom in front of their families and friends, vowing to love him and cherish him 'till death us do part'.

How the years had flown by since. Helen was forty-eight now and Tom would have been celebrating his fiftieth birthday in April, a milestone that would now go unmarked.

After Tom's memorial, Helen had invited close friends and family to the Seaview for a bite to eat as a way to say a final farewell to the man they'd all adored. Around her now lay the detritus of half-eaten sausage rolls and glasses stained by wine and beer. Her best friend, Marie, had offered to clean up before she left, but Helen wouldn't hear of it. As the afternoon had dissolved into evening, she had tried hard to disguise how relieved she was when everyone started to leave. She wanted to be on her own, for she had a lot on her mind.

She slid her legs along the window seat and noticed a ladder in her stockings above her right knee. Her calves shone in sheer black nylon seven-denier, smooth as silk and now ruined. She pushed her bobbed hair behind her ears and caught a reflection of herself in the window. Her big brown eyes stared back at her; she was surprised that she didn't look as tired as she felt. Her black jacket hung on a chair and her black shoes lay at the end of the window seat. She'd kicked them off after everyone had left, but when Suki had padded into the lounge, she'd had to lift them from the floor. Suki had a thing about shoes; she liked to chew them and Helen had to be careful about what she left lying around. Suki was sprawled on the floor like a pool of liquid caramel. She was a retired racing greyhound, all long limbs and soulful eyes.

Helen turned back to look out of the window. The sun was beginning to rise now, turning the sky milky blue.

Tom had been ill for months, cancer eating away at him at a cruel, relentless pace. When Helen could no longer manage his pain and care, he'd been moved to St Paul's Hospice. She'd visited daily, sometimes taking Suki so that Tom could see the dog through the floor-to-ceiling window by his bed. Suki would stand outside, cocking her head, staring in at him. As he'd neared the end of his life, Helen had promised him she'd carry on running the Seaview, but he'd been too ill to notice her cross her fingers when the words slipped from her lips.

The small, family-only funeral at St Mary's Church that had marked the end of Tom's life had done him proud. Afterwards, at the crematorium, his favourite hymn had been sung, hugs given and tears wiped away. When his coffin had disappeared behind the curtains, the first soulful notes of his favourite Elvis ballad had played, his only request. He had been an Elvis fan all his life. On the wall of the lounge in the Seaview was a jukebox filled entirely with Elvis songs, but it hadn't been touched since the day Tom was moved to the hospice. Now, more than three months after the funeral, Helen still couldn't bring herself to play it for fear of the emotions that would overwhelm her if she did.

She took a sip of whisky. After the funeral, she had felt unable to cope with her grief. So when Tom's sister Tina had invited her to stay with her and her family on their farm in a remote part of Scotland, she had jumped at the chance. The farm was in the middle of nowhere, far from Scarborough, far from the sea, far from everything that reminded her of Tom. She'd locked up the hotel, bundled Suki into her car, packed a suitcase, put her foot to the accelerator and driven like a woman possessed. She couldn't get away quickly enough.

She'd told Tina she'd only stay a few days, but those days became weeks and ended up turning into three months. Tina had insisted she stay for Christmas, and Helen gratefully accepted her invitation; she couldn't face returning home to spend Christmas on her own. Being on the farm proved restorative for her. She'd helped feed the chickens, and walked the dogs through fields and along streams each morning. Being around Tina's teenage sons, with their energy and vitality, had helped bring her out of herself.

When she'd finally felt strong enough to return to Scarborough, she'd decided to hold a memorial service for her beloved husband, a chance to fully celebrate his life now that she was about to face her future alone. However, something at the back of her mind was troubling her now as she remembered the guests arriving at the Seaview for drinks. It took her a few moments to remember what it was. Two of her best friends, Sue and Bev, had seemed distant with each other and she couldn't figure out why. Had she imagined it, or did Sue make a deliberate show of walking out of the lounge each time Bev walked in? She shook her head to dismiss the thought. She had more pressing things on her mind.

She set her glass on the table and ran her hands over her face. She still had her make-up on, her mask from the day before. But there was no one here to see how crumpled she knew she must look, no matter what her reflection in the window said. In front of a mirror in the harsh light of day, she knew her soft, round face would be pale, and the skin under her eyes dark from lack of sleep. Her plan was to take Suki for a walk, then head to bed to sleep. The Seaview had no guests booked in. Once Tom had taken ill, Helen hadn't the heart or the energy to run the place; it became too difficult even with the help of her staff. She had cancelled all the bookings, emailing the news that due to a family situation the Seaview was taking a break.

Now it was early March, the Easter holidays were around the corner and the holiday season was about to begin, but for the first time in decades, the Seaview was quiet. When asked by disappointed guests, whose holidays she'd had to cancel, if she could recommend somewhere else for them to stay, she gave them the number of the hotel next door. This was the four-star Vista del Mar, run by Miriam Jones, a woman who thought herself and her hotel a cut above Helen and Tom's three-star Seaview. But it wasn't Helen and Tom's now; it was just Helen's, and that scared her more than she dared admit. Because despite the promise she'd given Tom on his deathbed, she wasn't sure she wanted to keep it. What kind of life waited for her on her own in a hotel that catered for families and fun?

She glanced out of the window again. The tide was rolling in, frothy waves breaking. Early-morning surfers, clad head to toe in black to keep out the worst of the North Sea's icy chill, were making their way to the beach.

Helen often felt as if her heart would never recover from losing Tom. He'd been her husband, lover, soulmate and best friend. He had been her life, her everything, for decades. In the early days of their marriage, she'd fallen pregnant twice, but hadn't been able to carry her babies, first a daughter and then a son, to full term. The raw pain never left her, and she and Tom agreed they wouldn't put themselves through more agony by trying again. That was when they'd bought the Seaview. Now, with Tom gone, could she carry on running it alone? Did she even want to?

Her thoughts wouldn't stop; they churned in her mind and kept her awake at night. Her head was all over the place, but she needed to focus because people were depending on her. There was Jean, the cook Tom and Helen had inherited when they took over the hotel. There was single mum Sally, who did the housekeeping and in the past had relied solely on the Seaview for every penny she earned. And could she really defy the deathbed promise she'd given Tom and walk away from everything they'd built up? Everyone had told her not to make major decisions while lost in her grief. But each day she struggled with her instinct to run.

She sighed deeply, glanced back at the sea and lost herself in the comfort of watching the waves, as regular as a heartbeat. And that was when her phone rang.

'Good morning. Is that Mrs Dexter?' a deep male voice said.

Helen glanced at the clock above the bar. It was 8.30. She wondered what sort of person called so early in the day. Was it one of their suppliers? Perhaps it was a guest wanting to book, unaware that the Seaview was temporarily closed despite the notice she'd added to the website.

'Who is this?' she asked.

'Frederick Benson.'

The name meant nothing to her.

'From Benson's estate agents in town,' he continued.

Helen's head felt heavy from the whisky, her eyes were drooping after another night of lost sleep; her whole body felt as if it had done ten rounds in a boxing ring.

'Let me see if she's in,' she said, giving herself a moment to prepare for a conversation she didn't want to have. She leaned back against the window frame, looking out at the surfers. Scarborough was coming to life, with traffic on Marine Drive and early-morning out-of-season tourists out for a stroll. She held her phone at arm's length for a few seconds, trying to focus her mind, before putting it back to her ear.

'Helen Dexter here,' she said as brightly as she could manage.

'Ah, Mrs Dexter, how are you this fine morning? And what

a beautiful morning it looks set to be. Not bad for the time of year.'

Frederick Benson spoke with forced cheer. Helen didn't know the man, yet he was talking as if she was an old friend. It could only mean one thing, and her heart sank. Scarborough was a town with many hotels, a place where business properties changed hands often. Estate agents in the town called every now and then asking whether she'd consider using them if she decided to sell. She felt her hackles rise. The last thing she wanted to do was play along with a sales call at any time, never mind at 8.30 in the morning when she was in such a state.

'Mr Benson, I'm a busy woman,' she said, reaching for her whisky glass. 'If you could get to the point, I'd appreciate it.'

Frederick Benson cleared his throat. 'Ah yes, of course. Well, here's the thing. We've been given a rather unusual instruction relating to the hotel owned by yourself and Mr Dexter.'

Helen kept quiet. There was nothing to be gained by pointing out to someone she didn't know that there was no Mr Dexter any more.

'What instruction?' she said, confused.

'Mrs Dexter, before I continue, could I ask you, in confidence, of course, whether you and your husband might consider selling the Seaview Hotel?'

'Selling?' she said cagily. 'What is this? Are you touting for business?'

'Not in the way you might imagine.'

Helen thought she heard a note of caution in his voice, but put it down to the fact that she needed to sleep. It had been a very long night.

'Mrs Dexter, we've received an offer to buy your property.'

'It's not for sale,' she said. The words came out of her more aggressively than she'd expected.

'Our client has asked if you might be prepared to sell.'

Helen sat up straight. 'Who is it?' she asked.

'I'm afraid I can't reveal that information; it's confidential,' Mr Benson said. 'But they have offered a substantial sum. It's far above the market value for a property such as yours.'

Helen had to grip the side of the window seat when Mr Benson revealed the offer. It was enough money for her to start again. She could buy an apartment on Scarborough's South Bay, one of the really posh ones with a balcony looking out over the sea and a garden for Suki. She could afford regular holidays, even a new car. She could have everything she'd ever dreamed of. But it would be an empty life. Nothing she could buy would ever bring Tom back. She pressed her eyes closed and swallowed a lump in her throat.

'There is one thing, Mrs Dexter,' Mr Benson continued. 'The buyer has stipulated that they receive a response by close of business today or their offer will be withdrawn. That's why I called you the moment I arrived at my desk, so that you have the whole day to reach your decision. We close at five thirty.'

There was a beat of silence before Helen spoke again. 'Why does your buyer want the Seaview so badly?' she said. 'There are hotels for sale all over town. It doesn't make sense.'

'It's not the business they are interested in, Mrs Dexter.'

'They want the building, is that it? But they could have any building in Scarborough. Some of them are cheaper than the Seaview, even if it was up for sale. Which it's not,' she added

8

defensively. 'And why do they need to know by five thirty? What's their hurry? Surely if they want the building so badly, they'd give me ample time to consider their offer?'

'I'm afraid I'm not at liberty to comment any further,' Mr Benson said. 'But the clock is ticking, Mrs Dexter, and the decision is in your hands.'

Chapter 2

Helen stood under the shower and let the water pound her head, neck and shoulders. She tried to focus, tried to make sense of what Mr Benson had told her, but it seemed too bizarre to take seriously. Plus, there was her hangover to contend with and the effects of another night without sleep. She couldn't think straight; nothing made sense. But there it was, an offer to buy the Seaview. An offer that would leave her comfortably off. But was it an offer she would accept?

She'd had many thoughts about selling up and moving on since Tom had gone into the hospice, but now it felt as if she was being forced into making a decision. It was too soon to decide, too quick, she thought. She didn't want to be coerced. If she ever sold the hotel, she wanted to do it after looking at an offer from every angle. But here she was being told she had less than eight and a half hours to make a decision. It was ludicrous and she felt angry with herself for being in no fit state to think, never mind make a decision that might change her life.

She moved her neck slowly from side to side, letting the hot water ease her aches after her night on the window seat watching the velvet night disappear into a new day. She wondered who was after the Seaview, and why. It could only be a developer, she reasoned, but why did they have the Seaview in their sights? Why not another hotel?

The place had its merits, of course. It was one of eight three-storey buildings on Windsor Terrace, which stood high on the clifftop above North Bay. The buildings had been built as private homes before being converted into hotels in the nineteenth century to cater for the tourists that Scarborough attracted as the country's first seaside resort. Back then they had come to take the spa waters. Now they came for fish and chips, bright and breezy weekends, concerts at the open-air theatre and two glorious wide sandy beaches.

Along Windsor Terrace, each hotel was similar in size but painted a different colour. The Seaview was a muted green amongst the red, blue and whites of its colourful neighbours. Each hotel had a basement, which was where Helen's apartment was, with doors opening onto a sunken courtyard. The first-floor public lounge had a wide bay window to make the most of the sea views. However, while the hotels on Windsor Terrace were similar in shape and size, there was something different about the Seaview. It stood at the end of the row, the last one before the terrace curved towards the ruins of Scarborough Castle. Across the road from it was the dilapidated Glendale Hotel, which had closed for business months ago. Now its windows were boarded up and weeds grew through cracks in the path. A FOR SALE sign had gone up after the elderly owners had moved away, and the place had stood empty and unwanted ever since.

Helen turned the shower off and grabbed a towel. She wondered if there was a connection between the broken shell of the Glendale and the offer she'd received. It must be a developer, she thought again. It had to be. Who else would offer such a ridiculous sum? And why the urgency?

She dried herself and pulled her dressing gown over her warm, damp skin, then automatically reached for her toothbrush – and stood stock still. It was Tom's toothbrush she held, not her own; she'd picked it up by mistake. She'd bought him a new toothbrush when he'd moved into the hospice. She'd bought him new everything then. Shower gel, toothbrush, soap, pyjamas; everything was fresh and clean. Which meant that all his belongings were still here: in the bathroom, their bedroom, everywhere she looked. He was there in the slippers that sat by his side of the bed, in the wardrobe where his jackets brushed against her dresses, in the Elvis tracks on the jukebox. And now his toothbrush was in her hand.

She couldn't let go; her hand felt paralysed, her fist like iron. She forced herself not to cry, not again. She'd done her crying, she had to move on. Tom wouldn't want her to dwell. He'd want her to get on with her life, to embrace every minute and make the most of each day. Her chest shuddered as she struggled to hold back her tears. Slowly, carefully, she placed the toothbrush back in its holder. She'd have to make a start at some point on moving Tom's things, packing his clothes away, but she knew she wasn't ready yet.

Half an hour later, dressed in jeans, walking boots and fleece jacket, Helen clipped Suki's lead to her collar and headed out into the mild March day. The dog trotted obediently at her side as they walked to the beach. When they had first taken Suki from the rehoming centre, she wasn't allowed off the lead, her instinct to chase too strong. If there was another dog in the distance, she'd be off like a shot, with Helen and Tom in pursuit, red-faced and out of breath, trying to get her back. There were plenty of other dog walkers on the beach, their pets walking at their owners' side, chasing stones, bounding through the waves or digging holes with their front paws, spraying sand in the air.

Helen took greedy gulps of sea air as she strode along.

'Where shall we go for breakfast, Suki?' she asked the dog.

Suki turned her head at the mention of her name.

'What's that, Suki? You reckon we should try the Harbour Bar? Good girl, I was hoping that was what you'd say.'

Helen glanced at her watch. As Mr Benson had warned her, the clock was ticking. If she wanted to accept the offer on the hotel, she'd have to make up her mind pretty sharp. The problem was, she still wasn't sure what to do. She slowed Suki to a stop and the dog sat obediently on the sand. Helen turned her face to the weak sun trying to poke through the clouds. She closed her eyes and the sound of the ocean roared in her head.

'What shall I do, Tom?' she whispered. Her words were taken by the breeze. 'You know I can't go on at the Seaview without you. But neither can I leave it behind. I need a sign. If you can hear me, if you know what I'm going through, help me, Tom, please.'

She waited, willing herself to feel a touch of his hand on her arm, his face next to hers, his breath in her ear. But there was just the roar of the ocean and the whisper of the wind as it danced across the sand.

'Come on, let's go and eat breakfast.'

*   *   *

13

Helen walked along Foreshore Road towards a brightly painted yellow and red café. The Harbour Bar was a favourite haunt of tourists, who called in to eat award-winning ice creams, knickerbocker glories, chocolate sundaes piled high with cream, or warm waffles oozing with syrup.

'Bacon sandwich and a large coffee, please,' she said to the elderly waitress dressed in a sunshine-yellow uniform. 'I'll sit outside with the dog. Any chance of a couple of sausages for her, too?'

The waitress winked at her. 'I'll see what I can do.'

Helen tied Suki's lead around a table leg and settled into a chair. Foreshore Road was busy with walkers out for a stroll. It was a Thursday morning in early March, but it seemed to her that there were a lot more tourists than usual for the time of year. The fair weather forecast for the weekend might have something to do with it, she thought. On the table in front of her was a folded copy of the *Scarborough Times*. She picked it up and scanned the headline that warned of a strike by the town's bin men.

Within a few minutes, a mug of steaming coffee arrived along with Helen's sandwich. The waitress placed a metal plate on the ground beside Suki with sausages cut into chunks.

'Thanks very much,' Helen said.

'No problem,' the waitress replied, not moving. She stood with her hands on her hips, looking out over the busy harbour. 'Beautiful morning, isn't it?'

'Gorgeous,' Helen agreed.

'I wouldn't want to live anywhere else. I love Scarborough. It's busy this morning, mind you. Probably the convention that's on at the Spa this weekend that's pulling the tourists in.'

'What convention?' Helen asked. She was normally aware of events going on in the town. But being away in Scotland for so long, she'd fallen out of the loop of what was going on.

The waitress laughed. 'What convention? Only the biggest event Scarborough's ever had.'

Helen gave a puzzled look and shrugged.

'Have you been living on Mars, or what? I've had my ticket for the big gig on Saturday night for months.'

'Who's playing?' Helen asked.

'The King himself,' the waitress said with a note of reverence.

Helen's heart plummeted. Now she remembered. With everything that'd happened in the past few months, she'd pushed it to the back of her mind. Tom had talked excitedly about it when it was first announced, before he became ill.

'Elvis impersonators from all over the world are coming,' the waitress continued. 'It's going to be great. You should get along there and enjoy yourself, love. If you don't mind me saying so, you look like you could do with cheering up.'

Chapter 3

The songs of Elvis Presley had provided a soundtrack to Helen and Tom's lives. They'd spent happy nights dancing to his music in the hotel lounge. Each summer the Seaview hosted Elvis nights, Elvis parties and Elvis fancy dress competitions. Tom would dress up in his white suit, leg shaking, lip quivering, being a terrible Elvis who'd never win a prize no matter how hard he tried. And oh boy, did he try. He couldn't hold a tune, that was Tom's downfall, but that didn't stop him singing along to the jukebox. He knew every word, every note, when to pause, when to raise the roof as an anthem soared, when to bring it back slowly with a catch in his voice. Helen would watch her husband in his element, enjoying every second of those summer nights. She humoured him, encouraged him, and danced in his arms as the King's music played in the lounge.

'Your dad would have loved the Elvis convention, wouldn't he?' she said to Suki now between sips of coffee. Suki was too busy eating the sausage to reply.

Just as Helen was about to tuck into her bacon sandwich, her phone rang with a number she didn't recognise. She swiped it into life.

'Hello?'

'Mrs Dexter?' a woman asked.

'Yes.'

'Greenlands Crematorium here. I'm calling to say that Mr Thomas Dexter's ashes are available to collect. We've been trying to contact you for some time, ever since the funeral.'

'They are? You have? Oh, I'm sorry. I've been away and haven't been answering my phone.'

'Well, they're here for you to collect, Mrs Dexter, whenever you'd like to call for them. Just ask at the office and bring some ID.'

Helen hung up. 'What do you reckon, Suki?'

This time Suki looked up and cocked her head to one side. Helen drained her coffee, paid the waitress and decided to walk to Greenlands with Suki and make the most of the warm day.

She was just about to set off when her phone beeped with a text message. It was from Benson's estate agents, and her face clouded as she read. Mr Benson was urging her to call him to accept the offer on the Seaview Hotel before it was too late. His words sent a chill through her. What did he mean, too late? Five thirty was the deadline he'd given her, wasn't it? His message was curt, which wasn't unusual in a text, she knew that, but there was an edge to his words that made her feel uncomfortable. She threw her phone into her handbag, and started walking.

When she reached the crematorium, she checked her phone again, surprised to see another message from Benson's. This time it was a voicemail, even more hostile than the text message, with Mr Benson pushing hard for her reply. She wondered what he was playing at and who was pulling his strings. Did someone really want the Seaview so badly that they were forcing the estate agent to text and call her regularly and aggressively? What on

17

earth was going on? She shook her head to try to dismiss Mr Benson for now. She had something more important to do.

There was something comforting about the crematorium, Helen thought. The peace and quiet of the grounds, with its manicured lawns and canopy of trees, helped calm her mind after Mr Benson's unsettling messages. Inside the small office, the business of handing over the urn was done in a brisk, efficient manner. Helen showed her ID and in return received a sturdy black cardboard bag with handles. She lifted it from the counter and felt the weight of it for the first time.

'Oh,' she gasped. 'No one ever tells you how heavy someone's ashes are going to be.'

The young woman behind the counter smiled weakly and tried to pretend she hadn't heard that comment before.

Holding Suki's lead in one hand and the bag in the other, Helen walked out of the crematorium grounds. She had expected it to feel odd, creepy even, to be holding the remains of her husband in a bag. But it was soothing in a way she hadn't anticipated. Tom was back with her at last, and she knew there was only one place to take him.

'Back to the beach, Suki?' she said out loud. 'Dad loved it there, didn't he? Let's take him one last time.'

Helen stood on the golden sand of South Bay beach, waves bubbling at her feet, Suki at her side. Around them were the amusement arcades, candyfloss kiosks, whelk stalls, fish and chip shops, merry-go-rounds, swing boats, donkey rides and trampolines. From behind her came the call of the bingo, two little ducks and two fat ladies reaching her on the breeze. With each gritty handful she scattered to the sand, with each wave that came to take Tom away, tears streamed down her face. 'You're with our babies now,' she whispered to the breeze. And then the urn was empty, the ashes gone.

She stood a while in silence before returning the urn to the bag, then began to walk from the beach. She glanced at her watch and her heart lurched when she saw the time; it was much later than she'd expected, almost lunchtime. She hadn't given serious thought to Mr Benson's offer, and he'd texted her again demanding a response. Whoever was after the Seaview wanted it badly. But she couldn't think straight, not yet. Oh, she could do with the money, of course, and all it could bring her if she sold up. But being forced into making a decision within hours was too much to bear. To try to help her focus, she decided to head back to the Seaview and make a start on clearing up the mess in the lounge.

When she arrived home, the first thing she did was brew a cafetière of coffee to help clear her head, which was still foggy from too much whisky and not enough sleep. The fresh air and the walk with Suki had perked her up a little, but not enough to get her through the rest of the day without more caffeine. Another phone call from the estate agent pulled her up short, and this time she took the call.

'Ah, Mrs Dexter.' Benson's voice oozed like oil into her ear. 'It appears you've been ignoring my messages. I was calling to find out if you've reached a decision on the sale of the Seaview?'

Helen felt an anger rise. She was being forced into making a decision when she hadn't yet given the offer the attention it deserved. 'Not yet, Mr Benson.'

'And when do you think you'll be in a position to give me your answer?'

Helen thought for a moment. 'About the same time as you're in a position to give me the reason the buyer needs to move so quickly,' she replied.

Mr Benson gave a throaty chuckle, said he couldn't supply those details and begged her to ring him again before the deadline of 5.30.

Helen threw her phone onto a chair. She wouldn't be rushed into this, no matter what Mr Benson said. If his buyer was so desperate to get their hands on the Seaview, then surely there'd be other offers coming in the future, offers she wouldn't be pressured to accept, when – or if – she put it up for sale. She made herself a sandwich and filled Suki's food bowl.

It was mid afternoon by the time she made a start on clearing the plates and glasses – so many glasses – from the lounge. She sent it all down to the kitchen using the ancient dumbwaiter they'd inherited when they had taken the Seaview on. The lift was noisy and slow, but it saved walking up and down stairs carrying heavy trays. She loaded up the dishwasher, then headed back up to the lounge with polish and a duster. So much for spending the day catching up on her sleep. Her mind wouldn't stop going over the estate agent's call.

She forced herself to look at the clock. Just two hours before she had to give him her decision. She couldn't ring him yet, not when she still wasn't certain.

She polished the tables, then took the vacuum cleaner out and gave the carpet the once-over, hoovering up dropped crisps and crumbs. Another nervous glance at the clock warned her there was ninety minutes left. Then seventy-five. She continued to potter about, all the while trying to force herself into a decision. Suki lay on the lounge carpet watching her pace the floor. Forty minutes. She wanted to move out and sell up, didn't she? Wasn't that what she'd told herself she should do? Thirty minutes. She forced herself to stop and stand still. The sun that had been fighting the clouds all day had finally won its way out, and just for a second, a ray of sunshine flooded in, bathing the jukebox with soft, golden light. Helen walked slowly towards it. With each step she took, her heart hammered. She knew what she was going to do.

The metal buttons gave way at her touch. Number 158, Tom's favourite Elvis song of all time. It was the song that had played at their wedding, when he had taken her in his arms and held her tight on the dance floor, whispering in her ear, gently moving his body next to hers as the King's words fell like stardust around them. The jukebox sprang into action and the first notes floated out. It was a slow song, a ballad, one Helen hadn't listened to in months. As the music filled the lounge, she wasn't sure whether she sat or fell into the seat at her side. Her legs seemed to give way as the melody wrapped around her and squeezed at her heart. It rose in an almighty crescendo before petering out slowly, quietly, and then it was gone.

Helen couldn't move. Suki padded across the carpet to her and rested her head in her lap just as the phone rang. She gently nudged the dog's head away and reached for the receiver.

'Seaview Hotel,' she said as evenly as she could. She was feeling raw, tearful, with the last lingering notes of the song on her mind. A man's voice responded immediately.

'Hello? I'm calling to ask if you have any vacancies this weekend?'

She opened her mouth to reply, to say no, but she was cut short by the caller, who didn't stop for breath.

'I know it says on your website that you're temporarily closed, but it's an emergency, otherwise I would never have bothered you, and I do apologise. We need somewhere to stay this weekend and everywhere's full. I've stayed at the Seaview in the past, I know the hotel, and I wondered if, you know, perhaps you'd reopened and you hadn't updated your website, or if there might be a chance, I mean, just a small chance, you might be able to take us for two nights? Like I say, I wouldn't ask if we weren't desperate.'

'Sorry, I'm . . .' Helen tried to chip in, but without much success.

'I've tried everywhere else. You're my last hope. There's a group of us coming in for the Elvis convention. We're a band of Elvis impersonators and we're playing on Saturday night at the Spa. We were supposed to be booked into caravans at Cayton Bay, but Elvis Six made an error with the booking – he's no good with computers, I knew I should have done it myself – and now we've got nowhere to stay.'

'Elvis Six?'

'Didn't I say? There are twelve of us in the band. We're called Twelvis.'

'Twelvis?' A strange sound came out of Helen's mouth, and it took her a few moments to realise she was laughing. It had been a long time since she'd had anything to smile about, never mind laugh.

'I'm Jimmy,' he said. 'Otherwise known as Elvis One. So, er . . . would you have any rooms available?'

Helen looked at the clock. Fifteen minutes.

'Hello?' Jimmy said. 'Hello? Are you still there?'

Suki sat at Helen's feet, gazing up at her. Fourteen minutes. She glanced at the jukebox, glinting in the weak sun.

'We've . . . I've got ten rooms,' she said quickly, before she could change her mind. 'Some of you will have to share. Breakfast's included.'

She heard Jimmy give an enormous sigh of relief. She pulled a notepad and pen towards her, wrote down the twelve names and the time they were due to arrive the next day, then added a note to herself, a reminder to call Sally and Jean the minute she came off the phone. But there was someone else she needed to call first. With four minutes to spare, she dialled Benson's estate agents.

'Mrs Dexter,' Frederick Benson cooed with fawning profes-sionalism. 'How lovely to hear from you. I trust you're calling with good news?'

'Well, it's good news for me, Mr Benson, yes.'

'Splendid. I knew you'd see sense,' he said. 'Now let me just get the paperwork and—'

'No, Mr Benson, you won't need any paperwork. Because no matter how high the offer, I'm calling to tell you that the Seaview isn't for sale.'

There was a pause. Helen was certain she heard Benson gasp before he cleared his throat and began again. This time there was no trace of his earlier friendly tone.

'Very well, as you wish,' he said. 'But let me warn you that my client will not be happy to hear this, Mrs Dexter. I fear you've made a terrible mistake.'

Chapter 4

Helen hadn't liked the tone of Mr Benson's voice but had put his coolness down to the fact that he'd probably been banking on a hefty commission from the sale of the Seaview and was more than a little put out.

'What have I gone and done, Suki?' she asked. She found herself speaking to the dog more than ever since Tom had died. But all Suki did was cock her head to one side. Helen sighed. After months of to and fro, worry and anxiety about whether she should sell up or stay, she'd finally made her decision. Or rather, the booking from Twelvis had made it for her.

Twelvis. The name made her smile, something she hadn't done a lot of in the last few weeks. And now she had just hours to get the Seaview ready for guests. When she'd cancelled bookings after Tom had moved to the hospice, the Seaview's rooms had been left bare. All the bedding had been washed and folded away, and the rooms hadn't been touched. There was cleaning to be done in the bedrooms, en suites and dining room. Helen knew she couldn't do it on her own. There was only one thing for it. She picked up her phone and rang the woman she trusted implicitly and who knew the Seaview like the back of her hand.

'Jean? How are you? It's Helen.'

'Helen, love,' Jean said warmly. 'I'm fine. How are you? How did Tom's memorial service go? I'm sorry I couldn't make it. I didn't dare leave Mum on her own at the care home, not with her legs the way they are.'

There wasn't much about Jean's mum's legs that Helen didn't know. It was Jean's favourite subject and one she talked about often. Jean was a no-nonsense Yorkshirewoman who worked at the Seaview as its cook. She'd worked for the previous owners, and when Helen and Tom took the place over, she'd showed them the ropes. She was in her late sixties, stocky and short, with a round, plump face and glasses that she kept pushing up the bridge of her nose. She had cropped blonde hair and was a powerhouse of a woman who kept the kitchen spotless.

Her mum lived in a care home, where she was bad with her legs, and Jean herself had been a widow for many years. The Seaview was her life, and she took pride in her work, and especially in her breakfasts. Her full English was the talk of the town – well, that was what Jean reckoned after reading an online review that mentioned it: *Great location. Fantastic breakfast. Can recommend. We'll be back!* She'd been so chuffed when Tom had shown it to her that she'd asked him to print it out, and it was now stuck on the fridge door, held in place by a magnet in the shape of a model train from the North Bay miniature railway. Jean's breakfasts were no-frills, honest-to-goodness sausage, bacon and eggs with all the trimmings. Helen would never forget the look on her face when she and Tom had once suggested they offer porridge or kippers as an alternative. Jean was firm with them. She told them she did what she did well, or not at all. Kippers and porridge never made their way onto the menu.

'Your mum's still not well, then?' Helen asked.

'She's been up and down to the hospital that many times,' Jean sighed. 'But never mind Mum; how are you, love? Tell me all about the memorial service.'

'It went as well as could be expected,' Helen said. 'It was nice, you know. Dignified, a real celebration of his life.'

'Did he have that Elvis song played like he wanted?'

'He did, Jean. The same one that was played at his funeral. There wasn't a dry eye in the house.'

'You've lost a good 'un in Tom, but I think you know that already,' Jean said.

'He was one of the best. I'll never meet anyone like him again. Not that I want to.'

'Ah, you say that now. You're grieving. It'll take time to recover, but you'll get there. You'll carry him with you always, you know, like a heart-shaped pebble in your pocket. Well, that's how it was when my Archie went. Anyway, what can I do for you, love?'

'I'm thinking of reopening the hotel.'

There was silence, and Helen could imagine Jean in her living room in her tidy semi-detached on Dean Road, taking in the news.

'Good lass,' she said at last. 'I knew you would.'

There were times when Helen wondered if Jean knew her better than she knew herself.

'When?'

'Well . . .' Helen began. 'It's a bit short notice. I've just received a booking that'll fill all ten rooms. It's a group of men.'

'Oh Helen, it's not a stag do, is it?' Jean sighed. 'You know how much bother they are. I thought you and Tom had stopped taking in stag and hen groups?'

'No, they're Elvis impersonators, a band of twelve. Twelvis, they're called.'

Jean burst out laughing. Her laugh was infectious, and it set Helen off again.

'I know, what a name, eh? Twelve Elvises in the hotel. And what's even more crazy is . . .' She paused. 'Are you ready for this?'

'Go on, give it to me. I was brought up in Hull, I'm tough enough to take anything you can chuck at me.'

'They're coming tomorrow for two nights.'

'Tomorrow?' Jean cried.

Helen crossed her fingers and waited. There was silence, so she carried on.

'I'm going to ring Sally next, see if I can get her in to help with the cleaning first thing in the morning. With three of us here, we'll get it done. What do you say, Jean? Will you come and help?'

'Tomorrow?' Jean squeaked the word out this time.

'They're not due to arrive until the afternoon,' Helen said, trying her best to reassure the woman. 'It'll give me plenty of time to go to the cash-and-carry and buy everything we need – biscuits, tea and coffee for the rooms, soaps, breakfast stuff. It's almost as if we'll be starting all over again. Come on, Jean. Please? I can't do it without your help.'

'By, lass, you're a hard taskmaster, I'll give you that,' Jean said. 'But I'll be there. You can count on me, as always. What time do you want me? Will seven do you?'

Helen's shoulders dropped as she finally began to relax. She mouthed *thank you* to the ceiling.

27

Glenda Young

'Seven will be perfect. Thank you, Jean. You're an angel.'

The next call, however, wasn't so straightforward.

'Hello?' a little voice answered.

'Hello there. Is this Gracie? Can I speak to your mummy?'

'Mummy's in the toilet.'

Helen tried to suppress a laugh. 'This is Auntie Helen,' she said, using the honorary title that Gracie had bestowed on her as soon as she'd learned to talk. 'How are you, Gracie?'

'Auntie Helen!' Gracie squealed. 'Auntie Helen! I've been to school today.'

'Have you? And what did you do at school?'

'I did some maths and some drawing and some fighting with Adam cos he said I was sitting in his seat but I wasn't, Auntie Helen, I wasn't and he said . . . he said . . .'

Helen heard Sally's voice in the background.

'Give me the phone, Gracie. Hello?'

'Sally, it's Helen. How are you?'

'Helen, hi. Sorry about that. Gracie grabbed my phone while I was in the, er, kitchen. I shouldn't leave it lying around. Once she starts talking, she can jabber on for England. I'm doing all right. What about you? I mean, after Tom's memorial service and everything.'

'I'm doing all right; well, as best I can. Thanks, Sally. Listen, I was wondering how you're fixed for work at the minute?'

'Oh,' Sally said. 'Gracie, stop that. Put the cat down. No, don't pull its tail. You know it doesn't like it when you do that. Gracie, no! Sorry, Helen, what was that?'

'I said I'm wondering if you're working or not, and whether you'd like to come back to work here again?'

28

There was silence.

'Sally? Are you still there?'

'Honestly, Helen? I wasn't sure when you'd be opening again, or whether you would at all after, you know, Tom and everything,' Sally began hesitantly. 'And you know how I'm fixed with Gracie, I've got to earn money to support her. And with the Seaview shut for a while, I needed money, so . . .'

Helen's heart sank. 'Are you saying you've got another job?'

'At the Traveltime Inn. I'm sorry, Helen. I had to. I've got my college evening class to pay for, and there's Gracie's clothes – she's growing like you wouldn't believe – and the rent on this poky little flat, plus my bus fares and food and—'

'I understand, Sally, honestly.'

The Traveltime Inn flashed through Helen's mind. It was a square box of a place on the outskirts of town, by the noisy ring road, one of the new breed of chain hotels spreading like a pox around the country's seaside resorts. Small, traditional hoteliers weren't keen on the chain hotels, which undercut them by offering basic rooms at very cheap rates. None of the Traveltime Inns had a dedicated landlady or landlord; they had a customer relations manager, based in Dusseldorf of all places and contactable only by phone. Some of them didn't even have a check-in desk; guests entered their credit card number into a machine – a machine! – in the lobby to receive their room key. And none of them offered breakfast. All they provided was a bed and TV in a square white-washed room with a plastic cubicle for a bathroom. Each room was identical to the one next door to it, the one above it and below. None of them came with views, and Traveltime Inns were often tucked away in the roughest, cheapest part of town.

Helen thought for a moment.

'How much are they paying you?'

'Minimum wage, what else?' Sally sighed.

'I'll add fifty pence an hour,' Helen said quickly.

'Make it a pound. Gracie! Don't pull the cat's ears!' Sally yelled.

'Sixty pence,' Helen offered.

'Eighty.'

'Seventy-five?'

'Done! When do you want me to start?'

'How are you fixed for tomorrow morning at seven?' Helen said, holding her breath.

'Bloody hell, Helen, talk about short notice.'

'We've got twelve Elvis impersonators coming in tomorrow afternoon for two nights. They're playing at the Spa; there's an Elvis convention on this weekend.'

'I can't just walk out on Traveltime Inns,' Sally said. 'I'll have to check to see if I need to give my notice. They've been good to me so far.'

'Good? How?' asked Helen.

'They gave me a nice new duster.' Sally laughed. 'And a lovely yellow bucket.'

'Have you signed a contract of employment?' Helen asked.

'I'm on zero hours,' Sally replied sadly.

'Then you owe them nothing.'

'But it's too risky for me to leave on the promise of a weekend's work with you. As much as I'd love to come back, Helen, I can't drop Traveltime Inns just for two days cleaning up after twelve Elvises.'

'I take your point,' Helen said, thinking quickly. She knew she had to reel Sally in or lose her forever. 'Well, it wouldn't only be for the weekend. A hotel's for life, not just for Elvis.'

'Are you saying you'll be staying open after they leave?'

'That's exactly what I'm saying,' Helen said, making her mind up with each word she spoke. 'And I'll offer you a contract until the end of the summer season.'

There was silence, and she knew Sally was taking her time to think things through.

'Then I'll be there at seven. Is Jean coming back too?'

'Yes, it'll be the three of us working together again, just like the old days.'

'Gracie!' Sally yelled. 'Put the cat down and take the pencil out of its ear. Now! Sorry, Helen, I'm going to have to go. She's giving the poor cat hell. I'll see you tomorrow, right? Look, I know things are going to be different, you know, without Tom. But I'm here for you, Helen. And there are brighter days ahead.'

'It's not like you to be so profound.'

'Profound? Me? Oh . . . er, no. I meant the weather forecast for this weekend looks really good for the time of year.'

Helen's face creased into a smile. Immediately she felt a stab of guilt over feeling happy, for the first time, without Tom.

Chapter 5

That night, Helen slept better than she'd done in weeks. She was excited about the weekend and taking in the new guests. More than that, she was glad to be returning to some sort of normality, although without Tom, her new life was going to take some getting used to.

While Helen slept soundly, however, in the dark of the night something moved outside the hotel. Suki's ears pricked up and her eyes opened. She padded across the living room towards the patio doors that opened to the sunken courtyard. Heavy curtains hung against the doors, but she pushed her face through the gap in the middle, her nose twitching, eyes searching, her whole body alert. A crashing noise startled her, and she gave a low growl, ready to bark. But then there was silence and she relaxed. She walked back to the bedroom and lay down on the floor at the end of the bed as Helen carried on snoring, blissfully unaware.

The following morning, Helen woke feeling rested and happy. Oh, she still ached for Tom and often reached out in bed for the warmth of his body. But that morning, she felt refreshed and renewed in a way she hadn't in a long time. There was a purpose to the day ahead; the Seaview reopening was a new start, and she was looking forward to seeing Sally and Jean. It'd be different without Tom, there was no getting away from that. And because there'd only be three of them working instead of four, it'd be tougher; they'd need to pull together better than they'd ever done before. But Helen felt confident they could do it; she had a great team to rely on.

She glanced at the clock by her bed. It was 6 a.m. She had an hour to get showered, eat breakfast and walk Suki on the beach before Jean and Sally arrived. She pulled her dressing gown on, walked into the living room and drew the curtains to let in the light. That was when she noticed a smashed plant pot on the ground. Compost spilled from it along with green daffodil shoots. She tried to make sense of it. It couldn't have been the wind that knocked the pot over; the sunken courtyard was sheltered, and the wind rarely made its presence felt, no matter how gusty the Yorkshire weather. Had a cat jumped in during the night and knocked it over? Surely not. It was a hefty pot and heavy with soil. Perhaps it had been a dog, or a fox.

She stared at the debris. There was something about the soil, the way it was scattered, flattened against the paving stones . . . She gasped when she noticed the outline of a footprint, and her heart began to race. Someone had been in the courtyard during the night. An icy chill went through her as Frederick Benson's words ran through her mind. He'd said she was making a terrible mistake not accepting the offer for the hotel. Was someone trying to frighten her into selling? Was that what his rather threatening texts and phone calls were about? Or was it purely a coincidence; maybe a random intruder had been trying to break in?

She pulled her dressing gown tight, unlocked the patio doors and stepped out into the cold morning air. Apart from the smashed pot, nothing else was out of place. She inspected the door handles for any sign of them being forced, but they looked as they always did. Suki followed her outside, sniffing the air. Helen glanced around, looking for a clue as to who had been there, but the courtyard gave nothing away.

Heading back indoors, she brewed coffee, toasted bread and checked her phone. There was a long message from her best friend, Marie.

How are you, love? Give me a ring when you feel up to it. Just wanted to say I'm thinking of you, sending love, and hope you're OK. And I'm wondering if you noticed anything odd about Sue and Bev at the memorial service? I think they've had some sort of fight. They should know better at their age. Listen to me, OUR age, I mean, ha! All OK here. Daran's working away a lot, hence he couldn't be at Tom's memorial, I don't know if I explained. And when he IS home, he's always tired and, I dunno, distant? Be lovely to see you and Suki. Maybe I'll come for a walk on the beach with you one of these days – just need to find the right shoes! Love you xx

She smiled at the thought of Marie offering to come for a walk, because her friend never walked anywhere if she could help it. She was wedded to her car, a gorgeous little 1960s cherry-red convertible with a black hood. As for finding the right shoes, Helen had never seen Marie wear anything other than heels at least four inches high, usually red, strappy and expensive.

Suki had disappeared while Helen was reading the message, and now returned with one of Tom's slippers in her mouth and collapsed in a tangle of limbs in front of her.

'Suki, leave it!' she ordered.

Suki looked up, and Helen whipped the slipper from the dog's mouth. She wondered again when the time would be right to start packing Tom's belongings away. Would there ever be a right time?

She glanced out of the patio doors again. Should she report the intruder to the police? She shook her head. It might just have been kids, running wild and knocking things over. Plus, she already had enough on her mind with the Seaview reopening and the Elvis impersonators coming in. The last thing she needed, today of all days, was to get the police involved. Since Tom had moved to the hospice, she'd wondered about installing cameras at the back and front doors, but it hadn't seemed important so far. She'd always felt safe and protected. But now she was living on her own, was it time to think again about security?

She showered, then dried her bobbed hair in front of the bedroom mirror. It was the same hairstyle she'd always had: quick to dry and easy to look after, and it flattered her big brown eyes, or at least that was what Tom always said. She had it cut and styled once a month at Chez Margery, the only salon she'd ever used and one she trusted to maintain her hair the way she liked it. She dressed, then fastened Suki's lead to her collar. Just as they stepped out of the front door, she spied her neighbour Miriam, from the Vista del Mar.

Miriam was a woman of indeterminate age that Helen guessed was at least sixty-five. She wore her years well, with her long greying hair always stylishly curled. She sported oversized glasses that gave her the look of a gracefully ageing Bridget Bardot, if the Bardots had lived in North Yorkshire and their Bridget had grown up to run a seaside B&B. She was down on her knees polishing the glass in her front door. Helen couldn't fail to notice that even so early in the day, she was in full make-up, with her hair perfectly set.

Helen pulled her fleece jacket around her and pushed her bobbed hair under a hat.

'Morning, Miriam.'

Miriam stopped what she was doing and looked up. She smiled at Helen, then stood, stretching her back.

'Morning,' she said briskly. 'It's good to have you back from Scotland. Are you coping all right?'

Helen knew she'd have to get used to these types of questions. 'Just about,' she replied. 'Thanks for keeping your eye on this place while I was away. Miriam, did you hear anything in the night, any noise?'

Miriam shook her head. 'What sort of noise?'

'A crash, I guess. Not glass, but a plant pot. When I got up this morning, one of my daffodil pots was smashed in the courtyard.'

'Maybe a cat got in?'

Helen didn't want to alarm Miriam, so she kept quiet about the footprint. 'I'm reopening today,' she said. 'Just for the weekend, to see how it goes.'

'Good on you, dear,' Miriam replied. 'I'm fully booked this weekend too. It's the Elvis convention; there are lots of fans coming in. Course, I'm only taking the discerning ones, none of the riff-raff that might end up elsewhere.' She cast a critical eye towards the front door of the Seaview, a look that didn't go unnoticed by Helen. 'I had my Cheltenham ladies in last week on one of their Yorkshire experience holidays,' she continued. 'I always enjoy having them. They're such exclusive guests and refuse to stay

36

anywhere other than my Vista del Mar. Well, I am the only hotel around here with consistent four-star reviews.'

Helen had read some of the Vista del Mar's reviews on the HypeThatHotel review site. Getting good reviews on such sites was essential for B&Bs like those owned by Helen and Miriam, and it was important to keep their ratings high. However, some of the reviews for the Vista del Mar left a lot to be desired: *Fantastic location, great sea views. Comfy rooms. Watch out for the woman who runs the place, though, she's a scream! A proper snobby old bag.* One reviewer even called Miriam *a right old dragon.*

'You really should do something about the Seaview's three-star status, Helen,' Miriam often moaned. 'You're letting the whole street down. We're a four-star location and yours is the only hotel along here that's not up to scratch.'

Helen couldn't let Miriam's snobbery go without telling her about her own guests. 'Well, I'll see your Cheltenham ladies and raise my Elvis impersonators who are coming in this afternoon.'

'Impersonators?'

'Twelve of them. They're a tribute band called Twelvis.'

Miriam pursed her lips. 'I hope you won't be playing that dreadful rock and roll music and having one of your parties.'

'I hadn't given it any thought,' Helen said.

'I'd appreciate it very much if you could keep the noise down, dear. I don't want my guests upset. The Vista del Mar is an exclusive establishment. Speaking of which, the local paper reckons the bin men might be coming out on strike. If it goes ahead, I don't want you using my bins at the back after yours gets full.'

'I'd never do that, Miriam,' Helen said, affronted.

She heard a chattering sound coming from Suki at her side; it was the noise the dog made when she was excited and happy. She knew Suki would be aching to run on the sands. Before she headed out to the road, though, she turned back to Miriam, who was finishing off cleaning the glass panels in her door.

'Miriam? Have you heard anything from Benson's estate agents about someone wanting to buy properties along here?'

'No, and I'd give them short shrift if I had,' Miriam replied. 'Why, have you?'

'Yes, but I think it might have been a developer pushing his luck.'

Miriam pointed across the street to the ramshackle Glendale Hotel. 'Strange you should ask, though. I saw a couple of men in suits going in there last week. Didn't think anything of it, to be honest, forgot all about it until now. Maybe it's been sold? Anyway, I can't stand here all day chatting, I've got to start breakfast, and my guests like their fresh croissants warm from the oven.'

She disappeared inside, and Helen set off towards the North Bay beach.

'Croissants for breakfast?' Helen said to Suki. She could only imagine what Jean would say about that.

Chapter 6

The morning passed in a blur of cleaning, polishing and scrubbing. Fresh linen was laid on each bed, clean towels and bath mats were placed in the bathrooms, windows were opened to let in the surprisingly warm air of the early March day. The weather forecast had got it right, Helen thought; maybe there *were* brighter days ahead. The three of them worked like army tanks, unstoppable, unflappable, letting nothing get in their way. They knew their routine and what was expected. By lunchtime, all ten rooms were ready and Sally had even set up the dining room with tablecloths and cutlery ready for breakfast the next day. Helen found an old photo of Tom wearing his white Elvis suit. She kissed it gently, then stuck it on the wall behind the bar in the lounge.

'Wish me luck, Tom,' she whispered.

Downstairs in the basement, she sat at the kitchen table with Jean and Sally.

'Good work, girls,' she said. She brewed coffee for the three of them and opened a packet of chocolate digestives. Suki lay under the table, watching and hoping for dropped crumbs.

'Are you going to be all right on your own, lass, when the guests arrive?' Jean asked, dipping a biscuit into her mug.

'I'll be fine,' Helen said. And the truth was, she was feeling confident about welcoming guests to the hotel for the first time in months. She also knew her bank manager would be happy that the Seaview had reopened. There was money left in the business account to keep it going, but only just enough.

Sally stood up and took her apron off.

'I've got to go and pick up Gracie,' she said.

'Give her my love,' Helen said. 'And thank you for all you've done today. I couldn't have reopened without you and Jean.'

'We're hashtag Team Seaview, aren't we?' Sally smiled.

'We're hash what?' Jean pushed her glasses up the bridge of her nose.

'You need to get yourself on social media, Jean,' Sally said.

'I'll do no such thing,' Jean huffed.

Helen smiled. Oh, how she'd missed their company.

'What time are they due?' Jean asked. 'Are you sure you don't need me to stay and help with the check-ins?'

'They're due about two. Or at least that's what Elvis One said yesterday on the phone.'

'Elvis One?' Sally cried. 'What are they, the Red Arrows?'

Helen shrugged. 'They're all numbered, apparently. Might be easier than remembering their names.'

Sally put her coat on, and Helen hugged her warmly.

'Thanks again, Sally,' she said.

Jean took another chocolate biscuit and dunked it in her mug. 'Well, if you're sure you don't need me, I'll head home after I've had my coffee. I'll call in on Mum at the care home, see how her legs are.'

Once Jean had left too, Helen took a moment to appreciate the silence after the morning's activity. She made herself a sandwich, fed Suki and opened the laptop to deal with the bookings that were starting to arrive now she'd updated the website. But there was one email that caused her concern. It was a notification from HypeThatHotel saying that a new review had been left for the Seaview. It must have been written by someone who'd stayed there some time ago, because the place hadn't been open since before Tom had died, and that was over three months ago. She clicked the link to read the review, and her mouth dropped open.

Shoddy place. Dirty. Food dredful. Bad staff. Sory. Do not stay here.

She stared at her screen in disbelief. The date that the reviewer – Porgy42 – said they'd stayed at the Seaview was in the past week. But that wasn't possible! She scrolled down the page to see if there was a link she could click on to make a complaint and get the review removed. But if there was such a thing, it proved hard to find. She was getting frustrated with the site and its lack of transparency, and could feel her hackles rising. Finally she found the link and fired off her complaint, receiving an auto-confirmation email to say that her message had been received and would be acted on in the coming days.

Just at that moment, the doorbell rang. She closed the laptop and headed upstairs, closing the door behind her to keep Suki in the basement. As she approached the front door, she caught sight of a group of men through the glass panes: the first guests at the Seaview in months, the first guests since Tom had died. She paused at the mirror in the hallway and stared at her reflection. Her hair was as neat and shiny as always. She wore a touch of make-up, just enough to stop her from appearing too pale, her big brown eyes shining back at her. She smiled, happy with the way she looked, then put a welcoming smile on her face. 'Come on, Helen, you can do this,' she whispered.

She unlocked the door, opened it wide and looked out at a group of twelve men. There were old men, young men, thin men and fat men. There were bald men and men with grey hair. One man was smoking and two were holding hands. None of them looked like Elvis. A tall man who she guessed was about her own age, with dark hair and a pleasant, open face, stepped forward with his hand outstretched.

'Elvis One at your service,' he said. 'Or you can call me Jimmy, if you like.'

Jimmy was good-looking, rugged in a kind of past-his-best sort of way. She noticed a touch of grey in his dark hair, saw the lines around his mouth and the way his eyes twinkled when he smiled, and he smiled a lot. She found herself holding on to his hand for just a moment longer than necessary, and he didn't seem to want to pull away. She felt a flutter in her stomach when her eyes locked with his, and chided herself for being so ridiculous. She was acting like a schoolgirl with a crush! It was just the excitement of Twelvis's arrival, wasn't it?

'I'm Helen,' she said, beaming at him, then she turned to the other men. 'Please, come in.'

As each member of Twelvis shuffled forward, Jimmy introduced them.

'This is Elvis Two,' he said as an overweight young man heaved himself over the threshold, using the walls as support.

'I'm Kev. Pleased to meet you.' He shook hands with Helen.

'Elvis Three is Alan and Elvis Four is his brother Stuart. They'll share a room.'

'Sure is a pleasure to be here, ma'am,' Alan drawled in what Helen assumed was supposed to be an American accent, although it seemed to have drifted in from Wales.

'Ignore my brother, he talks Elvis all the time,' Stuart said, gripping Helen's hand.

'Elvis Five is Brian,' Jimmy said.

A wave of cloying aftershave hit Helen seconds before a broad, stocky man in his mid sixties with clipped brown hair walked past her.

'Nice place you've got here,' he said, glancing around the lobby appraisingly. He turned to Helen and looked her up and down, appraising her too. There was a moment when his eyes rested on her breasts and stayed there for a few more seconds than they should have done, making her feel very uncomfortable. 'You've got a big corner plot,' he added, as if she didn't know.

She fixed her smile as the next Elvis stepped inside.

'Elvis Six is Big Al,' Jimmy continued, like a mother hen parading her chicks for Helen's approval.

'Afternoon,' Big Al said. Helen wondered where the nickname came from, as he was the shortest man there.

'Elvis Seven is Ginger, the best singer of us all.'

A portly middle-aged man with wisps of red hair and a freckled face stepped into the lobby. He smiled warmly at Helen.

'Lovely place,' he said politely.

'Elvis Eight, where are you?' Jimmy called. 'Put your cigarette out and get yourself in here, Davey.'

A young man stepped inside and nodded towards Helen. He was skinny, far too thin to be Elvis even in his white suit days, Helen thought. He had long brown hair tied in a ponytail, and his bare arms revealed a jangle of coloured bead bracelets.

'Elvis Nine is young Colin,' Jimmy said.

Colin bounded inside like an excited puppy, eyes wide, looking around him as if he'd never been in a hotel before. He appeared to be the youngest of them all.

'Smashing place this, isn't it? I love Scarborough, me. My mum and dad used to bring me here when I was a kid. Haven't been back in years. Is the crazy golf course still open on the seafront, the one with the lighthouse on the last hole? I got a hole in one there one year, won a prize dolphin. A plastic one, I mean, not a real one, that'd be wrong. A real dolphin, can you imagine?'

Helen noticed Jimmy shooting Colin a look, and the lad quietened down.

'Elvis Ten is Bob and Eleven is his husband Sam.'

The two men holding hands wore matching checked shirts and jeans. One of them was tall and sported a neatly trimmed beard.

'I'm Bob,' he said.

'And I'm Sam,' the shorter man added.

'And last but by no means least, it's Elvis Twelve.'

A man in his fifties, well dressed in a dark blue suit and blue tie, stepped into the lobby, which was now crammed with men, luggage and suit carriers that Helen guessed held their Elvis outfits.

'But you can call me Tim,' he said, offering his hand.

'And there you have it, we're all in,' Jimmy said, smiling. 'Twelvis is in the building.'

Helen burst out laughing. Never in all her years running the Seaview Hotel had she received guests quite like these. It was clear to her that Jimmy was in charge, a scoutmaster looking after his troop.

'Let me check you all in and I'll give you the keys to your rooms,' she said.

She busied herself with paperwork, dishing out keys and dispatching the Elvises to their rooms. Jimmy hung back, waiting until she had dealt with them all. Only then did he step forward to receive his own key.

'You said on the phone you'd stayed here before?' Helen said.

'Oh, many years ago,' Jimmy replied. 'I remember you and your husband, and the Elvis parties you used to throw. You had a jukebox on the wall, if my memory serves me right, full of Elvis songs.'

'It's still there,' she told him.

'My little girl used to love the parties. She always insisted on dancing with your husband, said he looked just like Elvis in his black wig and white suit.'

Thousands of visitors had walked through the doors of the Seaview in the years since Helen and Tom had bought it. She took a good look at Jimmy's face. It was a kind face, a handsome, friendly face, but not one she could recall.

'Do you and your husband still run the Elvis parties?' he asked.

Helen stopped what she was doing and closed her eyes for a second to gather herself. This was something she was going to have to get used to.

'I'm afraid he passed away at the end of last year,' she said.

Jimmy dropped his gaze to the carpet. 'I'm sorry to hear it. I remember him as a very nice man.'

'Thank you,' Helen said. 'He was.'

Jimmy glanced around the lobby, then stepped into the lounge. 'I remember some good times in here, great party nights,' he said. 'But life changes us all. My wife and I separated years ago.'

'And your little girl, how old is she now?' Helen asked.

'Almost thirty,' he replied. Then he turned his head away, putting an end to their conversation.

'Here you go, you're in room eight,' Helen said, handing him two keys attached to a large white plastic fob. 'It's at the back but it's got a great view over the town and South Bay beach. The other key on the ring opens the front door; you can come and go any time. If you or your friends have any problems, give me a call on my mobile. I live just downstairs.'

Jimmy took the keys and his eyes lit up.

'Number eight,' he said approvingly. 'The King's birth date. Something tells me this is going to be a weekend I'll never forget.'

Chapter 7

While the men settled into their rooms, Helen headed to the lounge. She looked at Tom's photo – 'So far, so good,' she whispered – then moved to the window seat and sat down, gazing out at the North Bay beach and the rocky headland of Scalby Ness.

A young girl's voice carried into the lounge from the street.

'I hate Scarborough, it's minging!'

She glanced out to see who was disparaging the town she loved. Outside the Vista del Mar, a man and woman were busy unloading suitcases and bags from their car. The man was thin and slight; he wore small round glasses, and wisps of grey hair were scraped across his head. Helen noticed that he walked with a limp. The woman beside him looked younger, vibrant and attractive with cropped dyed silver hair. Beside them, tapping furiously into her phone, was a young girl Helen assumed was their daughter. She looked about twelve or thirteen years old, with long brown hair and a pretty round face.

'Daisy, come and help me and Mum with the luggage,' the man called, but the girl ignored his request. She now had her phone clamped to the side of her head.

'It's all right for you, you get to stay at home,' she yelled into the phone. 'Just cos you're the eldest. It's not fair. I wanted to stay at home too. Why did I have to come to Scarborough? It's rubbish here. There's nothing to do.'

'Daisy,' the woman said sharply. 'Stop talking to your sister and come and help.'

'No!' Daisy yelled. 'I hate Scarborough and I hate you.'

Once the warring family had disappeared inside the Vista del Mar, Helen watched the rolling sea, soon lost in her thoughts about Tom. As her memories threatened to drag her to tears, she heard someone cough. Spinning around, she saw Jimmy at the door.

'Come on in. No need to stand on ceremony. I'm just sitting here thinking about . . .' She stopped herself. From now on, there needed to be two versions of Helen: the helpful and friendly landlady, and the other, real Helen, who had to learn to be tough and strong enough to face her future on her own. She walked towards the bar. 'What can I get for you?'

'Oh, nothing yet, not for me,' Jimmy said. 'I'm just waiting for the boys and we'll head out for sea air and fish and chips. But if it's all right with you, I'll ask them to meet in here this evening, say about six, and we'll have a few drinks before we go out on the town. I thought we'd go for a curry tonight, then find karaoke in a pub. The lads love karaoke, especially young Colin. Once he's up singing, it's hard to get him to sit back down.'

'Sounds fun,' Helen said. 'The Scarborough Arms often has karaoke on, as does the Black Bull.'

'Is the Newcastle Packet still open on the seafront?' Jimmy asked.

'Oh, it's still there; it's a Scarborough institution, that place,' Helen replied. 'They do karaoke too.'

Jimmy thought for a moment. 'I might take the lads there. We're not performing at the convention until tomorrow night, so it'll be good to have a night off tonight, to be ourselves before we start work tomorrow.'

'Is it your job, then, impersonating Elvis?' Helen asked. She was intrigued to know more.

Jimmy pulled a chair from a table. 'May I?' he said.

Helen nodded. 'Be my guest.'

He sat a respectable distance from her as they talked. 'For me, it's a part-time job,' he explained. 'I took early retirement from my work in IT and haven't looked back since. I've been a fan of the King since, well . . .' his face creased into a smile, 'since before I can remember. My old mum used to say I came into the world dancing to his songs.'

He dropped his gaze to the carpet and Helen saw a blush of red creeping up his face. There was something about Jimmy that she found herself warming to. He had a way about him that was self-effacing and humble, yet he was clearly the leader of Twelvis, the one who kept them all in check.

'For most of the lads, being Elvis earns them money in some form or another, and some of them perform tribute gigs as other singers – Roy Orbison, say. All they need is a different wig.'

Helen laughed out loud as he carried on.

'We perform as Twelvis at gigs and festivals, but when the fee has to be split twelve ways, it doesn't go far. And some of the fans at those gigs can be obsessive; things often get intense. I remember one guy in particular turned nasty when we wouldn't let him into the green room. He pulled a knife on Big Al and we had to get the police involved, but he was a slippery fella who did a runner before the cops arrived.' Jimmy shuddered at the memory. 'We've had to run out of gigs with hordes of screaming women and a fair number of men chasing us. It can get quite scary at times. Mind you, some of the lads, the younger ones, they love all the attention.'

'What about you?' Helen asked.

'All I want to do at the end of a gig is sit down with my feet up and have a cup of tea. Kev, the big lad who came in after me when we arrived, Elvis Two, he's what we call a comedy Elvis; he does it for the laughs and free pints. He works full-time as a plumber. And at the other end of the scale there's Alan, the one whose brother Stuart is with him. Now Alan lives and breathes Elvis. I mean, you heard him when he came through your door. He thinks every word that comes out of his mouth sounds like the King, and we haven't the heart to put him right. He's happy, so why spoil it?'

There was a clatter of footsteps on the stairs, the banging of doors closing, and one by one the remaining members of Twelvis gathered in the lobby. Jimmy stood and smiled at Helen.

'Six o'clock all right for you in the bar?'

'I'll see you all then,' she replied.

Helen turned back to the window and watched the men walk out of the Seaview. They stood in a huddle on the pavement, some pointing up the street, some pointing down, trying to agree on the best route to take. Finally five of them headed right with Jimmy leading, four of them turned left, and two crossed the road to take in the stunning view, leaving one man on the hotel steps. It was Brian, the man who'd eyed her up and down and made her feel uncomfortable. She assumed the two men taking in the scenery were waiting for him, and was puzzled when they began to walk off without him. She saw him looking at his phone and noticed he kept glancing across the road, watching the others disappear. Once they'd gone, he did a most peculiar thing. He walked down the steps of the Seaview, but instead of heading away, he turned towards the Vista del Mar.

How bizarre, Helen thought. Through the wall that separated the Vista del Mar and the Seaview, she heard Brian knock at Miriam's door. She shook her head. What was she thinking? She had better things to do than pry on her neighbour and one of her guests. She was about to walk away, really she was, when she heard the door of the Vista del Mar open and Miriam's voice ring out.

'You bastard!'

Helen walked into the hallway and pressed her ear against the wall.

'We need to talk,' Brian said firmly.

'I've got nothing to say to you.'

Helen felt her heartbeat quicken as the conversation continued.

'Miriam, please.'

'What do you want, you slimy son-of-a-bitch?'

Helen gasped. She'd never heard her neighbour swear before, and yet the profanities were coming thick and fast. Miriam, who always spoke as if she had a plum in her mouth, was turning out to have taken language lessons from a foul-mouthed docker.

'I'm in town for a couple of days, got a bit of business to do. It's purely coincidence, I swear, but I'm staying next door. I couldn't not call in to see you, not when I was so close.'

'You're staying at the Seaview? In that dump?'

Helen's mouth dropped open.

'It's not that bad,' Brian said.

She nodded in agreement.

'The woman who runs it seems a tidy piece.'

Helen had been called many things over the years, but this was a new one. She could picture the online review: *Fantastic views, great breakfast, landlady's a right tidy piece.* She had to cover her mouth to stop herself giggling.

'You'd better come in,' Miriam said. 'But only because I refuse to be gossiped about, and if anyone sees you on my doorstep, they'll have a field day.'

Helen heard the door slam shut. She prayed they wouldn't walk into the Vista del Mar's lounge and out of earshot. Fortunately, though, it sounded as if Miriam wasn't going to allow Brian the luxury of getting any further into her precious domain.

'I've no time for small talk, Brian. Out with it. What are you doing here?'

There was silence for a few moments before he spoke.

'I've come to give you this.'

'You think that's going to make everything all right? After all these years of neglect? Well, you can think again. I'm not the soft touch I used to be, Brian. You can't fob me off with cash.'

Helen's eyes opened wide. Why was he offering Miriam money?

'Here, look, I've got more,' Brian said.

There was silence again until Miriam spoke.

'No matter how much you offer, I won't take it, not now or ever. I told you back then I didn't want anything to do with you, and I meant it.'

'Miriam, love—'

'Don't you dare call me that,' Miriam spat. 'Don't you bloody well dare! You lost the right to call me anything the day you walked out on us. It's been over thirty-five years, Brian. Not once . . . not once in all that time did you send money for me and our child. And now you just waltz back in here, knocking at my door.'

Helen felt her knees buckle with the shock of what she was hearing. Listening in was wrong and she knew it. She shouldn't be prying on Miriam's private life, but she couldn't seem to pull herself away.

'How is she?' Brian said.

'She's thirty-bloody-seven years old, that's how she is,' Miriam screamed. 'I've done all right on my own. I've done right by my daughter.'

'Our daughter,' Brian said.

'She's *my* daughter!' Miriam roared. 'Where were you when she needed new shoes or new clothes? When she was hungry and cried for food? When she needed her father? Where were you when I needed a husband?'

Helen's mouth, which had hung open during the exchange, now snapped shut. She'd never known Miriam was married. There'd been some talk about a daughter, she remembered, but Miriam had said she was working in Spain.

'You got your divorce, just like you wanted,' Brian said. 'I gave you that at least.'

'It's the only bloody thing you ever did give me,' Miriam said. 'Now go, Brian. I won't ask you again. And if you won't go, I'll call the police. I'm sure they'll be interested in what I've got to tell them.'

'You've got nothing on me,' Brian said.

'Nothing? How about decades of neglect? How about years of avoiding paying child maintenance for your daughter? How about using fraudulent addresses to stop my solicitor getting in touch with you when I needed money to feed our child, who you walked out on when she was only two years old? You're a rotten sod. That's what you are. Rotten to the core. Get out, Brian. Go on, get out.'

Helen heard a scuffle in the hallway.

'Don't say I didn't try to make amends, Miriam,' Brian said.

'With a couple of hundred quid, almost forty years too late? Don't make me laugh.'

The door opened, then there was more scuffling, as if a body was pressed against the wall.

'If you change your mind, Miriam—'

'I won't.'

'I'll be staying next door for two nights.'

'Bugger off. You might as well be staying on the moon as far as I'm concerned.'

'Will you tell our daughter you've seen me? Will you give her my love?'

'Not on your nelly.'

'Miriam, please!'

'Go and crawl back into the cesspool you came from.'

'You don't mean that,' Brian pleaded.

'Oh, I do,' Miriam said. 'I never want to see you again. I wish you'd never come here. In fact, I wish you were dead!'

Chapter 8

Helen was about to head down to her apartment when a flash of red caught her eye through the glass panes in the front door. She peered out and saw her friend Marie parking her sports car. She waved and held the door open. As Marie stepped out of her car and walked towards her, Brian stormed out of the Vista del Mar.

Marie was Helen's oldest friend. She had long and expensively coiffured brown hair, kept herself in shape with regular visits to the gym, wore designer clothes and heavy make-up and ran a successful nail bar in town. Helen sometimes felt a little dowdy in comparison; she always had, ever since they were best friends at junior school, which was a very long time ago now. Marie was tall and slim where Helen was average height with a body that women's magazines described as pear-shaped. Even though she hadn't been eating well since Tom became ill, and had lost even more weight while grieving, her body wasn't toned like Marie's; she looked and felt every bit of her forty-eight years, whereas Marie could pass for five years younger.

Where Helen's face was round and pale, Marie's was slim and olive, her cheekbones enhanced by the most expensive make-up she could buy. Her hair was long and luscious, curled to perfection; she looked as if she'd just walked out of a top-class salon after being pampered to within an inch of her life. Helen, in comparison, had the same bobbed cut that she'd worn since she was a child and didn't feel any need to change the way she looked, though there were times, usually on the days when Marie wafted into her life in a cloud of expensive perfume, when she felt a pang of regret at not making more of her looks. But even if she did, she'd be a fool to think she could ever look as glamorous as Marie. She didn't have time to spend on hair and make-up when she had a hotel to run. As long as she looked presentable and welcoming, that was all that mattered. Besides, Tom had always said he wouldn't change a thing about the way she looked, and that had been good enough for her. But now that Tom was gone, there was no one to tell her she was doing just fine or looking nice.

Helen greeted her friend and hugged her tight, welcoming Marie's embrace. It felt good to be held. No words were exchanged; their hug said everything they needed to say.

'Come downstairs, I'll put the kettle on,' she said.

'That fella I just passed coming out of next door was a right old lech,' Marie said as she followed her down. 'He looked me up and down as I passed him and flicked his tongue at me. Nasty old perv.'

'He's not staying next door, he's staying here,' Helen said. 'He did the same to me when he arrived, except I didn't get the tongue. Must be losing my touch. Anyway, coffee or tea?'

'Better make it coffee. I didn't get much sleep last night. Daran rolled home drunk at half past one and sat downstairs with the TV on.'

Helen had never much liked Marie's husband Daran. She

thought he was too flash by half, always bragging about how much money he was making, although she wasn't sure exactly what he did for a living. He was always working away. She often wondered what Marie saw in him, apart from the money, of course.

'How is he?' she asked.

Marie shrugged. 'Same as always. When he's not out drinking or throwing his money away in the casino, he's away on golfing holidays on the Costa del Sol with his dodgy mates exiled in Spain. Or he's off working. I never see him, and if I'm being honest, his absence suits me down to the ground. Actually, I think he might have found another woman.'

'How do you know?'

'On the rare occasions he is at home, he comes in with this smell on his skin, sickly and sweet, like strawberry perfume.'

'Have you asked him about it?'

'Do you want the truth? I don't care any more. There's no love left between us; hasn't been for years.' She bent down, pulled off her scarlet high heels and began to massage her toes. 'These shoes don't half hurt,' she moaned. 'Anyway, life's better when Daran's away. We've got nothing to say to each other. I don't know why I married him.'

'I do,' Helen said sagely. 'And if you're honest with yourself, you know fine well too. There were half a million reasons you went after Daran Clark, and all of them had the Queen's face on them.'

'Well, a lot of cash can turn a girl's head. What can I say?'

'Never mind turning your head, you've had to turn a blind eye to what he gets up to.'

Marie waved her hand dismissively. 'So, I run my nail bar—'

'Which he bought for you,' Helen chipped in.

'But it's in my name, Helen, and so is my car. If anything ever happens between me and Daran, I've got the nail bar to rely on for income. So what if I use his money to decorate the house how I want it, spend his cash on furniture I like? What's wrong with that? I've turned our house into a palace.'

Helen set a cafetière and two mugs on the kitchen table. 'But don't you get lonely?' she asked. 'Wouldn't you prefer it if he was a proper husband? When was the last time you two did anything together, like go for a walk, or hold hands? When was the last time he took you out for a meal?'

Marie ignored the question and carried on rubbing her sore feet.

'You'd better pick your shoes up off the floor or the dog'll have them,' Helen warned. 'She had one of Tom's slippers in her mouth yesterday. I managed to whip it away from her before she ripped it to bits.'

'Ugh.' Marie shivered. 'Dog saliva everywhere. I don't know how you cope.'

Helen poured coffee into the mugs. 'I'd be lost without Suki.'

Over their coffee, she told Marie all about the strange offer from Benson's estate agents. Then she told her about Twelvis, about reopening the hotel and about the smashed pot in the courtyard and the footprint in the soil. She also told her about scattering Tom's ashes on the beach. Marie was a good listener, chipping in at just the right times, staying silent when she should.

'What's going on with Bev and Sue, then?' Helen asked at last. 'When they were here after Tom's memorial, it was as if neither of them could bear to be in the same room as each other.'

'Search me,' Marie said. 'All I know is they haven't spoken to each other for over a week, but neither of them will tell me what's wrong.' She leaned across the table towards Helen and carried on in a whisper. 'But I've heard that Bev's husband has left her.'

'No!' Helen cried. 'Should we go and see Bev, make sure she's all right?'

Marie leaned back in her chair and took a sip from her mug. 'I'm inclined to leave them to sort themselves out.'

'Oh, you can be heartless at times,' Helen chided. 'I might give her a ring later.'

'Fancy dinner in town tonight? On me?' Marie offered.

'On Daran's credit card, you mean,' Helen laughed.

'Might as well make the most of his money,' Marie said, glancing at her watch. 'We could go to the Eat Me café.'

Helen shook her head. 'Can't. I'm working tonight in the bar. Got to serve drinks to the Elvis impersonators.'

'Are any of them single? Good-looking?' Marie said.

'You're a married woman, Marie Clark. Now who's being an old perv?' Helen laughed.

'Well, are they dishy or not?'

It was Jimmy's face that came to Helen first, along with his kind and gentle manner and the way he'd made her feel when he arrived. She decided not to say anything about that to Marie, or anyone; she was still grieving for Tom and it didn't feel right to admit she had . . . what was it exactly? . . . a childish crush on one of her guests.

'Some of them are all right,' she said. 'Two of them are married to each other. But none of them look like Elvis. Mind you, I haven't seen them dressed up as him yet.'

'I never saw his appeal, to be honest. You know I've never been a fan of his music.' Marie reached across the table, took Helen's hand and looked into her eyes. 'Look, are you really going to be all right?'

'Without Tom, you mean?'

'And running this place on your own.'

'I've got Jean and Sally.'

Suki whined under the table.

'And Suki.' Helen squeezed Marie's hand. 'And I've got you as my best mate to lean on, and Sue and Bev, when they sort themselves out.'

'What about Mrs Posh Drawers next door; has she been in to offer her condolences?' Marie said, slipping her feet back into her shoes. 'Cost me a fortune, these did, and they really pinch my toes.'

'Miriam? We had a quick word on the doorstep this morning.' Helen cast an admiring glance at the scarlet stilettos, then her gaze rested on her own down-at-heel black boots. 'What do you really think of this place, Marie?'

'Scarborough? I love it!'

'I mean the hotel.'

'Why do you ask?'

'I overheard something I shouldn't have earlier; someone called it a dump. And there's a review that's been left online calling it shoddy and dirty. I think they've written it about the wrong hotel; you know I haven't been open since before Christmas.'

'Well, that's just rubbish,' Marie said dismissively. 'The Seaview is always as neat as a pin and as clean as a whistle. I hope you're following it up with the review site to get it removed. They can't say that about you.'

'So you think the place is all right as it is?'

Marie took her time before replying. 'Well . . .' she began hesitantly.

'Spit it out, come on,' Helen said. 'It's not like you to hold back.'

'It's just it's a little . . .'

'What? For God's sake, Marie, just tell me!'

Marie bit her lip and took a second before she replied. 'It's stuck in a time warp. There, I've said it. When you walk in through the front door, it's like walking back into the eighties, and not in a good way.'

Helen rocked back in her seat, taking a moment to let Marie's words sink in. 'You think I should redecorate?'

'Yes, I do. And I think you should update the curtains, carpets, bedding, everything. New dining tables, crockery, tablecloths. I mean, everything's very clean and tidy, but it needs something new. It doesn't feel fresh any more. And you should go after that four-star rating. Oh God, have I said too much? I'm sorry, but you did ask, and I can't not be honest – you know what I'm like once I start. I just think you're going to have to up your game, especially if the new Traveltime Inn opens over the road—'

Helen held her hand up to stop Marie saying more. 'What?'

'The new Traveltime Inn,' Marie said. 'You must have heard, surely? Traveltime Inns are interested in buying the Glendale to convert it into one of their chain hotels.'

'How do you know?' Helen asked.

'Daran told me last week.'

Helen's heart sank. Do you think Traveltime Inns and the offer to buy this place might be connected?'

'It might be. You should try to find out; that's what I'd do,' Marie replied.

Helen thought for a moment. Yes, that was Marie's style: go straight into things, gung-ho. Marie was a woman who got things done. Helen wished she had half of her friend's get-up-and-go.

Marie drained her cup. 'Thanks for the coffee, Helen, but I'm sorry, I really must get to the salon.'

They hugged on the doorstep.

'Save an Elvis for me, the best-looking one.' Marie winked as she walked away. 'And remember, find out what's going on with Traveltime Inns.'

'I will, I promise,' Helen replied.

She watched her friend's sports car pull away. But then she caught sight of Brian walking towards the Seaview, and her stomach twisted.

'Afternoon,' she said as brightly as she could, forcing a smile.

'Ah, Mrs Dexter,' Brian said as he stepped inside. 'Could I have a word in your shell-like?'

'Is everything all right with your room? No problems, I hope? I know the shower in there can be a bit tricky, but if you twist the knob all the way, you'll be fine.'

'It's not the shower, Mrs Dexter,' he said firmly.

Helen didn't like the way he spoke, and felt unnerved by his stern look. There was no way he could have known she'd been listening in on his conversation with Miriam, so what was it?

'I need to speak to you in private,' he added.

'We can talk in the lounge,' she said.

Brian sank into a chair and Helen sat opposite, but not far enough away to escape his sickly cloud of aftershave. He was broad and stocky, and when he sat down, his stomach heaved against his brown leather jacket. He was clean-shaven and chubby-faced, with dark hair with a bald patch at the top. He looked respectable in every way, Helen thought, the kind of old-fashioned man you'd expect to be a solicitor or a bank manager. But there was something about him she didn't like, not least because of what she'd overheard through the wall. She noticed he wore a wedding ring. She was more than a little curious and a touch nervous as to what he was going to say.

'Allow me to be frank,' he began. 'I'm acting on behalf of an interested party.' He reached into his jacket and brought out a long blue leather wallet, which he placed on the table between them. 'There's five thousand pounds in cash in there, Mrs Dexter, and it's all yours.'

She eyed the wallet suspiciously. 'Mine?'

'And there's a lot more where that came from. Of course, I expect something from you in return.'

Helen sat up straight in her seat and pressed her feet to the floor. Her words came out of her in a very measured tone. 'I am *not* that kind of woman and the Seaview is *not* that kind of hotel. Whatever you think you're paying for here, you're wrong. I run a decent establishment. So put your money away and don't insult me again.'

She stood and headed for the door, but Brian caught her by her wrist and stopped her in her tracks.

'Get off me,' she hissed.

A wicked smile played around his lips. 'Oh, Mrs Dexter. I wasn't offering to buy your womanly charms, as appealing as they are. I'm offering to buy your hotel.'

Chapter 9

'It's not for sale,' Helen said through gritted teeth.

Brian loosened his grip on her wrist. 'Everything's for sale, at the right price. Even your precious hotel.'

'Who do you think you are?' Helen said, her voice rising. She eyed him suspiciously. 'What's going on?'

'Let's just say a friend of mine is interested in taking this place off your hands.'

'What do you mean?'

'I mean I represent someone who wants to buy the Seaview, Mrs Dexter.'

Helen felt her heart begin to pound as she tried to process his words. Why was one of her guests offering to buy her hotel? 'Has this got anything to do with Benson's?' she demanded, doing her best to think straight.

'Benson? Who's Benson?'

'The estate agent in town.'

'Never heard of them,' he said.

Her mind raced. Two offers in quick succession from two different sources was too much of a coincidence for her liking. Something fishy was going on, something she wasn't aware of. She was confused, and her state of mind wasn't helped by Brian's attitude, which made her feel vulnerable. Was he working for the person who had made the original offer?

'Who is it who wants the hotel? I demand that you tell me, now,' she said, her voice more assertive than she felt.

'I've told you, it's a friend of mine.' Brian smirked. 'That's all I'm at liberty to say.'

Helen had been nervous before, even a little scared. But Brian's smirk riled her up and sent her over the edge. Now she was angry. 'You think this is a joke, don't you? Sitting there smiling. Well, you've picked the wrong woman to mess with, Elvis Four or whatever your name is.'

'It's Brian, and I'm Elvis Five.'

Helen leaned towards him until she was just inches away from his fat face. His aftershave caught in her throat. She poked his shoulder with her forefinger as hard as she could, and with each word she spat, she poked him again. 'Leave. Me. Alone.' She stood up straight. Her finger hurt and she wondered if Brian had even felt it through his thick jacket. 'The Seaview is not and nor will it ever be for sale. And you can tell whoever it is that's given you the money to stick it where the sun don't shine.' She squared her shoulders, glaring at him with her hands on her hips. 'Got it?'

He had the decency to look a bit flustered, and Helen knew she'd won the battle if not the larger war that was taking place with her unknown combatants. Just who was after the Seaview and why did they want it so badly? Was it the Traveltime Inns people? Her heart was jumping out of her chest, but she was determined not to blink first.

'I said, have you got it?'

'Got it,' he mumbled.

Helen nodded towards the lounge door. 'Get out.'

'Oh, I'll go,' Brian said. 'But I must warn you, Mrs Dexter, that my friend is not the sort of man to take no for an answer.'

'Get out!' Helen yelled.

He left without another word. Helen listened to his footsteps as he climbed the stairs. She waited until she heard the door of his room open and close before she sank into a chair, legs shaking. She sat a few moments trying to pull herself together, wondering what to do. Should she call the police? But what exactly would she tell them if she did? That a middle-aged Elvis impersonator had offered her cash to buy the hotel? She shook her head. It was absurd; they would just laugh at her. But combined with the smashed plant pot and the footprint in the soil, she was feeling unnerved. She put a hand on her chest to steady herself after her encounter and looked at the photo of Tom behind the bar.

'What shall I do?' she said out loud, but Tom just stared back in silence.

Once she'd calmed down, she stood and walked to the window, trying to make sense of what had happened. She saw someone sitting on a bench on the clifftop opposite the hotel, but they weren't gazing out over the sea, making the most of the view. Instead they were staring right into the Seaview's lounge. They wore a black anorak with the hood pulled up, and when they realised they'd been spotted, they jumped up and ran, hands in pockets, skinny legs pounding the pavement. It was too much for Helen, another shock, another alarming incident. She took a glass from behind the bar, pushed it up against the brandy optic and downed the drink in one.

I'm still grieving, she told herself sternly. That's why things aren't making sense. I'm not myself. Didn't everyone warn me this is how it would be? I need to pull myself together, stop seeing things where there's nothing to see. But the fact was, after what had just happened with Brian, she was feeling panicked.

She headed downstairs. Suki was waiting for her with the remains of Tom's slipper hanging from her mouth.

'Oh Suki, no!' she cried.

Suki dropped the drool-covered slipper.

'That's Daddy's,' Helen chided.

Suki cocked her head to one side.

'Oh Suki. It's not your fault. It's my fault for leaving it where you could find it.'

She slid the slipper under the sofa out of Suki's reach, then opened her laptop and fired up a browser, typing in *Traveltime Inns*. In amongst the publicity pieces about the hotels, she found the corporate site she was looking for. She scanned its pages, searching for the owner of the company, and there he was, his picture beaming from the screen: a rat-faced man called Leon Weber. The name meant nothing to her; she'd never heard of him before.

She closed the browser and opened her emails, hoping that the routine of doing something so ordinary would help calm her down. There were more bookings coming in for the Easter holidays and even into the summer, which pleased her a lot. There was also an email from the review site, and she hoped it was a reply to her complaint. But it wasn't a reply; it was a notification to say she had a new review. Her hand shook as she clicked the link, nervous about what she would find.

Sory, this hotel is not good. I do not recamend. This one had been left by someone calling themself Pudding&Pie. Helen fired off another complaint, this time with stronger wording.

When she'd cleared her inbox and made sure all the bookings were entered in the diary, she turned towards Suki.

'Come on, I think we could both do with some fresh air.'

Within minutes, she was heading down the steps of the Seaview. As she glanced across the road towards the Glendale, her blood ran cold. Two men were standing there. Both had their backs to her, but she recognised Brian's brown leather jacket and stocky build. She didn't know who the other man was. He was taller than Brian, younger, slimmer, with dark hair and ears that stuck out just a little too far. He was dressed in what looked to her like a cheap shiny suit. She watched them a moment, wondering whether she had the nerve to storm over and demand to know what was going on.

'Come, Suki,' she said at last, her decision made.

She began walking towards the two men. But as she drew near, she could hear raised voices, angry words being yelled. She ducked behind a bright red postbox and did her best to hide, praying the pair wouldn't turn and spot her.

'You were supposed to get the stupid bitch to sell up, Brian!'

'She's a lot tougher than she looks. She wasn't in the least bit interested in taking the cash. Said the place isn't for sale and won't ever be either.'

'And now I have to go back to the boss and tell him he can't have his new Traveltime Inn?' the other man said, shaking his head. 'We've got no chance of developing this dump without demolishing the Seaview. We need the land for a car park or the deal doesn't go through. You know how tight the planning regulations are these days. Boss isn't going to be happy with you, Brian.'

Helen bristled indignantly behind the postbox. So that was why there'd been interest in her hotel! The chain wanted to knock it down and build a car park!

'I've told you, I tried my best. She won't budge,' Brian yelled.

From her spot behind the postbox, Helen saw him hand over the blue wallet. The other man slipped it inside his jacket.

'You've failed him, Brian. He'll be very disappointed. And you know how angry the boss gets when he doesn't get his own way.'

Brian stormed off in the direction of town, then the man in the cheap suit jumped into a black Porsche and disappeared with a squeal of tyres. Helen watched the car speed away, her blood pounding in her ears, her mind working hard to put the pieces of a puzzle together after what she'd just overheard.

'Come, Suki,' she said, pulling the dog's lead. She wanted to get to the beach quickly; she needed the wide-open space to think and make sense of what had happened. Who was the man in the Porsche? Was it Leon Weber himself? Or was Leon Weber the man that he'd referred to as the boss? And what was Brian's involvement? Nothing made sense!

When they reached the sands, Helen let Suki off her lead and the dog bounded to the shoreline as she thought things through slowly and carefully. She ran over again what she'd heard. Whoever wanted the Seaview sounded ruthless, she figured, if the man with Brian was one of his flunkeys and was being paid enough to afford a Porsche. He had referred to someone called the boss, and a chill ran down her spine. She didn't like the sound of it at all. If this boss was rich and powerful, what could an ordinary woman like her do to keep him from getting his hands on the hotel? If she refused to sell, would he ramp up the bullying, send in someone more threatening than Brian next time? She shuddered at the thought of just how far he might go to get what he wanted, which was clearly the Seaview Hotel. *Her* Seaview Hotel.

The sea roared as she walked, the seagulls cawing overhead while her thoughts whirled in her mind. As the reality of the situation began to sink in – that someone, whoever it was, was willing to threaten her to get her to sell – she began to feel alarmed. She couldn't protect herself against someone like that. All she could do was let the police know, but she suspected that if she told them, they'd laugh at her for spying on one of her guests, and from behind a postbox too. The whole thing was ridiculous, but unnerving and scary too.

At the end of the walk, she put Suki back on her lead to head back to the Seaview, feeling apprehensive about what, or who, she might find there. Since Tom died, she'd often felt a vulnerability that she'd never felt before; this time she felt more alone than ever, and unsure of what to do.

Chapter 10

Back in her apartment after the walk, Helen fed Suki and picked up Tom's slipper. The matching one that Suki had chewed to bits was still under the sofa, where she had put it out of Suki's sight. She got down on her hands and knees, pulled it out and sat with the pair of slippers in her hands. She still wasn't ready to pack Tom's belongings in a box and clear out his clothes. But she knew she had to make a start somewhere. She walked into the kitchen and flipped up the bin lid, ready to let the first part of him go. Closing her eyes, she pulled the slippers to her chest, then let them fall from her hands.

She had just enough time to check her emails and feed Suki before she needed to get ready to work behind the bar. She was relieved to see that no more fake reviews had been left but disappointed that there wasn't a reply from the site. She changed out of her jeans and T-shirt into a blue dress that had been one of Tom's favourites, and began putting on make-up. It felt strange to think about opening the bar without him at her side. She couldn't decide whether it was a milestone to achieve or a hurdle to be overcome. But he would be there, she reminded herself; he'd be right behind her, looking down on her, keeping watch from the wall.

She glanced at the clock. She still had half an hour before she was needed upstairs. Suki was dozing by the sofa. Helen picked up her phone and dialled her friend Bev's number.

'Bev? It's Helen, how are you?'

'Oh, Helen. Hi. Look, I'm sorry I haven't called. Things have been a bit, er, difficult. Do you need anything? Is there anything I can do?'

'I'm fine, honestly, still crying myself to sleep every once in a while, but that's to—'

'Be expected, yes,' Bev interrupted.

'Bev? Can I ask you something?'

'You know you can ask me anything.'

'I saw Marie earlier and she said she's tried ringing both you and Sue but neither of you will tell her what's going on?'

Bev sighed deeply. 'I've not been feeling too good.'

'What is it?'

'Probably nothing. Just feeling a bit tired, you know.'

'Have you seen the doctor?'

'Got an appointment next week.' There was silence for a few moments before Bev spoke again. 'How's Suki?'

'Oh, she's in good form. She's keeping me sane, truth be told, with all the walks on the beach and feeding her. She keeps me to a routine, which is—'

'Just what you need,' Bev interrupted. 'Tom's memorial service went well, I thought. And his funeral was lovely. The church was gorgeous; those flowers they did were beautiful.'

Helen swallowed back an unexpected lump in her throat. 'Yes, they were,' she agreed. 'Look, Bev, is there anything else going on that you want to tell me? I mean about you and Sue?'

There was silence.

'Bev? You still there? It's just . . . after Tom's memorial, when you were here, the two of you didn't seem to be speaking, and I wondered if you'd fallen out. Can I do anything to help?'

'Clive's gone,' Bev said.

Helen sat up straight in her seat. 'Gone?'

'We've split up.'

'God, I'm sorry,' Helen said. She was shocked to have Marie's earlier news about Bev's marriage confirmed.

'Don't be, it's for the best. He's staying with his mum until things sort themselves out. The kids don't know yet; they're still away at uni. We're going to sit down and talk to them next weekend when they're home.'

'Is there a chance he might come back?'

'I don't want him to,' Bev said firmly.

'Is there someone else involved?' Helen asked.

'Look, Helen, I'm really not ready to talk. I'm going through ten types of hell here; my life's been turned upside down . . .' Bev gasped. 'I'm sorry, forgive me. What's happening to me is nowhere near what you're going through. I can't even imagine it. You two were set for life. And I want that too, you know? I want to feel as happy with someone as you were with Tom.'

Helen screwed up her eyes. Now was not the time to burst into tears. 'Call me when you're ready to talk, OK?'

'Have you spoken to Sue?' Bev asked.

'No, do you think I should?'

'She's gone away on one of her yoga retreats.'

'How do you know? Are you two speaking again?'

'I've texted her,' Bev replied. 'She's getting her chakras realigned and her bank account emptied. The woman's a fool to herself.

Fancy getting involved with those hippy-trippy yogis or whatever they call themselves. I thought she had more sense.'

'We all need to have something in our lives to make us happy. I should know that better than anyone, but I still don't know if I've done the right thing.'

'Why? What *have* you done?'

'I've reopened the Seaview, and this weekend I'm playing host to twelve Elvis impersonators.'

Bev burst out laughing. 'You're not!'

'Oh, I am. In fact, I'd better go. I've got to get up to the bar; they'll be coming in for drinks soon.'

Helen left Suki snoozing and headed upstairs. She was surprised to see four men already in the bar; it was still only 5.40.

'Sorry, fellas.' She smiled, psyching herself up to be the gracious host after the hellish day she'd had. 'I bet you're all dying of thirst. What can I get for you?'

As she emptied bottles of lager into glasses and poured gin and tonics, the lounge began to fill. The men were in good spirits, looking forward to their night on the town.

'Could we play your jukebox, little lady?'

She looked up from pouring a vodka and Coke into a tall glass and stared at the jukebox. She'd been so busy today, she hadn't given it a moment's thought, but of course they'd want to play it once they saw the Elvis songs inside. She forced a smile. There had to be a first time for it to come back to life. In front of her stood the man she remembered Jimmy said always spoke like Elvis, but try as she might, she couldn't remember his name.

'Elvis Three, right?' she guessed.

'Alan Smith at your service, ma'am,' he drawled. 'My older brother Stuart and I are sharing room ten at the top of the stairs. It sure has pretty views.'

Helen flicked a switch behind the bar and the jukebox lit up. Alan walked towards it, the first to pick a tune.

'One of my all-time favourites, and surely one I love to sing whether onstage or off,' he said.

Music floated around the lounge, bringing a cheer to the Seaview that had been missing for months. Some of the men sang along to the song, tapped their feet or swayed with their drinks in their hands. All kinds of emotions bubbled up inside Helen. She wasn't sure whether to laugh or cry. It was horribly, achingly painful to hear Tom's favourite songs again, and yet there was an odd kind of joy in seeing the tunes enjoyed by her guests. Wasn't this what the Seaview was all about? What she and Tom had aimed for, and worked hard to achieve? She swallowed hard, then turned her back to the men while she gathered herself. When she turned back, Jimmy was waiting to be served. She smiled when she saw him, but then Brian walked in and the smile dropped from her face.

'Just a bottled beer for me, whatever you've got,' Jimmy said.

'Brian? What would you like?' Helen asked, as politely as she could manage. Brian asked curtly for a bottle of lager, then turned his head away, dismissing any attempt at conversation. Helen poured the lager into a glass, watching him carefully, looking for any sign, any clue, as to what he was really about, for there was clearly more to him than just being an Elvis impersonator. Just then, the song on the jukebox changed.

'From the film *G. I. Blues*, 1960,' Jimmy said, as quick as a flash.

'"Wooden Heart", it's a stomper,' Brian said.

As the song played, Helen continued to eye Brian. 'Do you sing this one onstage?' she asked him.

He seemed surprised that she was addressing him directly. 'Yes, I do. What of it?' Helen saw the look that Jimmy shot him.

'Manners, Brian,' he said quietly. 'Don't forget we're guests in Mrs Dexter's hotel.' He looked at Helen. 'Matter of fact, Brian sings this one beautifully. He even sings the bit in the middle in German; it's his second language.'

'I grew up in Dusseldorf,' Brian said, pulling nervously on his collar. He took the glass of lager from the bar and walked away to find a seat.

Dusseldorf? A distant bell rang at the back of Helen's mind. Wasn't that where the headquarters of Traveltime Inns was based? Just as she was trying to make sense of it, Jimmy leaned towards her.

'Sorry about that,' he said. 'Brian's got a few problems at home. His wife's ill; she's bed-bound, poor thing. I'll have a word with him later. He shouldn't be rude at any time, not when he's representing Twelvis, and especially not to someone who's been as welcoming as you have.'

He smiled at her, and she felt the familiar flutter in her stomach that she'd felt when she'd first laid eyes on him. She chided herself again for being so taken with the man.

When all the guests had been served, Helen sat on a stool behind the bar. She glanced across the room towards Jimmy and wondered if she should tell him about Brian offering her cash for the hotel. But then she dismissed the thought. It wasn't Jimmy's business and he didn't need to know.

More drinks were served, more tunes played, and the men finished with an Elvis singalong before getting up to leave. As they walked out of the lounge, Brian sauntered towards the bar, keeping one eye on the men heading out of the door. He positioned himself between Helen and his bandmates and spoke quietly, as if he didn't want to be overheard.

'Please don't let your cleaner enter my room. I'd like not to be disturbed. I've arranged my show clothes and I don't want anyone touching them.'

'Of course,' Helen said as politely as she could manage, although a flicker of doubt ran through her mind. Was there something he was trying to hide? She shook her head to dismiss a thought that presented itself. She'd never snooped in her guests' rooms in all the time she'd owned the Seaview, and she wasn't about to start now. She told herself to get a grip and stop being paranoid.

'Elvis Five, you're always chatting up women!' a voice called.

Helen turned to see the youngest lad, Colin, grinning.

'Come on, Brian, put the landlady down and leave her alone,' he joked. 'What happens in Scarborough stays in Scarborough, eh?'

'Brian, leave Mrs Dexter in peace,' Jimmy said.

Colin and Brian walked out of the lounge, but Jimmy hung back. 'I can only apologise,' he said with a rueful smile. 'They're grown men, but sometimes it's like managing a bunch of big kids.'

Chapter 11

Left alone in the bar, Helen collected glasses, straightened chairs and wiped tables. She turned to the photo on the wall and ran her fingers across it.

'That's the first night over, Tom,' she said. She thought about telling him about Traveltime Inns wanting to demolish the Seaview to make way for a car park. However, she knew he would have a few choice words to say, so she kept quiet.

Once the bar was tidy and the glasses washed, she headed to her apartment and found Suki pacing, teeth chattering, a telltale sign that she needed to go out. Helen pulled her zip-up fleece jacket over her dress, picked up her hat and scarf and clipped Suki's lead to her collar. Once outside, she saw the tide was in and knew there was no point heading to the beach. Instead she walked along King's Parade towards the North Riding, Tom's favourite pub, where he'd loved to sit in the small, square snug at the back. He'd take Suki and chat to the pub's owner about local breweries and beers. Suki pulled at the lead when they reached the pub, her instinct to head inside, just as she'd always done with Tom.

'Not tonight, Suki,' Helen said. 'Not any more.'

She turned right onto Victoria Road, past the indoor bowls centre on one side and a crazy golf course on the other. She heard a rustling noise behind her and what she thought was footsteps, but when she turned, she was surprised to see no one there. She spotted a shadow moving beside the shrubbery that ran along the crazy golf course, and swallowed hard, trying to calm herself down.

'Who's there?' she called, but was greeted only by silence.

She retraced her steps, unnerved by the thought that someone might have been following her, after all that had happened. But there was no sign of anyone.

'Must be my imagination playing tricks again,' she said out loud to Suki, knowing full well it was herself she was trying to convince.

She carried on walking down the hill to Peasholm Park, glancing behind her just in case. The park had been designed on an Oriental theme, with beautiful gardens, waterfalls and a putting green. It had always been one of Helen's favourite places to walk with Tom, hand in hand and eating ice creams on a summer's day. In the centre of the park was a tranquil lake where green and red pedalos designed to look like Chinese dragons could be hired. They were tied up by the boathouse now, bobbing in the water as she walked past, their dragon heads bowing down to her. In the middle of the lake was a bandstand where brass bands came to play, with players and their instruments ferried to the stage by the dragon boats. Beyond the bandstand was an island with an old wooden bridge across a stream. Helen had walked around the island many times with Tom. It was pretty there, lit with fairy lights on summer nights.

It was turning cold now, and her thin dress under her fleece provided little in the way of warmth. After she'd walked Suki around the lake, she headed towards the exit, which meant walking past rows of green wooden benches. A group of kids were sitting there, smoking and giggling. A man and a woman were gazing out at the lake, the man's arm draped across the woman's shoulders. Helen looked up at the darkening sky, at the stars that hung there like diamonds. She saw moonlight reflected in the lake, felt the silence of the park surround her in the soft velvet night. What she would have given for Tom to be by her side.

'I miss you,' she whispered.

As she reached the Buttercup Kiosk, she saw a man sitting alone, some way back from the lake. She didn't give him much thought until he called out her name.

'Mrs Dexter?'

She peered to see who it was. 'Jimmy?'

He gave her a mock salute. 'Elvis One at your service.'

Helen walked towards him and sat to one side in the row in front. Suki lay down on the cold, hard ground.

'What are you doing here? Why aren't you out with the boys?'

Jimmy laughed out loud. 'I left them drinking in the Newcastle Packet. Colin was happy up on the karaoke. Stuart and his brother had a falling-out over something or nothing. Brian disappeared off on his own. Tim was on his phone to his wife; he's missing her like crazy. Ginger went to the convention at the Spa to meet up with friends. And Bob and Sam went to find a gay bar. As for the rest of them, they're either chatting up women or getting drunk. I can't be doing with it. I don't drink much these days. I fear I'm getting too old or stuck in my ways for nights out with the boys.'

'Well, you did say they were like a group of teenagers,' Helen reminded him.

'Tell me about it,' Jimmy sighed.

'But what brought you to the park?'

He tapped the seat at his side. 'I came to see my old man.'

Helen gave him a puzzled look.

'We scattered his ashes here fifteen years ago.'

'In the park?'

'Right here, under this seat. Dad loved Scarborough; he knew the place like the back of his hand. His parents used to bring him here for holidays when he was a nipper. They stayed in a guest house on Trafalgar Square. When he died, my mum, me, my sister Jenny and brother Jack came to Scarborough for a long weekend and brought him with us, in his urn. We did all the things Dad loved to do: went to his favourite pub, had fish and chips on the seafront, ate ice creams at the Buttercup Kiosk and watched the miniature naval battle on the lake. Dad used to sit here and listen to the brass bands. Right here in this seat. Fourth row back, third seat in. That was his seat, he used to say. He always made a beeline for it and woe betide anyone that was already sitting in it. He would shoot evil looks their way.'

'He sounds a character,' Helen said.

'Oh, he was. And he was a big Elvis fan too.'

They both fell silent and looked out over the lake, where the reflection from the coloured lights strung around the edge shimmered in the water below.

'I scattered my husband's ashes this week,' Helen said. 'On the beach in the South Bay.'

'It's a beautiful place, Scarborough,' Jimmy said.

Helen smiled. 'As a Scarborough lass born and bred, I can only agree. Anyway, I'd best be getting back.'

'Could I walk with you, Mrs Dexter?'

'On one condition.'

Jimmy looked at her.

'That you stop calling me Mrs Dexter. Please, call me Helen.'

As they walked, they talked about Scarborough and about the Elvis convention taking place at the Spa, and Jimmy explained about the Twelvis gig.

'We play a ninety-minute slot with an interval. We start a cappella and end up rocking and rolling until the audience is dancing in the aisles.'

'Where are your instruments?' Helen asked. She couldn't recall seeing any when the band checked into the Seaview.

'Instruments?' Jimmy laughed. 'We use backing tracks. Not many of us can play a tune, although Ginger's very good on guitar and one or two of the others can play piano. But we don't use instruments for the band. It's all smoke and mirrors, I'm afraid.'

'How long have you been in Twelvis?'

'Probably too long. But it's not something you leave until you need to. There's a waiting list of people ready to join as soon as someone drops out. So once you're out, that's it, there can be no going back.'

'You make it sound like a secret society,' Helen said.

'It can get quite intense,' Jimmy muttered darkly, keeping his gaze fixed firmly ahead.

As they walked to the hotel, Helen noticed a hand-made poster stuck on a lamp post with a heartfelt plea for help to find a missing cat. When they reached the Seaview, she turned her key in the lock and was about to step indoors when the door at the

Vista del Mar was flung open. Miriam stood on the doorstep looking, to Helen's eyes, as infuriatingly glamorous as ever. She wondered where her neighbour found the time to pamper herself so lavishly, with her hotel to run too. Heaven knows, there didn't seem to be enough hours in the day sometimes.

'Ah, Helen dear. Two parcels arrived for you,' Miriam said, eyeing Jimmy standing behind her. 'While you were out with your, er, friend.'

Helen bristled at what Miriam seemed to be implying.

'Parcels? So late in the day?'

'They were delivered to the Victoria Seaview by mistake and someone from there walked round with them. I offered to take them in after they couldn't get an answer at your door. We must have a new delivery man on the route who doesn't know the difference yet between the two hotels.'

Helen tutted and rolled her eyes. It wasn't the first time that parcels for her had been delivered to the Victoria Seaview, and vice versa.

'Excuse me, Jimmy,' she said, preparing to walk past him down the steps. But Jimmy was ahead of her.

'I'll get them for you.'

'Miriam, meet Elvis,' Helen said.

Miriam stiffened. 'Oh. So, you're one of those impersonators, are you?' she sniffed.

Jimmy held his hand out for her to shake, but she simply looked at it as if it was a dirty cloth and left it hanging mid air. Helen felt her stomach turn with embarrassment on Jimmy's behalf. He pulled his hand back and ran it through his thick dark hair, as if that had been his intention all along.

'Yes, I'm Elvis One, Jimmy Brown. Pleased to meet you,' he said.

Helen was impressed by how polite he was to Miriam, especially when she'd been so rude towards him. Miriam handed him two brown cardboard boxes, then closed the door without a word. Jimmy walked back to the Seaview and gave the boxes to Helen.

'Thanks, Jimmy.'

He nodded towards the stairs. 'I think I'll go up,' he said. 'It's a big day tomorrow. Lots of preparation to do. What time's breakfast in the morning?'

'Any time from eight till nine thirty,' Helen said.

Jimmy thought for a moment. 'I remember when I used to come here years ago, the breakfasts were worth getting out of bed for. And it was either the full English or nothing, that was what your cook said.'

'And that's exactly how it still is,' Helen laughed. 'We've still got the same cook. I'll pass on your compliments.'

'Night, then, Mrs D—' Jimmy paused. 'Helen.'

'Night, Jimmy. Sleep well.'

He headed up the stairs and Helen went into the lounge with Suki. The long walk had done them both in, and Suki collapsed in a heap by the window seat as Helen sat down.

'He seems like a nice man, eh, Suki?' she said, scratching the dog behind the ears and making her groan with pleasure. She thought about how much she'd enjoyed talking to Jimmy, someone who didn't know her as well as her friends did, didn't know the depth of her grief for Tom or how difficult it was to force herself to look forward now and take control of her life. It had felt surprisingly refreshing.

As she sat there, she heard noises outside, a girl's voice.

'I hate it here; I want to go home. I'm missing all my friends. Look . . .'

She glanced out of the window and saw Miriam's guests heading up the path to the Vista del Mar, the same family she'd seen unpacking their car earlier: the mum with her cropped silver hair and the dad walking with a limp. Their daughter, Daisy, held her phone out to her father, begging him to look at something on the screen.

'Daisy, just get inside and shut up, will you?' the mum said. 'You've done nothing but complain since we got here.'

'That's cos I want to go home,' Daisy sulked.

Helen was more than relieved that the family were staying next door with Miriam and not at the Seaview.

She looked at the two boxes that had been delivered. She recognised the pet company logo on the smaller one and knew it would be vitamins for Suki that she'd ordered online. The second box had no logo on it, just a typed label on the front addressed to Mrs Dexter at the Seaview Hotel. She wasn't expecting anything; hadn't ordered anything else that she was waiting for. She peeled the tape from the top of the box and lifted the cardboard flaps at one end. Inside, brown paper packaging was scrunched around the contents. Helen was bemused; what could it possibly be? She looked again at the box, but there was nothing there, not even a postmark to give a clue to where it had been posted. She lifted the brown paper from the box to reveal a cheap fluffy toy, the kind you'd win on the funfair or in one of the bingo parlours on the seafront. It was a cartoon dog toy, made of brown fur, not too dissimilar to Suki's colour. And then she spotted the needle piercing the dog's belly. It looked like a small knitting needle, slicing right through the toy. She gasped and threw the dog to the floor. Suki immediately thought it was a game and leapt up to chase it.

'Leave it!' Helen yelled. She got to the toy dog before Suki did, her heart pounding, her knees shaking.

Meanwhile, outside the Seaview, a skinny figure in a black anorak with its hood pulled up walked slowly past, staring into the hotel lounge.

Chapter 12

Helen didn't sleep well that night. She'd checked the bolts on all the doors twice before she headed to bed, and only then after she'd had a brandy to help calm her nerves. Was this someone's idea of a sick joke? Was it connected to the Traveltime Inns and their offer to buy the Seaview? Was Brian behind it?

When she woke the next morning, it was the smell that hit her first, the unmistakable aroma of bacon and sausages cooking under the grill. It could only mean one thing: Jean was already at work. She felt safe knowing someone else was there, relieved not to be on her own after the unsettling events of the previous day. She decided to put the stupid dog toy to the back of her mind, along with Brian and Traveltime Inns. But there was a problem: the back of her mind was becoming awfully busy and full. She forced a smile onto her face; she wouldn't let this get her down, Tom wouldn't want that, and she was determined to face the day bravely. It had been a while since the Seaview had served up Jean's famous full English. 'We're back in business, Tom,' she whispered as she tumbled out of bed and into her dressing gown.

She popped her head around the kitchen door. Sure enough, there was Jean, wearing a floral apron, her short blonde hair tucked under a black chef's cap. She had a knife in her hand and was slicing her way through a small mountain of mushrooms. A large tray of brown eggs sat on the counter, ready for the frying pan. If anyone requested otherwise, Jean would grudgingly turn her hand to poaching or even scrambling, but that was as far as she diverged from her norm. In the dining room, guests could help themselves to fruit juice and mini boxes of cereal while tea or coffee was served, before the main event of sausages, beans, bacon, egg, tomatoes, mushrooms, fried bread and hash browns. And as a concession to those who didn't eat meat, a concept Jean still struggled with, a box of vegetarian sausages waited in the fridge, just in case. After the cooked breakfast, if guests wanted more, there were tiny glass jars of apricot or strawberry jam and neatly wrapped pats of butter to spread on toast.

'Morning, Jean. You're a sight for sore eyes. It's good to be getting back to some sort of normal.'

Jean pushed her glasses up the bridge of her nose and peered at Helen. 'Morning, love. My word, you look tired.'

Helen pressed her hands to her face and rubbed her eyes. 'Cheers, Jean. Give me half an hour to shower and take Suki out. Everything all right?'

'Everything's shipshape, Captain.' Jean smiled. 'It's good to be back.'

'How are your mum's legs?' Helen asked.

'Not good,' Jean sighed. She shook her head and returned to slicing the mushrooms with a little more vigour than before.

Over the next hour, the men began to drift downstairs. It looked set to be another fine day and the sky was eggshell blue. While Jean cooked, Sally and Helen stood at the entrance to the dining room, guards in floral tabards with the hotel's logo, a curling wave and a cheery sun, embroidered across the right breast. Some of the men wandered across the road to take in the view that drew guests like a magnet. Others sat in the lounge, checking their phones or reading leaflets about upcoming Scarborough events: plays at the Stephen Joseph Theatre or new exhibitions at arty Woodend and the Rotunda Museum.

It was Jimmy who walked into the dining room first, a general leading his men.

'Morning, Helen.'

This was what Tom would have wanted, Helen thought, his precious Seaview up and running again. As the men filed in, each one giving a polite greeting, Helen felt more certain than ever that she'd done the right thing. She could never sell the Seaview, not in a million years. What on earth had she been thinking? Grief really did do strange things.

Once all the men were seated, she smiled at Sally.

'Ready?' she said.

Sally winked. 'Let's do this!'

Breakfast passed in a bustle of plates and cups, teapots and fried bread, one accepted request for beans on toast, two denied requests for porridge, and many requests for tea. Cooked food from the kitchen was sent up to the dining room in the dumbwaiter before it took the dirty dishes back down. Helen and Sally worked efficiently, silently, slotting effortlessly into their roles. But there was someone missing from the dining room; only eleven of the band were downstairs.

'Will Brian be coming down?' Helen asked Jimmy when she placed his plate in front of him.

Jimmy seemed unconcerned. 'He must be having a lie-in. I expect he'll be down later.'

As Helen filled the dumbwaiter with plates and cups, Sally walked towards her. Mention of Brian prompted her to tell the other woman what he'd said the night before.

'There's no need to clean room seven this morning,' she said. 'He's asked not to be disturbed; says he'll have his Elvis clothes hanging up and he doesn't want them touched.'

'Fair enough,' Sally said. 'I'll make a start on the rooms as soon as they all leave.'

'Thanks, love.'

'Helen?'

She turned to look at Sally.

'It's good to be back.'

Not for the first time that morning, Helen had to choke back her tears.

Alan walked over to where the two women were chatting.

'Good lordy, that was a mighty fine feast of a meal,' he said in his peculiar drawl. 'Please give my highest regards to your cook.' And with that, he headed up to his room, leaving Sally gawping.

'Yes, he talks like Elvis,' Helen whispered. 'You'll get used to it.'

With breakfast over, the dining room emptied. Some of the men headed back to the lounge, but most of them went up to their rooms.

'Remember to assemble in the lobby at ten,' Jimmy called as they dispersed.

'Are you all at the convention today?' Helen asked.

'Not until this evening. I thought I'd show the boys around Scarborough, take them on the North Bay mini railway, maybe travel up the South Bay hill in one funicular and come down in another. There's a lot to see; some of them have never been here before. We're not due at the Spa until six. Our gig's at eight but they want us to do some publicity shots, all twelve of us, before we go onstage. The mayor's coming to shake our hands and have his picture taken with us for the *Scarborough Times*, and there's a meet-and-greet with fans. You should come.'

'Me?' Helen said, surprised. 'But I haven't got a ticket.'

'I've got spares,' Jimmy said. He turned towards Sally. 'Would you like to come too?'

Sally looked from Jimmy to Helen. 'Oh no . . . I can't. I've got my little girl to look after. Mum has her while I'm at work and I can't ask her to babysit tonight as well. Besides, I'm not really an Elvis fan.'

Jimmy took an exaggerated intake of breath, pressed his hands to his heart and pretended to stagger backwards. 'You're not a fan? I'm wounded! How about it, Helen? Would you like a couple of free tickets for you and a friend?'

Helen couldn't remember the last time she'd had a night out. It was long before Tom had become ill, she felt sure of that. But with all her guests out that evening at the concert, she decided to make the most of it.

'Yes, I will. Thanks, Jimmy. I appreciate it.'

Downstairs in the kitchen, she helped Jean clear away plates and bowls. The local news on the radio was giving an update on the bin men's threatened strike.

'Fancy coming out with me to see the Elvis impersonators tonight, Jean? I've just been offered two free tickets. We could make a night of it – what do you say?'

Jean lifted her floral apron over her head and folded it carefully. 'I can't, love. I've got to go and visit Mum in the care home, and I'll be plumb tuckered for the rest of the day. But I appreciate the offer. Will one of your friends go with you instead? Seems a shame to waste a free ticket.'

Helen knew there was no point in calling Sue, as she was away on her yoga retreat, and an Elvis tribute gig was definitely not Marie's cup of tea. She decided to try Bev, thinking that a night out might be just what her friend needed. But Bev's phone went straight to voicemail. Helen left a message, asking her to call back, then joined Sally upstairs cleaning rooms, replacing towels and making beds. She heard noises coming from room seven and assumed Brian was up and about.

When everything was done, she put the kettle on in the kitchen and prepared a cafetière of coffee. Sally sank into a chair at the table.

'Well, that's better than working for Traveltime Inns,' she said. 'It really is great to be back.'

'I've got your contract for you to sign,' Helen said, pushing a brown envelope across the table.

Sally slid the sheets of paper from the envelope and read them, then raised her gaze to Helen.

'You're offering me guaranteed work until after New Year? This is great, Helen. Before, you said it'd just be for the summer season. What's changed?'

'I'm staying open, Sal. I've got to.'

'For Tom?' Sally said.

Helen nodded. 'For Tom, me and the bank manager.' She smiled. 'Listen, I was thinking of going after four stars for the hotel. I've been reading up on it and I'd have to redecorate and update the place, maybe even put security cameras at the back and front doors.'

Security had been on her mind more than ever since she'd found the smashed pot in the courtyard. Plus there'd been the stranger hanging around outside the hotel, staring into the lounge, and now the unsettling brown furry toy dog pierced by a knitting needle. If she wanted to face the future with as much strength as she could, she had to feel secure.

'I can't afford to do anything yet,' she continued. 'But if we have a good summer season, I could think about making some changes before Christmas.'

'Good idea,' Sally said.

'Sally, do you think the Seaview is a bit old-fashioned?' Helen grimaced. 'A bit eighties?'

'Well, it's really not my place to say, but . . .'

'Go on,' Helen said gently.

'Well, if you're sure you want me to be honest, then yes. It's spick and span, I make sure of that, but it's been looking old and tired for years.'

'Aren't we all?' Helen sighed, and glanced around the kitchen. 'Mind you, going after four stars will mean I'll have to strong-arm Jean into expanding her breakfast menu.'

Sally laughed out loud. 'Good luck with that.'

* * *

Murder at the Seaview Hotel

As the day wore on, Helen's phone remained quiet, with no call or text from Bev. On her walk with Suki that afternoon, she reached a decision: she would pluck up the courage to head out to the Spa on her own. There had to be a first time to go out and do things without Tom, so why not tonight of all nights?

She changed into black jeans and high heels, the first time she'd dressed up in months, then went to the bathroom to make a start on her hair. The sight of Tom's toothbrush stopped her in her tracks. She stared at the blue plastic brush as if challenging it to a fight, then she picked it up, returned to the bedroom and, before she could change her mind, dropped it into the drawer where he'd kept his socks. She slammed the drawer shut and sank onto the bed, her heart hammering. Throwing his slippers in the bin . . . and now this. What was she thinking? How callous she felt, erasing Tom bit by bit from her life when what she wanted more than anything – more than everything – was to have her husband back.

Chapter 13

Hair done and make-up on, Helen stood in front of the bedroom mirror. The woman staring back at her was wearing black jeans with heels and a long-sleeved floaty white top decorated with forget-me-nots. She pushed her sleek brown bobbed hair behind her ears.

'You've lost too much weight,' she told the woman in the mirror. It was hardly surprising. After Tom had moved to the hospice, she hadn't had time to cook at home, instead grabbing food on the go: a sandwich from one of the shops on Eastborough or a carton of chips from the nearest fish and chip shop. In Scarborough, you were never far away from one of those. And then after he died and she moved to Scotland to stay with his sister, she couldn't eat at all; all she'd wanted to do was cry. But slowly, with Tina's nurturing support and loving care, not to mention her wonderful home-cooked food, she'd begun to find her appetite. She'd also gone walking each day with Tina, and helped out on the farm, and all the fresh air and stillness had done her the world of good. But she was still a long way off the size she had once been.

She took a belt and threaded it through the loops on her jeans. 'I'm turning into you, Suki, all skinny limbs and big eyes,' she told the dog, who was lying on the floor. 'I'll be chattering my teeth next if I'm not careful.'

Heading to the bar, she flicked the switch to turn on the jukebox. She picked a quiet, soulful tune and sang along. Jimmy had told her that Twelvis would be meeting in the bar in their stage outfits, ready to head out en masse. Taxis had been booked to pick everyone up at a quarter to six for the short ride to the Spa, and Helen had been invited to join them. But the gig didn't start until eight and she wasn't sure what she was going to do in the meantime. She didn't want to hang around looking like a desperate groupie. Besides, Twelvis had to shake hands with the mayor and meet and greet fans.

She knew there was a bar at the Spa, and she could wait there while they were busy. Or she might even go for a walk, as the night was mild. The South Bay by the Spa was quiet, and she thought of walking along past the funicular cliff lift and beach huts to where the outdoor seawater pool had once stood. She had learned to swim there as a child, wearing her bright orange armbands and a pink plastic cap. The pool had been demolished decades ago and in its place was a wide-open space from where you could view the whole of the South Bay in striking panorama. The area was old, made up of narrow streets of fishermen's cottages around the harbour, next to cheery amusements and fish and chip shops on the seafront. And above it all stood the magnificent castle high on the clifftop overlooking both bays.

The song on the jukebox ended and Helen was about to choose another when she heard doors slamming upstairs and the clatter of footsteps. She walked into the lobby, and as the men descended towards her, her mouth dropped open in shock. She'd never seen them dressed as Elvis before.

'You all look . . .' She paused, too shocked to speak. Each

and every one of them looked absolutely stunning. 'Amazing,' she said at last. There was a fat Elvis, thin Elvis, Hawaiian Elvis, Vegas Elvis, jailbird Elvis, GI Elvis in khaki uniform and peaked cap. There was a black-leather Elvis from his famous comeback show of 1968. There were sideburns, high collars, black wigs, blue suede shoes, silk scarves and scarlet shirts unbuttoned to reveal hairy chests and navels; neckerchiefs, wide belts, oversized glasses, heavy make-up and dark eyeliner. The problem was, now they were disguised by wigs and glasses and goodness knows what else, Helen couldn't tell who was who. She was relieved when one of the Elvises dressed in the iconic white suit stepped forward and began to speak. That was when she knew which one was Jimmy.

'Line up for uniform inspection. You know the drill, by now,' he said.

Helen watched as the men arranged themselves in a semicircle in the lounge. Jimmy walked from one end of the line to the other making sure each Twelvis member was properly attired.

'All present and correct,' he announced, then turned to Helen. 'What do you think of my boys?' he said proudly.

'You all look incredible. I mean absolutely fantastic.' And they did, they really did. But what she kept quiet about was that despite their wigs and clothes, snarls, quivering lips and shaking legs, none of them actually looked like the King of Rock and Roll. They looked like a bunch of men wearing impressive fancy dress, ready for a good night out.

Outside, a car tooted its horn.

'The taxis are here,' Hawaiian Elvis said. Helen stood to one side as the men filed out. Vegas Elvis went first.

'Elvis has left the building!' he yelled as he stepped out of the Seaview.

He was followed by a white-suited Elvis.

'Elvis has left the building!'

1968 Comeback Elvis was next.

'Elvis has left the—'

'That's enough of that, lads,' Jimmy said sternly. 'I'm sure Mrs Dexter doesn't want to hear all this.'

'Oh, but I do,' Helen laughed. 'It's the best thing that's happened to the Seaview in years!'

Two Elvises wearing matching white suits with an emerald-green flash down their trouser legs left together, one with his arm slung around the other's shoulders.

'Elvis has left the building!' Bob and Sam called out.

An older, fatter Elvis walked from the lounge to the lobby. He wore white trousers topped by a blue satin jacket with elasticated cuffs. He had a blue satin scarf around his neck. As he locked eyes with Helen, she breathed in his cloying scent and a chill ran through her. It was Brian. She noticed he was the only one of the twelve men to step out of the hotel in silence.

The first three taxis filled up and sped off. This left Helen waiting for the final cab outside the Seaview with Jimmy and Brian. As they waited, a black Porsche drove slowly by. She recognised the driver as the man from Traveltime Inns she'd seen arguing with Brian outside the Glendale. Just then Brian gripped his stomach and lurched forward.

'Jimmy, I think I must've eaten something at lunchtime that's starting to disagree with me. I need to go back indoors and use the khazi.'

'Hurry up,' Jimmy said, pointing along the road. 'The taxi's coming. We'll wait.'

'No, it's best if you go on without me. I'll follow you as soon as I can. I'll call another cab.'

'I'm not going without you.'

Brian pulled his keys out of his pocket. 'Jimmy, please. I'm really not feeling too well.'

He headed back up the steps of the hotel just as the taxi stopped outside.

'Come on, let's go,' Jimmy said. He held the back door of the taxi open for Helen and took the front seat.

'You off to this convention at the Spa, then?' the driver asked.

'Quick as you like, pal,' Jimmy said anxiously, aware of the time.

In the back of the cab, Helen turned to look at the Seaview. Brian was still on the doorstep, which she thought odd after he'd claimed to be in desperate need of heading indoors. Why was he hanging about? Then she saw him walk back down the steps to the road. The Porsche pulled up at the kerb and he disappeared inside. It was none of her business what her guests did, she knew that. But after what had happened earlier, she was more than a little suspicious.

'Jimmy?'

'What is it?'

She pointed out of the back window towards the Porsche as the taxi sped away. 'I've just seen Brian getting into that car.'

'Are you sure it was him?'

'How many Elvises are on the street this time of night? Of course it was him.'

'Turn the car round,' Jimmy ordered the driver. 'Follow that Porsche.'

But by the time the cab had done a U-turn and headed back to the Seaview, there was no sign of the car.

'Wait here a minute,' Jimmy said. He jumped out and ran up the steps, unlocked the door and headed inside. Helen followed and heard him calling for Brian.

'He's not here, is he?' Jimmy said when there was no response.

'Let me get the master key; we can check his room.'

As she headed downstairs, she heard Jimmy call out to the cab driver: 'We'll not be a minute!'

With the master key in her hand, she went straight to room seven with Jimmy following. He banged on the door, calling Brian's name, just in case he was inside. But when he was greeted with silence, he asked Helen to unlock the door. She turned the key, then stood to one side to let him enter.

'He's not here,' Jimmy cried. 'Where on earth has he gone? He can't have disappeared. Come on, we need to get to the Spa as quick as we can. Maybe he's turned up already.'

Helen locked the door, slipped the key into her handbag and headed back to the cab. Jimmy tapped his knee impatiently all the way. Within ten minutes, they'd pulled up in front of the large, ornate Victorian edifice. It had been built around the source of Scarborough's spa waters and in its day had been very grand. It was still a beautiful building, a Scarborough landmark, with a stunning outdoor sunroom where the Spa Orchestra played. It was used now as a venue for family entertainment, and for this weekend in March, it was home to the Elvis convention.

Jimmy paid the driver, then held his arm out for Helen as she unfolded herself from the car. She couldn't remember anyone ever doing that for her before, not even Tom. It was a charming gesture, old-fashioned, and one she appreciated.

The other ten members of the band were waiting for them in the foyer of the Spa. Jimmy strode over to them.

'Where's Brian? Has he turned up? Anyone seen him?'

Heads were shaken. No one had seen him since they left the hotel.

'Who's brought their phone?'

'I sure do have mine right here, sir,' Alan said.

'Call Brian. Find out where he is and tell him to get his fat arse here now.'

Helen noticed nervous looks being exchanged.

'He's not answering,' Alan said.

'Try him again,' Jimmy ordered.

'Where's he gone?' GI Elvis asked. 'Shall I go back to the hotel and see if I can find him?'

Jimmy checked his watch. 'No time. We'll just have to hope he turns up before the gig starts. Alan, keep trying his phone.'

'Jimmy, can I have a word, in private?' Helen said.

He was red in the face, anxious and sweating. She took his arm and discreetly manoeuvred him away from the lobby to a secluded spot behind the grand staircase.

'Look, I don't want to worry you, but . . .'

'What is it?' Jimmy said, concerned.

'It's about Brian,' she said. 'There's something I think you should know.'

Chapter 14

Helen was just about to tell Jimmy about the man in the black Porsche and Brian's connection to Traveltime Inns, but before she had a chance to say a single word, Alan came rushing towards them.

'I sure am sorry to interrupt you and the little lady, Jimmy, but the Mayor himself is waiting.'

'I'll be right there,' Jimmy said. He straightened his spine, then jerked his shoulders and arms forward, shooting his cuffs and making his collar stand up straight. 'I've got to go,' he told Helen. 'Hopefully Brian will turn up soon.'

'I hope so too,' Helen said, although she sounded more confident than she felt.

She watched as Twelvis headed towards a room cordoned off by a red rope slung between two brass poles. A hefty-looking bald man unfastened one end of the thick rope to allow the men to enter. Helen looked at her watch. She had almost two hours before the gig began. From the lobby she could see into Farrer's café bar, which was open for pre-gig drinks. It looked inviting with its twinkling lights and windows overlooking the sea, but it was empty and she didn't much fancy being the only customer. She was finding it hard enough being out for the first time since Tom's death; she certainly didn't feel brave enough to sit in a bar on her own. She wished Bev had called her back. They could have gone to the bar together, shared a bottle of wine and made the most of the time to have a really good chat. But Bev hadn't rung or texted, and so Helen was here alone.

She went outside and headed past the sun court for a stroll along the prom. The night had turned chilly after such a mild day, and she pulled her jacket tight around her as she looked out over the South Bay, twinkling with lights as darkness fell. The amusement arcades on the seafront flashed red and green next to neon signs advertising bingo and twopenny slots. Behind them, high up the hill, lights from cafés and bars shone like sprinkled glitter alongside those from the old town and harbour. Above it all was Scarborough Castle, a formidable and solid presence, floodlit on the cliff.

She walked past the ticket office for the funicular lift that ran up and down the cliff between the Spa and the Esplanade. The Esplanade was where Scarborough's more affluent visitors stayed, in the likes of the luxurious Crown Spa hotel, a decorative white building that reminded her of an iced wedding cake. The funicular ticket office was closed, as she had expected at this time of night, but a brightly painted sign declared it the oldest funicular in the UK and that it would open early the next day.

'Miss you, Tom,' she whispered into the night air.

She thought briefly about heading down to the beach, as the tide was far out, but then dismissed the idea; her high heels weren't the right sort of footwear for picking her way on the sand. She began to feel the cold keenly and decided to head back to the Spa. Perhaps there was a quiet corner in the bar where she could sit unobserved.

As she walked back, she noticed that the place was busier now, with people turning up for the gig. Some were heading to the bar, some straight to their seats inside the concert hall. Helen felt it was still too early to go inside to the gig; she would have to brave the bar. As she walked in, she saw a woman with cropped silver hair berating a young girl, and recognised them as Miriam's guests. She wondered if the family ever stopped arguing. She had to stand behind them in the queue for the bar and had no choice but to listen to them.

'I don't want to go in, Mum,' Daisy seethed.

'You'll do as you're told, young lady,' her mother replied.

'But it's old-fogey music. Can you imagine what my friends are going to say if they find out I'm here to see an Elvis concert? I mean, Elvis? Really? Who even called him that? That can't be his real name.'

'You know your dad's an Elvis fan.'

'Oh, and we've got to keep *him* happy, haven't we?' Daisy said sarcastically. 'Never mind about what I want.'

'You can drop that tone right now,' her mother said.

Helen saw Daisy whip her phone from her back pocket and begin texting, putting an end to the argument. The queue shuffled forward politely and silently. Ahead of Helen, it was Miriam's guests' turn to be served.

'A pint of Wold Top IPA for my husband,' the woman said. 'A gin and tonic for me and . . . Daisy, what would you like to drink?'

'Triple vodka with extra vodka,' Daisy said without lifting her gaze from her phone. Helen suppressed a smile.

'She'll have a Coke,' her mother told the barman.

Once served, Daisy lifted her drink from the bar and the woman took the amber beer and the goldfish-bowl-sized glass of gin.

'Come on, Daisy, there's a table by the window. Dad shouldn't be long.'

'Where's he gone anyway?' Daisy asked.

The woman shot her a look. 'To get you the ice cream you've been banging on about all flaming day,' she replied, barely concealing her anger. 'Now get over there, find a table and sit down.'

She turned to Helen and shook her head.

'Give me strength. Teenagers, eh? Who'd have 'em?'

A shiver ran down Helen's back. I would, she thought. Her own babies would have been in their twenties by now; maybe she'd even be a grandmother. She managed to offer a weak smile to the harassed mum before the barman asked her what she'd like, shaking her out of her reverie.

She ordered a large glass of dry white wine and retreated to a table for two. She positioned herself so that she could see the whole bar, then raised her glass and muttered 'cheers' under her breath. She wondered if Brian had turned up yet and hoped very much that he had. Whatever she thought of him, which admittedly wasn't much after the way he'd spoken to her, she didn't want Jimmy and the boys let down. She sipped her wine slowly, flicking through the Scarborough tourist guide that she'd picked up in the foyer. There were full-page ads inside for the North Bay miniature railway and the Alpamare water park on the edge of town. Then she turned the page and her blood ran cold.

There in front of her was a double-page ad for a new Traveltime Inn in the centre of town. It showed an artist's impression of what one of the beautiful Victorian terraced hotels that Scarborough was renowned for would look like once Traveltime got their hands on it. Their publicity pictures looked impressive, she had to admit, with lush green trees and well-dressed people strolling by the hotel. It seemed to her that Traveltime were on a mission to buy up as many old buildings as they could and turn them into soulless hotels. It was no wonder they were so keen on getting the Seaview, if they wanted to bring the Glendale into their brand.

She flicked over the page and read instead about guided bike rides through Dalby Forest and penguins at the Sea Life Centre. There was an advert for the beautiful Crown Spa hotel showing the kind of pampering the guests there could enjoy in luxurious surroundings, and more adverts for smaller, family-run B&Bs. An idea struck her and she popped the booklet into her handbag. Well, if she was thinking of going after four stars, maybe it was time to start thinking about posting adverts in the guide that tourists picked up at the Spa.

With half an hour to go before the gig began, she left the bar and walked into the concert hall. There was an excited murmur in the air as it filled up. It was an old-fashioned venue, with red velvet curtains closed across the stage. She looked at her ticket and headed to the front of the hall, where her seat was in the middle of row C.

'Excuse me, thank you. Excuse me, thank you,' she said as she made her way along the row, causing those already seated to gather bags, coats, sweets and drinks as they stood to let her past. When she reached her seat, she took her jacket off, sat down and smoothed her top. Just as she was getting comfortable, however, a woman in the row behind tapped her on her shoulder.

'Excuse me, I think that man's trying to get your attention,' she said.

Helen looked in the direction the woman was pointing and saw Jimmy standing in the aisle. He looked distressed, she thought, and he was beckoning her towards him. She picked up her bag and coat and headed towards him, causing everyone to stand up again. What on earth had happened to make him so upset?

'What is it? Has Brian arrived?' she said.

'No,' Jimmy whispered, glancing nervously around. 'He's not here and we're on in just over twenty minutes. We need another Elvis. We can't go on as Elevensis; we'll be a laughing stock.'

'There must be someone you know who can help?'

'We only know one person in Scarborough,' Jimmy replied. He stared at her long and hard, and the horrible truth sank in.

'No,' she said quickly. 'Oh no. No, no, no.'

'Yes, Helen, you can do it.'

'I can't.'

He laid his hands on her shoulders. 'We need someone we can trust.'

'But I can't sing!' she squeaked.

'You don't need to. We'll cover you. Brian only had one solo, and I'll sing it for him. You'll just be a backing singer. The audience need to see twelve of us, Helen, and you know all the songs. Please, I'm desperate.'

'But I don't look like Elvis! I'm not dressed up; I don't have the clothes. I'm not even a man!'

Jimmy dropped his hands from her shoulders. 'I know. There's a woman behind the scenes working in wardrobe; she'll help you look the part.'

'No, Jimmy. I can't.'

'Helen, please, I'm begging you. It's just until Brian turns up. You can go offstage the second he arrives.'

Still protesting, Helen felt Jimmy gently take her arm, and then somehow her legs were carrying her away from the aisle. Before she knew it, she was at the side of the theatre, walking through a door covered by a red velvet curtain, following a green sign to backstage.

'All you have to do is stand at the back; follow Colin, he'll look after you. Dance like he dances. If in doubt, wave your arms and sway from side to side, gyrate a bit.'

'That's all?' Helen gulped.

'Well, there is something else . . .'

She stiffened and glared at him. 'What?'

'For our last song, there's a grass skirt with coconut shells to wear while you do the hula across the stage. It brings the house down.'

Helen felt her legs go weak. 'Coconuts?'

'Come on, Helen, please,' Jimmy pleaded.

She looked at him and saw tears in his eyes. She knew how much this meant to him. 'Am I really your only hope to save the show?' she asked.

He nodded. 'Believe me, I wouldn't have asked if you weren't.'

She took one long breath after another to steel herself. 'OK, I'll do it. Jeez, I must be mad.'

If only Tom could see me now, she thought. She knew exactly what he'd tell her to do.

She smiled at Jimmy and cried out at the top of her voice, 'Helvis is in the building!'

Chapter 15

A young woman dressed head to foot in black, with fierce black eyebrows and dark hair piled messily on top of her head, eyed Helen up and down.

'I'm Alison, the wardrobe manager,' she said. 'And I'm guessing you must be a size ten?'

'I've lost a bit of weight recently,' Helen began. 'I'm usually a size—' but her words were cut off when a tape measure was looped around her waist and pulled tight. She stood mute with her arms stretched out while Alison measured her hips and chest.

'Come with me,' Alison said. 'We haven't got much time. This has been sprung on me at the last minute.'

'You and me both,' Helen said.

She followed Alison along dark corridors that twisted and turned.

'In here,' Alison said, pushing open a door into a tiny room crammed floor to ceiling with shelves. The room was hot and smelled of sweat and in the centre was a rail of clothes. Helen saw mannequin heads on the shelves sporting Marilyn Monroe wigs, Elvis wigs, Bowie wigs and flamboyant Elton John glasses. Alison pulled a black wig from a shelf, and, to Helen's horror, two coconut shells, a grass skirt and a flower lei. Then she rifled through the wardrobe rail and handed over a red nylon jacket and white trousers.

'This is what you'll wear for most of the gig. They should fit. The Hawaiian song comes on at the end of the second half. With a bit of luck the missing Elvis will have turned up by then and you won't need the grass skirt and bra. He usually does it as a comedy sketch.'

'You've seen Twelvis perform before?' Helen asked.

'Just online. Come on, you need to get changed now,' Alison urged. 'They're due onstage in fifteen minutes. We're going to have to do the best we can.'

'Where's the changing room?' Helen asked.

'You're in it. Come on, strip off. I'll help you get kitted out.'

'I have to get changed in here?' Helen cried. She looked around the poky room.

'I'll wait outside,' Alison said. 'Give me a shout when you've got the clothes on, then I'll fix the wig for you.'

Helen quickly changed into the clothes, which were miles too big for her slim frame, then pulled the door open. 'What do you reckon?' she said.

'I reckon I've got five minutes to get you looking as much like Elvis as I can. Stand still while I sort you out, and then I'll take you up to the stage.'

Alison worked quickly, crouching on the floor to pin up the trousers, which were far too long. 'How come you ended up doing this anyway?' she asked.

'I have no idea,' Helen said. 'The only thing I know is that I'm terrified of going out onstage.'

'Don't be. Drink some of this.'

Helen looked down. In her free hand, Alison was holding a plastic beaker containing a familiar-looking dark liquid.

'Is that red wine?' she asked, surprised. 'Where did it come from?'

'As wardrobe manager I've learned to be resourceful. I always keep a spare bottle or two in here. It'll get your engine revving. Just don't spill it on the trousers.'

Helen wasn't sure she wanted her engine revving, but there was no harm in getting her windscreen wipers working. She took a long gulp of wine while Alison worked around her, pinning and tucking the clothes to fit.

'Now for the wig,' she said.

Just then a disembodied voice boomed into the cramped room from a speaker high on the wall. 'Ten minutes to stage. Ten minutes to stage.'

Helen finished the wine in a single gulp, then Alison worked her magic on the wig, securing it with tape and grips.

'Don't nod too vigorously,' she warned. 'You ready to go out onstage now?'

'What shall I do with my handbag and clothes?'

'Leave them in here. I'll lock the door; they'll be safe.'

'Thanks, Alison. I appreciate it.'

'Follow me. Quickly,' Alison said as she set off at something close to a run along the dark corridors.

When they reached the wings, she handed Helen over to another young woman dressed head to foot in black, with fierce black eyebrows and dark hair piled messily on top of her head. This one wore a headset with a microphone placed at the corner of her mouth, and carried a clipboard.

'This is Amelia, the floor manager. She'll look after you now.'

'Thanks,' Helen breathed.

'You look great,' Amelia said.

'Do I?'

'Five minutes to stage. Five minutes to stage,' the voice boomed again.

Helen closed her eyes and took a moment to pull herself together. When she opened them, Jimmy and his men were in front of her.

'You look fantastic, Helen,' Jimmy said. 'Thanks for doing this for us.'

'Has anyone heard from Brian?' she asked, hoping there might be a chance he'd turned up and she wouldn't have to go on.

'I've been calling him, but he ain't answering,' Alan said.

'What about his family? Maybe he's headed back home?'

Helen noticed Jimmy and Colin share a look.

'We, er, we haven't called his wife. She's not well. We don't want to alert her to anything untoward until we know for sure what's going on,' Jimmy said.

'One minute to curtain. One minute to curtain.'

'That's our call; come on,' Jimmy said. 'Helen, you stay at the back and do your best, that's all we can ask. And I can't tell you how grateful we are to you for saving our show.'

'You sure are a wonderful lady,' Alan said.

The eleven Elvises and Helen walked onto the stage, which was still hidden from the audience by the red curtain. Jimmy took his place at the front; the others arranged themselves in rows behind him, with Helen right at the back. She could hear the audience beyond the curtain, could imagine their excitement at waiting to see the band perform. She only hoped they wouldn't be too disappointed if they noticed her dancing out of step.

'Ladies and gentlemen!' a voice rang out into the auditorium. 'Tonight! We are delighted to bring you not one, not two, not three . . .' Helen could hear the audience joining in with the chant as it went on to reach its final crescendo.

In the row ahead of her, Alan turned round. 'You doing OK back there, little lady?'

'. . . not five, not six, not even seven . . .' the voice boomed.

Helen raised both thumbs in reply.

'. . . not ten, not even eleven Elvises!'

By now the audience were going wild.

'Tonight! We bring you . . . Twelvis!'

The audience roared, clapped, screamed, hollered and whistled. The red velvet curtain slowly began to rise, and the stage was flooded with light. Helen blinked. She'd expected to see hundreds of faces staring at her, but she was blinded by the glare. Oddly, though, it helped calm her.

Jimmy had told her that Twelvis always kicked off with an a cappella song, and when it struck up, she began to mouth the words. This gave her the confidence to start singing and swaying, just as Colin and Alan were doing. She followed their every move, shadowing their steps. And then the audience were on their feet, cheering and clapping. She'd done it, she'd got through the first number. She allowed herself a moment to breathe. With no idea of what song was coming next, she kept her eyes firmly on Colin and Alan, ready to copy whatever they did. At the front of the stage, Jimmy was the consummate showman and held the audience in the palm of his hand.

'Ladies and gentlemen, let me, ah, introduce you to the band,' he said.

114

Murder at the Seaview Hotel

One by one each member of Twelvis stepped forward to take a bow as Jimmy called their name. Helen's heart jumped as if it was trying to escape from her chest.

'And now, ladies and gentlemen, let me introduce you to a special member of the band. Tonight, for one night only, let's give it up for Scarborough's very own Helen Dexter as . . . Helvis!'

She bowed from her spot on the back row to raucous applause. And then it was time for another song, a faster number this time. The backing track kicked in and the crowd went wild.

Helen sang and danced her way through the first half of the gig. She was too nervous to enjoy it, aware that she was there to make up the numbers and not let Twelvis down. At the interval, she was first off the stage. The minute she stepped into the wings, Alison was at her side, pinning and tucking her clothes and re-arranging the wig.

'Try Brian again!' Jimmy yelled as soon as he was offstage.

Alan held his phone up. 'I'm calling him now, Jim, but I'm afraid there ain't no answer.'

'Do you want me onstage again in the second half?' Helen asked Jimmy.

'Please, Helen,' he said. 'Listen, earlier you said you had something to tell me about Brian. What was it?'

'Let's leave it till after the show,' Helen said. She didn't want to upset Jimmy more than he already was over Brian's disappearance, especially when he had to go back out and perform.

After the interval, the lights in the auditorium went down and a hush descended on the audience. A blue light filled the stage as the Elvises took up their positions. The curtain rose to the beat of a drum. The audience erupted and jumped from their seats.

115

They were dancing, jiving, singing and waving their arms in the air. Helen began to relax, even started to enjoy herself. When the penultimate song began, stage manager Amelia beckoned to her from the wings. This was it, her cue to shimmy offstage, out of the silk top and trousers and into the grass skirt and coconuts.

'Stand still, let me do the work,' Alison ordered as she stripped Helen down and helped her into the change of clothes. 'Jimmy's given instructions that all you have to do is hula your way from left to right across the stage as the song starts, and do it again in the other direction at the end. Think you can manage it?'

Helen gulped.

'Here, drink this,' Alison said.

Helen took the plastic beaker of red wine and had a very long drink. 'You really are resourceful, aren't you?'

And then she was back onstage, this time at the front beside Jimmy. She waved her arms out to one side, then the other, doing her best approximation of a hula dance, her grass skirt waving to the beat of bongo drums. Once offstage, she stood in the wings until the end of the song and then shimmied her way back. The boys took their final bow, then filed offstage, leaving the audience screaming for more.

'Let's give them a moment before we do the encore,' Jimmy said.

Amelia stepped forward, nervously clutching her clipboard. 'I'm afraid you can't go back on,' she said.

'Why not?' Jimmy asked.

Two stern-faced men stepped forward. One was tall and distinguished-looking with grey hair, the other short with a round, plump face and dark hair.

Helen looked from one to the other. 'What's going on?'

'We want more! We want more!' the audience screamed.

The taller man cleared his throat. 'I'm Detective Sergeant Hutchinson and this is my colleague, Detective Constable Hall.'

'Evening, all,' DC Hall said.

'We understand from the Spa manager that your band is missing an Elvis impersonator who was due to perform with you this evening,' DS Hutchinson said.

'That's right,' Jimmy said. 'His name's Brian McNally. What's he done now?'

'I'm afraid the body of a man dressed as Elvis has been found this evening.' DS Hutchinson flipped his notepad open. 'He was wearing a blue nylon jacket and white trousers.'

Helen gasped.

'Yes, that's what Brian was wearing,' Jimmy said, 'along with his blue suede shoes. Officer, just to clarify, when you say a body was found, do you mean . . .?'

'Yes, sir. A dead man has been found floating in the lake at Peasholm Park. We believe he's your missing Elvis.'

Chapter 16

The audience was still cheering and screaming for an encore as the shock news sank in backstage. Amelia muttered something into the microphone at the side of her mouth, and within seconds a voice boomed out in the auditorium.

'Ladies and gentlemen, Twelvis has left the building!'

Beyond the red velvet curtain, the audience gave an almighty groan and the house lights came back on.

'How did he die?' Colin said. 'I mean, if it *is* Brian?'

More questions were fired from the men.

'Did he fall in the lake?'

'Was it suicide?'

'Who found him?'

'And when?'

DS Hutchinson held his hands up to calm them down. 'We can't say any more until we know for sure who it is, which means we'll need someone to identify the body.'

Helen watched the men shuffle uncomfortably and glance nervously at each other.

'I'll do it,' Jimmy said.

'And your name is?'

'James Brown.'

DS Hutchinson tried and failed to stifle a smile. 'Elvis Presley is telling me his real name is James Brown. I've heard it all now.'

Helen stepped forward and crossed her arms in front of her chest. 'These men might have lost a good friend tonight. The least you can do is show a little respect,' she said sternly.

DS Hutchinson glared at her and she felt heat rise in her neck.

'Right, Mr Brown. You need to go with my colleague.'

'This way, sir,' the short detective said. Helen watched as Jimmy followed him.

'The rest of you will have to come to the station with me,' DS Hutchinson said.

'Are we under arrest?' Sam asked.

'Of course not.'

'Then I'm sure you don't need me to tell you that we don't have to go to the station. We've all had a terrible shock and would appreciate returning to our hotel. If you need to interview us as witnesses, perhaps you could speak to us there.'

DS Hutchinson glared at him. 'You seem to know a lot about the law, lad.'

'I should do. I'm a solicitor,' Sam replied coolly.

DS Hutchinson nodded slowly, letting this sink in. 'Where are you staying?'

'The Seaview Hotel, and a mighty fine place it is too,' Alan said.

DS Hutchinson stared at him for a very long time. 'Are you taking the mickey, talking to me like that?'

'No, sir,' Alan said, dropping his gaze.

'This is my brother Alan, and that's how he speaks,' Stuart said. 'He doesn't mean any disrespect.'

DS Hutchinson turned his steely gaze from Alan. 'So you're all staying at the Seaview? Is that the one on Windsor Terrace?'

Helen stepped forward. 'Yes, that's it. It's my hotel. These men are my guests.'

DS Hutchinson's gaze fell on Helen's coconuts and he cleared his throat. 'Miss? You might want to cover yourself up before you head outside.'

'My clothes are backstage,' she said quickly. 'I'll go and get dressed.'

She went in search of Alison, and found her backstage. 'Thank goodness!' she breathed. 'I need my clothes, as quick as you can.'

'I've just heard what happened,' Alison said. 'I can't believe it.'

Helen followed her to the room where earlier that evening she'd changed out of her jeans and floaty top.

'I'll wait outside and lock up once you're done,' Alison said. 'And if you need something for the shock, there's a bottle of red behind Tina Turner's hairpiece.'

Once Helen was ready, she followed Alison back to the auditorium, where the ten remaining members of Twelvis were sitting. DS Hutchinson was standing in front of them.

'All ready, miss?' he said when Helen walked towards them.

'It's Mrs,' Helen said. 'Mrs Dexter.'

'As you wish,' he replied curtly. 'Everyone, please follow me.'

Helen and the Elvises did as they were told, all of them too stunned to speak. Helen felt sick. If the dead man turned out to be Brian, she knew she'd have to tell the police about his argument with the man from Traveltime Inns and his offer to buy her hotel. She wondered if he'd been in trouble before, for Jimmy

120

had assumed he'd been arrested. *What's he done now?* he had asked the detectives.

A police van was waiting outside the Spa. DS Hutchinson opened the back door.

'Everyone in,' he ordered. 'Not you, Mrs Dexter. You can sit in the front. It'll be more comfortable for you.'

One by one the men clambered into the van. Kev, being on the large side, had to have assistance, as did Big Al, the shortest man there. There were no seats inside.

'There's nothing for it, boys, we're going to have to sit on the floor,' Sam said.

Once everyone was seated, the van roared into life.

'He's not going to put the blue lights and siren on, is he?' Davey said.

'I hope not,' Bob replied.

In the front of the van, Helen kept her eyes on the road.

'Been singing with the Elvis band long, have you, Mrs Dexter?' DS Hutchinson asked as he drove.

'No. I just did it as a favour tonight.'

'How long have you known them?'

'Since yesterday.'

'Any of them strike you as unusual?'

Helen glared at him. 'There are ten men dressed as Elvis sitting in the van behind me. Most of them make their living pretending to be the King of Rock and Roll and one of them even speaks like Elvis. Now I don't know about you, DS Hutchinson, but none of that strikes me as usual.'

'There's no need to take a tone, Mrs Dexter,' he replied, in what she definitely would have said was a tone.

121

He drove the rest of the way in silence before pulling the van to a stop outside the Seaview. 'Everyone out,' he ordered, flinging the door open.

It took a while for the Elvises to unfold themselves from the van in their capes and wigs. Helen slid her key into the lock of the Seaview's door, and they filed into the hotel behind her.

'We're going up to our rooms to get out of our show clothes,' Sam told DS Hutchinson. 'We'll meet you in the lounge in a few minutes and you can ask us any questions you like. That is, of course, if the dead man is indeed our band member.'

As the men headed upstairs, DS Hutchinson sank into a chair. Helen switched the lights on in the lounge.

'Would you like a drink?' she asked.

'I shouldn't, not while I'm working.'

She pushed a glass against the brandy optic. 'Excuse me if I have one. It's been one hell of a night.'

DS Hutchinson looked around the lounge. 'Nice place you've got here. It reminds me of something.'

'The eighties?' Helen muttered under her breath. She downed the brandy in one, then rested both hands on the bar as she waited for the heat of the liquor to hit the back of her throat.

'Was the missing Elvis sharing a room with anyone?' DS Hutchinson asked.

'No, he had his own double room at the top of the stairs, number seven.'

'Keep it locked,' he ordered. 'Just in case the dead man turns out to be your guest. Forensics will need to inspect it and take his belongings as evidence.'

'Forensics? Evidence?' Helen cried.

'The crime scene is Peasholm Park, but we will need to account for his movements before his death. His belongings may offer vital clues.'

Slowly the men began to head downstairs. Their Elvis capes and trousers, buckles and belts were now replaced by jeans and shirts.

'You doing all right there, little lady?' Alan asked Helen when he walked into the lounge.

'I think so. I'm all shook up. Sorry, no pun intended.'

'We all surely are upset, Mrs Dexter.'

'Would you like a drink, Alan? It's on the house, anything you boys want, just ask.'

'Why, thank you kindly. A little darn whisky might just hit the spot.'

Helen busied herself pouring stiff drinks for the men. It was almost two hours later when DC Hall and Jimmy returned to the Seaview. When she heard the car outside, and then the noise of the door as the men walked into the hotel, she saw Jimmy ashen-faced. She didn't wait to be asked. She poured a large whisky and slid it across the bar. He downed it in a single gulp. All eyes were on him. He lifted his gaze and with a nod confirmed everyone's worst fears.

'No!' Colin cried.

There was silence for a few moments.

Sam turned to DS Hutchinson. 'You said he was found floating in the lake at the park?'

'That's right, sir.'

'Then how did he die? Did he fall in the water? What happened?'

The detectives exchanged a look. DS Hutchinson gave a nervous cough. 'He was found floating face down. He'd been strangled with his scarf.'

'Was he still wearing his Elvis outfit?' Colin asked.

'Yes, he was still dressed as Elvis,' DS Hutchinson confirmed.

'Not quite,' Jimmy said darkly. 'He was missing his blue suede shoes.'

Chapter 17

'Are you dredging the lake to see if—' Sam began.

DS Hutchinson sighed impatiently. 'Yes, we're dredging the lake. First thing in the morning. We're expecting to find the shoes and hopefully some evidence to help explain what happened.'

'I sometimes walk my dog in the park at night,' Helen said. 'There are usually other dog walkers around. Did no one see anything?'

'Apparently not,' DC Hall replied. 'Most of Scarborough was at the Elvis concert. It's been the talk of the town for months. The park, like everywhere else in town tonight, was deserted.'

Ginger walked towards Jimmy and laid his hand on his shoulder. 'Someone's going to have to call Brian's wife.'

'The police have already rung Brian's daughter to give the family the news,' Jimmy said.

'Perhaps I'll ring her too,' Ginger offered.

'Good idea.'

Ginger walked to the dining room and closed the door to make his call in private. A few moments later, he returned, wiping the back of his hand across his eyes. 'Worst phone call I've ever had to make in my life.'

Helen poured another whisky and slid the glass towards him.

'What do you need to ask us?' Sam asked the detectives.

'I'll take individual statements. Even if you think you know nothing about what happened tonight, it'll be useful for us to hear a little about the deceased, about the kind of man he was.'

'Stop calling him "the man", "the deceased". His name was Brian,' Big Al said with a catch in his voice.

'Brian, er, yes,' DS Hutchinson corrected himself. 'We need to know how you knew him, when you last saw him, how he seemed to you, what he said, whether he had any enemies, that kind of thing.'

Big Al shook his head. 'Enemies? Brian? No, you've got the wrong man. He was the sort who wouldn't hurt a fly.'

Helen wondered how much Twelvis really knew about their bandmate.

DS Hutchinson rose from his seat. 'I'll set myself up in the dining room across the hall, if that's all right with you, Mrs Dexter?'

'That's fine,' she said. 'Would you like coffee bringing in?'

'Please,' he replied. 'DC Hall, you stay here and send them in to see me one by one.'

Helen swallowed hard. 'Will you need to take a statement from me too?'

'Yes,' DS Hutchinson said.

She took another slug of brandy. 'Then I'd like to go first.' She tried to keep her voice from quivering. 'Because . . .' She felt her legs go weak and had to steady herself against the bar.

'Because you've had too much to drink?' DS Hutchinson said in a misplaced attempt at a joke. No one laughed; everyone was looking at Helen.

'Because I know something about Brian, something that no one else in this room knows.'

'Will you tell them about the black Porsche?' Jimmy said.

'I'm going to tell them everything.'

'I think you'd better follow me into the dining room, Mrs Dexter.'

DS Hutchinson chose a table in the middle of the room, from where he could see through the glass-paned door into the lobby. Helen moved the cutlery that Sally had laid neatly on the table for breakfast the following day.

'Now then, Mrs Dexter. Let's start at the beginning and you can tell me everything you know.'

She spoke hesitantly at first; it was the first time she'd told anyone about Brian's threatening offer to buy her hotel. But once she'd started, her words tumbled out. DS Hutchinson scribbled notes on his pad as she talked. She told him about the strange offer from Benson's estate agents, about Brian's offer of cash and the blue leather wallet, about him grabbing her by the wrist, about the argument with the man outside the Glendale Hotel, the man she suspected was working for Traveltime Inns. Then she told him what had happened earlier that evening, when Brian had feigned illness just as he was about to step into the cab that would have taken him to the Spa.

'And how did he seem to you as a person? Did he act like a regular hotel guest?' DS Hutchinson asked.

Helen shook her head. 'He was lascivious.'

'Las . . . what?'

'Lascivious,' Helen repeated.

She watched as DS Hutchinson's pen scrawled on his notepad in an attempt to spell out the word before giving up.

'What exactly do you mean?' he said.

127

'You know, he was a lech. Some men are; they look at your breasts instead of your face when you're talking to them. He was one of those. A creep. My best friend Marie visited me yesterday and she passed him outside on her way in to see me. She said he did the same to her. He even flicked his tongue at her. I mean, what sort of pervert does that?'

'Did you find him attractive?'

'What's that got to do with anything?' Helen said, raising her voice.

'So you didn't reciprocate his lecherous overtures?'

She sat back in her chair, crossed her arms and stared hard at DS Hutchinson, giving him her answer. 'But there *is* something else I should tell you,' she said.

'Go on.'

'I think I had an intruder this week. I woke up and found that a heavy plant pot had been knocked over in my courtyard. And there was a footprint in the soil where it had spilled on the ground. It's probably not connected to what's happened tonight – I mean, it can't be, can it? And then I saw someone looking into the lounge, staring in from the street. It was probably just a kid, but all things considered, and with what's happened tonight, it's left me feeling on edge.'

'Anything else unusual going on?'

She nodded. 'I received a toy in the post, a fluffy dog the same colour as my greyhound.'

'A toy dog? What's that got to do with a murder?'

'Maybe nothing, but the dog had a needle poked through its middle. I think it was sent to me as a warning from whoever is after the Seaview. There was nothing on the box to say who'd sent it, no postmark, no address label, nothing.'

'Do you still have it? I'll take it away with me, let forensics examine it. We'll follow up with the delivery man too, and we'll call Benson's estate agents to find out who made the offer to buy your hotel.'

DS Hutchinson scribbled more notes in his pad, then looked up at Helen. 'Surely you've got security cameras on the premises?'

'No,' she said.

'Then think about having them installed.'

There was a knock at the dining-room door. Helen swung around and saw DC Hall standing there.

'Hutch, forensics are here.'

'Right, thanks, pal.' DS Hutchinson looked at Helen. 'Would you show them which room the deceased man was staying in?'

'Of course,' she replied.

'Has anyone been in the room apart from the deceased? A maid, perhaps?'

'He specifically asked for the cleaner not to go in there. He said his show clothes were out and he didn't want them disturbed.'

'Oh, did he now?' DS Hutchinson said, making a note.

'Jimmy went in, though, just for a few seconds, when we came back here looking for Brian after we saw him getting into the Porsche. But he didn't touch anything, I watched him all the time he was in there.'

'Can you remember any numbers or letters from the Porsche's number plate?'

'Sorry, I can't.'

'But you're sure it was a Porsche?'

'Oh yes, quite sure. My friend Marie—'

'The one who visited you yesterday?'

'Yes. She had a similar one, though hers was bright red. She drives a red sixties convertible these days.'

DS Hutchinson stiffened. 'I know that car. It's the only one of its type in Scarborough. What's your friend's surname?'

'Clark. Why?'

'Is she related to Daran Clark?'

'She's married to him. Why do you want to know about Marie?'

'I don't,' DS Hutchinson said. 'It's her husband we're interested in. Seems his name keeps cropping up at the station in connection with one dodgy scheme after another.'

'Well, I wouldn't know anything about that,' Helen said, although she wasn't surprised to hear it.

'Right, well, I think you can go and let forensics into the room, Mrs Dexter. While you're out there, ask DC Hall to send James Brown in.'

Helen did as instructed and led two young women up to room seven. She unlocked the door, opened it wide and then was asked to leave. She headed downstairs and returned to the lounge.

'Would anyone like another drink? I know I could do with one.'

Her offer was taken up by every man in the room; even DC Hall had a glass of orangeade and a packet of dry-roasted nuts. When everyone had their glass filled, Helen excused herself and went down to her apartment. As expected, Suki was waiting by the door, teeth chattering.

'Oh, my love, I'm sorry. You'll be wanting to go out, won't you? Come on, I'll take you out to the grass. We can't go for a walk, but I'll make up for it tomorrow morning, I swear.'

She clipped Suki's lead to her collar and headed outside. The cold air hit her hard and she breathed in sharply. 'This is all too much,' she whispered into the cold night. 'Just when I'm getting back on my feet, why does this have to happen?'

Helen had lived in Scarborough all of her life and this was the first time she'd ever had an encounter with the police. It scared her. Murder was supposed to be something you heard about on the news, read about in the papers or watched on TV in a Sunday-night drama. She shut her eyes tight. Maybe if she kept them closed long enough, when she opened them again she'd find out she'd dreamt the whole thing.

As Suki sniffed the grass verge and stretched her legs, Helen turned her back to the sea, leaned against the blue metal railings and looked at the Seaview. A light was on in the room where the forensics team were working. She saw the dimmed lights in the lounge. And then the front door opened and Jimmy walked out. She watched as he pulled his phone out of his pocket. She saw the light illuminate the side of his face as he began speaking, and she wondered who he was talking to.

She tugged on Suki's lead. 'Come on, Suki, let's go back in.'

Jimmy was still standing on the steps, speaking on his phone. As Helen passed him, he turned his head away, but she caught a snippet of his conversation.

'It's done. Everything's going to be all right.'

Then he walked down the steps and away from the hotel with his phone still clamped to his ear.

Helen walked into the Seaview. In the hallway, Big Al was coming out of the dining room.

'The copper wants to talk to you again,' he said to Helen.

'Did he say why?'

He shook his head.

Helen led Suki into the dining room. 'Sorry, I promised to bring you coffee and I forgot all about it. I've had a lot on my mind.'

'It's not coffee I'm after, Mrs Dexter. Please have a seat.'

Helen sat down. The chair was still warm from Big Al's small bottom. Suki lay down under the table, a little too close to DS Hutchinson's boots for Helen's comfort. When she saw the dog start licking the boots, she pulled at the lead. The last thing she needed was for her to start chewing them.

'What is it?' she asked.

'When we spoke earlier, you said your friend Marie passed Mr McNally, the deceased man, as he left the hotel when she was coming in to see you. I just wondered if you could tell me a little about how he seemed when he left the Seaview?'

'Oh,' Helen gasped. She shook her head. 'No. He didn't leave here. He left next door, the Vista del Mar.'

'But he's staying here. Why would he be exiting a different hotel?'

She slumped back in her chair. 'I forgot all about it. With everything that's happened, I honestly forgot.'

'What is it? If you know something, now is not the time to withhold information.'

Helen took a deep breath and looked him straight in the eye. 'He was leaving next door after having an argument with the woman who runs the place.'

'And how do you know this? Did she tell you?'

She dropped her gaze to the table. 'I was listening to them through the wall.'

'Is this something you usually do?'

She sat up straight. 'No. I've never done it before.'

'Then why do it now?'

'Because I heard the landlady shouting and swearing. That's something she never does. I was intrigued to know what was going on.'

'And you heard them arguing?'

'Every word.'

'Mrs Dexter, getting information from you is rather like getting blood from a stone.'

'You think I'm proud of myself for eavesdropping on my neighbour and a guest?'

'Just tell me what they said.'

'Well, Miriam . . . that's the landlady's name . . . she said something about him turning up out of the blue after thirty-odd years, and it was clear she wasn't happy to see him. It turns out they used to be married.'

DS Hutchinson scribbled manically in his notepad. 'And so they argued for, what, ten minutes? Half an hour?'

'About five minutes or so,' Helen said.

'Raised voices?'

She nodded.

'Angry?'

'Yes.'

'Did anyone else hear them arguing?'

'How would I know?'

'No one else was with you?'

'No, I was alone.'

'And how did the argument end?'

'She told him she never wanted to see him again, and then she said . . .' She stopped, a chill running through her as she remembered Miriam's words.

'Mrs Dexter,' DS Hutchinson said, exasperated. 'Please carry on.'

Helen looked him in the eye.

'She said she wished he was dead.'

Chapter 18

DS Hutchinson snapped his notepad closed. 'I think I'm going to have a word with this Miriam. What's her surname?'

'Jones, Miriam Jones.'

'And she runs the place next door?'

'Yes, she's been there longer than we've been here at the Seaview.'

'Who's we?' DS Hutchinson asked.

Helen closed her eyes and swallowed a lump in her throat. Her grief was like the ocean inside her, always moving, churning, the tide coming in and going out, sometimes stormy, seldom calm, but always there. It was a wave of darkness and pain that threatened to overwhelm her when she least expected it. She reached for Suki's head and stroked the dog's ears to help calm her racing heart.

'My husband and I ran the place together. He died a few months ago.'

'I'm sorry to hear it,' DS Hutchinson said.

Helen looked into his eyes. 'Thank you.'

DS Hutchinson stood, and Suki darted for his boots, trying unsuccessfully to get her jaws around the heel.

'Suki, leave!' Helen ordered.

She followed DS Hutchinson to the lounge, where he told DC Hall to continue taking statements. 'I'm going next door to have a word with the landlady.'

Helen glanced at the clock behind the bar. It was getting on for midnight and she knew it was unlikely that her neighbour would still be up. Miriam went to bed early, claiming she needed her beauty sleep. Helen's stomach churned with anxiety. Had she done the right thing telling the detective what she had heard? She told herself she had no choice. This was murder after all; police business didn't come much more serious. But had Miriam really meant it?

She sank into a chair with Suki by her side. She could hear DS Hutchinson knocking at the door at the Vista del Mar. She could picture Miriam in her curlers and dressing gown, shocked to find a detective on her doorstep, scared most likely too. And she could only imagine what the other woman would think of her when DS Hutchinson told her that she'd listened to her arguing with Brian. Lost in her thoughts, Helen became aware of someone sitting at her side.

'You look done in,' Ginger said.

Helen gave a weak smile. 'When you rang Brian's daughter, did she say she'd give her mum the news tonight?'

Ginger nodded slowly.

'Poor woman,' she sighed.

There was a noise on the stairs and she went to investigate. The two forensics officers were heading down, both carrying large white bags. One officer headed straight outside and the other turned to Helen.

'We've taken all the dead man's belongings. The room is now yours to do as you wish with, cleaning or whatever. We're finished in there. We won't be troubling you again.'

'Thank you,' Helen said.

She was about to head down to her apartment to turn in for the night when Colin, Sam and Bob, who were sitting in the window seat, turned and pointed outside.

'Look, he's putting her in the van,' Colin cried excitedly.

'Is he arresting her?' Bob wondered.

'He'll be taking her in for questioning,' Sam said.

Everyone flocked to the window to see what was going on. When Helen saw what was happening, she couldn't believe her eyes. Out on the road, DS Hutchinson was holding the back door of the police van and a stony-faced Miriam was stepping inside. Her head began to throb. She didn't know how much more she could take.

'I'm calling it a night, boys,' she said. 'See you all at breakfast.'

'Night, Helen,' the men chorused.

She waited outside the dining room until Davey came out from being questioned, then popped her head around the door.

'Do you need me for anything else?'

DC Hall smiled when he saw her. 'No, I think we've got everything we need. Have forensics finished in the room?'

'They've just left.'

'Then you can retire, Mrs Dexter.'

Helen closed the door quietly and headed downstairs.

The next morning dawned cold, wet and dark. Helen woke to the welcome aroma of sausages and bacon cooking on the grill, but her heart sank at the thought of having to give Jean and Sally the tragic news about their guest. She lay still, listening to Suki's gentle snores.

'What's going on, Tom?' she whispered.

Twelvis were supposed to be leaving after breakfast, as they'd only booked in for two nights. Could she really go through the motions of preparing the Seaview after they'd left, turning the place around to welcome more guests after what had happened to Brian? She still had a few weeks' breathing space, as the next guests weren't due in until the start of the Easter holidays. She was anxious about losing the bookings, for once news got out about a murdered man having stayed at the Seaview, she felt certain that some people would cancel. But life must go on, she told herself. It was what Tom would have wanted.

She urged herself to remember the reasons why she hadn't sold up and moved on, reminded herself what the place had meant to Tom, told herself over again that the Seaview was her life. Just two days earlier she'd been preparing to take in her first guests, running the place on her own. But now, after Brian's death – no, worse than just a death; his murder – could life at the Seaview ever be normal again? The murder would make the news. She could see the headlines now, a perfect mix of the death of the King of Rock and Roll in the queen of seaside resorts. She screwed her eyes tight. Would the papers mention the Seaview? She'd have to cross that bridge when she came to it. And news wasn't exclusive to papers any more; these days it made its way online with lurid headlines, clickbait and scant regard for truth.

She groaned and pulled a pillow towards her to wrap her arms around. She felt something nudge her back and knew immediately what it was. She turned.

'Morning, Suki,' she said, looking into the dog's glassy grey eyes. 'How I wish I was you right now. All I'd have to worry about is whether I get walked and fed. Well, I promised you a long walk this morning after missing out on one last night, and a long walk is what you'll get.'

She quickly showered and dressed and headed to the kitchen. Jean was busy opening a catering-size tin of baked beans.

'Morning, Jean. How are your mum's legs?'

'Not so good, Helen. I've been back and forward to the care home and haven't had a minute to myself since I left here yesterday. As soon as I got home last night I went straight to bed and when my head hit the pillow I was out like a light.'

'Have you heard what happened last night?'

'Last night? No, what's gone on?'

'You haven't heard the news or seen it on TV this morning?'

'I don't bother much with the news. What's happened?'

'You might want to sit down, Jean,' Helen said.

'Is it that bad?'

'I'm afraid so.'

Helen told Jean about the dead Elvis impersonator found floating in the lake at Peasholm Park.

Jean's mouth dropped open and then she crossed herself. 'Bloody hell.'

Helen pulled a chair from the kitchen table. 'What have I done, Jean?'

Jean eyed her suspiciously. 'I don't know, love. What *have* you done?'

'This place. What was I thinking? I wanted to keep it open, and I thought I could, you know, I thought I'd be all right, but now this awful thing happens to one of our guests and I don't know if I can cope. I'm not sure I can carry on.'

Jean flew to her side and put her arm around her shoulders.

'You *can* carry on and you will,' she said gently as Helen began to cry. 'Come on, love, don't let's have more tears. After my Archie died, I didn't think I'd ever stop crying, but I did, and you will too. You can't let this knock you back. And you're not on your own, so you can get rid of that silly notion right now. You've got me and Sally; whatever happens, we're a team, the three of us.'

At Helen's feet, Suki whined.

'And you've got that rangy mutt, too,' Jean smiled. 'Come on, love, pull yourself together.'

Helen dried her eyes. 'Thanks, Jean. I'm going out to clear my head with a walk on the beach with Suki, and as soon as I get back, I'll help you with breakfast.'

'No need, love. It's all under control,' Jean said.

Helen stood and hugged her. 'I don't know what I'd do without you.'

As Helen headed down the Seaview's steps, she pulled the zip on her fleece up around her neck. It really was a rotten day, typical weather for March, after the warm and mild day yesterday. A young woman she'd never seen before was walking along Windsor Terrace towards her. She carried an oversized black umbrella, holding it against the drizzly rain. She wore jeans, trainers and a beige raincoat with a black scarf tucked in at the neck. Her long brown hair was whipping around her face in the wind. When she reached the Seaview, she stopped, blocking Helen's way.

'Mrs Dexter?'

Helen looked up, startled. 'Yes?'

'Oh. You *are* Helen Dexter? Owner of the Seaview Hotel?'

There was something about the way the girl spoke that unsettled Helen. 'Who are you?'

'Rosie Hyde, *Scarborough Times*. I'd like a few words about the Elvis murder last night. I have a source who tells me the dead man was a guest at your hotel.'

'You're a journalist?' Helen said, shocked. 'I've got nothing to say to you.'

'Mrs Dexter, please. Just a word? A quote? Don't you want to put your side of the story?'

'There is no story,' Helen spat. 'What there is is a dead man whose family and friends are grieving. Now, please, have some respect.'

But the girl wasn't prepared to give up. 'Mrs Dexter, how long have you owned the Seaview Hotel?'

'Leave me alone,' Helen said. She tried to push past, but the large umbrella made it difficult for her to manoeuvre her way through.

'Will you be keeping the hotel open, under such terrible and tragic circumstances?'

'Move out of my way,' Helen commanded.

But the girl didn't move. She was tenacious, Helen had to give her that. Just as she was thinking of heading back inside and leaving through the back door instead, she heard a voice behind her.

'I'll report you for harassment if you carry on that way.'

She turned and saw Jimmy walking towards her. 'Jimmy, I can manage perfectly well on my own,' she said through gritted teeth.

Jimmy reached out and tipped the girl's umbrella, spilling rain onto her face. It wasn't a threatening gesture – it was almost comical – but it upset the young journalist no end.

141

'Now who's harassing who?' she hissed, wiping rain from her face.

'Get off my property, or I'll report you to the police,' Helen said.

The journalist glared at Jimmy, then reached into the black leather satchel slung over her shoulder. She pulled out a small white card and offered it to Helen. 'If you change your mind and want to talk, here's my number.'

Helen took the card, ripped it in two and thrust it back into the girl's hands. 'You can stick your flaming number where the sun doesn't shine. I've got nothing to say to you.'

Chapter 19

The journalist stormed away.

'Thanks, Jimmy, but I really could have coped on my own.'

'Sorry. Guess I waded in without thinking. I couldn't sleep last night. Brian's death has rattled all of us; none of us are in our right minds. That's why I'm up so early. I thought I'd take a walk to clear my head before breakfast.'

Helen and Jimmy began to walk in step with Suki between them. The wind and rain bit into them as they headed to the beach. Helen saw Jimmy gaze out over the dark, choppy sea.

'I expect the boys will be heading home after breakfast,' he said. 'After you turned in last night, the police told us we're free to leave, but I thought I'd stay on for a few days at the Seaview, if that's all right with you.'

Helen was surprised. 'Well, I've no more guests booked in until Easter, so you can stay as long as you like until then. But don't you want to go home?'

'I've nothing much to go back for,' he said, avoiding her enquiring gaze. 'Brian's death's hit me hard, if I'm honest. I'd like to stay on in case the police turn up any clues. Last night you said you had something to tell me about him; was it the same thing you told the police?'

'It was, but let's talk later, once everyone's left and my staff have gone too. It's probably best if we're not overheard.'

Once they reached the beach, Helen let Suki off the lead and the dog bounded towards the waves.

'Think you'll have any more trouble from the journalist?' Jimmy asked.

'I hope not.'

'If you do, let me know.'

Helen shot him a look. 'Thanks, but I'm big enough to look after myself.'

She didn't want to sound ungrateful, but she felt strongly that it was something she needed to handle on her own. She had to prove to herself that she could get through whatever negative publicity might land on the Seaview because of Brian's death. She had to stand tall and face all kinds of things on her own now.

Jimmy nodded. 'OK. Noted. Look, it's probably best if I go back. It's chilly; I really should've brought my coat.' He turned and headed back to the road.

Helen carried on alone, thinking about Brian and Miriam, about Brian and Traveltime Inns, about everything that had happened. Her thoughts were churning like the waves out at sea. And as she ran through the argument that she'd overheard between Brian and Miriam, going over each sentence, every word she could recall, another piece of the puzzle appeared, as if she didn't have enough on her mind. She remembered what DS Hutchinson had asked her. He'd wanted to know if anyone else had overheard Brian and Miriam arguing. She'd said she didn't know, she'd been on her own, of that she was certain; all the members of Twelvis had left the Seaview. But what if . . . what if someone inside the Vista del Mar had overheard Miriam wishing Brian dead? What if someone had overheard her accusing him of being a fake and a fraud? And if someone else *had* listened in to the harsh words they'd flung at each other, what might the eavesdropper do with that information?

Back at the Seaview, Helen dried seawater from Suki's coat. Then she donned her tabard with its cheery sunshine logo and headed to the kitchen. Sally was already there, and she threw her arms around Helen. 'Jean's just told me about the dead man. I can't believe it.'

'Me neither,' Helen sighed. 'None of it seems real.'

'Are the others still planning on leaving this morning?' Jean asked, counting hash browns onto a large metal tray.

'Yes. Apparently the police don't need them for more questioning and they're free to go.'

'They've got cast-iron alibis, that's why,' Jean said sagely. 'They were onstage, weren't they, at the time of the murder.'

'There's something else I need to tell you. The police took Miriam in for questioning last night.'

Jean and Sally stared at her. Jean stood stock still with a hash brown in her hand.

'Miriam next door? That Miriam?'

Helen nodded.

'I always knew there was something not right about her,' Jean said caustically. 'All them airs and graces she gives herself. Makes you wonder what she's hiding underneath.'

'She used to be married to him – the dead man, I mean.'

145

'No!' Jean shook her head and tutted loudly. 'Well, I never,' she exclaimed. 'It's true what they say, you never know what goes on behind closed doors.'

'How do you know they were married?' Sally asked.

'I heard them arguing; they were really going for it, as loud as you like. I could hear them quite clearly through the wall.' She kept quiet about how she'd had to put her ear to the wall to listen in. Neither did she mention that Miriam had wished Brian dead. She was still feeling guilty and anxious after eavesdropping. But what if Miriam really had murdered Brian? She knew she could hardly have kept quiet about what she'd overheard.

'I wonder if they kept her in overnight,' Sally said. 'Do you think she's been arrested?'

'I'll go and check on her later,' Helen said. 'Forensics came last night and cleared out room seven. They said it was fine for us to go in there and clean. They won't be back.'

Sally wrinkled her nose. 'I'm not sure I like the idea of cleaning a dead man's room.'

Jean pushed her glasses up her nose and gave Sally a hard stare. 'Don't be so daft, lass,' she said.

Helen and Sally took up their positions outside the dining room as the men began to file in for breakfast. None of them looked as if they'd had a decent night's sleep; their faces were crumpled, their eyes bleary and red. Each man nodded towards Helen or offered a weak smile. They ate in silence and Helen and Sally worked quickly to clear their plates.

Once they'd eaten and finished packing, they headed back down to the lobby, returning their room keys to Helen. She told them that under the circumstances she wouldn't charge them for their stay, but they all insisted on paying. Every single one of them gave her a hug, many of them kissed her on the cheek and some even cried. Helen had to bite back her own tears. Since Tom's death, she'd been doing that a lot.

'We wanted to, uh, give you a token of our appreciation,' Alan said. 'For all you did for us last night onstage. You saved our bacon, little lady. We sure couldn't have performed without you.'

He handed her a small paper bag with white and neon pink stripes. Helen recognised the logo; it belonged to a trinket store on Foreshore Road.

'It's just a fun little gift,' Alan explained.

'Oh, there was no need to buy me anything,' Helen said.

'We hope it'll remind you of Twelvis,' Ginger added.

As if Helen would ever forget. She opened the bag and pulled out a plastic Elvis figurine dressed in a white suit with a black microphone in his hand.

'Press his head down and he shimmies his hips; it's the darnedest thing,' Alan said.

Helen placed plastic Elvis on a table and pressed his head. Sure enough, he shook from side to side. 'Thanks, everyone, I'll treasure it.'

'Consider it a good-luck charm,' Ginger said.

Slowly and quietly the men picked up their luggage, hugged Jimmy farewell and said their goodbyes before leaving the Seaview. Helen stood at the door with a heavy heart, Jimmy beside her, watching the ten men leave. How different it was from their noisy, joyous arrival less than two days ago. So much had happened since then. One of the men had died in the most horrible circumstances, leaving Helen unsure once more about her future at the Seaview. And now all the rooms had to be cleaned, and just like Sally, she wasn't looking forward to going into room seven.

Later that morning, Helen and Sally stood outside Brian's room. They'd left this one till last.

'Ready?' Helen asked.

Sally nodded. Helen unlocked the door and pushed it open. Neither she nor Sally wanted to be the first to step inside. They stood on the threshold peering in.

'Looks normal,' Sally said. 'Empty.'

'Forensics took all his belongings,' Helen told her. She stepped into the room. Despite the bitter wind outside and the rain spitting in the air, she headed to the window and flung it wide. 'Needs some air in here.' She noticed Sally still hadn't moved. 'If you don't want to come in, I'll clean it myself, love. I don't want to make you feel anxious.'

Sally put one foot into the room. 'I'm fine,' she said, not sounding fine at all. 'I'm not scared of an empty room.'

'There's nothing to be scared of,' Helen said gently. 'He slept here, that's all. Look, I'll change the bed and clean in here, and you do the bathroom. How does that sound?'

Sally nodded and headed into the en suite with her bucket and rubber gloves as Helen began work stripping the bed. She pulled a pillow towards her and peeled off the pillowcase. It reeked of the aftershave Brian had worn, unmistakably cloying. His fat face flickered through her mind; she saw him leering at her breasts, flicking his tongue out at Marie, grabbing her by the wrist. A shiver ran down her spine. She picked up the second pillow. This one smelled strongly too, but it wasn't Brian's after-shave this time. It was different, a sickly-sweet smell that reminded her of strawberry gum. But that wasn't all. There were strands of hair on the pillow, long hair as black as Whitby jet. It didn't take much for Helen to deduce that Brian must have shared his bed with a woman, one who wore strong strawberry perfume and had long black hair.

She stood still. No, it couldn't be, could it? Hadn't Marie mentioned something about strawberry perfume? Wasn't that what she said Daran came home smelling of when he'd been out on the town? She shook her head to dismiss the coincidence. She hadn't slept well again; her mind was playing tricks. But still, something didn't seem right.

When Helen and Sally's work was done, they headed to the kitchen, where Jean had the kettle on to make coffee. A packet of custard creams lay open on the table.

'All done and dusted?' Jean asked, popping a biscuit in her mouth.

Helen sank into a chair, picked up her phone and sent Marie a message.

Seen the news about dead Elvis? You free? I need to talk. Any word yet from Bev or Sue?

Marie texted back immediately.

Shocked and stunned here. You OK? Will pop in this afternoon. Not a peep out of either of them. PS Think Daran's having a midlife crisis. He came home wearing blue suede shoes.

Chapter 20

'Sorry, Jean, what was that?' Helen said, staring at her phone in shock. Surely Marie's husband wasn't connected to Brian's murder? But if he was innocent, what was he doing with Brian's shoes?

'I said are you all done and dusted?'

Helen's hands were shaking as she laid her phone on the table. She forced herself to look at Jean, to answer her, as her mind whirled with what she'd just read. 'Yes, I'm all done,' she said.

Jean walked towards her and Helen quickly turned her phone to hide Marie's text. She needed time to think about what she'd just learned. It felt like she was mentally putting pieces of a jigsaw puzzle together while wearing boxing gloves.

'Are you all right, love?' Jean asked. 'You've gone as white as a sheet.'

'I'm fine, thanks, Jean.' Helen forced a smile and got back to business. 'Room seven is shipshape again. I'm going to have to get the lock changed, though.'

'Goodness only knows where the key ended up,' Jean said. 'It's probably sitting on the bottom of the lake in Peasholm Park. But you can't take any chances. It might have been lost and it's best to be on the safe side.'

'It gave me the creeps being in there after what happened to the poor man,' Sally said.

Murder at the Seaview Hotel

Helen poured coffee into three blue stone mugs that she and Tom had bought from the Coast art gallery in the nearby pretty village of Cloughton. It had been an autumn morning, crisp and bright, and they'd kicked their way through leaves in the gallery's car park. It was strange, she thought, how something as ordinary as a mug could trigger a rush of emotion. She handed one each to Jean and Sally and cradled her own in her hands.

'Listen, both of you. I had a run-in with a journalist this morning; she was trying to fling some dirt about the murder and make it stick to the Seaview. I'm telling you this in case she comes back. If she does and she sees either of you leaving the hotel, she might pounce on you for a quote.'

'She'll get nothing out of me,' Jean said, dunking a biscuit into her mug.

'I won't say anything either,' Sally said.

'Oh, and Jean, we've got one guest staying for the next few days.'

Jean raised her eyebrows. 'I thought you weren't taking anyone until the Easter holidays began?'

'I wasn't going to, but one of the Elvis impersonators wants to stay, the one in room eight. I think he's upset about what happened and wants to be here in case the police turn up any clues.' Helen's shoulders slumped. 'Maybe I should have suggested he stayed somewhere else. I wish I knew what to do for the best. Since Tom moved to the hospice, there isn't a day that's gone by when I haven't thought about selling this place, you know.' She held her thumb and forefinger an inch apart. 'I was this close to selling up. I even received a decent offer from Benson's. You know the Glendale Hotel over the road?'

'That dump?' Sally said. 'It's been empty for ages.'

151

'Traveltime Inns have got their eye on it. They want to buy the Seaview to pull it down and turn it into a car park.'

'Well I never,' Jean said. 'And you never said a word to us about it.'

'I didn't know what to do, Jean. But after I picked up Tom's ashes and scattered them on the beach, I came back here and sat in the lounge and did a lot of thinking. When the booking came in from Twelvis, I decided to open up again and try to keep the place going. It was a spur-of-the-moment decision. That's when I rang both of you to ask if you'd come back to work. I thought I had the courage to run the Seaview on my own.'

Jean took another biscuit.

'Are you saying you're still thinking of selling up and we might be out of a job?' Sally asked.

Helen looked at her. 'I'm saying I thought I'd done the right thing keeping the Seaview open. But now . . .'

'I knew there was a *but* coming,' Sally sighed. 'I just knew it.'

'One of our guests was murdered,' Helen said, her voice rising. 'How on earth can I come back from this? That journalist's not going to give up, and if I don't give her a quote, she'll likely make something up. You know what newspapers are like.'

'It's the *Scarborough Times*, love, not the *News of the World*,' Jean said. She pushed her mug and the packet of biscuits aside, and turned her chair so that she was facing Helen straight on. 'Now listen to me,' she said sternly. 'You and Tom turned this place into something special and I won't let you give it up. Let the police sort things out as far as the dead man's concerned and don't get involved. Even if the hotel does get mentioned in the papers, it'll be old news eventually, and it's not as if he was murdered here. Yes, you might lose some business; some folk will be put off staying here. But in time, people will forget what happened, you mark my words.'

'I agree with Jean,' Sally said. 'You've got to keep going and reach for the stars.'

'I appreciate the sentiment—' Helen began.

'I'm not being sentimental,' Sally said. 'I mean you need to get the Seaview its four-star rating and show Scarborough you mean business. Show everyone you're not afraid to stand your ground and won't be put out of business by something that wasn't your fault.'

'You're right, it wasn't my fault, was it?' Helen said softly. 'I just feel so . . .'

Sally pointed towards the patio doors. 'Go out there with your head held high.'

'Come on, Helen, you can do it,' Jean urged.

'We'll help you all we can,' Sally added. 'You can't give up before you've even begun.'

Helen closed her eyes and swallowed a lump in her throat. She opened her eyes to find her friends staring at her, waiting for her to speak.

'Well?' Sally asked.

'What'll it be?' Jean said. 'Closing down and hiding away? Or staying open and grabbing your four stars by the scruff of the neck?'

Helen felt her stomach turn over. 'It's not going to be easy, and I can't afford to make major changes until after the end of this season . . .'

'Does that mean you're going to do it?' Sally said, smiling.

Helen took hold of Sally's hand with her left hand and Jean's with her right.

'What is this, a séance?' Jean laughed.

'Think of it more as the three of us looking into the future.'

Sally pulled her hand away and punched the air. 'Yes!'

Jean placed her free hand on top of Helen's. 'Good lass. You're making the right decision. I know you're having a rough time of it, love. On top of Tom's death, this awful thing has happened, and you feel as if you'll never recover. But let me tell you now that if you give up, you'd never forgive yourself.'

'Do you really think I'm doing the right thing?' Helen asked.

Jean stood, bent down and kissed her on the cheek. 'I know you are. And if Tom was here, he'd say the same thing.' She clapped her hands together. 'Right. I can't stay here all day chatting. I've got to walk up to the care home to see Mum; they're trying her on different tablets for her legs. Then there's a Burt Reynolds film on telly this afternoon that I'm going to settle down and watch. I'll be back in the morning to do breakfast.'

'What about me, Helen?' Sally asked. 'Do you want me back too if there's only one bedroom to clean?'

Helen sat up straight. 'Yes, I want you back. I know there's not much work, but we signed a contract, and I won't go back on my word.'

After Jean and Sally had left, Helen popped into the lounge in case Jimmy was waiting to speak to her. However, the room was empty, and she felt relieved. She didn't feel ready for a conversation about Brian. She'd deal with Jimmy in her own time. She placed the plastic Elvis ornament on the bar underneath Tom's photo-graph, then stood with her hands on her hips, looking out of the window at the grey North Sea, mulling an idea over. Once her decision was made, she knew that the sooner she got it over and done with, the better, so she walked out of the Seaview and headed to the Vista del Mar.

When the door opened, Miriam stared out from the hallway, but she wasn't the woman Helen knew. Her long curly hair, usually so glossy, was scraped back in a ponytail. Her eyes were rimmed red and her face looked heavy and pale. It was the first time Helen had seen her without her full make-up and trademark glasses. Normally clad in high-end department-store chic, she was wearing a black velour leisure suit.

'Oh, it's you,' she said softly.

Helen wasn't used to seeing her looking so vulnerable and lost, and her heart went out to her. 'I came to see if you were all right.'

Miriam held the door open wide. 'You'd better come in.'

Helen stepped inside the Vista del Mar. Its layout was a mirror image of the Seaview, but the decor was different. Where the Seaview hallway was pastel and beige, the Vista del Mar was lined with oppressive floral wallpaper, the type Jean would call blowsy.

'Come downstairs, we can talk in private.'

Helen followed Miriam to her apartment, where there were more floral prints, too many for Helen's liking. Obscenely red fuchsias were captured and framed on the wall, clashing with yellow tulips on cushions and damask roses climbing curtains. Miriam indicated for Helen to sit on one end of a sofa covered with a trailing ivy print. Ferns in pots of all shapes and sizes were dotted around the room, giving it a swampy, tropical feel that made Helen feel claustrophobic. Miriam took the armchair opposite.

'I think you owe me an explanation,' she said. 'I've spent the night in the police station, accused of murdering my ex-husband. And the police aren't finished with me yet. They say I'm a person of interest relating to the case.' Her hand fluttered towards her heart. 'A person of interest? Me?' She looked deflated, shrunken, a curled leaf of a woman amongst her living-room flora and fauna. 'I've even been told I can't leave the country. They think I'm a flight risk.'

'Miriam, I—'

'You heard our argument, I know. The police didn't need to tell me who'd been listening in. It could only have been you; noise travels through these walls. Why do you think I complain about the music from your Elvis parties each summer?'

'I'm sorry,' Helen said. 'Truly I am.' And she was. She felt dreadful. All she wanted was for the lurid sofa cushions to swallow her up and take her away. 'I didn't mean to listen in.'

'But you did.'

She nodded. There was no point in lying. 'I did. And once I did, I couldn't unhear what I'd heard. I had to tell the police after what happened last night.'

Miriam took her time to reply. 'Words said in anger, eh? Oh, the trouble they can cause.'

'I knew it was just a figure of speech. I knew you didn't mean what you said.'

'Oh, but I did!' Miriam cried. 'It would have suited me if Brian had never turned up in my life again. Did I wish him dead? Yes,

I did, with all my heart.' She narrowed her eyes at Helen. 'But did I kill him? No.'

'I had to come to apologise,' Helen said. 'I feel awful.'

'Well, that'll teach you to mind your own business then, won't it?'

Helen noticed a flash of the old Miriam coming back and had to stifle a smile. 'Listen, Miriam. I'd like to do something to make amends.'

'What?'

'I've only got one guest in next door. He's staying for a few days. I'm not reopening fully until the start of the Easter holidays. And my cleaning girl, Sally, she's competent, hard-working, very intelligent. She'll be kicking her heels without enough work from me to keep her busy. If you need help in here, let me know, and we can come to some arrangement about you paying for her time. It'll keep her occupied until I reopen fully.'

'That's very generous of you,' Miriam said, thinking the offer through. 'The flower-arranging society from Durham are booked in from midweek, and I've got some guests here already, a family with a young daughter.'

'The ones who are always yelling at each other?'

'Oh, you've heard them, have you?' Miriam smiled wryly. 'The poor man couldn't eat his breakfast this morning after he heard the news about Brian on the radio. Mind you, none of my staff know of my connection to Brian, or where I spent last night.' She glared at Helen. 'And I'd like to keep it that way. I'd be very grateful if you wouldn't mention it to anyone. The sooner this blows over, the better. I won't have it affecting my business.'

157

'Of course,' Helen said.

'What happened last night has taken its toll. I'm not as young as I used to be and it's fair to say I could probably do with an extra pair of hands. This Sally . . . she's honest, is she? I've had trouble in the past with young girls working here, taking things they shouldn't.'

'Sally's a gem, as honest as the day is long,' Helen said.

Miriam stood, and with a sweep of her hand towards the door that led upstairs, indicated that her audience with Helen was over.

Chapter 21

Helen walked quickly back to the Seaview, anxious to get out of the rain and cold wind. There was still no sign of Jimmy in the lounge, so she headed to her apartment, opened up her laptop and began to make a start on admin and emails. She was heartened to see that more bookings had arrived. She entered them in the diary, hoping they wouldn't be cancelled in a few weeks' time if the Seaview was mentioned in connection with Brian's death. There were emails from the review site too, notifications that new reviews had been left but still no reply to her complaint about the fake reviews. With a heavy heart, she forced herself to click through to the site, bracing herself for more negative comments. But when she read the first review, her mood began to lift.

Great breakfast, mighty fine views, friendly place, and just the most lovely little lady who runs it. Highly recommended indeed, yes.

It could only have been a Twelvis member who'd left it, posting it from his phone as he headed home on the train. It sounded like Alan, and she read it in his Elvis drawl. Encouraged by this, she clicked on another.

Clean, good location, you won't be disappointed. Five stars!

She read on, feeling happier.

Comfortable bed, free and fast Wi-Fi, sea views. If they offered kippers for breakfast, it'd be perfect.

But then her mood came crashing down when she saw another review left by the fake reviewer Porgy42.

Sorry. Do not stay here.

She stared at the screen, and her heart began to pound as anger flooded through her. She took a few breaths to calm herself. Just who was Porgy42 and why did they have it in for her? She could hardly complain to HypeThatHotel about a fake review this time, because the hotel was up and running. It was infuriating! She slammed the lid down on her laptop, causing Suki to raise her eyes from her spot in front of the patio doors.

At that moment, the doorbell rang, and Helen headed upstairs. She opened the door to find Marie yelling into her phone.

'. . . and I want you gone by the time I get home, got it? No. No . . . you listen to me, you two-timing toerag. I want you and all your stuff gone. All of it. Yes. What? No, you can't take Alexa, she's mine. No, I bought it, Daran. I paid for it. Yes, I've got the bloody receipt. I paid for it with MY money that I earned slogging MY guts out in MY nail bar. I earn my money the hard way, the old-fashioned way, do you remember that, Daran? A little four-letter word called work. Eh? What did you just call me? Well you can fu— Daran? Daran?'

Helen watched as Marie stared at her phone, her face like thunder.

'He's hung up on me. He actually hung up,' she hissed. She stormed past Helen, muttering obscenities as she went, and was heading to the stairs that led to Helen's apartment just as Jimmy came into the lobby.

'Is now a good time to talk?' he asked.

'No, Jimmy, sorry. I'll catch you later,' Helen said, rushing after Marie.

In Helen's living room, Marie paced back and forth, gripping her phone like a weapon. 'He's gone too far this time,' she growled. Each time she walked close to Suki, the dog inched her head towards Marie's high-heeled scarlet shoes.

'What's happened?' Helen said.

'Sandra bloody DeVine, that's what's happened!' Marie yelled at the patio doors. 'She's been having it away with Daran for the past six months and I'm the fool who's last to know. I got the whole story out of Daran's mate Gav just now.'

It took Helen a moment to make sense of what was going on. 'Sandra DeVine who works at Seaside Sam's fish and chip shop? That Sandra?'

'Do we know another Sandra with such a ridiculous surname?' Marie screamed. 'And it's not even her real name. Sandra Potts, that's what we called her at school, with that stupid twitch she used to have at the side of her mouth. Her surname's as fake as the rest of her.'

An image of Sandra DeVine flashed through Helen's mind. She was tall and skinny, with oversized breasts and a nipped-in waist. Her long hair was dyed as black as midnight and swept up like a whip of candyfloss. Her eyes were always perfectly made up with smoky eyeliner, and her lips painted blood red. The whole effect was a compelling, if somewhat unsettling, presence to behold, especially when she was serving fish and chips.

'You know, some months ago Bev told me something about Sandra,' Helen said. 'I didn't want to believe it at the time, but

I guess we all have to make a living where we can. Apparently she's on the game.'

'That new quiz show on TV?'

Helen laughed out loud. 'No. You know, she's part of the oldest profession in the world.'

'She's a window cleaner?'

'Jesus, Marie. Where's your head today?'

'In pieces,' Marie said sadly.

'I'm sorry, love. What I mean is that Sandra's a lady of the night. A prostitute. A call girl. A sex worker or whatever the politically correct term is these days.'

'Funny, but Gav didn't mention that,' Marie said, puzzled.

Helen walked towards her with open arms, ready to give her a hug, but Marie stepped away, straightened her spine and flicked her long brown hair over her shoulders. 'Don't be sorry,' she said. 'I told you last time I saw you that I thought something was going on. It's the end of my marriage, that's for sure, but it won't be the end of my world.'

'Sit down, Marie,' Helen said calmly. 'You need to tell me all you know about the blue suede shoes that Daran brought home.'

Marie clamped her hand against her forehead. 'Oh my God, the shoes. He's going through a midlife crisis, I'm sure. He doesn't even like Elvis.'

'Those shoes signify something more important than a midlife crisis,' Helen said gravely.

Marie arched an eyebrow. 'What do you mean?'

'The dead Elvis impersonator was wearing blue suede shoes when he left here to head to the concert. But when they took his body from the lake, his shoes had gone.'

Marie's mouth opened, but no words left her lips for a few moments as the magnitude of Helen's words sank in.

'So you're saying Daran might be walking around in a dead man's shoes?' she said at last.

'I think we need to be careful about what we assume. We both know Daran's involved in shady businesses around town, but is he the sort of bloke who would really kill a man?'

Marie shook her head. 'Not Daran. He doesn't have it in him. He doesn't like getting his hands dirty, see. He likes to stay one step removed from whatever's going on so that no evidence sticks. But he knows people, bad people. I won't have them in the house. I told him right from the start, what he gets up to is his business, and I'm not getting involved. I've turned a blind eye to what he does for a living all my married life.'

Helen reached a hand to her friend's arm. 'Are you really going to split up?'

'I want him gone, Helen. I won't give him a chance to make a fool of me a second time. Sandra DeVine is welcome to him. She can be the one who stays at home wondering where he is and how much money he's gambling or drinking away every night.'

'Are you certain that leaving him is what you want?'

'Oh, I'm certain,' Marie said. Helen noticed a mischievous smile playing around her lips. 'And when I'm finished with him, he'll not know what's hit him. I'm going to take him for every penny I can get.' Her face dropped. 'There's only one problem.'

'What?' Helen asked.

'I don't know a good solicitor. The one I use for the nail bar specialises in property. I've never had anything to do with marital law before. Do you know anyone in town I could speak to?'

'Just the firm we used when we bought this place,' Helen said. But then she had an idea. 'I can recommend someone, though.'

'Who?'

'One of the Elvis impersonators who's just left. Sam, his name was. He's a solicitor. Lovely guy.'

'Would you text me his details?'

'I can do better than that; I'll give you one of his business cards he left with me. How long are you giving Daran to clear his stuff out?'

Marie turned her arm, and Helen saw the silver designer watch around her slim wrist glint in the light.

'I'll give him a couple of hours.'

'Then I'll stick the kettle on. Fancy having some lunch while you're here? I can pop something in the oven and knock a salad up to go with it. To be honest, I could do with someone to talk to. There's been some weird stuff happening and it's making me nervous.'

Marie finally stopped pacing and sank onto the sofa. 'Lunch sounds great, thanks. But if you ask me, Helen, you need to be eating more than salad these days. You're starting to look a bit gaunt. Look, I'm sorry for banging on about me; it's all I've done from the minute I walked through your door. I'm here because you said you wanted to talk. What weird stuff's going on? What's happened?'

'Come into the kitchen. We can talk while I fix lunch.'

Ten minutes later, one Mediterranean vegetable tart had been taken from its box and was warming in the oven. Two generous portions of green leaves and shoots were laid out on plates. One bottle of red wine was half empty, two glasses were half full and Marie's mouth was hanging open in shock.

'You think the man from Traveltime Inns killed Elvis? And Miriam's somehow involved? I'm struggling to get my head around this.'

'You and me both,' Helen said. 'There's worse stuff going on too. I think I've got a stalker. Someone keeps walking past the Seaview and staring into the lounge. And there was that intruder on the patio who smashed a pot and left a footprint in the soil.

'You should tell the police.'

'I already have. But what can they do? They can't arrest someone for looking at a hotel. There's something else, too. A parcel arrived for me with one of those kids' toys inside, a fluffy dog, the same colour as Suki.'

'And?' Marie said.

'And it was pierced by a small, sharp knitting needle.'

'Bloody hell, Helen.' Marie took a long swig from her glass.

'I'm afraid it doesn't end there. There's something I haven't told the police.'

'Withholding information? Isn't that illegal?'

'I'm not sure it *is* information, not really. But this morning I was cleaning the room where the dead man stayed . . .'

'Urgh.'

'. . . and I can always tell, you know, when someone else has been in a room. Sometimes it's because toiletries are left in the bathroom. Sometimes I see a girl sneaking out; they're not often subtle. But this morning there was something different, a smell on the pillow – perfume, I mean. There are always two pillows in each room—'

'Just two? No wonder you've only got three stars,' Marie said.

Helen ignored her and carried on. 'And one pillow smelled of his aftershave. I'd know it anywhere; it gives me the creeps just thinking about it. The other pillow reeked of perfume.'

'Chanel? Dior?' Marie said.

'As if I'd recognise either of those. No, this was a cheap and nasty scent, sickly sweet . . .' she locked eyes with Marie, 'like strawberry gum.'

Marie's eyes widened. 'No!'

'Yes. And there's more. Long black hairs on the pillow.'

'Are you thinking what I'm thinking?' Marie breathed.

'It could be a coincidence, and we have no proof,' Helen warned. 'That's why I've kept quiet. But it struck me as odd that the perfume should linger so long. I remembered what you'd said about Daran coming home reeking of the same stuff.'

'Bloody Sandra DeVine!' Marie said.

Helen nodded. 'And if it is her perfume in Brian's bed, it means she slept here with him on Friday night. No wonder he didn't want Sally to clean his room. He was frightened of what she might find. He didn't come down to breakfast on Saturday morning either. Do you really think we should tell the police?'

Marie thought for a moment, then jumped off the stool at the kitchen counter. 'Not yet. I'll find the evidence to hang my cheating husband myself. I'll have to be quick, though, if I'm to catch him before he packs his bags and leaves with the blue suede shoes. Once I've got them, we'll tell the police what we know.' She headed to the stairs.

'Don't you want lunch first?' Helen called after her.

'Have my half of the tart. You could do with feeding up,' Marie cried.

Helen followed her to the hall, then watched from the lounge as her friend sped off in her sports car. She was about to turn away from the window when something caught her eye outside the Glendale. Jimmy was standing close to someone who had their back to her. They wore a black anorak with its hood pulled up, and had skinny legs and dirty trainers. She might be mistaken, but she had a feeling she'd seen them before.

Could it be the same person she'd caught staring into the Seaview? Her heart fell to the floor. She liked Jimmy; he seemed like a really nice man, someone, if she was honest with herself, she could let herself fall for, when the time was right. But maybe she'd been fooling herself. If the person he was speaking to was the same one who'd been staring into the Seaview, and it looked very much like it was, then what was Jimmy's connection to them? The fact that they were meeting outside the Glendale set more alarm bells ringing. Was Jimmy somehow involved in the Traveltime Inns situation that Brian had been caught up in? Had Traveltime sent another Twelvis member to play good cop to Brian's bad, trying to wheedle his way into Helen's affections by being friendly, hoping to force her to sell? She felt sick with anxiety at the thought that Jimmy might be involved in something so seedy. And she felt angry that she'd almost let herself succumb to his charm.

Chapter 22

Helen turned to the photograph of Tom above the bar. 'I'm not thinking straight, Tom.'

She heard the front door open. Someone was coming in and it could only be Jimmy, as she wasn't expecting Sally or Jean until the following day. Sure enough, he appeared at the lounge door. Helen sensed his uncertainty as to whether he should enter the room.

'Come in, Jimmy. It's probably time we had that talk.'

He walked in, removed his damp coat and hung it on the back of a chair. Helen settled at one end of the window seat and Jimmy sat at the other.

'Would you like a coffee? Tea? Anything from the bar?'

'No, I'm good, thanks,' he replied.

Helen's stomach was churning with anxiety after seeing him talking to the stranger outside. She knew she had to tackle him to clear the air before their conversation about Brian began. 'I saw you outside the Glendale Hotel just now.'

Jimmy stiffened and his smile dropped. 'Yeah, there was a kid there asking for directions. They were a bit lost.'

Helen stared at him. She noticed that he'd crossed his arms, then his legs, defensive against her. But she wasn't about to give up. 'I've had a problem with a kid who looks just like that, hanging around outside the hotel, staring in.'

'Have you?' Jimmy said. Helen noticed the surprise in his voice.

'And I think I've had an intruder as well. Someone was in the courtyard outside my apartment; they broke a plant pot and left their footprint in the soil.' Jimmy shifted in his seat as she continued. 'Now, I'm not saying the intruder was the same person who was staring into the lounge, or that the person you were talking to outside is the one who was here, but—'

'I don't think it could be the same person,' Jimmy said quickly. 'Like I say, they were lost. They wanted to know how to get to the train station, that was all.' He kept his arms tightly crossed. Helen was no expert in body language but even she could tell he wasn't sitting comfortably and wondered if he had something to hide. She searched his face for any telltale signs that he might be lying, but in truth she had no idea what she was looking for. A nervous tic? A clenched jaw?

'It was just the anorak they were wearing, you know, it looked familiar,' she said at last.

'Lots of kids wear that kind of coat these days; there must be hundreds of them in Scarborough,' Jimmy said.

Helen felt as if he was giving her the brush-off, wanting the conversation to come to an end. She pressed her back against the wide window frame and gazed out at the sea. Was he telling the truth? Oh, if only she knew.

'Do you know how long you'll be staying?' she asked at last.

'Until the police solve Brian's murder or at least come up with some clues. I've let DS Hutchinson know I'm here in case he needs me to provide more information. I knew Brian better than anyone else in the band. I knew his secrets, his dark side.'

He'd relaxed in his seat now and uncrossed his arms. Helen

decided to push him for more. Perhaps then she'd discover how much she could trust him.

'Did you know that Brian offered me cash to sell this place?'

Jimmy's mouth dropped open in shock and his face clouded over. In that moment, Helen knew that he had no clue about what Brian had done. He couldn't be all bad, she thought, her hopes rising a little. Either that or he was a very good actor.

'What? Why would he do that? He was broke, Helen. I mean, seriously deep in debt, ever since his wife took ill. She needed twenty-four-hour care, and he refused to let her go into a home. He paid for private carers to come to their house. You can imagine the cost of that. It bled him dry, so he went to the bank for a loan but ended up being unable to make the repayments. Then he went to a loan shark, and that's when his problems really started. Those people aren't in the business of lending money because they've got big hearts and a caring disposition. So I can't imagine where he got the money from to offer to buy your hotel. I don't think it could have been his own. He didn't have any savings, nothing like that.'

Helen thought through this new knowledge about Brian. With hindsight, she realised it tied in with his desperation in pushing her to sell. Someone higher up the chain had been threatening him, but this didn't excuse his behaviour. She was heartened that Jimmy was confiding in her, though; it helped put some of her suspicions about him on the back burner. However, she still felt she should be cagey about what she said next. She didn't want to give too much away, just in case. 'Have you ever heard of Traveltime Inns?'

He shook his head, and Helen continued. 'They're interested in buying the Glendale Hotel over the road, but they would need to have parking for their guests. That's why they're after my hotel, to demolish it for a car park.'

'What does this have to do with Brian?' Jimmy asked.

'That's what I'd like to know. He was offering me cash to sell up, and he wasn't exactly polite about it. He said he had a friend who was interested in buying the place, a friend who wouldn't take no for an answer.'

'Brian threatened you?' Jimmy said, his voice rising.

'Yes, and afterwards I saw him outside the Glendale with an official-looking fella carrying a clipboard. That's why I needed to know who you were talking to just now. So many peculiar things have happened, Jimmy, I have to know the truth.'

'And I've told you, it was just a kid I was speaking to,' he replied. But as the words left his lips, he crossed his arms again, closing himself off.

Helen ploughed on, trying to draw him out, still wondering how much she should trust him. 'Brian and the man in the suit were arguing, and then the man drove off in a black Porsche.'

'The car you saw Brian getting into yesterday, before the gig?'

'The very same. I told the police all this, of course.'

Jimmy uncrossed his arms and sat back in his seat, letting Helen's words sink in. She wondered if she'd said too much. Had she played her hand too openly when she should be holding back, just in case? Two days ago, she'd never met Jimmy Brown. And now here she was talking to him about a dead man. While he seemed nice enough, she was only too aware that she didn't know him at all.

'You seem surprised to hear this about Brian,' she said, watching him closely.

'Surprised? I'm shocked. All I can think is that his dealings with loan sharks and goodness knows who else have led him into doing some dodgy work for Traveltime Inns.'

'Well, I've now told you everything I told the police. You said you knew Brian's secrets and his dark side,' she ventured. 'Is there anything else *you* told the police that might help them find the person who killed him?'

Jimmy ran a hand through his hair. 'Look, I want to be honest with you, Helen.'

She was encouraged to hear this, but something still niggled at her. There was something a little off about Jimmy, something she felt he was holding back on, but she couldn't put her finger on what it was. 'Go on,' she said.

'Brian liked the ladies. I mean, his wife wasn't well. Not that I'm excusing what he did, but he . . .' He blew air out of his mouth. 'Well, this is embarrassing.' He smiled nervously.

'Take your time,' Helen coaxed.

He proceeded with caution, barely able to meet her eyes. 'Brian used dating sites.'

'To meet women?'

He nodded. 'He'd arranged to meet a woman this weekend. He showed me her picture when we were on the train on our way here.'

'Don't tell me, let me guess,' Helen said. 'She had jet-black hair done up in an old-fashioned beehive, bright red lips and dark eyes.'

Jimmy leaned forward. 'How on earth do you know?'

There was a beat of silence before she spoke again. 'I wasn't going to tell you, but there's no point in keeping quiet now. This morning when I cleaned his room, I knew he'd had a woman in. There was a smell of perfume still lingering, long dark hairs on the pillow, that sort of thing. And I think I know who the woman was.'

'She was called Sandra,' Jimmy said. 'With a strange surname.'

'DeVine,' Helen said.

'That's it! Sandra DeVine. I remember I was making fun of her name when he showed me her profile on the site. But would forensics have missed hair on the pillow when they searched his room?'

'They bagged up his clothes and belongings and took them away but left the sheets and pillows undisturbed. However, my trained landlady eye misses nothing.'

'Have you told the police?'

'Not yet.'

'Then you can't tell them, Helen, please. It'd devastate Brian's family if they found out what he was up to. His wife is already reeling from the news of his death. As far as his family are concerned, he's a loyal husband and dedicated father. If the truth comes out and they discover he was sleeping with other women . . .'

Helen held her hands up. 'I'll keep quiet, for now.'

Jimmy leapt from his seat. 'Oh my God, I can't believe I've been so stupid.'

'What is it?'

'What if this woman, Sandra . . . what if she was the one who killed Brian?'

Helen thought this over for a moment. 'Unlikely,' she said. 'I used to go to school with her, I know her family. She's a sex worker these days, but I can't see her as a murderer.'

'A sex worker?' Jimmy said, surprised. 'I don't think Brian knew that. I don't imagine he could have afforded her services, unless he'd borrowed more money from the loan sharks. I'm sure that her profile on the dating site said she worked in . . .'

'. . . a fish and chip shop?'

'Yeah, something like that.'

'Listen, Jimmy. I know Sandra and I know where she works. Leave her to me, I'll go and speak to her. I'll be able to tell if she's lying.'

'How?'

'I'll just know,' she said firmly, giving nothing away. She remembered when she, Marie and Sandra were friends at school, although it *was* a lifetime ago. When Sandra was late for class and lied to the teacher about where she'd been, when everyone knew she'd been having a sly fag behind the gym, her mouth would start twitching. She couldn't lie; her twitch gave her away every time.

'What a mess this all is,' Jimmy said.

'I won't disagree with you there. Can I ask you something else about Brian?'

'Ask me anything, Helen. I want to be as honest as I can.'

Helen thought of the person in the anorak outside the Glendale. Something still didn't seem right about it. Was Jimmy really as honest as he claimed? She wished she knew for sure.

'Brian's wife . . . is she his first wife? I mean, did he ever mention being married before?'

'As far as I know, he's only been married once.'

'And he's never mentioned any children from a previous relationship?'

'No, never,' Jimmy said. 'Why do you ask?'

Helen searched his face again; from what she could make out, he seemed to be telling the truth. 'I just wondered if there was something in his past that might have come back to haunt him,' she said as lightly as she could. She was thinking of what she knew about Miriam and Brian's daughter, but she didn't feel able to trust Jimmy enough to share more.

'If I hear anything from DS Hutchinson, I'll let you know,' he said.

'I appreciate it, Jimmy. Thanks.'

He glanced out of the window at the dark, menacing sky. 'Don't suppose you've got an umbrella I could borrow? I thought I'd make a night of it and go a bit wild with a visit to the indoor bowling centre.'

'I'll leave a brolly in the lobby, no problem.'

'Thanks, Helen,' he said.

Once Jimmy had headed up to his room, Helen went downstairs and prepared to take Suki out for her walk. She was looking forward to clearing her head in the fresh air and mulling over what Jimmy had told her. He'd seemed to be telling her the truth, but each time she mentioned the person walking past the hotel, the one in the anorak, the one he'd been talking to outside the Glendale, he'd clammed up and crossed his arms against any further questions. She wished she knew what was really going on. She couldn't seem to make sense of anything any more; her mind was in a whirl.

'Come on, before it starts raining again,' she called, and the dog padded towards her, pushing her head into Helen's hands.

As the tide was in and there was no point in going to the beach, Helen turned right when she came out of the Seaview and headed to the old town. The cobbled streets above the harbour were lined with a mix of tall, narrow houses and fishermen's cottages. She loved this part of town, and with its stone walls and cobbles, it was easy to imagine what Scarborough life had been like centuries ago. She followed Castle Road to St Mary's church, where Tom's funeral and memorial service had been held. A small group of tourists were milling in the churchyard, pointing out Anne Brontë's grave. She walked past the church and along Paradise, the street name that always made her smile. The origins of Paradise were connected to an ancient monastery that had once stood on the site, but now it was a quaint cobbled street at the top of a hill that looked over the South Bay, with views of the beach and the Spa.

As she walked, she thought of Jimmy and Brian, of Traveltime Inns, of Daran and Sandra and the missing blue suede shoes. It felt as if she had the pieces of a puzzle in her head, but none of them would fit together, no matter how much she moved them around. Each time she thought of Jimmy, she scolded herself for being taken in so quickly and easily by his warmth and charm. For all she knew, he could be involved in Traveltime Inns' underhand plot to force her out of the Seaview. She found herself crossing her fingers and hoping that he wasn't.

She turned and headed back towards the church. When she reached it, she peered over the wall and saw that the door was wide open. It looked as if Sunday service had ended. She walked down the path and glanced inside. A couple of middle-aged women were bustling about, collecting hymn books from deserted pews.

'Here, Suki,' Helen said, leading the dog to the church gate and tying her lead to a metal post. As she walked away, she heard Suki whine. 'I'm coming straight back,' she said before she disappeared inside.

She slid into a pew at the back of the church. One of the women acknowledged her and smiled encouragingly. Helen bent her head and closed her eyes to quieten her mind. She kept her eyes closed and thought about Tom. It didn't feel right to tell him about Jimmy or worry him about Traveltime Inns. She just wanted, more than anything, to feel close to him. If the women in the church were watching her, sitting alone, eyes closed, hands pressed together, head bowed, they would assume she was praying. And she was, in her own way. But she wasn't offering thanks to an unseen being. She was whispering a silent message to the only man she'd ever loved.

'I'm keeping the Seaview open, Tom, but I know it won't be easy. I'll work hard, you know that. I'll do everything I can to get those four stars. I'll even ask Jean to make porridge.'

Chapter 23

When Helen left the church, she saw Suki standing by the gate. Normally the dog would be lying down waiting for her, but today she was licking something off the ground, then chewing whatever she'd found.

'Come on, you,' Helen said, untying the lead. 'Whatever that is, leave it.' It looked like someone had dropped chips, and Suki was busy munching through them. 'If you get an upset stomach, don't come running to me.'

The rain that had been spitting all morning now began to turn heavy. Helen picked up her pace as she headed to the Seaview, but Suki seemed slow and lethargic and she had to encourage her to walk quickly. Normally the dog would be trotting at her side, but for some reason she was lagging behind.

'Come on, girl,' Helen said encouragingly, but Suki didn't heed the command and Helen ended up almost dragging her home.

'What it is, Suki?' she said when they reached the hotel. She got down on her haunches and ran her hands over the dog's head. Suki's eyes seemed to be a strange milky colour instead of their usual grey. 'Let's get you inside,' she said.

She stood and pulled at the lead. Suki didn't move, so Helen tried again. This time the dog inched forward but suddenly began retching and drooling.

'Those bloody chips,' Helen cried. 'You can't leave anything alone, can you? You've always got to be eating things you shouldn't and I . . . Suki? Suki?'

Suki keeled over, her body convulsing, legs kicking out.

'Suki!' Helen screamed.

The door of the Seaview opened and Jimmy flew out. Helen fumbled in her pocket for her phone.

'What's going on? I was in the lounge and heard you screaming,' Jimmy said, running down the steps.

'I need to ring the vet, I need to call them now,' Helen cried. In her panic, her phone fell from her hands. Jimmy picked it up and handed it to her.

'What's happened?'

'I think she's eaten something she shouldn't. I've got to get her to the vet, Jimmy. I've never seen her like this before. My car's over there.' She pointed. 'The blue four-by-four.'

Jimmy stood beside Suki and braced his back and knees. Then he slid his hands under the dog's body and slowly began to lift her. She'd stopped convulsing now and went limp in his arms. Helen ran up the steps, pulled the hotel door closed and then darted across the road to her car. She unlocked it and lifted the tailgate, and Jimmy slid Suki inside. Helen's panic gave way to tears.

'Let me drive, you're in no fit state,' Jimmy said.

Without hesitation, Helen handed him her keys. Then she pushed the back seats down and clambered in next to Suki, stroking the dog's head, telling her everything would be all right. Suki's breathing was shallow, her eyes closed, legs twitching. Drool was pouring from her mouth and she kept trying to retch.

Glenda Young

'Which way, Helen?' Jimmy shouted.

Helen gave directions, and as Jimmy revved the engine and set off, she took her phone out again. This time she managed to swipe it into life and got through to the receptionist to tell them she was bringing Suki in.

When they reached the vet's, Jimmy brought the car to a screeching halt. Jumping out, he went round to the back of the car and lifted the tailgate. He positioned his feet carefully to help get his balance and scooped Suki into his arms, carrying her slowly and carefully to the door of the surgery. Helen ran past him to give details of what she'd seen Suki eating and the dog's reaction. A tall man with sandy hair walked into the reception area. He was tying a green apron around his back and indicated to Jimmy to hand Suki over. Helen watched, her heart in her mouth, as her beloved pet was transferred to the vet.

'I'll go and park the car,' Jimmy said.

Helen sank into a chair, her legs shaking uncontrollably. After a few minutes, the receptionist approached her.

'Mrs Dexter?' she said. 'The vet's going to run some tests. We think it'd be better if Suki stayed here tonight so we can keep an eye on her.'

'Can I wait?'

'No, it's best if you don't. I'll give you a call as soon as we know what's going on.'

'Does the vet know what caused her convulsions?'

'It's too early to say. It might have been an allergic reaction.'

'But she's not allergic to anything I know of,' Helen said.

'Or she could have eaten something toxic. We'll find out very

180

soon; the vet's working on her now. Please, Mrs Dexter. It's better if you head home and leave Suki in our care. We'll do all we can for her.'

'And you'll ring me the moment I can take her home, right?'

The receptionist had been well trained and knew not to admit that animals brought in on an emergency call might not make their way home again. 'I'll ring you as soon as we've got news.' She glanced at her computer screen. 'Can I just confirm that your contact numbers are . . .'

She reeled off Helen's mobile number and the number for the landline at the Seaview. Then she read out another number. At first Helen didn't recognise it, but then, with a growing sense of unease, she realised it was Tom's mobile.

'. . . and that the two named contacts for Suki are yourself and Thomas Dexter?'

In all the trauma involved in getting Suki to the vet, Helen realised she hadn't once thought about Tom. For the first time since he'd been taken to the hospice, he had not been on her mind, and the realisation scared her.

'Mrs Dexter?'

'Sorry,' she said. 'I was miles away. Worried about the dog.'

'Of course. Now, if you could just confirm the numbers, that'd be great.'

'The last mobile number you read out . . . it was my husband's.' She swallowed a lump in her throat. 'My late husband.' It was the first time she'd used that phrase, and the words felt uncomfortable, cruel and wrong.

'I understand,' the receptionist said.

Helen saw the woman's finger slide to the delete key on her keyboard to remove Tom's number, and in one quick movement it was gone. This was how it would be from now on, she thought, Tom would disappear in tiny increments. His name removed from a computer screen at the vet's, his details deleted at the library, his life archived in records.

'You're free to go now, Mrs Dexter.'

Helen walked out of the vet's office and found Jimmy right outside the door with the engine running. She climbed into the passenger seat.

'Would you like to drive?' he offered.

She shook her head. 'No, I don't think I'm up to it. The shock's knocked me for six. Thanks, Jimmy. Thanks for everything you did.'

He pulled the car out of the car park and onto the road. 'Is she going to be all right?' he asked.

Helen stared ahead out of the window. 'I hope so. They're keeping her in overnight and said they'd ring when there was news. Do you have any pets, Jimmy? Turn left here.'

'Not me, no,' he said, indicating left to turn onto the main road that led back to the seafront. 'We had a hamster, I remember, when Jodie was little.'

'Is Jodie your daughter?'

'Yes, the one we used to bring on holiday to the Seaview. The one who used to love dancing with your husband.'

'I wish I could remember her, but we've had so many guests over the years. Does she have her own family now? Do you see a lot of her?'

The car arrived at a set of traffic lights just as they turned red. Jimmy braked a little more sharply than Helen had anticipated.

'I'd rather not talk about her, if that's all right with you.'

He drove the rest of the way in silence.

Chapter 24

Back at the Seaview, Helen and Jimmy headed into the lounge. Outside, the rain had eased, although the sky was still threatening and dark.

'I need to go to Paradise,' Helen said.

Jimmy shot her a look. 'Pardon?'

'Paradise, it's up in the old town, a gorgeous little street,' she explained. 'It's where I left Suki while I went into the church. I came out and found her eating chips from the pavement. Maybe I'll be able to find the remains of what she ate; I can collect them in a bag and take them to the vet. They could do tests on them, surely? It's got to help them find out what she's eaten. I know the chips weren't there when I tied Suki to the gate. I'd never have left her anywhere near food; I know what she's like for chewing things she shouldn't.'

'Are you sure it will help?' Jimmy said. 'Did the vet ask you to take the food in?'

'No, but I want to do all I can to find out what's wrong,' Helen said. 'I can't just sit here and wait for the phone to ring.'

'Would you like me to come with you?'

'Thanks, but I'll be fine on my own.'

'Well, if you don't mind me saying so, Helen, you don't look fine. You've had a bad shock.'

'It's been one shock after another this weekend.'

'I think both of us could do with some fresh air,' Jimmy said. 'And to be honest, I'd like to see more of Scarborough. When I used to come here with my family all those years ago, we never got much further than the seafront and the beach.'

'Are you sure you want to come?'

'Is it far? Do we need to drive?'

Helen shook her head. 'It's just five minutes' walk, past Anne Brontë's grave.'

'Anne Brontë the famous writer? The one who wrote *Wuthering Heights*?'

'That was Emily, her sister. Anne wrote *The Tenant of Wildfell Hall*. It's a good read.'

'Never heard of it, I'm afraid,' Jimmy said. 'I'm not much of a reader.'

'Well, if you're sure you want to come, it'd be good to have some company. Thanks, Jimmy.'

Walking always helped clear Helen's mind. This time, as well as looking for clues to help her find out what Suki had eaten, she was hoping to get Jimmy to open up, and to find out more about him. There was something he wasn't being honest about, of that she felt sure, and it made her uneasy.

She picked up the umbrella she'd left in the lobby, then checked her phone for a message from the vet, but all was quiet. They headed out, walking in silence for a while until Jimmy began asking questions about the old town and harbour, the castle and Scarborough's history. Helen was happy to share her knowledge and love of the town. She tried to turn the conversation to the stranger Jimmy had been talking to outside the Glendale, but as before, he quickly changed the subject. She was frustrated, but she knew that if she kept banging on about the Glendale, he might clam up completely.

They reached the church and the gate Suki had been tied to, but as she had suspected, there was no sign of any food.

'It was just here,' she explained. 'But it's all gone. Greedy seagulls have probably taken it. I thought I might be clutching at straws.' She turned her face to the sky. 'I couldn't bear to lose Suki. I don't know what I'd do without her. She's been my rock since Tom took ill.'

'The vet will be doing all he can,' Jimmy said gently. 'She's in the best possible hands. He knows what he's doing.'

'I know you're right, but it won't stop me worrying.' Helen looked ahead, where the cobbles of Paradise awaited. 'Do you need to get back, Jimmy? Or would you like a guided tour of the old town while we're here? It'd take my mind off Suki.'

She was relieved when he accepted her offer, and they set off along the narrow, winding streets, Helen pointing out quirky cottages built for the fishermen who'd once brought in Scarborough's herring and tunny fleet. Their walk ended when the rain began again. She opened the umbrella and angled it towards Jimmy so that he could take shelter too.

Once back at the Seaview, he removed his wet coat in the lobby.

'The . . . er . . . bowls club tonight,' he said. 'I don't know whether you like bowls or if you'd like to come with me, but it might make for a nice night, take our minds off things after what's been a pretty nasty weekend for us both.'

'Oh, I don't think so,' Helen began. Jimmy's reticence about the person he'd been speaking to outside the Glendale was still on her mind.

'I read online that they do food in there,' he carried on. 'Maybe we could get a bite to eat.'

'Jimmy, that's very good of you, but I need to stay here.'

He smiled kindly. 'And worry about Suki all night?'

Helen thought for a moment. She looked at Jimmy, his open expression, his friendly smile and his handsome face. What secrets did his soulful eyes hide? Maybe an evening with him at the bowls club might be just the thing to get him to relax and open up.

'Good point,' she said. She checked her phone. 'Still nothing from the vet.'

'Why not ring them to put your mind at ease? And then if you'd like to join me tonight, we could meet in the lounge, say about six? If you decide not to show, I'll go on my own. No pressure, just an open invitation you can refuse if you wish. How does that sound?'

'Sounds great, thanks, Jimmy.'

Jimmy headed up to his room and Helen went down to her apartment, where she immediately rang the vet. Suki was sleeping, she was told, and they still wanted to keep her overnight in case the convulsions started again. She hung up, then made herself a sandwich. She realised she hadn't eaten anything since breakfast; the day had gone by in a blur. She ran over Jimmy's invitation to the bowls club. She'd enjoyed his company walking around the old town, and he *had* helped save Suki's life. If she took him up on his offer, she thought again, it might be an ideal opportunity to talk more deeply than they're already done, and she could decide once and for all whether he was telling the truth.

*   *   *

At the bowls club later, Helen and Jimmy sat opposite each other at a table by the bar, watching a game going on. Jimmy had insisted on buying their drinks and paying for dinner. Despite Helen protesting that she would pay for herself, he wouldn't hear of it.

'I'm old-fashioned, Helen, humour me,' he smiled.

She raised her glass of dry white wine. 'Thanks, Jimmy,' she said.

While they waited for their food, they talked about the bowls game, keeping conversation neutral and away from tricky ground, but Helen was determined to find out just what kind of man Jimmy was. He was kind, that much was clear, and he'd helped save Suki's life. He was handsome, too, with a magnetic charm that she had felt the moment he'd stepped through the door at the Seaview. But there was something else there, something she couldn't figure out. She wanted to know more about him; she really wanted to trust him and set her suspicions to rest. But as before, when she brought up the Glendale, Brian and Traveltime Inns, he changed the subject, saying he hoped they could have a few hours together to take their minds off the distressing murder of one of his friends.

'Of course, I'm sorry,' Helen said.

'Let's leave it to the police,' Jimmy said.

The rest of the evening passed companionably, with conversation flowing easily on subjects ranging from Scarborough tourist attractions to Jimmy's home town of London. It was, Helen had to admit to herself later, one of the most pleasant nights she'd enjoyed in a long time.

* * *

Next morning, Helen found herself constantly checking her phone, waiting for a message from the vet. She was beside herself with worry over Suki and had been unable to sleep. She'd called the vet first thing when she woke, but was told they'd ring her back as soon as Suki had been examined. Now she sat on a stool at the kitchen counter talking to Jean, who was preparing breakfast.

'You went where?' Jean said, pushing her glasses up her nose. 'You? Bowling? I didn't know you liked that sort of thing.'

'Me neither,' Helen said. 'But after everything that's happened in the last couple of days, a night out was just what I needed to take my mind off things.'

'And you went with your guest, the Elvis impersonator?'

Helen couldn't fail to notice Jean's inquisitive tone. 'Jimmy. He's a nice bloke.'

'And that's all there is to it between you and him?'

'Jean, what do you take me for?' Helen scolded. 'I've no desire to take up with anyone, least of all one of my guests. I'm not ready for a new relationship; it's far too soon to start again.'

'And life's too short not to,' Jean said sagely as she opened the fridge door. 'Now, what'll I do with these vegetarian sausages?'

'Stick them in the freezer,' Helen said. 'And stop changing the subject. You know Tom was my life. I don't want anyone else, I'm still grieving, Jean. Jimmy's a nice man, that's all. We enjoyed each other's company. End of story.'

Jean unwrapped a parcel of pork sausages. 'When my Archie died, I had three fellas after me, you know. Clive used to take me to the bingo on a Friday afternoon. John took me to the pictures once a week, to the pensioner special where we got a free cup of tea. And Malcolm took me dancing at the Spa. I had a good time, but I promised none of them anything more than a couple of hours of my company once a week. It worked well for a while. Took me out of myself, got me out of the house, stopped me from thinking too much and becoming depressed.'

'What happened? Didn't you want to get serious with any of them?'

Jean shook her head. 'No. Archie was my life. No one could ever have replaced him.'

'And that's exactly how I feel about Tom.'

'Doesn't mean you can't enjoy yourself with Jimmy.'

'I don't want to enjoy myself with anyone, not in the way you seem to be insinuating. I've already told you I'm not ready to go out with anyone yet, I don't know if I ever will.'

'Ah, you will in time, you'll see,' Jean said. 'Now then, one sausage or two?'

'Two for Jimmy. Can you stick a couple under the grill for me, Jean, and do me a poached egg and beans? I need to start eating properly again.'

Jean looked at her. 'I'm happy to hear it, lass, because you look like you could do with feeding up.'

Helen's phone buzzed, and when she saw the vet's number displayed, she answered immediately.

'She is?' she breathed. 'Oh, that's great news. Yes, I'll come and collect her. Do you know what caused . . .? But that's awful. Why would anyone be so cruel as to do that? Well, thank you very much indeed. Yes, of course. Pet insurance? No. Oh. How much? Really? I'll bring my credit card. See you then. And thank you again, for everything.'

'Suki's on the mend, then?' Jean said once Helen hung up.

'She's fine, thank goodness,' but then Helen's face clouded over. 'What is it?' Jean asked.

'They said she'd been poisoned. Those chips she ate had some sort of toxic substance on them. Who would do such a thing?'

'There are some very odd people out there,' Jean said.

Helen's relief at Suki being well enough to collect cheered her up immensely. She was pouring tea from the pot for her and Jean when the kitchen door opened and Sally walked in. At her side was her young daughter, holding tight to her hand.

'Helen, I'm really sorry, I had to bring Gracie with me this morning. Mum's got one of her migraines and she couldn't look after her, and I've got to go to college to drop my assignment in once I've finished here. I had no one else to leave her with. I hope it's all right. I've only got one room to clean, you said, and the public spaces. It'll not take me long. She'll sit quietly and wait for me, I promise.'

'I won't be in the way,' Gracie chirped.

'Of course it's all right,' Helen said. 'You know I love seeing her.'

'Auntie Helen!' Gracie cried, and she let go of Sally's hand and ran full pelt towards Helen.

'Gracie, don't run!' Sally warned.

'I'll take her into the living room,' Helen said.

'I'll bring your breakfast through when it's done.' Jean turned to Sally. 'Will Gracie have a dippy egg and some soldiers?'

'Jean, that'd be smashing, thanks.'

Helen took Gracie's hand and led her out of the kitchen. As she walked into the living room, she stared out through the patio doors to the courtyard, remembering the smashed plant pot and the footprint in the soil, the stranger in the hooded anorak staring into the lounge and the pierced toy dog that had arrived in the post. And now Suki had been poisoned. A shiver ran down her spine. Was it possible these events were connected to Brian's death? Was Traveltime Inns using dirty tactics to scare her into selling up? She couldn't help feeling rattled and upset.

She helped Gracie take her coat off, then settled the little girl on the sofa in front of a cartoon on TV, trying to take her mind off it all with the pleasure of looking after her honorary niece. Then her phone rang again. This time it was Marie.

'I've got them.'

'The blue suede shoes?' Helen asked.

'Yes.'

'Bring them over and we'll decide what to do.'

'Now?'

'Later. I've got to go to the vet's first to pick Suki up.'

'Is she poorly?'

'She's . . . Look, Marie, I've had a rotten weekend, what with Brian being . . .' She glanced at Gracie, who was engrossed in the TV exploits of a yellow duck donning an astronaut's suit. She knew she had to be careful about what she said. Little ears were notorious for picking up things they weren't meant to hear. 'Well, it's been crazy, with everything that's happened. And I know this is going to sound mad and it'll make me sound paranoid, but . . .'

'What is it, Helen?'

Helen turned her head away from Gracie and whispered into her phone, 'I think someone tried to poison my dog.'

192

Chapter 25

'Where's Suki?' Gracie asked once Helen ended her call.

Helen sat on the sofa next to the little girl. 'She's not been very well, Gracie, and she's at the animal hospital. But she's better this morning and I'm going to collect her to bring her home.'

'Did she have a bad foot? Because my cat had a bad foot and I know how to fix it.'

'You do?'

'I fixed it myself, Auntie Helen. I wrapped Mummy's hanky around its poorly paw.' Gracie glanced around Helen's living room. 'You haven't got any toys in your house. Why not, Auntie Helen? I've got lots of toys in my house.'

'Well . . .' Helen began, trying to work out how to reply. 'That's because I don't have any children in my house.'

Gracie opened her eyes wide and stared at her. 'Why not?'

Helen's stomach turned over. How on earth was she going to get out of this one? 'Because I've got Suki to look after and I've got you to look after when you come to visit.'

The answer seemed to satisfy Gracie.

'Does Suki have any toys?'

'She has a ball she runs after on the beach.'

'I've got a ball, it's pink with princesses on it. I've got a princess dressing gown too. I've got *so* many princesses in my life.' Gracie sighed heavily, as if the responsibility for their welfare was a burden.

The two of them watched TV together for a while, with Gracie snuggled into Helen's side. They sat in silence, content with each other's company, until Gracie turned to Helen again.

'Mummy says Uncle Tom's gone to live with the angels.'

Helen leaned across and kissed the top of her head. 'That's right.'

'When's he coming back?'

'Oh darling, he won't be coming back.'

Gracie's eyes widened, trying to make sense of this. 'The angels must like him if they want to keep him,' she said.

Helen smiled. 'Yes, I think they must.'

And then the little girl was back to watching TV again, engrossed in the exploits of a bright orange mouse working on a high-wire act in a circus. The subject was dropped; there was no more talk of Tom or lack of toys. It brought Helen some comfort to know that as far as Gracie was concerned, Tom was living happily with the angels; that was all she needed to know.

Jean walked in with a tray containing Helen's cooked breakfast and a soft-boiled egg and toast for Gracie.

'Thanks, Jean, I really appreciate this,' Helen said.

'It's no problem, love,' Jean said.

Gracie took her own plate and smashed the egg with her spoon before dipping the slices of buttered toast in the runny yolk.

'I love eggs, Auntie Helen,' she said. 'And I love Suki and I love you and I love Mummy.'

'Love you too, Gracie,' Helen said as she tucked into the most tasty, filling meal she'd eaten since she'd returned from Scotland.

* * *

After Jean had finished breakfast and Sally had finished cleaning, Sally popped her head around the living-room door.

'Coffee, Helen?'

'Please,' she replied. 'Come on, Gracie, let's go and see Mummy in the kitchen. But remember, you mustn't run in there.'

Gracie jumped off the sofa and held tight to Helen's hand as they walked into the kitchen.

'He seemed chipper this morning,' Sally said to Helen.

'Who?'

'Your guest. Elvis. He was on good form when I took his breakfast in, asking me about Scarborough, where I'd recommend he goes for the best fish and chips, that kind of thing. He was really chatty.'

'Sounds like something's put a spring in his step,' Jean said. 'Or someone.'

Helen chose to ignore the remark. 'Anyway, changing the subject, I've had a word with Miriam next door,' she said.

'Oh, she's not been locked up then?' Jean said.

'Who's locked up?' Gracie asked.

'No one, sweetheart,' Sally said, rolling her eyes at Helen.

'They let her go after questioning her, but she's not off the hook yet. I don't suppose she will be until they found out who did it.'

'What's happened, Mummy?' Gracie said.

'Nothing, love,' Sally said, shaking her head.

'I said you'd help out next door; I hope you don't mind. It'd be payment at the usual rate.'

Sally shrugged. 'It's no skin off my nose where I work, as long as it pays.'

Helen noticed Gracie touch her nose.

'It's just while it's quiet in here, until our first guests come in at Easter.'

'Jesus brings chocolate eggs at Easter,' Gracie said.

'When does she want me? Not today, Helen, it's too short notice. I've got to go to college. The deadline for the assignment's this morning; if I don't get it in, I'll be in trouble.'

'It'll be later this week; she's got a coach party of ladies coming in from Durham. I'll give you a ring to confirm.'

After coffee and biscuits, Jean and Sally left. Helen walked to the door to see them out.

'Bye, Auntie Helen,' Gracie called.

Helen waved. 'Bye, Gracie. See you tomorrow, Jean, Sally.'

As she watched them head off down Windsor Terrace, she spotted Jimmy walking towards the Seaview.

'I've just been for a walk on the beach,' he explained. 'It's magnificent down there.'

'Isn't it?' Helen smiled. 'I'm lucky to have it on my doorstep.'

'Did you sleep well?' he asked.

The informal question took her by surprise. 'Yes, I did. Thank you. You?'

'Like a log. How's Suki this morning?'

'Fully on the mend, thanks to you.'

Jimmy shrugged. 'Ah, it was nothing. I only did what any right-minded person would have done.'

'Well, I can't tell you how much I appreciated your help.'

'You know, I really enjoyed myself last night,' he said 'It's been a long time since . . .'

He stopped and smiled at Helen, who knew instinctively what he meant.

'It's been a long time for me too. I'd never have thought watching a game of bowls could be so engaging. Thanks, Jimmy.'

Their night out had helped Helen form more of an opinion about Jimmy. She'd got to know him better, but even more importantly, especially after what he'd done to save Suki's life, she felt as if she could allow herself to trust him. Well, a little at least. She still had a niggle in the back of her mind about the person she'd seen him speaking to outside the Glendale.

'Oh, I had a call from Ginger,' Jimmy said. 'His wife is good friends with Brian's wife, and she's been supporting her. The poor woman's in a terrible state. He sends his best to you. And Colin texted and asked me to pass on his love to you too.'

'That's good to hear, thanks.'

Helen watched as Jimmy headed up to his room. She was just about to go down to her apartment when she heard the tinny strains of Elvis's 'Rock-A-Hula Baby' drifting down the stairs, the ringtone on Jimmy's phone. Then she heard him talking as he made his way up.

'Don't ring again,' he said. 'You won't get any more. I told you last time I'd given you enough.'

The door to his room opened and slammed closed. What on earth was going on? Just when it seemed as if she was getting closer to understanding him, was she learning that he had more secrets? It felt as if their friendship was taking one step forward then one step back. But she didn't have time to think any more about it, as she had to drive to the vet to collect the one thing in her life she *could* trust with all her heart. She grabbed her coat and bag, jumped in her car and went to pick up Suki.

* * *

'She'll be fine. Just take it easy with her today and only give her light food,' the vet instructed.

Suki stuck to Helen's side and whined when she opened the car's tailgate. It took no persuasion at all to get her in; she leapt up straight away, wagging her tail furiously. Helen was about to get into the driver's seat when her phone rang. She was surprised to see Benson's estate agents on the caller display.

'Helen Dexter here,' she said with more than a touch of frustration. All she wanted to do was get Suki safely home. She'd thought she was finished with Benson's; what did they want now? Was their call in connection with DS Hutchinson following up the enquiry from the mystery buyer?

'Ah, Mrs Dexter.' It was Frederick Benson's oily tones.

'What is it this time?' she snapped.

'Oh, please, Mrs Dexter, there's no need to be so offhand.'

Helen tapped her foot impatiently against the gravel of the car park, waiting for the man to get to the point. 'I'm in a bit of a hurry, Mr Benson.'

'Then I won't waste too much of your time. I'm calling to say we've received another offer from our interested party to buy the Seaview Hotel.'

'And I've already told you it's not for sale.'

'Now, Mrs Dexter, if I've learned one thing in over thirty years working as an estate agent, it's that everything has its price. Word on the grapevine is that the Seaview's online ratings are plummeting since one of your guests was found murdered.'

Helen gripped her phone so tightly her knuckles turned white.

'It's easy to see how these kinds of things can be bad for business, which might lead any right-minded person to think about selling up and moving on,' he continued.

'Not me,' Helen hissed.

'Let's not be too hasty, Mrs Dexter. As I said, we've received another offer—'

'From Traveltime Inns?'

'I'm afraid I'm not at liberty to divulge my client's details. Of course, this current offer isn't as high as the one put forward to you last time. But under the circumstances, my client feels that it's a fair price for a hotel that has been tainted by scandal and may never recover.'

Helen kicked the gravel and little stones went shooting everywhere. 'Now you listen to me, Mr Benson—'

'No, Mrs Dexter, you need to listen to me,' Mr Benson said, his voice moving from oily to threatening. 'Think carefully about this. It's my client's final offer and your last chance to sell up and move on and make something of your life. Because if you stay at the Seaview, things might just take a turn for the worse.'

'How dare you!' Helen cried. But it was too late; the estate agent had already rung off. She stood for a few moments letting her racing heart calm, scuffing her boots in the gravel. Something sinister was going on, something she didn't understand. She was scared, she was nervous, but more than anything else, she was determined that she wouldn't be forced into selling her cherished hotel.

When she pulled up outside the Seaview, she saw Marie's cherry-red sports car parked outside and Marie in the driver's seat. She blew her car horn to get her friend's attention, and Marie stepped out with a black plastic bag in her hand. Helen snapped Suki's lead to her collar and the dog jumped out of the car.

'How's the mutt?' Marie asked.

'Seems OK,' Helen said. 'Have you been waiting long?'

Marie shook her head. 'Just arrived.'

Helen nodded at the bag in her hand. 'Is that the shoes?'

'Yeah.'

Helen glanced nervously up and down the street before leading the way to the Seaview. She unlocked the door and was about to step inside when she noticed an envelope on the doormat. Nothing unusual there, she thought; the postman must have been while she'd been out. But it wasn't the usual slim brown or white envelope indicating a bill to be paid, a booking coming by post or a demand for taxes due. This was a square black envelope, which was most unexpected. She bent down, picked it up and turned it over. On the front, written in silver ink, were the words *Mrs Dexter, Seaview Hotel.* Suki was straining at her lead so Helen stuffed the envelope into her coat pocket and led the way downstairs, with Marie following.

Suki padded around the apartment, sniffing everything, making herself at home, before collapsing in a heap by the patio doors, where she promptly began to snore.

'Let's see the shoes,' Helen said.

Marie opened the bag.

'You haven't touched them, have you?'

'I used tongs to lift them; you know, the ones for turning sausages. They haven't got my fingerprints on them, but they will have Daran's. I nabbed them while he wasn't looking, when he was packing his stuff to leave.'

'Think he's moved in with Sandra DeVine already?'

'I don't know and I honestly don't care,' Marie said. 'The only thing I'm certain about is that I should have chucked him out years ago.'

Helen peered inside the bag and saw two large, clunky blue suede shoes. They had thick rubber soles and were tied with blue laces.

'This could be just what the police need to find the killer,' she said. 'I'll ring DS Hutchinson now and tell him we're on our way.'

She reached into her pocket for her phone but found the envelope she'd picked up from the doormat. Her mind was spinning; she had so much to think about, the last thing she needed was the emotion that would come from what looked like a very late condolence card over Tom's death. Reluctantly she ripped it open.

'What's that?' Marie asked.

Helen stared open-mouthed at the card with its picture of funereal lilies. Inside was a short handwritten message that sent a shiver down her back.

'Helen? What is it?'

She passed the card to Marie so that she could see the message for herself.

'*Seaview Hotel RIP*,' Marie read. 'Someone's got a sick sense of humour. Who on earth would send you something like this?'

'Someone who wants to knock down the hotel and destroy it, that's who,' Helen said, her mind working quickly. 'It's got to be from whoever's behind Traveltime Inns.'

She grabbed the card back from Marie, tore it up and marched to the kitchen bin, flinging the pieces and the envelope in.

'Well, whoever's behind this isn't threatening me,' she said, more boldly than she felt.

Helen and Marie headed to the police station in Marie's car. They left the blue suede shoes with DS Hutchinson and Marie gave a statement as to how they came to be in her possession. DS Hutchinson raised his eyebrows when he heard Daran Clark's name. Helen also told him about Suki being poisoned – it was too much of a coincidence after she'd received the soft dog toy with the needle through it – and about the card with the lilies that she'd just received. DS Hutchinson wasn't happy to hear that she'd destroyed the card and scolded her for not bringing it in, as it might contain a useful clue.

Once their business with the police was done, Helen asked Marie if she fancied joining her for coffee in town.

'I can't, love. I've got to get to the nail bar. Speaking of which, drop in any time and I'll give you a freebie. You need to think about smartening yourself up, Helen. You can't walk around in widow's weeds for ever.'

Helen looked down at her blue jeans and black boots. 'Weeds?'

'You know what I mean. You should think about giving yourself a makeover as well as updating the Seaview. You need to put yourself on display again, lay your best goods out on your front counter; that's what my old mum used to say.'

Helen raised a hand to her hair. 'I don't want a makeover. There's nothing wrong with my appearance . . . is there?'

'Just like your hotel, your look is stuck in the eighties,' Marie said.

'Oh, spare my feelings, won't you?' Helen laughed.

'Sorry, love, but you could do with a bit of freshening up. How about going blonde?'

'Never. I'm a brunette and always will be.'

'Then why not try something shorter, a pixie cut?'

'But I like my bob, it's neat and tidy. The stylist at Chez Margery looks after it well. You know I don't have much time to spend on hair and make-up when I've got the Seaview to run.'

'Then let me take you shopping for new clothes. We could get the train into York, make a day of it, have lunch.'

'Marie, listen to me, please. I'm happy with the way I am. Besides, I don't think I could afford the clothes shops you'd take me to.'

'Well, you need to do something to get out of the rut you're in. Besides, it'll take your mind off everything that's going on with Traveltime Inns. And you never know when a nice fella might catch your eye, once your grieving is done.'

'Not you as well? Jean's been having a go at me too. I'm not ready for any of that stuff. I don't know if I'll ever be. Or if I want to be. Although . . .'

Marie raised a perfectly shaped eyebrow. 'What?'

'I did go out last night with a man.'

'Helen Dexter! You dark horse. Who was it?'

'Elvis One.'

'Your guest?'

'Jimmy, yes. We went to the bowls club and had a bite to eat. It was nothing, we're just friends. He's a really nice guy.'

'He took you out for dinner?'

'I had pie and chips and gravy, Marie. It was hardly dinner.

And he did help me get Suki to the vet; you could say he even saved her life.'

'You really think someone deliberately poisoned her?'

'I think someone's trying to scare me into selling up, and they targeted Suki this time. They must have followed me from the Seaview to the church. It gives me the creeps to think someone's watching me.'

'You think the people from Traveltime Inns are behind it?'

'You heard what I told DC Hutchinson just now. Who else could it be? The calls from Benson's estate agents, Brian's odd offer, the intruder, the weird toy dog with the needle through it, and now the card. These things must be connected, surely?'

'We should ask DS Hutchinson for a security guard for you at the hotel.'

'Rubbish,' Helen said. 'As if they're going to spend money and resources on me. No, Marie, the Seaview is mine; I've got to deal with this myself. I can't cave in now.'

'Do you think we should have told DS Hutchinson about Sandra DeVine staying at the Seaview with Brian the night before he was killed?'

'No,' Helen said firmly, remembering what Jimmy had said about keeping Brian's womanising a secret for now. 'I plan to speak to Sandra myself. I've heard she still works in the chippy and I'll go there tonight. I'll ask her straight out what she knows about Brian, and I'll know if she's lying or not.'

'That twitch at the side of her mouth?' Marie said.

'Of course. Look, Marie, I've been mulling over the idea of getting CCTV installed, and I think now's the time to do something about it. It'll help put my mind at rest.'

'I'll text you Gav's number,' Marie offered. 'He's handy at sourcing and fitting things like that.'

'Will he offer mates' rates? I can't afford to spend much.'

'Can you afford not to?' she said sagely.

Helen sighed. 'It'll be legit stuff, won't it?'

'Legit enough.' Marie checked her expensive silver watch, then gave Helen a peck on the cheek. 'I've got to run. Take care, Helen. And if you hear anything from the police about the shoes, let me know.'

Helen walked from the police station to Westborough, the town's main shopping street. Towards the end of the street, she turned right into narrow Huntriss Row and headed to Bonnets, her favourite coffee shop. It was over a hundred years old, a quaint little place where the scent of hand-made chocolates greeted her. She threaded her way through the tables to the counter and ordered a large frothy coffee.

'Sitting in or out?' the waitress asked.

'I'll sit in, upstairs,' Helen said.

'I'll bring it up in a few minutes.'

Helen made her way up the stairs and settled herself at a table for two. As she waited for her coffee, she glanced around the room. That was when she noticed a woman sitting alone, a woman with dark eyes, full red lips, and black hair whipped into a beehive and lacquered to within an inch of its life.

Chapter 26

Sandra DeVine was tapping at her phone when Helen approached her.

'Sandra?'

She glanced up with a flash of her smoky eyes. 'Helen! How the devil are you?'

She wiggled out of her seat and enveloped Helen in a hug. Helen had to stop herself from gagging on a cloud of cloying strawberry scent. Sandra released her, then sat down and turned her phone over, hiding the screen.

'God, it must be . . . what? Two, three years since we last bumped into each other?' she said.

'Well, you could have seen me at the weekend when you spent Friday night at my hotel,' Helen said coolly.

Sandra froze. 'Are you here with anyone?'

'No, I'm on my own.'

'Then join me, please.'

Helen gathered her jacket and handbag from her table and settled into the chair opposite Sandra just as the waitress appeared with her coffee. She locked eyes with Sandra, remaining poised and still until the waitress was out of earshot, then leaned across the table and got straight down to business. Bumping into

206

Sandra DeVine like this was too good an opportunity to waste with small talk. 'What's going on?'

'Well,' Sandra replied cagily. 'I mean, it's good to see you and everything, and I'd love to catch up with half an hour of pleasantries, but as you've already come right out and said it, what did you mean about me staying at your hotel?'

'Look, I'm sorry for bringing it up like this, but I know you were at the Seaview on Friday night.'

Sandra leaned forward and narrowed her eyes. 'So you've just said. And?'

'And the man you . . . well, the man whose room you stayed in is the man whose body was found in Peasholm Park.'

Sandra's perfectly powdered face fell. 'No!' she cried. 'The dead Elvis? Are you sure it was definitely him?'

'I'm afraid so.'

'Do the police know who killed him?'

'Not yet,' Helen said, thinking of the blue suede shoes. 'But they'll find out.'

Sandra sank back in her chair, but Helen beckoned her forward, keen not to speak too loudly in case they were overheard. 'I know what you were doing at the Seaview, Sandra. I know about the dating site and the extra money you make from the services you provide. Plus . . . I know about you and Daran Clark.'

'Daran? I don't know what you mean.'

And then Helen saw it, the first twitch at the side of Sandra's mouth.

'Come on, Sandra, tell me the truth,' she said.

'So I do a bit of home working to make ends meet,' Sandra

said defensively. 'Think I can afford to look like this on what I earn at the chip shop? I need money to look after my kids. My two eldest are at York University, one doing physics, the other doing maths. Then there's Cassandra, who's at college in Scarborough, and Adam's doing A levels. They're great kids, but have their dads ever chipped in and offered to help out? Never. What a waste of space they turned out to be. I've brought my kids up on my own, paid for everything, and I won't listen to anyone who says that how I earn my living is wrong.'

Helen held her hands up. 'Hey, I never said it was wrong. What you do to earn cash is your business. But don't ever use the Seaview again.'

Sandra nodded, and her beehive shook. 'All right, I'll steer clear. But why did you bring up Daran Clark?'

'I know about you and him having an affair. I'm Marie's best friend, remember?'

'An affair?' Sandra said sharply. 'How can it be an affair when he got divorced months ago?'

'Divorced? Who told you that?'

'Daran.'

Helen shook her head. 'They're still married.'

'No, Daran said—'

'Daran lied to you, Sandra.'

Sandra gazed out of the window and Helen saw tears welling in her eyes. She dreaded to think what would happen to her immaculate make-up if the tears began to flow.

'He lied,' Sandra muttered. 'There's no way I would have started a relationship with him if I'd known he was married.' She stuck out her ample chest. 'I'm not that kind of girl.'

Suddenly Helen was seeing a more vulnerable side to her old schoolfriend than she'd ever seen before.

'Do you think I should go to the police to tell them what I know about the dead man?' Sandra said.

Once again Helen remembered Jimmy's warning about keeping Brian's womanising a secret from his family. 'It's probably best if you don't. That is, unless you know something that you think might help?'

Sandra thought for a moment, then shook her head. 'No, he was just a regular punter.' She narrowed her eyes. 'Which copper's handling the case?'

'DS Hutchinson and DC Hall,' Helen replied.

Sandra picked up her coffee cup and took a long sip. Was Helen mistaken, or was the cup trembling in her hands?

'Where were you on Saturday evening when the man died?' Helen asked.

'What is this? Are you going all Miss Marple on me?'

'Just asking, that's all.' She watched the side of Sandra's mouth, ready to spot the twitch that might reveal her lies.

'Let's see,' Sandra said. 'On Saturday I was . . . Oh.'

'What?'

'I'd rather not say.'

'Sandra, a man was murdered. You have to tell me the truth.'

'I was with someone, all right?'

'Working?'

'Yes, working. And not at the chip shop either. I was at the Seaview on Friday night with the Elvis impersonator and on Saturday I was with someone else.'

'Daran?'

'No.'

'Then who?'

'I can't say.'

'Because he's married?'

'Married? Divorced? Makes no difference to me when they pay. It's only when I find a guy I like enough to want to see outside my line of work that I make sure he's not involved with someone else. Flaming Daran!' Sandra said through gritted teeth. 'I believed him when he said he and Marie had split. Now I'm wondering what else he's lied to me about.'

'Sandra, why can't you reveal where you were on Saturday?'

'Because . . .' Sandra looked out of the window at the shoppers walking by on Huntriss Row. She took her time to reply. 'Because I was with DS Hutchinson.'

'Really?' Helen was shocked by Sandra's revelation.

'Are you happy now I've told you the truth? And don't you dare breathe a word to anyone about this. He's a very private man.'

'What time did you, er, conclude your business with him?' Helen asked.

'About seven,' Sandra replied. Her face stayed perfectly still, with not a twitch in sight.

Satisfied that she was telling the truth, Helen finished her coffee and told her she needed to get back to the Seaview. Sandra gave her another strawberry-scented hug.

As Helen took her leave, the waitress headed towards Sandra to collect the empty cups.

'Was everything all right?' she asked.

'Everything's just fine,' Sandra said. And her mouth began to twitch.

Back at the Seaview, Jimmy was waiting.

'I thought you should see this,' he said, handing Helen a copy of the *Scarborough Times*. Brian's murder was front page news. Helen's heart sank as she scanned the story. Sure enough, the Seaview was mentioned.

'I'm ruined, Jimmy.'

'No, you're not. Today's newspaper is tomorrow's fish-and-chip wrapping, isn't that what they say?'

'In the days before the internet, maybe,' Helen said.

'Who cares where a dead man stayed? It doesn't matter; it's not going to stop people booking in at the Seaview. It's not as if he was murdered here, is it?'

'Isn't it?' Helen's voice rose. 'You don't understand, Jimmy. This place is my life. It's all I've got. I can shrug off a few nasty reviews online, but this . . .' She waved the newspaper in the air. 'How am I going to come back after this?'

Her phone rang, and she stormed from the lounge to answer it in private.

'Helen, it's Bev.'

'Bev? How are you?'

'Never mind me, I've just seen the headlines. You must be devastated.'

Helen pressed her back against the wall. 'I don't know what to do, Bev. If it's not a weirdo staring into the hotel, a broken pot and footprints left outside my apartment, fake reviews being

211

left online, threats from whoever wants to buy this place, nasty stuff coming in the post or someone trying to poison my dog, now I've got headlines like this to contend with. I'm barely coping as it is without Tom. It's too much. I think I'm cracking up.'

'Ah, well, that's where your fairy godmother comes in.'

'Fairy what? What are you on about?' Helen snapped.

'We're taking you out tonight.'

'Who's we? Where?'

'Me and Sue and Marie are taking you to the Scarborough Arms. Marie says you need feeding up, so I've booked a table for a meal. See you there at seven.' And with that, Bev hung up.

Helen was leaning against the wall, trying to pull herself together, when Jimmy walked into the lobby.

'I'm sorry, I didn't mean to upset you,' he said.

'No, *I'm* sorry, Jimmy.' She smiled. 'I don't usually yell at my guests.'

Jimmy excused himself and headed up to his room. Helen walked down to her apartment, where she was happy to find Suki in good spirits and back to her old self. She snapped the dog's lead to her collar and set off to the beach. As she walked, she ran through her conversation with Sandra DeVine. What Sandra did for a living was her own business; Helen wasn't one to judge. But a murderer? No, Helen didn't think so. But if Sandra hadn't killed Brian, then who had?

At ten to seven that evening, Helen left the Seaview for the short walk to the Scarborough Arms. It was a historic pub with a good reputation for serving hearty home-cooked food. As soon as she walked through the door, she saw Marie, Bev and Sue at a corner table. She couldn't remember the last time she'd been on a girls' night out. As she approached the table, both Sue and Bev stood to embrace her, then she slid along the leather seat to sit next to Marie, who gave her a peck on the cheek. Helen thought Bev looked a little pale and drawn but didn't mention it; she was too relieved that Bev and Sue were friends again and sitting side by side.

'I've ordered a bottle of red at the bar,' Marie said. 'We weren't sure if you'd want something different?'

'No, red's fine for me. It's just what I need after the last few days,' Helen sighed.

She looked at Sue, who was the eldest of the four. Her grey hair was cut in a perfect short bob and she always had a peaceful, calm air about her that Helen admired.

'How was your yoga retreat?'

'Expensive,' Bev said before Sue could answer. 'She's always being fleeced by those hippies.'

'It was restorative,' Sue said. 'Helped me get my head around some things that were on my mind.'

'What's happening with you and Clive?' Helen asked Bev.

'He's not coming back; we're getting a divorce.' Bev looked from Helen to Marie. 'I've found someone else.'

'Who?' Marie said.

Helen noticed Sue and Bev exchange a look, then Bev took Sue's hand. Sue put her free arm protectively around Bev's shoulders, and the two women snuggled close, gazing into each other's eyes.

'You two? Really?' Helen gasped. She turned to Marie. 'Did you know about this?'

Marie shook her head. 'I'm as surprised as you are.'

'How long's it been going on?' Helen asked.

'Since Christmas,' Bev said.

'And you've kept it quiet all this time? Why didn't you tell us?'

'Because we didn't know for sure ourselves,' Sue explained. 'We've gone through hell, the two of us, agonising over our feelings. We've been friends for years, and it just felt right taking things up a notch. But it meant breaking up Bev's marriage. We had to consider her kids and Clive. We had to be sure it was what we wanted before we said anything to anyone else.'

Helen sank back in the leather seat, stunned by the news. The waitress arrived with the bottle of wine, four glasses and four menus. Helen poured wine into each glass then raised her own in a toast.

'To Sue and Bev,' she said. 'I wish you both all the love in the world.'

'Sue and Bev,' Marie repeated.

Bev and Sue smiled at each other.

'To us two.'

Bev set her glass carefully on the table. 'But I'm afraid that's not all of my news. There's something else. Sue already knows this, and she's been my absolute rock.'

'What is it?' Helen said, concerned.

'You know I told you I'd not been feeling well? Well, I've had tests done . . .' She faltered. 'The doctor sent me to see a consultant and . . .'

'Come on, you can do it,' Sue said gently, squeezing Bev's shoulder.

Bev raised her gaze to Helen and Marie.

'. . . and they've found a lump in my breast.'

Chapter 27

At the end of the night, Helen hugged her friends before the short walk back to the Seaview. She was reeling from the shock of Bev's bad news, and from Bev and Sue's relationship too. She hadn't seen that one coming. And yet the more she thought about it, the more it made sense, as the two of them had always been close. Her heart went out to Bev's husband Clive; he was a nice guy, quiet, a bit too timid for Helen's liking, but he'd always seemed genuine and he thought the world of Bev. She felt tired, more than a little drunk after all the wine she'd had. The bottles had kept coming as the four of them celebrated Bev and Sue's relationship and then drowned their sorrows and quelled anxieties over what might be in store for Bev once she received her biopsy result.

When she reached the Seaview, Helen was surprised to see the light was on in the lounge. She was even more surprised to find Jimmy watching TV, two football pundits discussing a game played that night. Two empty beer bottles stood on the table at Jimmy's side and a third bottle was in his hand. When Helen walked into the lounge, he sat up straight and reached for the remote control.

'You don't mind, do you? I'll pay for the beers, of course.'

She waved her hand dismissively. 'It's OK, Jimmy, don't worry.'

'I couldn't face sitting on the bed in my room watching TV so I thought I'd sit here instead. It's nice here, lovely view out over the bay.' He turned the TV off.

Helen pointed to the bottle in his hand. 'Would you like another?'

'Please.'

She opened a bottle for Jimmy and helped herself to a brandy. She had to put her hand on the bar to steady herself as she worked. She really had drunk too much already, but the brandy seemed too good an idea to refuse.

'Oh, you're on the hard stuff,' Jimmy teased.

'I've had a bit of a shock.' Helen set the beer next to Jimmy, then sat at one end of the window seat and raised her glass. 'Cheers.'

Jimmy picked up his beer. 'Care to talk about it?'

Helen gazed out of the window into the black night. At the bottom of the cliff a string of street lights on Marine Drive illuminated the shore. She took a long sip of brandy and let it warm her throat. 'No. You don't want to hear about it.'

'A problem shared is a problem halved and all that.'

She shook her head. 'No, it's personal.' She closed her eyes, thinking about Bev. She couldn't bear to lose her friend to the same disease that had stolen Tom.

'Are you all right?' Jimmy asked.

Helen blinked and realised, too late, that tears were rolling down her face.

'Here, let me get you a tissue,' Jimmy said, patting his pockets then desperately looking around the lounge.

'It's all right, I've got one here,' Helen said, opening her handbag and shaking a tissue from a pack. Her bag fell to the carpet and she reached to pick it up just as Jimmy had the same idea. His hand brushed hers and neither of them pulled away.

'I'm sorry,' he said at last. He lifted the bag and placed it on a chair.

'No, I'm sorry, Jimmy. I need to turn in for the night. I've had too much to drink. I'm feeling . . . what's the phrase? . . . tired and emotional.'

She stood to leave but tottered slightly and had to put her hand on a chair to steady herself. Jimmy stood too.

'Allow me,' he said, offering his arm. Helen took it gratefully, and arm in arm they walked across the lobby to the door that led to her apartment. As she fumbled in her bag for her key, Jimmy turned back to the lounge.

'Jimmy,' she called. He stopped and looked at her. 'Thanks,' she said. 'For everything.'

The two of them locked eyes for a few seconds longer than necessary. Then Jimmy walked slowly back towards her. His breath brushed her face as he leaned close, and Helen breathed in his aftershave of lemon and spice. She felt the roughness of his cheek against her skin, and then his lips on hers, delicate and fleeting, not pushing for more.

'Night, Helen,' he said, taking a step back. 'I'll see you in the morning.'

Her heart was jumping. What on earth had just happened?

'Night, Jimmy,' she said, then she turned the key in the lock and headed downstairs.

The following morning, Helen's waking thoughts turned to painkillers to help numb her hangover – that is, until she remembered the kiss. It was like being seventeen again, she thought, the morning after a night out with Marie, drinking in bars they weren't old enough to be in, snogging boys they'd only just met. And then waking up with the dawning realisation of the mischief they'd been up to. Except this time she wasn't seventeen. She was old enough to know better.

'Sorry, Tom,' she whispered as she stared up at the ceiling.

She clambered out of bed, stepped over the dog and headed to the shower. Once she was dressed and heading out with Suki for a walk, her phone beeped with a message from Marie.

Gav's on his way to fit CCTV. He's a nice lad. What a shocker last night! Call me if you hear from Bev about biopsy xx

Back at the Seaview after her walk on the beach, where Jimmy was on her mind, Helen called into the kitchen, where Jean was peeling bacon rashers from a pack.

'Any chance of a sandwich?' she asked.

Jean looked up. 'God, you look rough. Still not sleeping well?'

'Cheers. I slept like a log, but I went out last night with the girls and we ended up drinking too much.'

'It'll do you good to start getting out again.'

The doorbell rang and Helen and Jean exchanged a look.

'Not expecting anyone this early, are you?' Jean asked.

'It'll be Marie's friend Gav. He's fitting security cameras today.'

Helen headed upstairs and opened the door. The man in front of her was, she guessed, in his mid thirties. He was tall and lean, with long, dark wavy hair and a pleasant, friendly face.

'It's your man Gav,' he said, bounding into the hall and glancing around the lobby. 'Now, where do you want the cameras?'

Gav wore blue jeans and a short-sleeved black shirt that read

Gav's Cabs in large orange print on the back. Outside the Seaview, Helen saw a blue van with *Gav's Garden Services* printed on the side. She opened her mouth to speak, but he cut her short.

'Now, is that bacon I can smell cooking?' He patted his taut, toned stomach through his black shirt. 'It'd set me right up for a day's work if I had a bite to eat. Didn't have time for breakfast this morning before I left the house. You can take it off my bill.'

Helen nodded towards the empty dining room. 'Oh, go on then, wait in there. Full English? Mug of tea?'

'That'd be smashing.' He beamed and disappeared into the dining room. Helen headed downstairs to give Jean the news, then returned to talk to him about the work he was going to do.

'When you're installing the camera at the back, you'll have to work around the rubbish as best you can,' she told him. 'It doesn't smell too good out there.'

'Ah, the strike,' Gav said. 'Do you know, I put a tender in with the council to try to get a temporary contract until the strike ends, but I've not heard anything back.'

'You're a refuse collector as well as everything else?'

'I'll do anything if it makes cash,' he laughed. 'Drive a taxi, clean windows, fit security cameras and alarms . . . You name it, I'll do it.'

'Can you change locks on doors?' Helen asked, thinking about room seven, where Brian had stayed.

'No problem,' Gav said.

All the while Helen was talking to Gav, she kept glancing nervously at the dining-room door. She knew Jimmy would be coming down for breakfast soon and she was still trying to make sense of what had happened between them the night before.

219

'How do you know Marie?' she asked.

'Ah, she's an angel, she is. I know her through Daran; I did some work on their garden, put sprinklers in and dug a pond. And I tiled the bathroom while I was there.'

Outside the dining room the bell on the dumbwaiter rang, the sign that breakfast was on its way up. As Helen served Gav his food, she caught sight of Jimmy. But he wasn't walking downstairs as she'd expected; he was coming in through the front door.

'It's a bit nippy out there,' he said when he saw her.

'Morning, Jimmy.' She took a deep breath to calm herself. 'Full English this morning?'

'Please,' he said 'And Helen, I'm sorry about last night. I shouldn't have—'

She shook her head, then gave a discreet nod to the dining room, where Gav was squeezing brown sauce over Jean's perfectly cooked sausages.

Chapter 28

After Jimmy had eaten breakfast, sharing the dining room with Gav, Helen ushered him into the lounge and closed the door. They stood so close that she could smell the lemon and spice scent of his aftershave again. She pressed her boots into the carpet and pushed her shoulders back. Jimmy looked as tired as she felt, and she wondered if he was suffering a hangover too.

'Look, Jimmy, what happened last night shouldn't have happened,' she said sternly.

He nodded in agreement. 'You're absolutely right, and I'm sorry. I should never have—'

She held her hand up to stop him. 'It wasn't all your fault. I didn't exactly push you away. I'm not thinking straight at the minute, Jimmy,' she explained. 'There are all kinds of problems, strange things going on, fake reviews, threats to sell, and what with Brian being murdered . . . I'm feeling scared, like I'm going out of my mind.'

He let this sink in for a few moments. 'I understand,' he said at last.

'Do you?' Helen said. 'I don't think anyone understands what I'm going through right now. Not my friends, not my staff, no one. I'm only just managing to keep my sanity.'

Jimmy opened his mouth to reply, but was cut short when the lounge door burst open and Gav breezed in.

'Right then, missus! Where do you want these cameras?'

Helen ushered him out. 'I'll be with you in five minutes,' she said.

Gav looked from her to Jimmy. 'Oh. Right you are. I'll see if I can squeeze another drop from the teapot while I wait.'

Helen closed the door. She sat down next to Jimmy and laid her hand on his arm. He turned towards her and smiled, but his face dropped as soon as she began to speak.

'I think it might be best if you leave, Jimmy. I can't handle you being here, not while I'm trying to make sense of what's going on in my life. I'm struggling with feelings and emotions I don't know how to handle. I'm still grieving for my husband, and after what happened, our kiss, it feels like I'm betraying him.'

Jimmy took her hand. 'Then I'll go,' he said quietly. 'The last thing I want is to cause you any pain.'

She slid her hand free. 'Will you head home?'

He shook his head. 'I need to be here in Scarborough,' he said, rubbing the back of his neck. 'DS Hutchinson called to say he wants me to stay, in case any leads turn up. Besides, I'm getting to like the place.'

'There's no one waiting for you at home?' Helen asked.

'Just my friends in what remains of Twelvis, which reminds me, we'll have to go through the motions of admitting a new member to take Brian's place. It's a procedure mired in politics that I won't bore you with. There'll be Brian's funeral, of course; I'll go back for that as soon as I get a call from Ginger to let me know when it's taking place. Could be a while, though, as the police still have the body. But if you're asking if there's a woman in my life, the answer's no. There *was* someone after my wife left; we lasted a few years before we grew apart. I've been on my own since, rattling around a three-bedroom semi that's far too big for just me. I've been thinking for a long time about selling up and moving.'

'Me too.' Helen smiled.

'Oh, you can't leave this place,' Jimmy said. 'It's a little gem. And it takes a special woman like you to run it.' He stood. 'Well, I guess I'll go and pack my bags.'

'Where will you stay?'

'I'll go looking for a vacancy sign hanging in a window of a decent B&B. Would you recommend next door?'

'The Vista del Mar?' Helen hadn't told Jimmy that Miriam was Brian's ex-wife; she'd promised Miriam not to mention it to anyone. 'Probably best if you stay somewhere our paths might not cross.'

The lounge door swung open and Gav walked in again. 'Ready for me yet, missus?'

'Just a couple more minutes,' Helen said.

'Right you are then.' He closed the door as he left.

'Would it be all right if I asked to see you again?' Jimmy began hesitantly. 'Perhaps for a drink one night?'

'I'll think about it,' Helen said.

They sat in silence for a few moments.

'Have you heard anything from the police?' Jimmy asked.

'DS Hutchinson's promised to keep me updated, but he says they don't have much to go on.' She kept quiet about taking the blue suede shoes to the police station. She felt as if she'd already told Jimmy too much. What if he was involved with Traveltime Inns, even with Brian's murder? She tried to stop her emotions clouding her face. 'They'll ring as soon as they have news.'

'And will you call me when they do?' Jimmy asked.

'Of course I will. Look, Jimmy, I don't want us to fall out over what happened last night.'

The lounge door opened yet again and Gav stood on the threshold, not daring to enter this time.

'Missus?'

'I'm coming now,' Helen said. She turned to face Jimmy. 'Let's keep in touch while you're in Scarborough.'

'I'd like that,' he said. 'I'll leave my key on the bar when I go.'

Helen walked out of the lounge, forcing her feet forward. She kept telling herself she'd done the right thing asking Jimmy to leave. He was a nice man and a good man and if she wasn't grieving over Tom, if she didn't have the Seaview and her future weighing heavy on her mind, if she'd met him at any time in her life other than right now, it would be easy to fall for his charms.

She smiled at Gav. 'This way, I'll show you where I'd like the cameras fitted.'

Helen's morning was spent catching up on admin on her laptop, with Suki lying at her feet. Every now and then the dog stood, stretched and walked towards where Gav was working. At one point, when he was concentrating on setting up the display screen in the kitchen, Suki began gently gnawing the heels of his trainers.

'Suki, leave!' Helen ordered, returning to her emails. Her eyes were drawn to a list of five messages from HypeThatHotel. Four were notifications to say that more reviews had been left, and Helen clicked them open. Two were glowing: one from Sam and one from Jimmy. The other two were from Porgy42 and Pudding&Pie, and were identical in every way, even down to the same spelling mistake.

Dead man stayed here. Do not stay. Sory, hotel is no good.

This time, however, there was also an email from the review site in reply to Helen's complaint. It was an auto-generated response to say that she had to prove that the fake review violated the site's guidelines, and if it did, she could report it.

As she went through the motions of making the complaint once again, Gav popped his head around the door.

'Is that the kettle I can hear boiling? Is that the biscuits I can hear shouting my name? *Gav! Gav!* they're saying. I can hear them calling me all the way to the back door.'

Fuelled by tea and chocolate digestives, Gav worked steadily, and by mid afternoon his work was done and he was explaining to Helen how the security system worked. The screen in the kitchen would show and record views from each of the cameras, one by the back door, one at the front and one in the sunken courtyard. But each time he switched the display on, all she could see were flickering images.

'It's like one of those old black and white movies that jump all over the screen,' she said.

'It'll be all right, just needs a bit of tweaking,' he replied confidently. 'And if the kettle's boiling for another cuppa, it might be just what I need to help me concentrate and get this fixed.'

Helen obliged with another cup of tea and the remains of the digestives. But neither the tea nor the biscuits could fire up Gav to get the display working.

'This is proper, legit stuff, isn't it?' she asked. 'I mean, it's not knock-off?'

'Missus!' he cried in mock exasperation. 'What are you suggesting? That it fell off the back of the lorry? I bought it legit from Daran.'

'Well, I know how Daran Clark operates and I know he gets things cheap. I notice you didn't bring an instruction manual with you, or a guarantee.'

'No, I, er . . .'

'And I don't suppose I'm going to get a receipt or an invoice, am I?'

'I'd prefer cash, it makes things easier,' Gav said with a cheeky grin. He took a long slurp of tea, then wiped the back of his hand across his mouth. 'Leave it with your man Gav. I'll get it fixed. I'm going to have to send off for a part. As soon as I get it, I'll pop back and fix it.'

'When will that be?'

He shrugged. 'I've got a kids' party to do this week. Which reminds me, I need to find a bouncy castle from somewhere. And then I've got a garage roof to fix and a drive to lay in Scalby.' He rubbed his chin. 'I reckon I'll be back before the end of the week.' He set down his empty cup beside the flickering display unit. 'Give my love to Marie when you see her,' he said. 'Tell her if she wants her hot tub finishing, all she has to do is give me a bell.'

And with that, he was gone. Helen stood a few moments watching the flickering displays from each camera. She squinted, but it didn't help pull the display into focus. She walked to the living room and let Suki out to the courtyard, then went back to the console to see if she could spot the dog walking in front of the camera. All she saw was a fuzzy bear in a snowstorm prowling the patio.

She picked her phone up and was about to text Marie to tell her about her encounter with Gav when it lit up with a call. It was the police station. Helen girded herself.

'Helen Dexter,' she said as assertively as she could.

'Mrs Dexter, DS Hutchinson here.'

She couldn't stop an image of him with Sandra DeVine popping into her mind. She shook her head to dismiss it. 'Any news?' she asked.

'I'm ringing about the blue suede shoes you and Mrs Clark brought in yesterday.'

'And?' Helen urged, desperate to know.

'We've run some tests on them, Mrs Dexter. And they do indeed have Mr Clark's fingerprints all over them. However . . .'

Helen's heart sank. Just when it seemed as if the nightmare of Brian's murder might be coming to an end, it sounded like more bad news.

'. . . none of the fingerprints on the shoes belong to Brian McNally.'

'But . . . how . . .?'

'We've discovered a few other things about the shoes, Mrs Dexter.'

'What sort of things?'

'The pair you brought in were size nines, but we've received confirmation from Brian's daughter that he took a size eleven. Not only that, but he had very wide feet, and he had to have extra-wide shoes. The ones we have here are a regular fit. In addition, the shoes you brought in were lace-ups. Now, the Elvis troupe all wore the same shoes; they bought them as a job lot. They all wore slip-ons, Mrs Dexter. So while, yes, you brought us a pair of blue suede shoes, I can confirm they're not the ones we're looking for.' DS Hutchinson sighed heavily. 'It seems that slippery son-of-a-bitch Daran Clark is off the hook, again.'

'Could I ask that this new information is relayed to Jimmy as soon as possible, please?' Helen asked.

'No problem,' he replied. 'I've got his mobile number; I'll call him. I've also got his landline. It might be better to use that now he's gone home.'

'No, he's still here in Scarborough,' Helen said, confused. 'He told me he was sticking around in case you needed to speak to him about the case.'

'Me? I never said any such thing, Mrs Dexter. If Mr Brown is staying local, he's doing it of his own accord. It's got nothing to do with any request from Scarborough police, or anything to do with the case. I told all the Elvis impersonators they were free to leave after we'd questioned them at the Seaview. Can you think of any reason he's decided to stay, and, if I may be so bold, why he's lied to you about it?'

Helen's heart sank at his words. She was confused, angry and more hurt than she'd expected to be that Jimmy hadn't told her the truth.

'No, I can't think of any reason,' she said, and hung up.

Chapter 29

Helen called Marie straight away. Their conversation meandered its way from Daran's blue suede shoes to Bev and Sue's shock news from the night before, to concern about Bev's biopsy through to Gav's installation of the non-functioning CCTV, before ending on Helen's reveal that she and Jimmy had kissed and then she'd thrown him out.

'You did what?'

'He's gone to stay somewhere else. It's for the best. I'm having all sorts of feelings I can't make sense of. If he stayed here, he'd always be on my mind. I had to put some distance between us.'

'Has he gone home?'

'He's staying in Scarborough.'

'Will you see him again? Do you want to?'

'Yes, I want to, but . . . he's a man who's got secrets, Marie.'

'Show me a man who hasn't,' Marie said wryly. 'Do you want my advice?'

Helen laughed. 'No, but you're going to give it to me anyway, so let's have it.'

'I say you should go for it. Oh, and you'll never guess what happened.'

'What now?'

'Sandra DeVine has only gone and dumped Daran!'

Helen's next call was to Jean to tell her that Jimmy had moved out, although she didn't tell her why, or what had happened between them. Without any guests to cook for, there was no need for Jean to come back to work until Easter. Helen brushed aside Jean's concerns about her being alone at the hotel until the first guests arrived. But she knew she was kidding herself, trying to convince her friend that she'd be fine on her own. She could imagine Jean sitting on her sofa in her semi-detached on Dean Road, eyebrows knitted, tutting.

Half an hour after Helen's call ended, there was a knock at her kitchen door. She froze. No one was allowed downstairs to her apartment; the door from the lobby was kept locked, even when there were no guests. The only people with keys to the Seaview's front door and the door to the apartment were Sally and Jean, and she wasn't expecting either. She headed for the door just as Jean walked in pulling a small black suitcase on wheels. Helen's mouth dropped open in shock.

'You'll not know I'm here,' Jean said. 'I'll take the keys to room one, I've always loved the view from there. I'll cook for us both while I'm here. Someone's got to keep an eye on you, lass. Look at you, you're all skin and bone. I'll clean up after myself. I'll be as quiet as a mouse. I've brought my puzzle books and knitting. Now get yourself out for a walk and some fresh air. It's glorious out there. Looks like we're in for another spell of warm weather.'

'But . . .' Helen began.

'But nothing, lass. You need looking after. And I . . . well, I need someone to look after. Besides, it'll be like a little holiday for me, a home away from home. It'll help take my mind off Mum's legs.'

'Jean. I don't know what to say.'

Jean held her arms out. 'There's no need for words, love. I've been through what you're suffering, and I know how you feel. You're doing your best to stay strong, but my word, it's harder than you ever expect. When my Archie died, I thought I'd never be the same again. Come here and give me a hug.'

At Jean's insistence, Helen took Suki out for a walk in the sunshine. Knowing someone was in the hotel with her was a relief. Better still that the someone was Jean. Helen felt as if a warm blanket had been thrown around her shoulders. The tide was out, but instead of heading to the North Bay sands, Helen decided to make the most of the good weather and walk to the South Bay. She let Suki off the lead and the dog went splashing into the waves. When she reached the spot where she'd scattered Tom's ashes, Helen turned her face to the sun and closed her eyes, feeling the warmth on her skin. With her eyes shut, the cry of the seagulls seemed louder and the ocean began to roar.

She headed up the steps that led from the sand to the Spa. How different she felt now compared to the last time she'd been there, with Twelvis. So much had happened since then, still too much for her to process in any normal way, never mind while she was grieving. She walked along the prom past the Spa and noticed signs of the tourist season coming to life. The ice-cream shop was open, as was the stall offering deckchairs and wind breaks; flags fluttered in the breeze with buckets and spades for sale.

She walked on, following the path that led up the cliff to the big hotels on the Esplanade. The pathway twisted and turned, offering spectacular views of the bay and castle. It was a walk she and Tom had loved to take with the dog, and it was comforting to let herself imagine him by her side. The rose garden at the top of the cliff was one of her favourite places in summer, when sweet floral scents filled the air. However, in March the rose bushes were bare sticks poking through soil. She was about to walk past – there was no point in going in, not at this time of year – when she saw a man sitting alone on a bench, and she froze when she realised who it was. Suki pulled on her lead, expecting to carry on walking.

'This way, girl,' Helen said, and stepped into the rose garden.

It was a secluded, private place, surrounded by privet hedges. Wooden seats ran along a path, and Jimmy was sitting in the middle of one of them.

'Room for a little one on the end?' Helen said as she drew near.

Her words seemed to force Jimmy out of his reverie, and when he caught sight of her, he looked past her, beyond her, as if searching for something. She'd expected him to shift along the bench, at the very least, so that she could sit down. But he didn't move. She wondered if she'd upset him when she'd asked him to leave the Seaview.

'It's a lovely spot to sit in the sunshine,' she said encouragingly. 'The hedges keep the wind out. And you should see it in the summer; it's glorious when the roses are out.'

Jimmy looked around wildly. 'Helen, you should go,' he urged.

'I've just got here,' she said, confused. 'Did you find somewhere to stay?'

'The Grand Hotel,' he hissed impatiently.

Helen tried again. 'Did DS Hutchinson ring you with an update?'

'What?' Jimmy said distractedly, still trying to look past her. Just then, his eyes widened. He dropped his head. 'Oh no,' he muttered.

Suki barked, something she rarely did, and Helen turned to see what had caught the dog's attention. Someone was walking towards her and Jimmy, someone with skinny legs and dirty trainers, wearing a black anorak with the hood shielding their face.

Chapter 30

'Helen, this is my daughter, Jodie,' Jimmy said.

Helen's mouth opened and closed as she took in the slight figure in front of her. From the shape of her coat and Jodie's height, she was certain it was the same person she'd caught staring into the Seaview's lounge; the same person she'd seen Jimmy talking to outside the Glendale. A mixture of emotions and feelings rushed through her, but mainly relief. Jodie was the reason Jimmy had clammed up each time she'd tried to get him to reveal who he'd been talking to. He had been protecting his daughter. Did this confirm he wasn't involved with Traveltime Inns or with Brian's death? So many questions fizzed in her mind.

She took a good look at Jodie, trying to see a resemblance to Jimmy. It was there, but only just. The girl had Jimmy's dark eyes, but her face was pinched and her skin pale.

Suki took a step forward and began sniffing Jodie's shoes. Helen pulled her back, then glanced down at the shoes, which were nothing more than plimsolls, worn thin, with holes at the toes. One had a tear down the side. They looked loose and ill-fitting, tied with scraps of black laces.

'What are you staring at?' Jodie demanded.

Helen snapped her gaze back. 'Sorry,' she said.

Jodie turned her back on Helen. 'What's she doing here?' she

234

asked Jimmy. 'I'm not seeing another social worker; I've got one already.' She spun back round. 'And you can get that dog away. Is that what they're using for drugs dogs these days? I know the council are having cutbacks, but that's ridiculous. It's not even a dog; it's a rat on a lead. Anyway, I've been clean for years now. Dad, tell her!'

'This is Helen. She's a friend of mine. She's not a social worker,' Jimmy said calmly.

'Where is it, Dad?' Jodie said.

'Jodie, not here, please,' Jimmy whispered.

'Look, I'll go and leave you two alone,' Helen said quickly. 'I'll call you later, Jimmy.'

'Helen, no. Wait,' Jimmy cried.

'Dad? I need it!' Jodie urged. 'I'm starving.'

Jimmy dug into his back pocket and pulled out a leather wallet. He opened it, peeled off two ten-pound notes and handed them to Jodie, who bent down and stuffed them inside one of her shoes, forcing the money under her foot.

'See you, Dad,' she said, and began to walk away.

Helen and Jimmy watched her go.

'I wish you hadn't seen that,' Jimmy said.

'But I did. Talk about being in the wrong place at the wrong time,' Helen said wryly.

'I owe you an explanation; it's the least I can do.'

Helen glanced at her watch. There was nothing to hurry back for. Jean had offered to cook dinner and told Helen it'd be on the table for six. She had a couple of hours to kill before then.

'Fancy a coffee?' she asked. 'There's a café just a short walk away.'

'Thanks, Helen,' Jimmy said.

They left the rose garden together.

'Jodie's got a few problems, as you can probably tell,' Jimmy said.

'Does she live here?'

'She moved to Scarborough when she left home. She gravitated to the place she spent happy holidays when she was little, holidays at the Seaview.'

'I wish I could remember her,' Helen said. 'I wish I could remember you too, but I can't, not after all the guests who stayed at the hotel; we must have had thousands over the years.'

They headed to the Esplanade and walked back towards town.

'How old was she when she left home?' Helen asked.

'Fifteen,' Jimmy said. 'She left without a word to me or her mum. She'd got in with some bad kids at school; they were taking drugs and we tried to help her as best we could. But we didn't know what she was going through, not really. You try to help them, you know? They're your child, your world, you want to do what's best. When she disappeared, we called the police and they found her living here in a squat. We dragged her home, but she kept running off, and life was hell for a very long time.'

'Where does her mum fit into all of this?'

'She abandoned her. Said she couldn't cope. That was what led to us splitting up. Jodie's . . . well, you saw the state of her. She's got problems. She's been like that for years, living rough. The only time I see her is when she needs money.'

'Oh Jimmy, I'm sorry.'

'Not a day goes by when I don't feel like I've failed her,' he said.

They headed across the Spa Bridge to the St Nicholas Café in the shadow of the Grand Hotel. Helen tied Suki to the railings outside, then they ordered two coffees that Jimmy insisted on paying for and took seats at a window table overlooking the South Bay beach.

'Lovely little place,' Jimmy said, glancing around.

'It used to be a funicular cliff lift,' Helen explained. 'But after it was left empty for decades, they turned it into a café. There's another one at the bottom of the cliff too.'

The coffees arrived with fat circles of gold foil promising chocolate within.

'Jodie thought I was a social worker when she saw me,' Helen said. 'Is she getting help from social services?'

'They do what they can. And she's plugged into a community project that looks out for her too. When I knew I was coming here for the Elvis convention, I wrote to her – she lives in a hostel in town. She begged to see me and I knew she'd be asking for money. But how can I refuse her? She's my only child.' Jimmy stirred the frothy milk in his cappuccino.

'She's the person I saw you talking to outside the Glendale, isn't she?'

'Yes, she came asking for cash after I told her where I was staying. I'm sorry I lied to you about her. I had to protect her.'

Helen felt another rush of relief go through her with Jimmy's confirmation. Her hands began to shake and she steadied herself by placing them on her knees. 'She scared me witless once or twice staring straight into the lounge,' she admitted. 'I thought it was a kid looking to break in.'

'Yes, that was her,' Jimmy said. 'She came looking for me,

wanting money. When you told me you thought someone had tried to break into your apartment, I asked her about it but she swore blind it wasn't her. I have to believe her.'

'I think you're right,' Helen sighed. 'Whoever came prowling on the patio had bigger feet than Jodie and their shoes left a heavy imprint in the soil. Her tiny plimsolls wouldn't have done that.' She sipped her coffee. 'She's the real reason you stayed in Scarborough, isn't she? DS Hutchinson told me on the phone that he never asked you to hang around. He said you were free to go.'

Jimmy raised his eyes towards her. 'Well, now you know the truth. DS Hutchinson rang me this morning and told me about the blue suede shoes you found. If I'd known they weren't slip-ons, I could have saved you the bother of taking them to him in the first place.'

Helen sighed. 'I didn't tell you about the shoes because I didn't know if I could trust you. I felt you were keeping something from me. Now that I know about Jodie, I'm relieved. As for the shoes, not only were they lace-ups, they were also the wrong size and fit. Did DS Hutchinson say if he'd received any more clues as to who murdered Brian? No mention of anyone from Traveltime Inns or the black Porsche?'

'Not a dicky bird.'

Helen picked up the two golden coins. 'Want one?'

Jimmy nodded. She handed one to him and unwrapped the other herself.

'Before last week I hadn't seen Jodie in years,' he said. 'I kept in touch with her through the hostel. Christmas cards, birthdays, that sort of thing. When I saw her again, my heart broke, and

I wanted to stay near her for as long as I could. We started talking, were making headway; she even agreed to let me meet her social worker next week.'

'And then this morning I turned up and scared her away,' Helen said. 'I'm really sorry.'

'It's not your fault. She's edgy, flighty. I'll see her again soon. She knows I'm staying at the Grand now.' He pointed out of the café window. 'That's my room up there, third floor at the end.'

The Grand Hotel was a Scarborough landmark, visible from almost everywhere in town. It had been built in the nineteenth century for affluent tourists and was constructed on the theme of time. There were twelve floors to represent the months of the year, 365 rooms, one for each day, and four wings, one for each season. In its day it was the biggest hotel in Europe.

Jimmy sipped his coffee. 'I do understand, you know, why you threw me out.'

'That makes me sound like an ogre,' Helen laughed. 'I asked you to leave, that was all. It was for the best.'

The tinny strains of 'Rock-A-Hula Baby' cut into their conversation. Jimmy took his phone from his pocket and glanced at the screen. 'It's Ginger,' he said. 'I'll ring him back later.' He pocketed the phone and looked at Helen. 'I want to apologise again, Helen. I shouldn't have kissed you.'

'We've both got a lot on our minds,' Helen said. 'Maybe when we're thinking more clearly, we could try that kiss again.'

Jimmy flashed a smile and his whole face lit up. 'That'd be nice,' he said.

* * *

239

Much later, after more coffee, more chocolates wrapped in gold foil and a lot more conversation, Helen and Jimmy finally left the café. Helen untied Suki from the railing and the dog whined with pleasure at being back at her side.

'Well, this is me,' Jimmy said as he turned to face the Grand Hotel.

Helen walked with him to the wide flight of stone steps that led up to the impressive doors, and they stood awkwardly together before she brought him to her in a brief, functional hug. Neither of them knew what was expected of them; it was as if they were writing the rules as they were going along.

'I hope it all goes OK with Jodie,' she said. 'And ring me if you hear anything from the police.'

She waved farewell to Jimmy and set off through town. As she walked, she found herself looking forward not only to eating Jean's home-cooked meal but to sharing a table and chatting while she ate. She thought she might tell Jean about Jimmy and confide in her about Jodie. When she reached the Seaview, she spotted Miriam cleaning the steps of the Vista del Mar with a bucket of soapy water and a scrubbing brush.

'Miriam? You all right?'

Miriam stood, and Helen was pleased to see that she looked back to her old self, with her make-up immaculate and her long grey hair piled up on her head in a mass of curls. She peeled off her pink rubber gloves.

'Ah, Helen dear. Just the person I was hoping to speak to. I've had a bit of good news.' She glanced up and down the street, then beckoned Helen towards her. 'Leave the dog at the gate; I don't want her fouling my pathway.'

Helen tied Suki to Miriam's gatepost. 'What is it?' she asked.

Miriam leaned close. 'Strictly *entre nous*, the police have just told me I'm no longer a person of interest,' she whispered.

Helen's eyebrows shot up. 'Oh?'

Miriam glanced from left to right before she carried on. 'It turns out that your dead Elvis was seen getting into a car on the night he was murdered.'

'He's not my dead Elvis, Miriam. And I've already told the police that I saw him getting into the black Porsche.'

'No, this was another car, later. Apparently he returned to the Seaview and called a cab to pick him up to take him to the Spa. But when the driver turned up, he saw a man dressed as Elvis climbing into a car that drove off, leaving the poor cabbie waiting outside the Seaview for a fare that never arrived.'

'When did the police tell you this?' Helen said.

'About half an hour ago.'

Helen untied Suki and flew into the Seaview, pulling her phone from her bag. She knew she should call DS Hutchinson to find out what was going on. But instead she dialled Jimmy's number.

Chapter 31

'Jimmy? It's Helen. Has DS Hutchinson called you with news about the car?'

'What car?'

She told him everything she'd just learned from Miriam.

'He's supposed to be keeping me up to date with what's going on,' Jimmy said. Helen couldn't fail to notice his frustration. 'We should go and talk to him at the station.'

'I've got a better idea. We need to find the guy from Traveltime Inns, the one who drives the black Porsche.'

'And what good would that do? You've just said Brian was seen getting into another car by the cabbie who turned up at the Seaview.'

'I can't help thinking there's more to it than that. I think we should talk to the man with the Porsche.'

'I'm not sure about this, Helen,' Jimmy said warily. 'You really think we should collar the guy? I'm inclined to leave that to the police. You shouldn't get involved.'

'It's not getting involved . . . exactly,' Helen said. 'I mean, if I happen to be taking Suki out for a walk and he's there outside the hotel opposite my bed and breakfast, all I'd be doing is acting neighbourly if I went over to say good morning. There's no law against that, is there?'

'Helen, no,' Jimmy warned.

'Don't you want Brian's killer caught and this horrible situation brought to an end?'

'Of course I do, but—'

'But nothing, Jimmy. I'm going to speak to him tomorrow morning if he's there, and you can come with me if you like.'

There was a beat of silence.

'Tomorrow?' Jimmy said, deflated. 'I can't tomorrow, Helen. I have to leave first thing in the morning to head home. That's what Ginger was ringing to tell me: they've lined up auditions for a new Twelvis member.'

'So soon after Brian's death?' Helen asked.

'Bringing someone new into the group is fraught with difficulties, and it needs to be done quickly. Ginger also told me Twelvis have been offered a contract for some work later this year, and we need to talk it through before we get promotional photos taken with our new guy.'

'Will you be coming back?' Helen asked. She was surprised at how much she hoped to hear he was.

'I'll be away for a day or two, but yes, I'll be staying at the Grand again when I return.'

She felt a flutter of relief in her chest.

'I need to come back. I'm hoping to get close to Jodie again, to help her, you know?' There was a moment of silence before Jimmy spoke again. 'And I'd like to see you too.'

Helen remembered Marie and Jean's words of advice to take happiness where she could.

'Thanks, Jimmy, I'd like that too.'

'Wait until I return and we'll go and talk to the man from Traveltime Inns together.'

243

'No, I'll go tomorrow on my own,' Helen said decisively.

'Are you sure about this?'

'No,' she laughed. 'But I'll have Suki with me. You and I know she's as soft as a kitten, but there's no need for anyone else to find out. She can look quite scary when she bares her teeth. Besides, if this man is behind Suki being poisoned, I want to see the whites of his eyes and know whether he's telling me the truth when I confront him.'

'Just be careful,' Jimmy warned.

Helen hung up, then walked down to her apartment. 'Jean, I'm back!' How comforting it felt to announce her arrival and to hear someone's reply. It was the first time in months it had happened.

'I'm in the kitchen, love.'

She walked into the kitchen to find Jean with her sleeves rolled up and an apron tied around her stout waist. She was rolling pastry on a floured board.

'Chicken and mushroom pie all right for you?' she asked.

Helen felt tears prick her eyes. 'I can't tell you how grateful I am.'

Jean waved a floured hand dismissively. 'Ah, it's nothing. It's going in the oven in five minutes and it'll be ready in half an hour. I've made an apple crumble for afters too.'

'Jean, I could kiss you.'

'There's no need to get carried away,' Jean said sternly.

As Helen watched Jean lay a flat circle of pastry over the pie dish before taking a knife and expertly turning the dish to trim the excess, her phone rang with a number she didn't recognise. The call was short and to the point; it was yet another guest cancelling their booking and blaming the news they'd read about the murder. Helen sank into a chair with her phone in her hands. Was she really doing the right thing hanging on to the Seaview? She thought again of the offers that Mr Benson had put forward, then shook her head to dismiss the thought. No, no! She wouldn't allow herself to even consider them, no matter how bad business got. She'd weather this storm; she had to. Her phone rang again and this time her stomach turned when she saw the caller was Bev.

'I need to take this in private,' she told Jean, making her way to the living room. But when she put her phone to her ear, all she could hear was the sound of Bev crying. She sank into a chair and waited a moment, preparing herself for the worst.

'Bev?'

'Hel . . . Helen,' Bev sobbed.

Helen swallowed hard and closed her eyes.

'I'm . . . it's . . .' Bev tried again.

Helen put her free hand to her temple and squeezed hard. Listening to her friend crying was one of the most heartbreaking sounds she'd ever heard.

'Bev, I'm here for you, whatever happens. We're all here for you.'

She heard the shudder of Bev's breath.

'No . . .' Bev said. 'I've got . . .'

Helen braced herself for the hated word. Her heart began to pound and she felt a lump rise in her throat.

'I've got the results!' Bev cried.

'Bev?'

'It's . . . it's benign.'

And then she was off again, sobbing and crying, and Helen realised that they were tears not of sorrow but of joy.

'Oh Bev . . .' she breathed into the phone, and once her own first tear escaped, the rest followed without warning.

'I've been crying all day,' Bev said, sniffing. 'I'm still in shock.'

'Is Sue with you?'

'She's here, looking after me. I'm staying with her now; I've sort of moved in. I feel like I've been given a new lease of life, Helen. The nurses at the hospital and the consultant I saw, they were incredible.'

Helen squeezed her eyes shut. 'I remember Tom had good things to say about them too, when he was having chemo there.'

'I know I've been lucky, Helen, and I want to make the most of every single day. There's something else I want to do, too.'

'Make a bucket list, go swimming with dolphins, that sort of thing?'

'No, I want to raise money for the cancer ward at the hospital. I was thinking about doing a sponsored run or something. I'm not sure what exactly, it's just an idea.'

'I'd like to help too, in memory of Tom,' Helen said. 'We'll talk in a few days, get our heads together and come up with a plan. Give my love to Sue.'

Once she'd hung up, she pressed her head back against the sofa and sat in silence for a few moments before returning to the kitchen to share the good news with Jean.

A little later, Jean's chicken pie was enjoyed with friendly conversation and a bottle of red wine that Helen opened to celebrate Bev's news. After dessert, she insisted on clearing up and shooed Jean to the living room to watch TV with Suki, who was lying by the patio doors. She loaded up the dishwasher, tidied the kitchen and made a pot of tea, which she took into the living room on a tray. Suki moved to lie on the floor between the two women. Helen poured the tea and handed a blue stone mug to Jean. Jean nodded towards the TV.

'Look,' she said.

Helen's jaw dropped to the floor. The news reporter was standing right outside the Seaview, reporting on Brian's death, saying that the police were following up leads but no arrest had been made. The hotel's name was visible in big bold letters above the front door.

'They must have filmed earlier today. I didn't see anyone out there, did you?' Helen said.

'If I had, I'd have given them an earful,' Jean said.

Helen's heart sank. 'I'm ruined. Newspaper clippings and online stories disappear from people's memories. But this is television.'

'Local television,' Jean reminded her. 'It'll all blow over. See, they're already finished with that story; they're on to dairy cows now.'

Helen took a sip of tea. 'Jean, can I ask you a question?'

'Course you can, love.'

'When Archie died, I mean afterwards, how long did it take for you to start packing his things away, his clothes and shoes? I don't know what to do for the best. Part of me accepts that Tom's gone and I've got to get rid of . . . no, that sounds too final . . . I've got to move his clothes from where I see them each day. They remind me too much of what I've lost, and it hurts every time I see his jeans or his boots or his trousers. I remember when he wore them last, where we went, the walks we enjoyed with the dog.'

'And you'll never forget any of those things. But it's best if you can let things go bit by bit. Don't do it all at once; you'll only regret it. Take your time. Put things in a box first,' Jean advised. 'That's what I did. As you say, when their clothes are hanging in the wardrobe and you see them every day, it's hard. You feel like you're stuck in the past. I gave most of Archie's things to charity shops; there are plenty of places in town that'd be grateful for Tom's clothes. But I kept some things, special things – his cufflinks and his glasses, things I couldn't bear to let go. They're in a drawer I open every now and then. But I don't need things to remember him by.' She laid her hand on her heart. 'He'll always be in here.'

'Thanks, Jean, that means a lot to me to know.' Helen sipped her tea. 'Bev wants to do something to raise money for the cancer ward at the hospital. I said I'd help. I wonder if the hospital has a charity I can donate Tom's things to?'

'You could donate to them, by all means,' Jean said with a knowing look. 'But I can think of another way you can help raise money for them.'

Helen raised an eyebrow. 'You can?'

A mischievous smile made its way to Jean's lips.

'Come on, Jean, out with it.'

'Oh, let's just say it involves Elvis and a group of men led by a very handsome chap called Jimmy.'

Helen couldn't believe what Jean seemed to be suggesting. 'You mean Twelvis?' she asked, struggling to get her head around the idea.

'A charity gig. Why not?' Jean said.

Helen shook her head. 'No, I couldn't ask them. Not after what happened with Brian. I don't think they'll be in any rush to return to the town where their friend was killed. They're still in mourning; it's too soon. Shouldn't we at least wait until Brian's killer is found?'

Jean gave Helen a look. 'Well, if you ask me, it might be just what Twelvis – and the Seaview – needs to counter the bad publicity. Consider it a tribute to the poor man. It'd just be for one night; what's the worst that can happen?'

'I don't know,' Helen said, wavering. 'Besides, there's only eleven of them now. Jimmy's heading home tomorrow to recruit someone to replace Brian. Apparently there's all sorts of problems associated with bringing a new member in.'

Jean leaned forward, her eyes bright. 'At least think about it. I know one of the women who volunteers there; I'll ask her to put you in touch with the right person to speak to.'

'No,' Helen said, shaking her head. 'I can't ask Twelvis to do this. What if they say no?'

'There's only one way to find out. Why not speak to Jimmy and see what he says? Maybe you could split any donations received between the hospital and Brian's family? Didn't you tell me that his wife was ill, and her care costs a fortune?'

Helen was silent for a few moments. Despite everything, she was finding Jean's enthusiasm infectious.

'Well, you might have a point about garnering good publicity, and Jimmy might appreciate it,' she said cautiously. 'And I'm sure Brian's family would be grateful. I could think about it, I suppose. But we'd need to hire a room in town. The YMCA might help; they've got a small theatre they might let us use.'

'You don't need a theatre, lass.' Jean raised her eyes to the ceiling. 'Not when you've got a bar upstairs.'

'I can't hold a gig in here, it's far too small,' Helen cried.

'You've got the lounge, the lobby and the dining room,' Jean said. 'Think of it as one big concert space. We'll take the tables and chairs out of the dining room, and I'll put a buffet on. It'd be just like the old days, when you and Tom held the Elvis parties.'

'Oh, you know how to press my buttons, don't you?' Helen laughed. 'All right then. Let's do it. I'll ring Bev tomorrow to talk it through, and speak to Jimmy too.'

Jean raised her mug. 'To the King of Rock and Roll.'

'To Elvis,' Helen said. 'And to Tom.'

'And my Archie,' Jean added. 'May they all rest in peace.'

Chapter 32

The following morning, Helen woke to the sound of Jean singing. She smiled when she recognised the sixties pop song. Suki was lying on the floor at the end of the bed, and Helen could hear her snoring. She knew Tom wouldn't have approved of the dog sleeping in the bedroom; he'd always shut her in the kitchen overnight. But now that Helen was living in the apartment alone, she welcomed Suki beside her. When she woke in the night, it gave her some comfort to know that there was a living, breathing being in the room, even if it was just her dog.

She ran over Jean's suggestion of a charity gig. She'd need to call Jimmy first to ask him if Twelvis might be interested. She didn't hold out much hope, however, and refused to let herself get excited by the thought of hosting an Elvis party. And then she remembered what Jean had said about making a start on clearing away Tom's clothes. It was a horrible job, one she was dreading, but she knew it had to be done. Still, the thought of taking his shirts from their hangers and packing them away seemed too daunting. What had Jean said? Don't do it all at once. Wise words indeed. Getting some cardboard boxes and plastic bags would be her first step.

'Miss you, Tom,' she breathed as she clambered out of bed and walked towards the shower.

Once she was dressed, she headed to the kitchen, where she was met by the sight of Jean standing at the cooker stirring something with a wooden spoon. An open box of oats stood next to a carton of milk on the worktop.

'Are you doing what I think you're doing?' Helen asked, surprised.

Jean looked up from the pan. 'Morning, love. You're looking a lot better today. And yes, I thought it was about time I had a go at making porridge. I've never been able to master it in the past, but I'm beggared if I'm going to let it get the better of me this time.'

'I know our guests will appreciate an expanded breakfast menu.'

'Here, you can be my guinea pig,' Jean said. She spooned porridge into a bowl, which she pushed towards Helen. Helen dipped her spoon in while Jean watched like a hawk.

'How is it?' she asked.

'Well . . .' Helen began.

'Does it need more sugar? More milk?'

'Jean, it's perfect.'

Jean emptied the pan into a bowl for herself and sat next to Helen on a stool at the counter.

'You know what you need, Jean?' Helen asked while they ate.

'What?'

'A spurtle.'

'I beg your pardon?'

'A spurtle,' Helen repeated. 'It's a wooden stick for stirring porridge, a traditional Scottish thing.'

Jean looked at her across the top of her specs. 'And I'm a traditional Yorkshire thing, so I'll stick to using a wooden spoon, thank you very much.'

'You know that Miriam next door offers freshly baked croissants for breakfast,' Helen teased.

'Croissants?' Jean sucked air through her teeth and shook her head. 'That's taking things too far.'

After breakfast, Helen headed outdoors with Suki. It was another mild spring day with a beautiful clear blue sky. When she left the Seaview, she glanced towards the Glendale, but there was no sign of the black Porsche or any activity around the old hotel. She followed the sloping walkway down the side of the cliff that led to the North Bay beach. The tide was out, so she let Suki off her lead and the dog bounded into the waves. Helen strode along the sands, breathing in the sea air. She felt more herself than she'd done in a long time. As she walked, she thought over what Jimmy had told her about Twelvis, about the group's membership being strictly one out, one in. She wondered how much competition there was to win the coveted empty slot.

After an hour or so, she headed back to the Seaview with Suki on her lead. When she stepped back onto Windsor Terrace, however, she froze. The black Porsche was there.

She squared her shoulders and, before she could change her mind, walked up the path to the front door. The windows were boarded up, making the place look ramshackle, unloved. She knocked at the door. Within seconds, it flew open and she came face to face with the man she'd seen arguing with Brian. Her heart leapt into her mouth, but she forced herself to stand firm. There could be no wavering now. And yet, up close and personal with the man, she realised how young he was; little more than a boy really. His brown hair was cut short around his ears, which was what made them look as if they were sticking out. His face was blank, expressionless, and he wore a black suit that didn't hang right on his tall, skinny frame. It was an old suit that had seen better days, the jacket and trousers shiny and worn. Under the black jacket he wore a blue shirt and black tie.

'Oh, no . . . not you!' he cried, and slammed the door in Helen's face.

She tried the handle, but it wouldn't budge. She banged on the door with her fist. 'Get out here,' she yelled. 'I want a word with you.'

'Mrs Dexter, please go,' the boy pleaded.

'Oh, you know who I am, do you? Then you'll know why I'm here.'

'Mrs Dexter, if you know what's good for you, you'll leave now.'

'Don't you dare threaten me,' Helen said.

'It's not a threat; it's a polite request for you to go.'

'And if I don't?'

'I'll have you removed from the premises, and let me tell you now, it won't be pleasant for you. I've got men who don't care who they hurt.'

'Send them out here then. Go on,' Helen said with more bravado than she felt. She looked around, up and down the street, relieved to see passers-by she could call out to if needed. 'None of you can frighten me any more than you've done in the last few days.'

There was silence for a few moments.

'They're not here,' he replied. 'But all I have to do is call them.'

'So you're in there on your own?' Helen said. 'Then why don't we just have a nice chat, you and I?'

More silence.

'Open up!' Helen yelled. She banged hard at the door with her fist.

The letter box midway down the door tipped open and a voice floated out.

'Please leave me alone. None of this is my fault.'

Helen got down on her haunches, held the letter box open and peered in. 'We need to talk,' she said as calmly as she could. 'Why not open the door, let me in and we can discuss what's been going on?'

'No, I can't be seen with you.'

'Then we'll have to chat through the letter box. Is that really what you want? For everyone walking by on the street to hear what I've got to say?'

There was a scuffling sound, then the door opened slowly. Helen kept her eyes firmly fixed on the boy's smooth, unblemished face. She was trying to work out if it was the face of someone capable of poisoning her dog. There was an innocence about him that disturbed her; could someone like him really be the one who'd tried to scare her? She stepped into the Glendale, where the cold lobby smelled of damp.

'Please, come through to the back. There are chairs. We can sit,' he said.

Helen followed him into a room at the back with ornate red and gold art deco windows. These weren't boarded up, and the room overlooked a large garden rampant with weeds. There were two square tables and three white plastic chairs. Helen watched in astonishment as the young man took a perfectly folded white cotton handkerchief from his jacket pocket and ran it over a chair, cleaning dust from it. Then he indicated for her to sit, pulled up a chair for himself and sat opposite. Suki stood at Helen's side, alert, sniffing the unfamiliar air. Then she bent her head and nudged her nose towards the young man's shoes.

'Suki, no,' Helen said, pulling the lead.

She glanced at the black shoes; they were unusually long and pointed, almost like the winklepickers she'd seen some of the men in Twelvis wear when they weren't performing.

Once Suki was settled, Helen stared the man in the eye. 'I want to know what the hell's going on,' she demanded. 'Traveltime Inns have been after my hotel to demolish it to make way for a car park for this place. I received offers to sell, including one from a man who ended up dead in Peasholm Park. I believe an intruder tried to break into my apartment, some creepy things were sent through the post, and my dog was poisoned.' She gripped Suki's lead.

'Mrs Dexter, I can explain,' he said. 'But first let me introduce myself. I am George Weber, the son of Leon Weber.'

Helen immediately recognised the name. 'Leon Weber who owns Traveltime Inns?'

'Yes, that's right.'

Helen saw a scarlet flush make its way from the frayed collar of George's blue shirt up his neck. She eyed him keenly. 'What do you do for Traveltime Inns exactly?'

'I'm the executive digital vice president for online engagement.'

Helen stared at him. 'What's that when it's at home?'

'I look after Facebook, Twitter, all the company's social media. It's a job my father secured for me; he insisted I work for the family firm. But it's not what I want to do, it's not what I am. I want to be a musician and play the guitar.' He dropped his gaze and shook his head. 'Sorry, I talk too much when I'm nervous.'

Helen felt herself soften a little. 'But if you're the social media person, what are you doing here now? Your company doesn't even own the Glendale yet.'

'I'm taking pictures for our architect, that's all. The estate agent allows me to hold the keys as long as I return them to their office at the end of the day.'

'What were you doing here with Brian McNally?' Helen demanded. 'I heard you arguing with him in the street. You threatened him, saying your boss wouldn't be happy that he hadn't been able to convince me to sell the Seaview. You even called me a bitch! And I saw you drive him away in your Porsche on the night he was killed.'

George pulled at his shirt collar. 'How is your dog?' he mumbled, gazing at the floor.

'Stop changing the subject,' Helen snapped.

George picked at the skin around his fingernails. 'Mr McNally . . . Brian . . . he owed my father money . . .' he began hesitantly. 'A lot of money. When Father found out he was visiting Scarborough and staying at your hotel, it was too good a chance to miss. He forced him to approach you with an offer to sell. He knew Brian liked to socialise with women and he thought he could seduce you into selling your property. When it didn't work out, Father demanded to see him. That was why I was arguing with Brian, which was difficult for me.'

'Difficult? How?' Helen demanded.

George's hands fluttered at the side of his face as if fanning away a hot flush.

'Difficult emotionally. I'm not an angry person, Mrs Dexter. It takes a lot out of me to work for Traveltime Inns and carry out my father's demands.'

Helen ploughed on, undeterred by George's admission, determined to get to the bottom of what had happened the night of the Twelvis gig. 'And so you drove Brian to see your father?'

'Yes, I had to take him to Father's house in Scalby. Traveltime Inns is a huge company, and nothing must get in its way.'

'Not even me and my hotel?' Helen said.

George smiled weakly. 'Brian was dressed as Elvis Presley that night. When we arrived, Father taunted him and made him dance in front of his friends. It was humiliating, shameful.'

'Did your dad kill him?' Helen asked.

George sat up straight in his chair. 'No! My father is many things, but he is not a killer, Mrs Dexter. I can assure you of that.'

'So what happened after he treated Brian like a dancing bear?'

'I drove Brian back to the Seaview, he got out of my car and I left.'

'Did you see what he did next?'

George shook his head.

Helen stared hard at him. 'Did you try to break into my apartment?'

He looked at her blankly. 'No.'

'What about my dog? Was it you who tried to poison her?'

She saw his shoulders heave and realised, with a start, that he was crying.

'I didn't mean to. I didn't want to. Father made me do it, to scare you into selling. He can't buy the Glendale to develop it

258

into a Traveltime Inn unless it has a car park. Without the Seaview, he can't proceed.'

'You bastard!' Helen hissed. 'You almost killed her.'

At Helen's side, Suki began to growl. George pressed his back into his seat, trying to put distance between himself and the dog.

'I'm sorry, Mrs Dexter, truly I am. Please forgive me. It's my father, he makes me do these things and I . . .'

Helen stood, anger pulsing through her. She knew she had to leave before she ended up punching George's boyish face or slapping him around his big ears. She pulled at Suki's lead and walked back to the front door of the hotel, leaving George behind her in tears.

Chapter 33

Helen stormed back to the Seaview, threw her keys on the bar and sank into a chair in the lounge with her head in her hands. She couldn't help but feel responsible for Brian's death in some way. Twelve Elvis impersonators had arrived at the Seaview, but only eleven had left. Then there was the matter of the broken pot and the footprints in the soil outside her apartment. Had someone been trying to break in? With no evidence to go on, she still wasn't sure what had happened. She felt that George Weber had been truthful with her. He'd caved in too easily when she'd asked him about poisoning Suki; surely if he had been on her patio that night, he'd have confessed to that too? No, she decided, it didn't seem likely that George was the one who had tried to break in. But then who on earth was it?

As her mind spun with worry, Suki walked towards her and slid her head onto her lap.

'What would I do without you?' Helen said, and Suki whined in reply.

Helen pulled her phone from her pocket and called Scarborough police. She was immediately put through to DS Hutchinson, and she told him about her exchange with George Weber. She also gave him the registration number of George's Porsche, which she'd noted when she left the Glendale. DS Hutchinson promised to speak to George and his father, and assured her that his men were doing all they could to find Brian's killer.

'You said you'd update me about the case, but I know I haven't been informed about everything that's going on,' Helen said. She kept quiet about it being Miriam who'd told her about Brian getting into a second car on the night he was killed, not wanting to get the landlady into trouble.

'Mrs Dexter, I can assure you that as soon as we have news, we'll let you and Mr Brown know. Cutbacks at the station mean we're not as well equipped as we used to be to follow up leads and make calls. Our efforts are concentrated on painstaking detective work and we're doing all we can. We want the killer caught and the case solved as quickly as you do.'

And with that, he hung up, leaving Helen staring at her phone. She headed downstairs to her apartment and found a note on the kitchen table.

Gone to visit Mum, legs aren't so good. Cheese scones by kettle. Jean.

She put the kettle on, made a cafetière of coffee and was about to butter one of Jean's home-made blue cheese scones, still warm from the oven, when there was a knock at the kitchen door. Without waiting for a reply, Sally popped her head in.

'Just thought I'd call in and say hi. I'm on my way to do the cleaning next door.'

'Got time for a coffee and a bite to eat?' Helen asked.

Sally shook her head. 'No, sorry. I just wanted to say thanks, Helen. I'm really grateful for the work at the Vista del Mar.'

'Is Miriam treating you all right in there?'

'She's a funny old stick, but I think we already knew that.'

Sally smiled. 'Mind you, she's not as thorough with the cleaning regime in her rooms as you are in here.'

'Really?' Helen was surprised to hear this. 'I thought she'd be a stickler for cleanliness.'

'Oh, it's clean enough, but she told me to do just the bare minimum, nowhere near as much as I do for you.'

'Here,' Helen said, dropping two cheese scones into a plastic bag. 'One for you and one for Gracie, from Jean.'

'Jean's cooking for you? You're starting to look better, Helen, there's more colour in your cheeks.'

'Thanks, love. How's your coursework going at college?'

Sally beamed. 'Got a distinction for my business management assignment.'

'Well done. Keep up the good work.'

'You too. See you, Helen.'

'Bye, love.'

Once Sally was gone, Helen took her scone and coffee to the kitchen table and checked her phone. There was a message from Marie.

Thanks for recommending solicitor Elvis Sam. He's ace. Going to take Daran to the cleaners over my divorce settlement. He's asked me to take him back (Daran, not Sam, haha!) now Sandra DeVine's dumped him. NO chance of that! Ha! The sky's the limit for Marie Clark now I'm free and single. Any word from the cops? Great news about Bev's biopsy results. We should celebrate xx

Helen called Jimmy, but received no reply. She left a voicemail instead, asking him to call back when he could. Then she called Bev to tell her about Jean's crazy idea of a Twelvis gig to raise money for the cancer ward. Bev was excited to hear all about it, but Helen warned her not to get carried away and not to mention it to anyone yet. She still had to speak to Jimmy before they could consider it, and she wasn't sure he would agree.

She glanced at the CCTV display Gav had fitted. The image from the camera on the patio was perfectly still, while the one by the front door showed indistinct shapes moving past on the pavement. But on the feed from the back door there was blurred movement, someone walking towards Helen's bins. The bin men were still on strike, so it couldn't be them. The image was flickering and grainy, and she couldn't even tell if the person was female or male. She headed to the back door, pulling it open just in time to hear the back door at the Vista del Mar slam shut.

'Oi! Miriam!' she yelled, but there was no response.

'Using my flaming bins when hers are full. The cheek of it,' she muttered.

She headed back to the kitchen and finished her coffee and scone. Then she opened her laptop to catch up with admin. She was disheartened to receive more cancellations, several of them blaming the bad publicity over Brian's death. Her plans to reopen the Seaview with a bang for a successful spring and summer season were diminishing with each cancelled booking. Frustratingly, there was still no reply from the review site about the fake postings. Next she searched online for the number of the planning department at the council, and pulled out her phone, ready to ask what they knew about the future of the Glendale.

'Yes, I can confirm we've received interest from Traveltime Inns,' a very young, very high-pitched female voice squeaked.

'But nothing's been approved yet, no plans submitted?' Helen asked.

'No offer can be made until the car parking issue is resolved.'

'And can you confirm whether—'

'Oh, just one moment,' the girl said. 'There's an e-note on the file to say that Traveltime Inns have revoked their interest, just today.'

Helen's heart leapt with joy. 'You mean they're no longer considering buying the Glendale?'

'Yes, that's correct. The note says the issue with car parking couldn't be resolved and they no longer intend to purchase.'

'What'll happen to the Glendale now?'

'It's still up for sale. We've already got another developer interested and I'll be calling them this morning with the news that it's become available.'

'Does the new company want to develop it into a hotel?'

'I can't reveal details, I'm afraid. All I can say is that it's unlikely a hotel will be given permission on that site without a car park. The rules are very strict these days, not like they were when the hotels on that street were originally built. That's all I can say.'

'Thank you,' Helen said. 'You've been very helpful.'

She hung up and punched the air with delight. Then something on the CCTV display caught her eye, a fuzzy shape moving by the front door. The doorbell rang and she headed upstairs. Before she reached the lobby, the bell rang again.

'Hang on, I'm coming,' she yelled.

When she pulled the door open, she was greeted by an enormous bouquet of soft pink and creamy white roses, with a short, dumpy woman behind them.

'Mrs Dexter? Seaview Hotel?' the woman barked.

'Yes,' Helen replied. She couldn't take her eyes off the flowers.

Her first thought was that they were from someone expressing sympathy over Tom's death. Although she'd specifically asked for no flowers at his funeral and had requested donations be made to the hospice instead, not everyone might have known. But then a flicker of unease ran through her. Was this another underhand tactic from Traveltime Inns, their way of making her pay for refusing to sell? Would she accept the bouquet only to find something rotten inside? But it didn't look menacing, she thought; it looked a lot more jolly than that, and more, well . . . romantic.

She took the bouquet from the woman's hands and walked with it into the lounge. She never saw the woman turn and walk away, didn't notice her climb into her little blue van emblazoned with a garland of flowers. Neither did she notice a tall, stringy boy in a cheap black suit walk towards her front door with something in his hand.

The roses were old-fashioned blooms, long-stemmed and hand-tied with raffia. A tiny white envelope bore the handwritten words *Mrs Helen Dexter*. She opened it, took out a small card and read the words printed there.

From Jimmy x

She ran her finger across the card. How thoughtful and kind of him to make such a gesture. She appreciated the subtlety of the pink and white roses. She would have felt awkward had they been red ones, with their symbolism of passion and love. From the little Helen knew of Jimmy so far, the roses and the card were typical of him: respectful, old-fashioned, polite.

The rattle of the letter box at the front door pulled her out of her thoughts. She looked out of the window, expecting to see the postman. Instead, she was shocked to see George Weber, with his big ears and cheap suit, walking quickly away. She kneeled on the window seat, leaning forward so that she could see all the way to the Glendale Hotel, and watched as he got into his Porsche and sped off. Then she went into the lobby, where a single white envelope lay.

She turned it over in her hands and lifted the tucked-in flap. The card came out the wrong way up, with a bright yellow sticker showing that it had cost the grand total of 59p. She turned it over. On the front was a glossy photograph of a small white dog sitting on a lush lawn. She opened the card, stunned to read the single word inside.

Sory.

Chapter 34

Helen carried the bouquet from Jimmy and the card from George downstairs to her apartment. She rummaged in the cupboard under the sink, found a vase and arranged the roses. Then she took a picture and sent it to Jimmy with a note to say thank you.

She opened George's card again and stared at the misspelled word, and a shiver ran down her spine.

'Bastard,' she muttered. Not only had he admitted to poisoning Suki, but the evidence in the card pointed to him having left the fake reviews too. She ripped the card in two and threw it in the bin.

Just then her phone beeped with a message.

I'll call tonight after auditions for new Twelvis member. On train now heading home, phone signal not good in tunnels. Glad the flowers arrived OK. DS Hutchinson rang, brought me up to date on Weber and about Brian getting into the other car. I'll tell the boys tonight. Jimmy x

She pocketed her phone and breathed in the heavenly scent of the roses. Without Jean bustling about in the kitchen, she suddenly felt desperately alone. The apartment was too quiet and she was surprised at how quickly she'd become used to having someone else around. She decided to make a start on packing away Tom's clothes while Jean was still staying with her, in case she needed moral support. She'd head into town to pick up some boxes; it didn't seem right to use bin bags. It'd feel too much like throwing rubbish out, and Tom deserved better than that.

She glanced at the kitchen clock and wondered if she had time to call at Marie's nail bar and take her friend up on her free manicure offer. Ah, what the heck, she thought. She might as well treat herself to lunch in town too. She had nothing and no one to build her day around; just Suki to walk later.

She walked to the patio doors and tugged on each handle to double-check that they were locked. Ever since the intruder on the patio, she'd felt more than a little insecure. She looked out into the sunken courtyard. Her pots of tulips bulbs were showing strong green shoots. In other brightly painted pots, daffodils nodded gently, and cheery purple and white crocuses brightened up the view. She left Suki sleeping by the doors, grabbed her fleece jacket, scarf and handbag, and headed out for the walk into town.

Scarborough's main shopping streets were a mix of chain stores, charity shops and independent shops and cafés. Many of the streets came with the bonus of stunning views, whether of the castle on the clifftop or a glimpse of sparkling sea between ancient cobbled lanes. She called into the bookshop, asking for any old boxes they no longer needed. They offered her half a dozen and she said she'd call in for them on her way back to the Seaview.

During a coffee stop at Bonnets, which this time was thankfully free of Sandra DeVine, she texted Marie to ask when might be suitable for her to call at the nail bar, and Marie offered her a two o'clock slot. Helen walked the length of Westborough, window-shopping as she went, and when she spotted a home and hardware store, she went in and bought a porridge spurtle in the hope that she might tempt Jean to use it. Well, stranger things had happened.

She carried on up Westborough towards the art deco Stephen Joseph Theatre, where new works by award-winning playwright and Scarborough resident Alan Ayckbourn were given world premieres, and where his old classic plays were revived; then turned right into Hanover Road, where the hidden gem of the Eat Me café was tucked away. The small, friendly café had been one of Helen and Tom's favourites. However, today Helen headed towards it hesitantly, for it would be her first time there without Tom.

Inside, she was shown to a table for two in the window and put her handbag on the chair that would have been Tom's. She ordered a bowl of ramen broth with noodles, then spent a few moments people-watching from the window. She'd expected to feel lonely there on her own, and more than a little bit lost. But the cheery café, with its kitsch artworks and friendly staff, made her feel welcome, and she was relieved not to feel awkward at all. She knew Tom would approve of her getting on with her life, and hoped he could see her, wherever he was.

After lunch, she headed to the nail bar, where Marie had left a message to apologise as she'd had to go out on business. Instead, Helen was tended to by a young girl called Chelsey, who caressed and massaged her hands, soaked and moisturised her fingers, then buffed and polished her short, round nails.

Back at the Seaview, she set to preparing dinner, her way of saying thank you to Jean for looking after her. It was the first time she'd cooked in months, and she soon lost herself in the almost forgotten motions of chopping and peeling, adding spices and stirring as she brought a chicken curry to life. When Jean returned, the first thing she did was put the kettle on ready to make a pot of tea. Only then did she remove her coat, put her handbag down and point at the roses.

'From Jimmy?'

'How on earth did you know?' Helen said.

'There's not much gets past me, love. I've seen it all. Been there, done it, worn the rubber gloves to clean it.'

Helen laughed out loud. 'Yes, they're from Jimmy.'

'Must have cost him a pretty packet,' Jean noted. 'He obviously thinks you're worth it.'

And so another evening passed companionably. Jean filled Helen in on the status of her mum's legs (not good), while Helen told Jean about the boxes she'd collected in town. Tomorrow, she said, she'd assemble them ready for the next dreaded step. After dinner, the two of them watched the local news. Helen was tense in case the Seaview was mentioned again, but she needn't have worried. There was no mention of Brian's murder, and it was clear there was nothing new to report. After that, they watched the soaps together, with Jean bringing Helen up to date on all of the characters' love lives, drama and long-lost children who'd crawled out of the woodwork during the months when Helen had lost interest, her time taken up instead with daily trips to the hospice and worries over Tom. At around 9.30, Jean headed up to bed. Helen took Suki out for one final walk, and when she returned, Jimmy called, sounding upbeat.

'We found our new Elvis,' he said.

'That's great news. What's he like?'

'The youngest of us all. Even younger than Colin. He's just eighteen and training to be a fireman. We're working out how to spin that when he sings "Love Me Tender".'

Helen laughed out loud.

'So, you liked the roses?' Jimmy said.

'They're beautiful. But there was no need, Jimmy, really.'

'Elvis always sent Priscilla roses, you know,' he said.

'He did?'

'Ah, he surely did,' Jimmy said, doing his best Elvis impression, and Helen laughed again. She was doing a lot of that lately, and it felt good.

'Oh, and I need to thank *you*, Helen,' he added.

'What for?'

'For telling me about Anne Brontë and *The Tenant of Wildfell Hall*. I don't read many novels, but I thought I'd buy it from the bookshop and give it a try. It's not half bad.'

'That's great to hear,' she said. 'Jimmy, I was . . . erm . . . talking to a friend of mine.' She paused, choosing her words carefully. 'She's trying to raise some money for a local charity, and we were wondering if Twelvis might be interested in—'

'You want a free gig?' Jimmy said.

She sighed. 'I'm sorry. I shouldn't have asked. I told Jean it was too soon, but she said to mention it and now I realise I shouldn't have—'

'Yes, you should.'

'Sorry?'

'I think it's a great idea.'

'You do?' She sat up straight in her seat. 'I'd like to put it on here, at the Seaview.'

'It could work,' Jimmy said, thinking it through. 'We need to get our new member settled in with a soft gig. It might be exactly the right thing to do. There's only one problem.'

'What?'

'It has to be this weekend.'

'So soon?'

'You know I told you we've been given a new contract for some work? It starts sooner than expected. So we need to get Trevor, the new guy, performing with us as soon as possible, get his confidence up as a member of the team.'

'I'm not sure I can arrange something so quickly, Jimmy.'

'Why not?' He laughed. 'Strikes me you're the sort of woman who can do anything you put your mind to, Helen Dexter.'

'But this weekend? It's madness.'

'It's Twelvis,' Jimmy teased. 'We could all stay with you again, that's if your rooms are free?'

'Yes, they're free until Easter. Of course you can all stay here.'

Helen's mind began whirring and planning. She'd need to call Bev, speak to Jean, get Sally back from Miriam, plan a buffet, send invitations . . .

'How many do you reckon we can fit into the Seaview?' Jimmy asked.

'About fifty in the lounge and dining room. But only if we take the furniture out.'

'Not a bad number. You could ask for donations and send invitations to local VIPs.'

'But I don't know any VIPs.'

'I mean the people involved in your friend's charity: volunteers, fundraisers and organisers. Invite the mayor and council officials too, that kind of thing. It wouldn't do the Seaview any harm if they came, would it?' he pointed out.

'An excellent idea,' Helen said excitedly. 'And we can split the money received between the charity and Brian's family, if you think that'd work?'

'Helen, you're an angel. I'll call the boys tonight, see if I can persuade them to come to Scarborough for the weekend. It's short notice, so they might not all be free, but keep your fingers crossed. I'll let you know how many are coming just as soon as I find out. You all right if we arrive Friday and stay until Sunday as we did last weekend?'

'No problem,' Helen said.

'You know, I'm really happy with the new guy, he sings like a dream,' Jimmy said.

'I look forward to meeting him. You said the procedure of admitting a new member into Twelvis was tricky; did it go all right in the end?'

There was a long silence before Jimmy spoke again. 'Well, we auditioned six guys, but Trevor was far and away the best. He had the moves, the words, he knew all the songs. But he also had that elusive Elvis touch. We all like to think we've got it, but when we see it in someone else, we realise we're just pretenders to the throne. Trevor's got it in spades. He'll help take Twelvis into the future.'

'Six? Wow, that's a lot of people wanting to join the band,' Helen said.

'No, you don't understand. Those were just the six we

auditioned; there are still over fifty on the waiting list to be considered for audition next time a place becomes free.'

'Fifty?' she cried.

'We're an elite troupe,' Jimmy explained. 'People have always been desperate to join us, ever since I created the band. Some guys have even tried to bribe me to let them in. I've been offered substantial sums of cash. We had one who turned nasty when he didn't make the cut. He threatened Big Al that if he didn't get him in, he'd set some heavies on him.'

Helen was horrified by what she was hearing, but Jimmy wasn't finished.

'Another one stalked Ginger, followed him to work in his car. It all turned very weird and we had to get the police involved to get the guy to back off.'

A chill ran down Helen's spine. 'Jimmy?'

'Yeah?'

'When you say there's over fifty people waiting to get into Twelvis . . .'

'Fifty-three on our waiting list as of tonight. Big Al's in charge of keeping the list up to date, but he's not very good with computers. He was doing all right with it when it was just pen and paper. I really should give the task to one of the other lads. I think there are still some names on the list who shouldn't be there.'

Helen thought for a moment. 'This waiting list . . . You say that some of these men are desperate enough to threaten and bribe their way in?'

'I'd never take a backhander, if that's what you're suggesting.'

'No, of course it's not,' she said firmly. 'But let's say someone on your list became obsessed with joining Twelvis. What lengths might they go to in order to get into the band?'

'You know we only accept new members when a space becomes available – when an existing member leaves, or in this case dies. What exactly are you suggesting?'

'What I'm wondering,' Helen spoke carefully, 'is what might happen if a fan became so obsessed they'd stop at nothing. You say that some of these men have been on your list for years. Well, what if one of them feels he's waited too long? What if he's had enough of waiting for someone to leave? What if . . .' she gulped, 'what if he's desperate enough to kill?'

Chapter 35

'No!' Jimmy cried. 'You've got it wrong, Helen. These are family men, Elvis fans. They're not capable of murder.'

'How can you be sure? Do you personally know all of these fifty-three men?'

'No, but—'

'Then we should find out where each and every one of them was on Saturday night at the time of Brian's death.'

'It's a crazy idea. We can't investigate them all.'

Helen couldn't fail to pick up on Jimmy's frustration, but she had the bit between her teeth and wasn't ready to give up. 'Why not?'

'Because Brian's death is a matter for the police. It was murder, Helen. We can't go sticking our noses in and asking personal questions of all of those men just because you've come up with a half-baked idea.'

She bristled at his tone. 'And have you come up with anything better?' she said, feeling her anger rise. 'We can't leave this to the police. They've got no leads to go on so far; they haven't even found the blue suede shoes. When I last spoke to DS Hutchinson, he told me that due to cutbacks at the station, they can't even keep us updated, so there's fat chance of them ringing over fifty suspects. We need to do this ourselves.'

'No, Helen, this is madness,' Jimmy pleaded.

'There are twelve of you in the band, and fifty-three men to call. What's fifty-three divided by twelve? A handful of calls for each Twelvis member to make. All they have to do is ask each man one simple question: *Where were you on Saturday night?*'

'It won't work, we'd need alibis, evidence,' Jimmy said, exasperated.

'Then ask for it,' Helen said, trying not to explode. 'Make it a condition of staying on the Twelvis waiting list that they need to provide proof of where they were when Brian died.'

'We can't do it,' he said firmly. 'There's all sorts of privacy laws we'd be flouting. What about data protection and human rights and all that kind of thing?'

Helen's dander was well and truly up by now. 'So you're going to sit back and let Brian's killer go free?'

'No, of course not.'

'There's a woman who's lost her husband and a family who've lost their father, Jimmy. We need to do this for them. Plus, Brian's death is hanging over Scarborough like a black cloud; it's driving the tourists away before the season has even begun. I've already had bookings cancelled after the news got out. We can't let this carry on; we've got to do all we can to help find the killer. I suggest you get on the phone to Twelvis and tell them to start making those calls first thing in the morning.'

'Helen—'

But Helen had already hung up and dropped her phone on the sofa.

* * *

When Helen woke the following morning, the first person on her mind for the first time in months wasn't Tom. Her stomach turned when her conversation with Jimmy flooded back, word for stupid word. She knew she'd gone too far, pushing him to act on an idea that had come from nowhere. He was right: it was crazy, she hadn't thought it through. She showered and dressed, all the while planning to ring him to apologise as soon as she'd eaten breakfast. But when she picked up her phone after polishing off a bowl of Jean's porridge, she was surprised to see that a message had come in from him overnight.

Been thinking about what you said. Still think it's crazy but will speak to the boys. Will also ask them about charity gig at weekend and let you know asap. Jimmy x

She walked Suki on the North Bay beach under a dull sky with drizzly rain, and when she headed back to the Seaview, she was relieved to see that all was quiet outside the Glendale, with no sign of the black Porsche. She hoped she wouldn't see it again now that Traveltime Inns had retracted their interest in the place.

As she walked to her front door, she heard a voice behind her.

'Morning, Helen!'

She spun around to see Sally heading into the Vista del Mar. 'Morning, love.' She beckoned Sally to her. 'Listen, keep it to yourself for now, but we might be having the Elvis impersonators back this weekend. I'll let you know as soon as I hear from them.'

'Why are they coming back?'

'It's a long story,' Helen replied.

'Has the killer been found?'

'Not yet.'

Just then the front door of the Vista del Mar swung open and Miriam's perfectly made-up face, big glasses and curled grey hair appeared.

'Do come in, dear,' she said to Sally, then she cast a glance towards Helen. 'I won't have my help chatting like a common fishwife on the doorstep.'

Sally and Helen shared a look.

'Come in for coffee when you're done,' Helen whispered.

She went downstairs, fed Suki and told Jean that she'd put her idea of a charity gig to Jimmy and she'd let her know what was happening as soon as she received his reply.

Jean took a pad of paper and a pen from her handbag and began making a list. 'We'll need sausage rolls, bread buns, tuna mayo, egg and cress . . .'

'It might not happen, Jean; don't get carried away arranging a buffet,' Helen warned.

Jean winked. 'That Jimmy fella idolises you, love. Something tells me we'll be having a party this weekend.'

Jean returned to her list-making as Helen sat at the kitchen table and flipped the lid of her laptop open. She scanned her emails and her heart sank when she saw yet more bookings cancelled. It appeared the news of Brian's death had spread beyond Scarborough, even beyond Yorkshire. Social media had pushed the news further than it needed to go. Each news post online carried a picture of Brian dressed as Elvis, and to Helen's horror, she even saw some with a picture of the Seaview.

'I need a strong cup of tea, Jean,' she said, heading towards the kettle. But Jean got to it first.

'Sit yourself down, lass. Let me do it.'

'I've had more cancelled bookings,' Helen said. 'Not only do people not want to stay at the Seaview, but they don't even want to come to Scarborough.'

'Then we need this party at the weekend more than ever. It might just change all of that.'

'Do you think so?' Helen asked.

'I know so.'

Helen crossed her fingers. 'I hope you're right, Jean. Because I don't know how much more I can take.'

Later that morning, while Helen was working on a spreadsheet on the laptop with Suki at her feet while Jean read the *Scarborough Times*, there was a knock at the kitchen door and Sally walked in.

'That flaming woman!' she hissed through gritted teeth.

Helen raised her eyes from her screen. 'Miriam? What's she done now?'

'You should hear the way she talks to her guests; she treats them with disdain, patronises them. I'm surprised any of them come back a second time.'

'Has she got many guests in there right now?'

'There's a load of old ladies from Durham, who are lovely. And a family with a young girl who's always arguing with her parents.'

'Coffee and a slice of my chocolate cake for you both?' Jean asked.

'Please, Jean,' Helen said. 'Sounds like just what I need.'

Sally took a seat at the kitchen table. 'What's that?' she asked, pointing at the fuzzy images on the CCTV display.

'Would you believe it if I told you they were live pictures from security cameras I've had installed?' Helen said. 'The guy's supposed to be coming back to fix them, but each time I ring him, his phone goes to voicemail. Anyway, never mind that: tell us all about what's going on next door. I could do with a bit of idle gossip to take my mind off things.'

'There's not much to tell,' Sally said. 'Except I'm cleaning those rooms better than they've been cleaned in years. Miriam says she's impressed with my attention to detail, but I told her it's just standard stuff that I do here for you – you know, vacuuming under the bed, dusting the tops of wardrobes, that kind of thing.'

'She doesn't do any of that in the Vista del Mar?' Jean tutted.

'And the tops of wardrobes is where a lot of guests forget they've put things and go home without them. Oh, the amount of stuff I've found and had to send on after they've gone,' Helen sighed. 'After all my years in the hospitality business, I don't think I'll ever get used to the weird things guests leave in their rooms.'

'That family I told you about,' Sally continued. 'When I cleaned their room this morning, their daughter was still in there. She told me she'd been arguing with her mum and they'd threatened to go out for the day and leave her behind. She was sulking a bit.'

'All teenagers do,' Jean chipped in.

'She seemed a nice kid, though, bright. Sat on the bed and watched me while I cleaned, asked me questions like how much was I paid and did I like my work. When I told her I was working as a cleaner to put myself through college, she started asking me all about that. Said she hated Scarborough and hated being away from her friends and her big sister. She was on her phone constantly.'

'Kids are these days,' Jean said.

'She was kind of innocent, too. She had her teddy bear sitting next to her on the bed.' Sally cut into her slice of gooey chocolate cake with her fork. 'Then her dad came in while I was cleaning and told me how much his daughter loved Scarborough, and I thought to myself, that's not what she's just told me, mate.'

Helen bit into her cake. 'Jean, you've surpassed yourself, this is gorgeous.' Her phone rang, and she shot Jean a look when she saw who the caller was. 'It's Jimmy.'

Jean laid her fork down, waiting to hear the news.

'Jimmy? Fine, yes. You? No problem. You are? Oh Jimmy, that's . . . Really? All twelve? That's fantastic!' Helen nodded towards Jean, confirming that she'd been right after all. 'Tomorrow, yes, till Sunday,' she continued. 'We'll be ready for you.' Then her face clouded over. 'It's probably for the best. You've given them the list? DC Hall's ringing all fifty-three? Good one, Jimmy. Well, it's not often I have ideas like that, but I'm glad I have my uses. Yes, me too. Looking forward to seeing you.'

She put her phone down and looked from Jean to Sally. 'Twelvis are coming back!'

Chapter 36

'See, what did I tell you?' Jean said with a smile.

'They'll be arriving early tomorrow,' Helen said.

'Will they need breakfast when they get here?'

'No, Jimmy said they'll eat at a service station en route. He's secured them a live interview on local radio and the DJ wants them in the studio for the breakfast show, all dressed as Elvis too. The station's going to take photos and share them on social media and the station boss is liaising with DS Hutchinson. The police hope the publicity from having Twelvis back in town might generate some leads to catch Brian's killer.'

'It's a strange to-do and no mistake,' Jean muttered darkly.

Helen looked at Sally. 'What are your plans for the rest of the day?'

'I've got to collect Gracie from Mum, take her home and feed her lunch, and then I was going to take her to the pet shop to buy a new toy for the cat.'

Helen thought for a moment. 'How would you and Gracie like to spend the afternoon here with me? I could do with an extra pair of hands getting ready for Twelvis coming back.'

'But there can't be any cleaning to do, surely? No one's stayed here since they went home, and I left all the rooms immaculate.'

'There's just room one to do, where I've been staying,' Jean chipped in. 'And I'm more than happy to clean it and sort out fresh bed linen and towels in the morning.'

'It's not cleaning I need help with,' Helen said. 'It's ringing and emailing people to invite them to the charity gig. I might call that young lass from the *Scarborough Times*, the one who wanted a story on the Seaview and I turned her away with a flea in her ear. I'll have to lay the charm on pretty thick, though, and apologise for the way I behaved. I'll tell her it's an exclusive; that ought to do the trick and help butter her up. And there'll be party decorations to sort out – maybe Gracie can help colour in and make streamers, that kind of thing. Think you'd be up for it?'

'I'd love to help, it sounds right up my street,' Sally said. 'And I know Gracie will be over the moon to spend time here. She thinks the world of you. She's always talking about Auntie Helen and Suki.'

Helen laid her hand on Sally's. 'Thanks, love. We could do with going to the cash and carry. We could take Gracie and turn it into a bit of an adventure.'

'She'd love it!' Sally cried.

Jean stood and put her hands on her hips. 'Well, if we're having lunch here, I'd better get busy.' She pulled open a drawer, took out her apron and tied it around her stout waist. 'Quiche Lorraine all right for you both?'

Once Sally had left to collect her daughter, Jean switched the oven on and began flouring the pastry board. At the kitchen table, Helen took out her phone. The first thing she needed to do was call Bev to share the good news.

'This Saturday night? Blimey, that's short notice, Helen,' Bev cried. 'I'll get in touch now with the charity coordinator and email you a list of those to be invited.'

'Not too many, remember,' Helen warned. 'It's hardly the Royal Albert Hall in here.'

'Still no news from the police on finding the murderer?' Bev asked.

'Nothing, no leads at all,' Helen replied. 'Although Jimmy's spoken to them about a list of people waiting to join Twelvis.'

'Why? Does he think one of them might have killed Brian?'

'It's worth a try. Actually, it was my suggestion for the cops to check the list.' Helen sighed. 'Although in the cold light of day, I'm not so sure it was one of the best ideas I've had.'

'Better safe than sorry, eh?' Bev said. 'Listen, do you need any help preparing for the party?'

'Jean and Sally have got it all under control,' Helen said. 'Just turn up about six with your party frock on. And bring Sue, of course.'

'I wouldn't dream of coming without her.'

Once she'd ended her call to Bev, Helen decided to ring the journalist at the *Scarborough Times* to see if she could whip up some publicity for Twelvis, the cancer charity and the Seaview. She opened up a web browser on her phone and searched for the newspaper's site. On it she found a list of the staff with their photographs alongside. Bingo! There was the girl – Rosie Hyde – staring confidently from the screen. Her picture had an email address and phone number next to it.

Rosie's tone was somewhat cold at first when Helen introduced herself and mentioned the Seaview Hotel. But she soon softened when Helen revealed she had an exclusive story for her and gave her the news about Twelvis's charity gig.

'And of course, you'd be welcome to come along too,' she offered. 'It's my way of saying sorry for the way I spoke to you last time we met. It's the least I can do.'

'I might just take you up on it,' Rosie replied.

Sally returned within half an hour, holding Gracie by the hand.

'Auntie Helen! I've brought my colouring pens,' Gracie said excitedly.

Sally looked at Helen. 'It's all right, they're washable. She'll get them all over the walls if I don't keep my eye on her.'

Helen laid sheets of paper on the floor for Gracie to colour and turn into streamers. Suki lay down next to them, and Helen watched as Gracie coloured with her right hand and stroked Suki's head with her left. As Jean fried bacon and whisked eggs for the quiche, Sally settled herself into a seat next to Helen and pulled her phone from her bag.

'Right, I'll make a list of people to invite from the council,' she said. 'I know some of them through college; they're involved with the exam board. As it's very short notice, don't be surprised if not many come. Their diaries are usually booked months in advance.'

'But this is for charity, and it's positive publicity for Scarborough.' Helen smiled. 'They're all going to want to get their pictures in the paper.'

Helen and Sally worked fast and hard, sending emails, calling the council and even the local TV news. Bev's promised email arrived with a list of people to be invited from the charity.

'We need to design an invitation, but I'm no good at things like that,' Helen said.

'I'll do it,' Sally offered. 'We covered this at college. I'll need to use your laptop, though; I can't really do it on my phone.'

Helen turned the laptop towards her. 'Knock yourself out.' She got up and walked towards Gracie, watching her colouring circles and squares.

'Shall I close your emails down before I open the graphics software?' Sally asked. 'You've got a message here that's just come in. Do you want to read it?'

Helen sauntered back to the table and peered over Sally's shoulder. 'It's from the review site. I've been having a few problems with someone leaving fake reviews,' she said. 'Do me a favour, Sally, click into it and let's see what they've got to say.'

Sally did as instructed, and both she and Helen read the email. Helen had to read it twice to convince herself that what she saw was correct, and then she gasped in relief.

'Yes! They've gone!' she cried. 'They've actually gone. It says the fake reviews have been taken down.'

'Do you want me to click through to the site to make sure?' Sally asked.

Without waiting for a reply, she brought up the Seaview's page on the review site and they both scanned the reviews, which were all positive, glowing, five stars.

Helen smiled widely. 'Today just keeps on getting better.'

Her attention was caught by a moving fuzzy image on the display from the camera at the front door, then she heard the doorbell ring. 'I'll get it,' she called when she saw Jean wiping her hands on her apron. Upstairs, she pulled the door open, and without so much as a hello or good morning, Gav stepped inside carrying a large battered toolbox.

'It's your man Gav,' he beamed, as enthusiastic as ever. 'I found myself with a couple of hours to spare and I said to myself, who needs your help today, Gav? And do you know what? Here I am. Lead the way and I'll fix your wotsit. And if the kettle's on and the chocolate biscuits are calling, your man Gav won't say no.'

'Come on down,' Helen said. 'Although I wish I'd known you were coming. I've got visitors.'

He winked at her. 'If they don't bother Gav, then I won't bother them.'

Helen led the way and Gav followed her into her apartment. 'Jean, this is Gav, who's come to fix the camera display.'

'About time too,' Jean said sternly.

Her words didn't affect Gav one bit. 'I'm a busy man, missus,' he said.

To get to the display, he had to squeeze past the table where Sally was working.

'Hang on, I'll move, just a minute,' she said.

'No need, princess. You stay where you are,' he replied with a cheeky smile.

He set to work on the display, turning it off and unscrewing the back, and Helen noticed that as he did so, he kept glancing at Sally.

'You work here then?' he asked her.

Sally looked up from her laptop and smiled at him, and they began to talk and flirt. Helen busied herself around the kitchen, pretending not to listen to their conversation as Sally introduced Gav to Gracie. She saw him shake the little girl's hand, then he curtsied and waved regally, which made Gracie burst into giggles.

'Is that something cooking in the oven?' he said as he worked. 'I can always tell a good cook by the great smells in a kitchen.'

Jean peered at him over the top of her specs. 'Flattery will get you nowhere.'

'Jean's made a quiche for lunch,' Sally said.

'Has she now? And might this be Gav's lucky day? It might be just what I need to set me up to fix this display.'

Helen looked at Sally and raised her eyebrows in an unspoken question, to which Sally nodded in reply.

'Would you like to stay for lunch, Gav?' Helen asked. 'I think Jean's quiche is big enough for all of us.'

Chapter 37

As Helen tucked into Jean's freshly baked quiche, she took a moment to glance at those sitting around her: Jean on her left, Sally on her right, and Gracie and Gav opposite. She noticed Gracie intently watching Gav tuck into his food.

'Smashing grub this, missus,' he said to Jean.

'There's a trifle for afters,' Jean replied. 'But it's not coming out of the fridge until you've fixed those cameras for Helen.'

'There's not much I won't do for a spot of home cooking, and trifle's one of my favourites,' Gav replied. 'I'll get them fixed and working before I go, you'll see.'

'Do you live local?' Jean asked, straight to the point as always.

'Up on Filey Road.'

'Any family?'

'No, missus, I'm single. Footloose and fancy-free, me,' he said, smiling at Sally. 'I'm just waiting for the right girl to settle down with. Until I find her, all my time and energy goes straight into my work.'

'How many businesses have you got?' Helen asked.

'Six,' he replied. 'Might be seven soon. Just got to tie up some loose ends on a contract I'm signing.'

'Six businesses?' Sally said. 'What are they?'

Gav laid his knife and fork down and counted on his

fingers. 'Gav's Cabs, my taxi firm; Gav's Baths, my plumbing business; Gav's Cams, that's the security business I'll be billing you from for the CCTV, Helen.'

'And you'll be giving her a discount, I trust, after fitting stuff that didn't work,' Jean chipped in.

Gav ignored her and carried on. 'I've also got Gav's Grub, a sandwich shop in Filey; Gav's Garden Services, which speaks for itself; and Gav's Go-Karts on the seafront.'

'And what's the seventh business you're opening up?' Sally asked.

He concentrated on his plate, avoiding Sally's gaze. 'I'm not allowed to say until the contract's been signed.'

'You're a busy fella,' Helen said. 'I'm impressed.'

'Oh, I don't do it on my own. I employ good people. I look after them and treat them well.'

Helen was curious. 'What was the first business you set up?'

'The cab firm,' Gav replied with a smile. 'It's been running for over fifteen years now. One of my drivers was questioned by the police this week about the Elvis impersonator who . . .'

Helen shook her head, put her finger to her lips and nodded towards Gracie, who was unsuccessfully trying to stab a piece of bacon with her knife. 'Little ears,' she warned.

Gracie pulled her ear lobe with her free hand. 'Little ears,' she repeated.

'. . . about the Elvis impersonator who went to live on the farm in the country,' Gav continued.

'I went to a farm, didn't I, Mummy?' Gracie said. 'I saw chickens and pigs.'

'What did your cab driver tell the police?' Helen asked.

291

'The truth.'

'And you believe him?'

'I've got no reason not to. He's a good lad, that driver. I've known him for years. A call was received at base and he was dispatched to pick up a fare to go from your hotel to the Spa, booked in the name of Brian McNally.'

'No, silly. It's not McNally's farm, it's Old MacDonald's farm,' Gracie said.

'Eat your lunch, sweetheart,' Sally told her.

'When my driver arrived here, he saw a man outside the Seaview getting into a car,' Gav continued. 'Now, my driver didn't know that it was his fare that was being driven away, and the request for a taxi wasn't cancelled, so he waited. When no one appeared, he beeped his horn and then got out and knocked on the Seaview's door. Still nothing, so he radioed base, who called Brian McNally's phone, but there was no reply. My driver returned to base, and that was that until we saw the story about the, er, man who went to live on the farm in the country on the front page of the *Scarborough Times*.'

'Did he say what kind of car it was that Brian was driven off in? What colour? Did he see the registration?'

'The police asked him all of that,' Gav said, shaking his head. 'The only thing he can be sure of is that it was small and dark-coloured. He didn't notice the reg or the make, because he was concentrating on waiting for his fare.'

'And it was definitely Brian he saw getting into the car?' Helen asked.

'Well, obviously he didn't know the fella, so he can't be certain. But he said he saw a man dressed as Elvis in a jacket, a scarf, a pair of flared trousers and all the rigmarole the impersonators wear. And he said the man got into the car of his own free will.'

'Who's Elvis, Mummy?' Gracie asked.

'No one, eat your lunch,' Sally replied.

'Did he see the driver?'

'No.' Gav shook his head. 'Why? Do the cops think that whoever drove off with him . . .' He glanced at Gracie and chose his words carefully. 'Do they think he was driven to the farm in the country?'

'I'm afraid so,' Helen said.

'Don't be afraid, Auntie Helen,' Gracie said, looking up from her quiche. 'I'll look after you.'

After lunch, Gav returned to his toolbox, tinkering with the display unit, and after twenty minutes' work he called out to Helen.

'Gav's only gone and done it!'

'You've fixed it?' she asked.

He winked at Jean. 'Only cos I knew I couldn't have my trifle until I got it done.'

Helen walked towards him and saw three crystal-clear black and white images on the screen. 'That's fantastic, thanks, Gav.'

'Now you shouldn't have any more problems with it, but if you do, give me a call straight away,' he said. 'I'm in town a lot at the minute on a bit of business, so it's easy enough for me to call in.'

After trifle had been eaten, Gav began packing up his toolbox. Helen asked Sally if she and Gracie wanted to head to the cash and carry.

'Can I sit in the front of Auntie Helen's car?' Gracie asked, but she was disappointed when Sally refused.

'Here's my list for the party buffet,' Jean said, handing Helen a piece of lined paper.

When Gav was packed up, everyone headed upstairs, except Jean who insisted on staying behind to do the washing-up.

'There's a programme on the wireless I want to listen to while you're all out,' she said. 'Me and Suki will be fine. Besides, it'll give me a chance to read up on the best way to cook kippers.'

'Thanks, Jean. Our new breakfast menu's coming on leaps and bounds.'

At the front door of the Seaview, Helen spotted Gav's van parked a little way down Windsor Terrace.

'I'll be seeing you, bye for now,' he called as he headed towards it.

'Seems like a nice guy,' Sally said.

Helen helped her strap Gracie into the back of her car, then climbed into the driver's seat. She turned the key in the ignition and checked the rear-view mirror. She was surprised to see Marie's red sports car behind her. Well, if her friend was hoping to call in to see her, she was going to be disappointed. But Marie didn't pull into a parking space as Helen had expected, and she wondered what she was up to. As she watched in the mirror, she saw Gav walk up to Marie's car and slip into the passenger seat.

'What is it, Helen? Traffic?' Sally asked. She turned around and looked out of the back window.

What happened next shocked them both. Gav leaned across to Marie and kissed her on the lips. Then the sports car zoomed away. Marie was completely focused on the road ahead of her; she hadn't noticed Helen's car waiting to pull out.

'And he said he was single, the lying rat,' Sally said. 'What's he doing with that old tart? She looks old enough to be his mother.'

'I'm wondering the same thing,' Helen said, pinned to her seat with shock. She flicked the indicator on, waiting for traffic to pass before she could pull out. 'And by the way, that old tart happens to be my best friend.'

Sally's hand flew to her mouth. 'I'm sorry, Helen. I didn't mean anything by it. I was just surprised, you know?'

'It's all right, love. I didn't know they were seeing each other either. It's come as a shock to me too. I can't believe Marie didn't tell me; we always tell each other everything.'

'Just when I think I've found a nice lad, someone who doesn't mind me having Gracie in my life. Oh well, guess I can forget about seeing him again.'

'Who, Mummy?' Gracie piped up from the back.

'She doesn't miss a thing, does she?' Helen smiled.

Sally shook her head.

Finally there was a break in the traffic, and Helen pulled out.

'Oh, look!' Sally said, pointing ahead at the Glendale Hotel. There, standing tall and proud, was a SOLD sign from Benson's estate agents.

Chapter 38

Heading home from the cash and carry, Helen dropped Sally and Gracie off at their flat on Falsgrave Road.

'See you tomorrow, Sally. It's going to be a big day, with Twelvis coming back for the weekend.'

'You'll speak to Miriam to tell her tomorrow morning will be my last day cleaning for her until Monday?'

'Course I will,' Helen said. 'See you, Sally. Bye, Gracie!'

She drove back to the Seaview and with Jean's help unloaded the car. Downstairs in the kitchen they began packing the food into the freezer and fridge.

'Did you know the Glendale has been sold?' she told Jean. 'There's a SOLD sign gone up.'

'It'll need some love and attention from whoever takes it on,' Jean said sagely. 'Did the people from Traveltime Inns buy it after all?'

'I don't think so,' Helen said, remembering what the woman at the council had said. 'I might give Benson's a ring to see if they'll tell me anything.'

'Oh, I heard some good news on the radio while you were out,' Jean said. 'The bin strike's over. They're back at work today.'

'Thank heavens for that. The rubbish out there is starting to smell, and do you know what? Miriam next door had the cheek to use my bins.'

Jean shook her head and tutted. 'Never in the world.'

'Not only that,' Helen continued, 'but she'd already made a snide comment about me not using *her* bins when mine were full.'

'She's an odd one, that Miriam. Do you know, I always thought she'd be better suited to running a place somewhere a bit more genteel, like Bridlington.'

'Well, there's a lot going on with Miriam right now. I'm prepared to cut her some slack and forgive a certain amount. I know she's had a lot on her mind.' Helen looked around the living room. 'Suki?' she called.

'Oh, I let her out the back for some fresh air, love,' Jean said.

'You did what?' Helen cried. 'But Jean, I never let her out on her own. She chases things – other dogs, kids on bikes.'

She rushed to the back door, and was relieved to find Suki lying on the step, half in and half out of the door. The dog gazed up at her longingly, and Helen got down on her haunches and stroked her head.

'Good girl,' she said. 'Good Suki for not running away. Now come on inside.'

When she returned to the kitchen with Suki trotting after her, Jean gave a knowing look.

'See, I knew she wouldn't go far. You need to trust that dog more than you do; she's a lot more intelligent than you think.'

'But her instinct is to chase, Jean. I've got to be careful or she'll go running off, get hit by a car, and then where would I be?'

'You're too soft with her,' Jean said. 'But she's set me off thinking about getting a dog myself. I've enjoyed her company. I reckon it might be just the thing to perk me up.'

'It'll keep you fit, that's for sure, with all the walking dogs need. And you have to walk them whatever the weather, too. Mind you, greyhounds don't need that much exercise, despite their size. I walk Suki more for my benefit than hers; being on the beach in the fresh air really helps clear my head. I can give you the number of the rehoming centre where Tom and I got Suki from, if you'd like?'

Jean wrinkled her nose. 'Oh no, I don't think I want to be taking in a greyhound. It'd be far too big for my little semi.'

'They rehome all kinds of dogs, not just big ones. I'll find the number for you.'

Jean took her apron off, folded it and slid it into the kitchen drawer. 'Well, that's me done for today. I'm off to visit Mum. I'll be back in time to cook dinner.'

'What if I took you out for dinner instead to say thank you for looking after me? It's your last night here tonight. We could go for fish and chips on the seafront and walk Suki on the beach.'

Jean licked her lips. 'Fish and chips? Now there's a thought.'

Once Jean had left, Helen whipped out her phone and texted Marie.

You and Gav! What's going on? X

Left alone, she steeled herself for what she was about to do.

'Come on, Suki. I've put this off long enough,' she said. Suki cocked her head to one side and followed her to the bedroom.

At the foot of the bed, three large cardboard boxes gaped open. Suki lay down beside them. Helen slid the wardrobe door open to reveal Tom's shirts and trousers. Slowly she removed each shirt from its hanger, folded it neatly, then carefully placed it in the box. She worked steadily, without rushing, taking her time to hold Tom's clothes to her before she packed them away. She buried her face in his favourite jumper, the one he wore when he walked Suki on a winter's day. She could see him now, pulling it on, the static making his hair stand on end. It had a hole in the back and the cuffs were frayed, but she knew she couldn't part with it, and she put it to one side. The wooden clothes hangers rocked inside the bare wardrobe.

Next she packed away Tom's shoes, trainers, flip-flops and boots, taking care to keep the footwear out of Suki's reach. And then she saw it, a flash of white at the bottom of the wardrobe. Her heart turned over and she sank to the floor, lost in a wave of grief that threatened to overwhelm her. She thought she'd been doing well, coping, but as she pulled out the white nylon suit, her tears began to flow. Suki walked towards her and nuzzled her shoulder. Helen pulled the suit to her chest and let it soak up her tears.

At last her crying subsided, and memories flooded back to her of Tom dressed as Elvis at the Seaview parties. She stood up and faced the bedroom mirror. She didn't notice Suki slink out of the room. She tentatively held the jumpsuit against her body, kicking her feet behind the legs, moving it against herself, forming a shape. She held it out in front of her and took a good look. The hem on one trouser leg needed stitching. It was dusty, dirty, didn't smell good and had what looked like a red wine stain on the front. She wondered if Tom had thrown it in the wardrobe after their last Elvis party before he'd taken ill. An idea began to form, but she shook her head.

'No,' she breathed. 'I couldn't . . . could I?'

She spun back to the mirror, this time holding the suit against her more tightly, pulling it over her chest and legs. It would need altering, perhaps a belt, and the legs would need taking up. The longer she looked, the more her idea took hold. She marched to the kitchen, opened the washing machine, and flung the Elvis suit in.

Once the machine was switched on, Helen's phone pinged with a message. She hoped it would be a reply from Marie to explain what she was doing with Gav. But it wasn't from Marie; it was from Jimmy.

Arriving at Seaview tomorrow first thing after interview at radio station. Bringing a minibus this time for Twelvis to travel in style! Looking forward to seeing you again x

The message prompted Helen to head next door to the Vista del Mar to have a word with Miriam about Sally. Miriam opened her front door and invited her in.

'Have you seen the Glendale's been sold?' she said.

'The SOLD sign has just gone up today,' Helen said. 'Have you heard anything about it?'

'Not a dicky bird, dear,' Miriam replied, walking into the floral lounge. 'Take a seat, Helen. Now, to what do I owe the honour this time? It's not to do with my ex and the police again, is it? I don't think I can take any more. Do you know, he left me high and dry all those years ago, and once I managed to get over him, I never gave him a second thought, although it took a few years, admittedly. And then he turned up here on my doorstep and the next thing I know he's lying face down and quite dead in Peasholm Park. It's shaken me up.'

Despite Miriam's impeccable make-up and curls, in the harsh light of the lounge Helen could see how tired and done in she looked.

'No, it's not about any of that,' she explained. 'Although the Elvis impersonators *are* returning tomorrow and staying for two nights. They're going to be singing next door on Saturday night.'

'And there'll be all kinds of that awful loud music, I expect,' Miriam moaned.

'It's a party to raise money for charity, Miriam. I hope you won't mind too much. It's not as if it'll be going on until the small hours. It'll start at six and end by ten. I don't want to cause you or your guests any problems with noise. And you're more than welcome to come.'

'I'm not a party person,' Miriam said quickly.

'Well, if you change your mind . . . you never know, you might enjoy yourself.'

Miriam thought for a moment. 'If you've got guests coming in, you'll be wanting Sally back.'

'And that's the reason I'm here. She's happy to come and clean here for you first thing in the morning, and then she'll be back with me this weekend. If you'd like her after that until my first guests arrive at Easter – at least the ones who haven't cancelled so far – I'll speak to her about it.'

'I understand,' Miriam said. 'She's been a hard worker. You've got a good team next door with Sally and Jean. You're lucky. I can't seem to keep staff here very long. For the life of me I can't think why.'

Helen bit her tongue.

'Did you hear that the dreadful bin strike is over?' Miriam said.

'Yes, Jean told me this morning,' Helen said. 'Although I have to say it was very unfair of you to drop your rubbish in my bins. I wouldn't have minded if you'd asked. I'd have said yes. But it was a bit rich of you to do it without checking, especially as you'd already warned me not to use yours.'

Miriam sat up straight in her seat. 'Whatever makes you think I would do such a thing?' she bristled.

'Oh Miriam, stop it. I saw you,' Helen said. 'On my new security cameras.'

Miriam gasped. 'So, not content with listening to my conversations through the wall, you've taken to spying on me now with CCTV, have you?'

'Of course I'm not spying on you. After what happened with Brian and the intruder on my patio, I needed to beef up security, so I had cameras installed. One at the front, one on the patio and one at the back door. And I saw you, Miriam.'

'You didn't, dear,' Miriam said calmly. 'I can assure you that whoever you saw, it wasn't me. I would never do anything so common.'

'If it wasn't you, then who was it?'

'Surely your camera showed the person's face?'

Helen shifted uncomfortably. 'Well, not exactly. I had a bit of a problem with the display, but it's been fixed now.'

'Then how dare you come in here and accuse me when you don't have proof?' Miriam stood and walked towards the door. 'I think it's about time you left. I'm sure there must be things you need to be getting on with in your three-star abode.'

Helen sheepishly followed her into the lobby. Miriam held the front door open.

'Miriam, I'm sorry. Please come to the party on Saturday night.'

'Goodbye, Helen,' Miriam said firmly.

Helen heard the door slam behind her. She was confused. If it hadn't been Miriam dumping stuff, then who was it? But there was no point her raking through the bins looking for clues – to find what exactly? – as she'd put out too much other rubbish since then.

She headed into the Seaview and decided to take Suki to the beach. 'Suki!' she called, gathering the dog's lead. Normally Suki would come running to greet her, but there was no sign of her, and it was only after Helen's third call that she finally appeared, padding into the kitchen, head lowered, eyes raised guiltily, with a torn piece of blue satin hanging from her mouth.

Chapter 39

'Suki, drop!' Helen ordered.

The dog opened her mouth and the scrap of material fell to the floor.

'Where did you get this from?' Helen said.

Suki cocked her head to one side and whined. Helen scooped the material up; it was wet through with dog drool and she threw it in her kitchen bin, giving it no more thought. She fastened Suki's lead to her collar, headed upstairs and out to the beach.

On the North Bay beach, the tide was out and a wide expanse of sand lay ahead. The beach seemed busier that afternoon than it had in some time, and Helen recognised the signs of early spring tourists coming in, lulled into a false sense of security by the mild weather earlier that week. As she walked, she thought about Marie and Gav and struggled to make sense of it. She'd never had her friend down as the sort of woman to go after a toy boy, but then if Marie and Daran were starting divorce proceedings, who knew where her mind was these days? She pulled her phone from her pocket but was disheartened to see there was still no reply to her message.

She thought of Twelvis returning to the Seaview the next morning and smiled. But it would be a very different Twelvis to the group of men who had stayed with her the previous weekend.

No matter how much they sang and smiled at the charity gig, or how lively, enthusiastic and funny they came over in their radio interview, she knew that laughter would be hiding their heart-ache. Whatever she had thought of the way Brian had treated her, and the way he'd leched over Marie, he'd been a friend of the men, a friend of Jimmy's.

Somehow all her thoughts meandered back to Jimmy. She gazed out to sea, watching Suki pick her way through the shallow waves. He was a good-looking man, a kind and respectful man. But was she ready to become involved with him? She shook her head to clear the mist of her thoughts. Would she be ready for anyone when there had only ever been Tom? Could she live the rest of her life holding on to his memory? Should she? She thought about what Jean would tell her to do, what Marie would say, what Bev and Sue would advise. She knew they'd all say the same thing: they'd tell her to grab happiness where she could. She pushed her hair behind her ears and turned her face to the weak sun trying to break through the clouds.

'Miss you, Tom,' she whispered.

As she walked along the beach, she heard the whistle of the miniature steam train of the North Bay railway. It was a sure sign, if one was needed, that tourists were back in town. She looked up and saw the tiny green train chugging its way along the hilltop from Peasholm Station to Scalby Mills. At the back of the train, standing on the footplate and waving to passers-by, was one of the many volunteers who kept the heritage railway alive. She spotted that the cabin at the crazy golf course was open, flags fluttering in the breeze. And along the colourful rows of brightly painted beach huts, a young couple were hanging bunting around the door of a red hut. Outside a blue hut stood two cheery green and white striped deckchairs.

Helen called for Suki and clipped her lead on, then walked back along the prom. Before she began to climb the hill to the Seaview, she tied Suki to the railings outside a small café and headed in to order. Soon she was sitting at an outdoor table overlooking the sea with Suki at her feet and a mug of hot chocolate in her hands. She watched people going by, walking dogs, pushing prams, licking ice creams, chasing grandchildren and making them scream with delight. She saw the open-top double-decker bus making its way along Marine Drive, ferrying passengers from the Spa along the seafront to the North Bay café.

She sat outside the café for a long time, long after she'd finished her drink, watching life go on around her. This was how it would be from now on, she realised. Minutes and hours would pass; days and weeks would go by; seasons would blossom and fade, and it would all happen without Tom. Her mind turned to decorating the Seaview for the party on Saturday night. She'd hang Gracie's coloured streamers with balloons the little girl had chosen at the cash and carry. She smiled. She'd host the party as a tribute to Tom and make it the kind of do he loved.

She thought of Tom's white Elvis suit whirling around in the washing machine. She still wasn't sure if she had the nerve to wear it. But there was no harm in cleaning it, just in case. It would be too big for her, she already knew that. Tom had been taller than her, wider, his stomach full and his shoulders broad. She felt sure she'd find a belt in her wardrobe she could use. Or if not a belt, she could head into town to buy a strip of cheap satin from the market to tie around her waist or use as a scarf.

A scarf? Her face clouded over. She thought of the scrap of blue satin that Suki had found. The colour of it, the material . . . No, it couldn't be . . .

'No!' she yelled.

A woman at the next table looked over. 'You all right, love?'

Helen felt anything but all right. She scraped her chair back, untied Suki's lead and ran from the café and up the hill. She was soon out of breath, gasping for air. She raced up Albert Road and onto Windsor Terrace, Suki at her side, enjoying the pace. At the Seaview's front door, she fumbled for her key, dropped it, picked it up and tried again. Finally she got inside, where she rushed downstairs, flew into the kitchen and flipped the bin lid.

It was there: the piece of pale blue satin cloth, ragged around the edges. She stared hard at it, then gingerly picked it up, taking care to hold it by the edges; she didn't want any more of her fingerprints on it. It was dirty, stained and still damp from Suki's mouth.

'Where did you get this, girl?' she said out loud.

Suki wandered to the living room and lay down in front of the patio doors while Helen, heart racing, wondered what to do next. And then she remembered what Jean had said about letting Suki outside while she had been at the cash and carry. Was that where the dog had picked up the blue satin patch? Had she pulled it from the rubbish bags left next to the bins?

Helen unlocked the back door and looked out. In the back lane, a blue and white bin lorry was making its way to the end of the street. Her bins weren't in the yard; they'd already been taken and emptied, their contents now in the back of the lorry. She glanced around, looking for . . . what, exactly? A clue? More of the blue satin? She lifted old plant pots and wooden boxes that Tom had been meaning to throw out; there was nothing but spiders scuttling away. She headed back indoors and laid both hands on the kitchen worktop, staring at the patch of blue satin. She felt sick. She swallowed hard, pushed her hands through her hair, then ran the cold tap, filled a glass and took a long drink. She knew what she had to do next.

She found her phone and called the police. A switchboard operator answered efficiently and swiftly, and Helen asked to be put through to the person she needed. Within seconds, he'd answered her call.

'DS Hutchinson here.'

'It's Helen Dexter from the Seaview Hotel.'

'Ah, Mrs Dexter. How are you?'

'Truthfully? I'm not so good,' she said, eyeing the blue cloth. 'Something's happened. I've found something.'

'And this something is related to the death of Mr McNally, I assume?'

Helen felt her legs go weak, and she sank into a chair.

'Mrs Dexter?' DS Hutchinson asked. 'Are you still there?'

'Yes, I'm here. Sorry, I've found a . . . well, my dog found it really, and it's . . . it's all come as a bit of a shock.'

'What is it you've found?'

'I mean, it might not be his, you know?' Helen said quickly. 'I can't say for sure. I might be wrong.'

'Just tell me what it is,' DS Hutchinson said firmly.

She took a deep breath. 'I think I've found a piece of Brian's blue satin scarf. The one he was wearing on the night he was killed.'

Chapter 40

'His scarf?' DS Hutchinson said.

'Yes, I'm certain it's his. I remember how he was dressed the night of the gig; I was here when they all left the Seaview. I remember seeing him wearing a blue satin scarf.'

'But we've got his scarf here, Helen. Forensics have been over it already. They've got all his clothes and none of them are torn or missing any pieces.'

'What do you mean?' Helen said, staring at the scrap of material Suki had brought in.

'Everything is here, Mrs Dexter, and his scarf is intact.'

'All of it?' she cried.

'All of it,' DS Hutchinson said calmly.

'Are you sure?'

'After twenty-five years in this job, I think I know evidence when I see it.'

'But—' Helen began.

'Mrs Dexter, whatever you've found isn't Brian's scarf, or anything to do with it.'

'Shouldn't I at least bring it in so you can look at it? Don't you want to do tests?' she said.

'There's really no need.'

She sighed. 'You must think I'm losing the plot.'

'Not at all,' DS Hutchinson replied kindly. 'You've been through a lot and I know none of this can be easy on you or your business. I hear Twelvis are returning tomorrow.'

'Have you spoken to Jimmy?'

'Yes, we've talked. We're hoping that the band being back in town might jog people's memories about what they might have seen on the night Brian died. It might bring a few witnesses out of the woodwork.'

'Jimmy said he's given you a list of men on the Twelvis waiting list. Have any clues come from that?'

'We're working our way through the list as quickly as we can,' DS Hutchinson replied. 'But as you know, what with cutbacks . . .'

'I understand,' Helen said. 'Well, you're welcome to pop along to the party if you'd like, you and DC Hall.'

'Thank you kindly. I might just take you up on that.'

'Bring a partner if you wish,' Helen said, and Sandra DeVine's smoky eyes flashed through her mind. 'And tell DC Hall he's welcome to bring someone too – perhaps his wife?'

'I think he'd rather not,' he laughed. 'She left him for a fireman last summer and he hasn't seen her since.'

Helen hung up the phone and leaned back in her chair. She closed her eyes. How could she have been so stupid, seeking clues to a murder in a piece of tatty old cloth? She picked up the torn satin and returned it to the bin. Then she put the kettle on, brewed a pot of tea, took a couple of Jean's home-made ginger snaps from the biscuit tin and rang Benson's estate agents.

'Good afternoon? Benson's?' a woman's voice trilled, its upward inflection turning sentences into questions and setting Helen's already frayed nerves on edge. 'Janine speaking? How may I assist you today?'

'Could I speak to Frederick Benson, please?'

'And whom may I say is calling?'

'Helen Dexter, from the Seaview Hotel.'

'Of course. One moment?'

There was a click, a beat of silence and then the deep booming voice of the estate agent came on the line.

'Mrs Dexter, Frederick Benson here. What can I do for you?'

'I'd like to know who's bought the Glendale Hotel.'

'You're nothing if not direct, Mrs Dexter. But I'm afraid details of the purchase are confidential.'

'Is it Traveltime Inns? Did they get permission after all to redevelop without a car park?'

'Mrs Dexter, please. You know I'm not at liberty to divulge such information. However, if in the future you find yourself ready to sell the Seaview, I hope you'll consider using Benson's for all your estate agency needs. Now, is there anything else I can help you with today?'

'No,' Helen said sulkily. She hung up and stuffed a whole ginger snap into her mouth. She drank some tea, walked into the living room, stared out to the courtyard and then rang Marie. 'Marie? It's Helen. Why are you ignoring my texts?'

Silence.

'I know you're there,' she said. 'I can hear your nail varnish screaming.'

'I'm here,' Marie said. 'But I don't know what to say.'

'You could start by telling me what's going on with you and Gav.'

'I can't,' Marie said quickly. 'It's complicated.'

'I mean, I can see the attraction. He's young, he's fit, he's young, he's good-looking, he's fit, he's young . . .'

'Helen, don't, please.'

'Then what's happened? Tell me.'

'I can't, not yet.'

'What do you mean, not yet? Stop being so bloody infuriating and just tell me what's going on. Are you and he a couple?'

'Oh Helen, please . . .'

Helen sighed. 'I'm going to get nothing out of you, am I? Not when you're in one of your moods. I know you, Marie Clark.'

'It's Marie Davenport now.'

Helen's mouth opened in shock. 'You've gone back to using your maiden name? I take it this means your divorce from Daran is going through?'

'Elvis Sam is on the case, Helen. He's brilliant. He's really got Daran by the balls as far as his bank balance is concerned. He's threatened him with court proceedings to ensure the best divorce settlement he can get.'

Helen raised her eyebrows. 'Daran won't like that. It'll mean having his bank accounts inspected, and we all know how he likes to keep those hidden from the taxman.'

'You're right, he doesn't like it one little bit. In fact, he's offered me an out-of-court settlement instead. If I agree, it means I get to keep the house and my gorgeous little car; obviously the nail bar's in my name, so I can keep that going. And the settlement will give me enough cash to invest in something I've had my heart set on for years.'

This was news to Helen. 'How long have I known you, Marie?

You've never said a word to me about wanting to invest in anything before. Is it stocks and shares, that kind of thing?'

Silence.

'Marie?'

'I can't talk. I'm at work and I've got a client waiting. When are you free next? I'll call at the Seaview, or we could meet at the Angel for a drink.'

'I can't meet tonight, I'm taking Jean out for fish and chips. And tomorrow I've got the Elvis impersonators coming back for the weekend.'

'Really? Could I call in to meet Sam and say thank you?'

'You can do more than that. I'm throwing a party to raise funds for Bev's charity and Brian's family on Saturday night, and Twelvis are singing. Come any time after six.'

'You know I'm not an Elvis fan.'

'Ah, come on, Marie. It's for charity. You can make a donation and get some free publicity for your nail bar at the same time. I've got a journalist from the *Scarborough Times* coming.'

'Oh all right, I'll think about it.' There was a beat of silence before Marie spoke again. 'Can I bring Gav?'

'Really? You're at that couples stage already?'

'Helen, it's—'

'I know, it's none of my business. Course you can bring him. I'll just have to get my head around you having a toy boy, won't I? My world's weird enough at the moment; another strange addition won't make much difference.'

Jean returned to the hotel later that afternoon. She brewed a pot of tea and sank onto the sofa.

'How are your mum's legs?' Helen asked.

Jean shook her head woefully. 'Not good,' she said. 'The new medication's not helping as much as the doctor hoped. It's a rum do; she's never going to improve. She'll be in that care home until her dying day. The only thing that's kept me cheerful is the thought of you treating me to a fish and chip supper tonight.'

'Which chippy would you like to go to? It's my treat, remember. There're loads of them on the seafront. It's hard to keep track of who owns which one these days.'

'Well, we *could* go to the seafront,' Jean said, and Helen noticed a mischievous grin on her lips. 'But there's somewhere else we could head to where they serve the best fish and chips in Scarborough. We'd have to leave Suki here, though, and it's a bit of a walk.'

'Old Mother Hubbard's up on Westborough?' Helen said. 'It's been a while since I've eaten in there.'

'They're always getting good reviews in the paper,' Jean said.

'And online too,' Helen added. 'They've got their own social media hashtags now.'

'Hashtags?' Jean huffed. 'I'll have haddock and chips like I always do.'

The following morning Helen woke to the sound of rain belting against her bedroom window. She lay still, feeling safe and cocooned against the bad weather. Then she heard Jean singing from the kitchen, a ballad this time, one she recognised from the seventies. The unfamiliar smell of kippers cooking on the grill greeted her, and she smiled at the thought of Jean trying to master yet another item to add to the breakfast menu. She clambered out of bed and was met by Suki stretching and yawning.

'Morning, Suki,' she said, stroking the dog's head.

Suki whined in reply. Helen walked past the cardboard boxes, which were now full to the brim with Tom's clothes, though she hadn't had the heart yet to tape them up. What was it Jean had advised her to do? Step by step, she'd said, and that was how it was going to be. She was in no hurry to move the boxes and she'd do it only when it felt right.

As she showered and dressed, she realised just how much she was looking forward to Twelvis returning. And yes, she acknowledged to herself, much of that was tied up with seeing Jimmy again. She headed to the kitchen, where Jean had the radio tuned to the local station's breakfast show.

'Morning, Jean. Kippers, eh? I haven't had those in years. Tom used to love them.'

'Thought I'd try grilling them with a poached egg on the side; how does that sound?'

'Like heaven,' Helen replied. She picked up a paper bag from the countertop. 'I forget to tell you, I bought you this.' She handed the bag to Jean, who peered warily inside before pulling out a long wooden stick, rounded at one end and fashioned with a handle grip at the other.

'What the devil's this?' she cried.

'It's a spurtle, for making porridge,' Helen replied.

Jean put it to one side. 'New-fangled gadgets,' she complained, then nodded towards the radio. 'What time are the boys doing their interview this morning?'

315

'Jimmy said they'd be speaking live on the breakfast show, so it should be any time now.'

'Oh, I saw Sally this morning,' Jean said. 'When I opened the curtains, she was heading to Miriam's next door. I knocked on the window and gave her a wave.'

'I expect she'll be calling in here for her morning coffee after she's done at the Vista del Mar,' Helen said.

'She's a nice lass, that Sally,' Jean said. 'You want to try to keep her on here for as long as you can.'

'She is, and I will,' Helen replied.

'And that Gav fella who was here fixing your cameras. I know he's a bit loud, but he seemed to have a heart of gold. He's a hard worker too. Sally and him really hit it off when he stayed for lunch. I reckon they'd make a nice couple.'

Jean returned to the kippers and buttered two slices of toast while Helen gazed out of the patio doors, watching rain bouncing off the flagstones.

'Sally and Gav?' She shook her head. 'I think that ship has sailed.'

Chapter 41

As the rain continued to pour down, a song played on the radio with sunny lyrics promising brighter days to come.

Jean raised the butter knife and jabbed it towards the window. 'Springtime sunshine in this flaming rain?' she snorted. 'Don't make me laugh.'

As the song was ending, the DJ's cheery voice chipped in to say he was taking a short break for news and weather and then he promised his listeners a big surprise.

'Do you think it'll be the Twelvis interview?' Jean asked.

'It might be,' Helen replied.

Jean handed her a plate. On it were two perfectly grilled buttery kippers with a poached egg and a slice of wholemeal toast. 'Eat up. And there's plenty of tea in the pot.'

'Thanks, Jean,' Helen said. 'You've really looked after me, and I appreciate it.'

'Ah, it's nothing,' Jean said.

'No, Jean. It's everything. You being here has meant the world to me. I don't know how I'd have coped this week if it hadn't been for you. You've cooked for me, cleaned – you've done more than you know. Having you stay here even gave me the confidence to start packing away Tom's things.'

Jean glanced at her. 'And how are you finding it, love?'

'Well, I cleared out his side of the wardrobe and his chest of drawers. Of course I couldn't bear to throw everything out; there are things I'll always keep. But I'm getting there. I've filled boxes and I'll take them up to the hospital next week.'

'You can have a word with my friend Dora from the charity; she's coming to the party. She'll be grateful for your support.'

'It's good to know his clothes will be helping raise money for a good cause.'

'Still hurts, though, doesn't it?' Jean said. 'It's never easy.'

'How long does it take for the pain to go, Jean?'

Jean laid her hand on Helen's arm. 'You never get over them, love. The pain dulls, but it'll always be there.'

Helen sipped her tea, then picked up her fork and pierced the poached egg, spilling yolk onto the toast. 'Jean, this is perfect. I'd like to add kippers and porridge to the breakfast menu this weekend while Twelvis are here. How about it? Think you can manage?'

'There's only one way to find out,' Jean replied.

'Excellent. I'll type up new menus this morning.'

On the radio, another song started up, one that Helen and Jean recognised immediately from its very first beat.

'This was one of Tom's favourite Elvis songs,' Helen said, tapping her foot.

The tune was short and sweet and it finished much too soon. The cheery voice of the DJ kicked in on the last note and he began talking about Twelvis.

'Here they are,' Helen said excitedly. 'This is it. Turn it up, Jean.'

Jean reached over to the radio and turned up the volume as the DJ asked each Elvis impersonator to introduce himself.

Jimmy spoke first, and Helen was happy to hear his voice. Kev was next, then Ginger with his polite, gentlemanly tone, then Stuart, followed by his brother Alan with his strange Elvis drawl, Big Al, laid-back Davey, enthusiastic Colin, married couple Bob and Sam, then Tim. They sounded happy, joking with one another, and it was easy for Helen to imagine them squashed into the studio, some of them sitting, some standing, all dressed in their black leather or white suits with their make-up and wigs on, diamantés and sparkles and goodness know what. Finally it was the turn of the group's new member, Trevor, to introduce himself.

'The new lad sounds nervous,' she said.

'Not without good reason. He's replaced a murdered man,' Jean replied.

And that was when the DJ's voice turned serious as he began to talk about Brian, asking for witnesses to come forward with anything they might have seen or heard last Saturday night that could help the police catch his killer. He reported that Peasholm Park had now reopened after the police had cordoned it off while they dredged the lake. And then he and Jimmy began talking about happier news: about the party to raise funds for the hospital charity and Brian's family.

'And where will the party be held?' the DJ asked.

'The Seaview Hotel on Windsor Terrace. It's the best little hotel in Scarborough,' Jimmy said.

Helen's heart skipped a beat and she beamed at Jean.

'I knew he'd slip a mention in,' Jean said.

'The Seaview is a mighty fine place with a breakfast to be proud of, and, uh-uh, the hotel is run by the best little lady in town.'

'Is that Alan?' Jean asked.

Helen nodded as Jimmy began to speak again.

'But it's quite a small place, not really the kind of venue for a full-on gig, and so we've had to restrict entry to those who've been invited,' he said. 'We've got dignitaries from the council and the local tourist board coming as well as volunteers from the charity we're raising money for.'

'Invitation only, eh? Mine must have got lost in the post!' the DJ laughed. 'Any chance of you guys returning to Scarborough in the future to do another gig that's open to all? Maybe somewhere bigger than a B&B next time? How about another sell-out gig at the Spa?'

'We'd surely be willing to look into that, sir,' Alan said.

There was more banter, more joking, and then the interview was over, bookended with another Elvis song, this one mournful and sad.

'I've put the bed linen from room one in the wash,' Jean said, breaking into Helen's thoughts. 'And I've cleaned the room and en suite so it's ready for the men coming in.'

'I wonder if any of them will want to stay in the room Brian stayed in last weekend?' Helen said. 'Or should we leave it empty as a mark of respect?'

'Leave it empty,' Jean advised. 'I'm sure they won't mind doubling up and sharing. There's plenty of rooms with twin beds or bunk beds.'

Right on cue, Helen's phone pinged with a message from Jimmy.

We're on our way to Seaview now x

Once breakfast had been eaten and the rain began to ease, Helen led Suki outside on their morning walk. It was nippy, and she pulled her fleece tight around her. She wondered about wearing Tom's old jumper the next time the weather was bad. Down on the beach, the tide was rolling in, the waves frothy and high. Surfers clad in black carried their boards out to the stormy sea. Helen walked along the sand as far as the café where she'd sat the previous day. Above it was a luxury apartment complex, one of the most expensive in town, its occupants rewarded with stunning views of the castle and sea.

Her phone was in her pocket and she felt it vibrate against her hip. She took it out and saw Marie's name.

'Marie? You all right?'

'No, I'm not!' Marie cried. 'I haven't been honest with you, Helen. There are things you need to know. I'm on my way to the Seaview now. Oh, and Gav's coming too.'

'Is he with you?' Helen asked.

'No, he's driving one of his cabs.'

And with that Marie rang off, leaving Helen staring at her phone, confused.

When she returned to Windsor Terrace, she saw the front door of the Vista del Mar open and recognised Miriam's guests loading their car: the thin, slight man with grey hair and glasses and the woman with cropped silver hair. Their daughter, Daisy, was sitting on the wall outside the Seaview, glued to her phone. As Helen drew near, she could hear them arguing, just as they'd done when they'd arrived.

'Daisy, come and help your mum load the car.'

'I'm busy!' Daisy yelled.

'Daisy! Now!'

'It's not fair,' she cried, still not moving. 'This is child abuse.

You're making me work after the crappiest week of my life in a place I never want to see again.'

Helen caught the mother's eye as she walked past the warring family.

'Kids, eh?' the woman said with a wry smile.

Helen smiled in reply and continued on to the Seaview.

As she headed down to her apartment, she could hear Jean's voice telling someone to calm down. Helen wondered who it was. She let Suki off the lead and walked into the kitchen, where she was surprised to find Sally, who was wearing a peach-coloured tabard over jeans and a T-shirt. The tabard had the Vista del Mar's logo on the front, a dolphin leaping out of the sea. Sally's face was flushed red; she looked agitated, angry.

'Sally? Are you all right? What's happened? Has Miriam said something to upset you? Because if she has, I'll go in there and wring her bloody neck.'

'No, it's not Miriam,' Sally said between gulps of air.

'Is it Gracie? Oh my God, what's happened?'

'She won't tell me a thing,' Jean said. 'She insisted on waiting for you to come back.'

Helen gently took Sally by the arm and led her to a chair at the table. She noticed that Sally was carrying a white plastic bag. Jean followed and they all sat down.

'Sally, calm down and tell me what's wrong,' Helen said.

Sally did as she was told, taking four or five breaths to calm her racing heart before she spoke.

'I was cleaning this morning, next door . . .'

Helen nodded encouragingly.

'. . . and there's a room I had to go into—'

Jean crossed herself. 'Oh my word, she's seen the ghost,' she cried. 'I knew the stories about Miriam's hotel were true.'

Helen looked at her aghast. 'I'm surprised you're daft enough to believe that old rubbish. Now come on, Sally, I'm listening.'

Sally gulped air. 'I was vacuuming and . . . and I had to move a small dressing table to do it properly, to get behind it. You trained me to clean rooms properly, Helen, and even though Miriam doesn't care if I move the furniture or not, I do it because I take pride in my work.'

'Well, what happened?' Jean said impatiently.

'Jean, give the girl a chance to explain,' Helen said firmly.

'The room was empty,' Sally continued. 'The guests had just left and so I moved the dressing table to give the place a good bottoming. But the vacuum cleaner started sucking up the edge of the carpet . . . it wasn't stuck down properly.'

'How shoddy,' Jean tutted. 'Miriam should know better. And her with four stars.'

'Go on, Sally,' Helen said calmly.

'The carpet got stuck in the vacuum cleaner, so I had to turn it off and get down on my hands and knees to clear the threads. And when I pulled at it, I could see that underneath, there was no underlay, just bare floorboards, and . . . and they were scratched and broken and . . .'

'Take your time, Sally, nice and easy,' Helen said.

'And the floorboard came loose – it'd moved after I'd vacuumed – so I tried to put it back, but it came away from the rest of the floor, Helen, and there was a hole there and then . . . then I found this bag.'

Helen and Jean exchanged a puzzled look as Sally bent down

to pick up the white plastic bag. Helen took it from her and looked inside, and her mouth dropped open in shock.

'What is it?' Jean asked.

Helen gulped. It was a pair of blue suede shoes. They were slip-ons, size eleven, in an extra-wide fit.

Chapter 42

'Brian's shoes!' Helen was barely able to breathe.

'I brought them straight over. Miriam doesn't know I'm here. As far as she knows, I'm still in there, cleaning.'

'Which room did you find them in?'

'Room six, second floor at the back.'

'And the guests have already gone, you said?'

'They checked out after breakfast. It was the family . . .'

'. . . with the young daughter and the woman with silver hair?'

'How on earth do you know that?' Sally said.

'I've just seen them packing their car outside.'

Helen stood up so quickly that she knocked her chair over and it clattered to the floor. She thrust the bag with the shoes in at Jean. 'Keep tight hold of these; they're evidence. Lock the door after I've gone, don't let anyone in who might try to take them. Oh, and keep them away from Suki.' She turned to Sally. 'Come on, we need to stop them from leaving. I just pray they haven't already gone.'

She whipped her phone from her pocket. 'DS Hutchinson, please. It's urgent.' As she flew up the stairs, she told the detective what had happened.

'Helen, calm down,' he said. 'Wait until we get there and don't do anything stupid. These people might be dangerous. I was going to call you this morning. We've had a lead, from the Twelvis waiting list that Elvis One gave us. All the men on the list are accounted for . . . all except one, a Mr Ken Solway. We've called his home, spoken to his daughter, and she told us he's on holiday . . .'

Helen dashed through the lobby, heading to the front door.

'. . . here in Scarborough. We're on our way now.'

Helen's heart was pounding as she and Sally ran out of the Seaview. In front of them, a small dark blue car was indicating to pull away from the kerb. The man was in the driving seat, his wife beside him in the front. In the back, Daisy was concentrating on her phone.

'Stop that car!' Helen screamed at the top of her voice, but her words were lost on the empty road. There was no traffic coming, no passers-by to help.

'It's just you and me, kid,' she said to Sally. 'Be careful. I don't know how we're going to do it, but we've got to stop them.'

Sally ran around the car and banged as hard as she could on the passenger door. The silver-haired woman stared at her as if she was mad. Sally tried the passenger door handle, but it was locked. Helen ran to the driver's door, but that was locked too. Inside the car, the family looked terrified, being assaulted on both sides by raving women.

Helen took a moment to come to her senses. 'We need to speak to you,' she said as assertively as she could. 'Please get out of the car.'

A look of fury passed over the man's face and he revved the engine. 'Get out of my way!' he screamed.

Helen looked at his wife. She appeared unnaturally calm. In

the back seat, their daughter was filming it all on her phone. 'I'm putting this online,' she laughed. 'It's the most exciting thing that's happened all week.'

Helen moved to stand in front of the car. 'You're going to have to mow me down if you want to leave, cos I'm not moving until you get out of the car.'

The engine revved again angrily, and this time the car leapt forward.

'You wouldn't dare!' Helen yelled.

'Yes, I bloody would!' the man roared.

'Get out of the car! We just want to talk.'

'I've got nothing to say,' he yelled.

The car crept forward again. Helen braced her hands against the bonnet.

'Who do you think you are, Wonder Woman?' he jeered. 'Move now, before you get hurt.'

She stared him down, but it was no use: the car inched forward again, forcing her to step aside.

'We can't let them go,' Sally cried.

Helen glanced around, hoping for a miracle, but Windsor Terrace was still deserted. The car inched forward again, its wheels turning as it pulled away from the kerb.

'They're getting away,' Helen said. 'Sally, stop them!'

'What am I supposed to do?' Sally cried.

And that was when Marie's red sports car screeched around the corner of Windsor Terrace. Helen ran into the road, waving her arms to get her attention.

'Stop your car! Stop your car!' she shouted. 'Block the street with it! Now!'

Marie didn't hesitate. She spun her car so that it blocked one end of Windsor Terrace. Inside the blue car, the driver's face fell. But Marie's small vehicle didn't fill the road completely, and Helen could see him trying to work out if he could squeeze through the narrow space. He revved the engine once more, and the car shot forward just as one of Gav's bright yellow cabs arrived, successfully blocking the gap.

'You bitch! I'll get you for this!' the man screamed at Helen.

Helen saw the woman lean across to her husband, saw her turn and look out of the rear window; then the car's white reverse lights came on and it sped backwards down Windsor Terrace. There was no traffic coming, nothing to stop it getting away. But just when it looked hopeless, when it seemed to Helen as if the man and his oddly calm wife would leave Scarborough for good, a silver minibus turned onto the street. It was emblazoned on both sides and the bonnet with white guitars and the words *Twelvis on Tour!*

The small car screeched to a halt, caught between Marie's sports car and Gav's cab at one end of the street and Twelvis's minibus at the other. The grey-haired man leapt out, unhindered by his limp, and looked wildly around, clearly seeking an escape route. There was only one way he could go, and it was over the clifftop that led down to the sea.

'Catch him!' Helen called out. 'He's the one who killed Brian!'

Jimmy, wearing his full Elvis white suit ripped open to the navel, jumped out of the driver's seat of the minibus.

'Come on, boys! Let's get him!' he cried.

One by one, Twelvis poured from the van, capes flying, belts jiggling, hairpieces lifting, eye make-up streaking, Hawaiian leis flying, leather jackets blowing, blue suede shoes skidding down the hill. The grey-haired man was wiry and quick but ultimately not fast enough to outrun twelve men in fancy dress. Helen and Sally stood guard beside the blue car to make sure his wife and daughter couldn't leave. Marie and Gav watched from the top of the cliff until the sound of sirens filled the air, getting louder.

'Come on, we need to move our cars to let the police in,' Marie told Gav.

Within minutes, Jimmy and Kev had tackled the grey-haired man to the ground. Stuart and Alan helped pull him to his feet and the four of them frogmarched him back up the hill, arriving sweaty, messy, dirty and out of breath just as DS Hutchinson and DC Hall stepped out of their police car. At the same time, the door of the Vista del Mar flung open and Miriam stood with her hands on her hips and her face like thunder.

'What on earth's all the noise for? What's going on?'

'I think you need to accompany me to the station to answer a few questions, Mr Solway,' DS Hutchinson said. 'It *is* Mr Solway, isn't it?'

'Four years I waited to get into Twelvis,' Mr Solway hissed. 'Four flamin' years!' He spat on the ground next to DS Hutchinson's big black boots. 'I only wanted a second chance! I didn't mean to kill him!'

'Well, Mr Solway. The sooner you come to the station and explain what you were doing with a pair of shoes belonging to a murdered man, the sooner all of this will be over and done with.'

DC Hall took one of Mr Solway's arms, DS Hutchinson the other, and together they led him to their car and secured him in the back seat.

'Call for backup,' DS Hutchinson ordered his colleague. 'Get them to take the wife and daughter to the station. I want the woman questioned too. Take it easy with the daughter; she's little more than a child.'

'Right, boss,' DC Hall said.

As DC Hall drove Mr Solway to the station, DS Hutchinson waited on the street with Helen and Sally, Marie and Gav, Miriam and Twelvis. Another police car arrived to take away a still calm Mrs Solway. Young Daisy was in tears, but although she was shaking and obviously scared by what had happened, Helen noticed that her mother gave her no reassurance; no arm around her shoulder, no kiss on the cheek, nothing.

'Are you all right?' Jimmy was at Helen's side.

'Yes, I'm just shocked. I don't think my legs want to work; they're shaking.'

He held his arm out and she took it gratefully.

At their side, DS Hutchinson coughed loudly. 'I need to come and collect the shoes as evidence, Mrs Dexter.'

'Of course,' she said.

'And can one of your lads move the minibus, Jimmy? It's still blocking the road.'

Jimmy put his hand into the pocket of his Elvis suit, pulled out a key and threw it towards Alan. 'Alan, can you move the van?'

'Right away, Elvis One,' Alan replied.

'Boys, assemble in the lounge,' Jimmy called, then Helen led everyone into the Seaview.

Chapter 43

DS Hutchinson left the Seaview carrying the blue suede shoes in the white bag. He promised Helen he'd be in touch to let her know what was happening with Mr Solway as soon as there was news.

'Their daughter was filming it all on her phone,' Helen said.

'We'll make sure it's deleted. I'll get forensics into the hotel next door immediately. I'll go and have a word with the landlady now.'

'Go easy on her,' Helen said. 'She can be a bit prickly, but she's got a heart of gold underneath it all . . . somewhere.'

Helen walked into the lounge, where Marie and Gav were sitting close together, whispering. Beside them, Sally was tapping at her phone. Twelvis were scattered around the lounge, some of them sitting forward in their seats with their heads in their hands, others with their eyes closed, all of them trying to come to terms with what had just happened.

'Have you eaten breakfast this morning?' Helen asked Jimmy.

He shook his head. 'We stopped off at a service station in the early hours, but it seems a long time ago now.'

'Well, we haven't prepped for a full breakfast for you, I'm afraid, but how does a round of bacon sandwiches and hot coffee sound?'

'Perfect,' he replied.

'Marie? Gav? Sally?' Helen called. 'Bacon sandwiches for you too?'

'Please, Helen. That'd be great,' Marie replied.

'Your man Gav's always hungry,' Gav added.

Sally stood and placed her phone in the pocket of her Vista del Mar peach tabard. 'I'll go downstairs and help Jean,' she said.

Helen turned to Jimmy. 'I'll give your boys their room keys and allow them time to get settled in and changed. I'll ask Jean to rustle up bacon butties for everyone in the dining room say in an hour's time? About the rooms, Jimmy, I was thinking of keeping room seven empty; it's where Brian stayed last time. That's if one of your boys doesn't mind doubling up with someone else?'

Jimmy looked around the room and his gaze settled on Trevor, the newest and youngest Twelvis member. Helen was touched by how innocent Trevor looked, and how startling his resemblance was to a young Elvis, with his smooth, clear skin, dark eyes and black hair.

'Trevor, you're in room eight, OK?' Jimmy said.

'Cheers, Jimmy,' Trevor replied. 'The King's birth date, nice touch.'

'That's the room you had last time,' Helen said.

'I'll share with Ginger this time; he had twin beds in his room. Everyone else will be fine to have the same rooms as last weekend.'

Helen handed out keys and slowly the men dispersed, bringing in their luggage from the minibus then climbing the stairs to their rooms. After checking on Jean and getting Suki settled, Helen walked back to the lounge. Marie and Gav were sitting on the window seat gazing out at the sea. Helen sank into a chair opposite.

'Jean's sending tea and coffee up in the dumbwaiter in a few minutes,' she said. 'What a morning it's been. I could do without another like it. Come to think of it, I never want another week as bad as this.'

'Have the cops arrested the man from next door?' Marie asked.

'DS Hutchinson's going to ring to tell me what's going on. He reckons all the evidence is pointing towards him being the killer.'

'But he looked so short and slight,' Marie said. 'And from what I remember about Brian, he was a stocky bloke.'

Helen shrugged. 'I've no idea what happened. We'll have to wait for the police to explain.'

Marie and Gav exchanged a look that Helen couldn't fail to notice.

'Well, you two,' Helen said gently. 'Do you want to tell me what's going on?'

Gav shifted in his seat.

'You're unusually quiet, Gav,' she said.

He looked at Marie. 'Do you want to tell her or shall I?' he asked.

Marie sat up straight in her seat and placed her scarlet six-inch heels firmly on the carpet. She flicked her long brown hair over her shoulder. 'Helen, you deserve to hear it from me.'

Helen steeled herself. 'Come on then, out with it.'

'It's the Glendale Hotel,' Marie said. 'We've bought it.'

Helen almost fell off her chair. 'You've done what?'

'I said it's the Glendale Hotel and we've—'

Helen held her hand up. 'I heard what you said. But I'm having trouble understanding it. You've actually bought the Glendale?'

Marie nodded.

'Both of you?'

'We're partners,' Gav said. 'You are now looking at the new directors of Maz and Gav Enterprises Limited. We've pooled our resources and now we own the Glendale outright.'

'I'm investing my divorce settlement in it,' Marie explained. 'I've got to look after myself and my future.'

'But what are you going to do with it? I know you won't get planning permission to reopen it as a hotel; it hasn't got a car park.'

'And that's exactly why Traveltime Inns pulled out,' Gav said. 'Leaving it ripe for us to develop.'

'Into what?' Helen said, still trying to make sense of things.

'Well, that's where you come in,' Marie said, raising a perfectly manicured eyebrow.

'Me?'

'We're going to gut it and rip its insides out,' Gav said.

'Apart from the original art deco windows at the back; they're staying,' Marie added firmly.

'Noted,' Gav said.

'Is someone going to tell me what the hell's going on?' Helen said, glaring at Marie.

Marie beamed back at her and took time to savour the moment before she delivered her news.

'We're going to open a tearoom.'

Helen rocked back in her seat.

'It's going to be retro and twee,' Marie carried on excitedly. 'Everything a good tearoom should be. Nice and cosy, you know? We'll serve the best local food and drink we can source. There's a garden at the back for outdoor seating. Think about it, Helen, there are no cafés over this side of the bay, not up here on the clifftop. Our guests will have a view of the castle while they eat; it's going to be great.'

Helen laughed out loud. 'You and Gav? Running a tearoom together?'

'It'll work, missus,' Gav said confidently. 'Gav never invests in anything that could fail. We've done our market research. We've got planning permission and we've already got three thousand followers online. With Marie's money and my business know-how, we're on to a winner.'

A smile played around Helen's lips. 'The pair of you are crackers. But do you know what? I think it might just work.'

She looked at Gav then at Marie. 'So . . . you're *business* partners? That's all?'

'What are you suggesting?' Gav laughed. 'That the two of us are having it off?'

That was exactly what Helen had been thinking. 'I saw you kissing, in Marie's car.'

Marie looked her square in the eye. 'We're just business partners,' she said. 'Nothing more. Anything physical you might have seen between us was down to our excitement at getting the Glendale at last; we've been after it for a long time.'

Helen looked hard at her friend and felt certain she was telling the truth. 'But there's still something I don't understand. Where do I come into this? I can't afford to invest, if that's what you mean.'

'Oh, it's not your money I'm after,' Marie said. 'It's your curtains and tables and chairs that you've had in here since the Ark was built. The furnishings in here are perfect for the old-fashioned look I'm aiming for in my tearoom.'

'Our tearoom,' Gav said.

'Noted,' Marie replied.

Helen looked around the lounge, at the carpets and curtains, the tables and chairs.

'You can't take all this!' she cried. 'I'd be left with nothing, and besides, who says I want to get rid of it? I can't afford to replace it all, no matter how dated it is.'

'Well, *you* might not be able to afford to replace things. But I can,' Marie said gently.

Helen eyed her keenly. 'What do you mean?'

'I mean I want to invest in the Seaview, Helen. I want to invest in *you*. Daran's divorce settlement is a lot larger than expected. Sam's squeezing him dry, and it means I've ended up with a lot of cash I need to invest.'

'And this investment in the Seaview, will it be coming from Maz and Gav Enterprises, or whatever you're calling yourselves?'

Marie shook her head. 'This would be coming from only me.' Marie turned to Gav. 'Gav, could you give me and Helen a few minutes on our own?'

'Course I can,' Gav replied. 'Helen, is it all right if I head downstairs? I could maybe, er, help Jean with breakfast.'

'Yes, that's fine,' Helen said. 'Although while you're down there, you might want to explain to Sally that you're free and single after all. I think some wires got crossed over what might have been going on between you and Marie.'

Once Gav had left the lounge, Marie leaned across the table and took hold of Helen's hands.

'You love this place, Helen. The Seaview was everything to you and Tom; you spent years building the business. I remember when you first told me you were thinking of buying it and I came to view it with you.'

'You warned us *not* to buy it, if I remember correctly,' Helen said. 'You thought it'd be a money pit and we'd end up losing all our cash. But I fell in love with the place the minute I walked through the door, and Tom felt the same way.'

'You and Tom were always of like mind. You were lucky to have each other. I hope I find someone who makes me as happy as he made you.'

Helen closed her eyes. 'Don't, Marie, please. You'll set me off crying again.'

'What I'm saying, Helen, is that you can't let the Seaview slide now you're on your own. You need to future-proof it, make it work for you. Get Sally in to manage it so you can take a day off now and then. You could even have a couple of holidays each year. We could go to Majorca on a girls' week away, take Sue and Bev too.'

Helen let Marie's words sink in. The idea was appealing, she had to give it that.

'Think about this place, Helen. Imagine how it would look with new furnishings, fresh decor and modern bedding. A lick of paint here, a new carpet there. It could all lead to the Seaview getting that extra star you've talked about. And you need a proper online booking system, one that links into all the new booking sites that keep popping up. I'll help pay for that too.'

'I'm intrigued, I have to admit. But I don't want to change the Seaview out of all recognition.'

'You won't be changing it. You'll be making the most of what you've got. Think of it as polishing a gem to make it sparkle and shine. Speaking of which, before the party tomorrow night, why not let me get you an appointment with my hairstylist, Paulo. He's fabulous. You could do with smartening up. What were you planning on wearing? Not your jeans and boots again?'

'I've got an outfit planned,' Helen teased, but said no more. She wanted to keep it a surprise. 'Look, Marie, this all sounds wonderful, and I'm grateful for your offer, but what would you want in return?'

'To become a sleeping partner. I promise I won't interfere in the business. I don't want to become a hotel landlady; that isn't the life for me. It'd ruin my nails, for a start. We'll have a contract drawn up and do it properly.'

Helen choked back a tear. 'You'd really do this for me?' she said.

'I'm doing it for both of us, and for Tom.' Marie glanced around the lounge. 'And for the Seaview. Family-run hotels like yours are a dying breed now that big groups like Traveltime Inns are spreading their tentacles into seaside resorts.'

Helen squeezed her hand. 'Then let's do it,' she said.

'And there's something else I need to tell you,' Marie said. 'The tearoom that me and Gav are opening in the Glendale . . . I've decided on a name for it, but I'd like your blessing first.'

'My blessing? Why? What's it going to be? Maz and Gav's Eatery?' Helen laughed.

Marie shook her head. 'I'd like to call it Tom's Teas.'

Chapter 44

A little later, Jimmy and the Twelvis boys began to amble downstairs, dressed in jeans and shirts, their Elvis clothes hung up in their rooms until the party the following night. As they made their way into the dining room, Helen was on the phone in the lounge, taking a call from DS Hutchinson. When she finally hung up, she followed them in to break the news she'd just been told. All eyes turned towards her as she raised her phone.

'I've just come off a call from DS Hutchinson,' she announced. 'They've charged the man from next door with Brian's murder.'

There was silence in the dining room as the information sank in.

'He's confessed to the killing,' she continued. 'On the night of your gig at the Spa, I was in the bar having a drink before the show began and I saw his wife and daughter there; they were arguing in the queue and I heard the wife say that her husband had gone to get his daughter an ice cream. It turns out that while he was out, his wife called to ask him to pick up her jacket from their room at the Vista del Mar. I remember that the night had got cold quickly after a lovely warm day. Anyway, when he came out of the hotel with the jacket, he saw Brian dressed as Elvis waiting for his cab. He guessed he was heading to the Spa and offered him a lift.'

'Did he recognise Brian as one of Twelvis?' Jimmy asked.

'I'm afraid so,' she said. 'Mr Solway knew all of you.'

'But how?'

'He auditioned to join Twelvis some years ago but was rejected for not being good enough. He'd waited over four years for that audition and he never recovered from being refused a place in the band.'

Helen looked around the dining room. 'Do any of you remember him from his audition?'

Heads were shaken and shoulders shrugged.

Ginger glanced up. 'Wait a minute . . . I recognise his name. Yes, I remember, he tried out for the band a few years ago, when we hired the community centre for a whole day of auditions. You must remember him, Jimmy. He was very intense, never cracked a smile, and he had piercing blue eyes.'

Jimmy began to slowly nod his head. 'I remember him, you're right. He couldn't hit the high notes.'

'That's the one!' Big Al said. 'I had to show him out in the end. He wouldn't leave; kept creeping back in and asking for another chance to sing.'

'Then what was he doing still on our waiting list?' Jimmy said, glaring at Big Al. 'You're in charge of auditions; why wasn't he struck off the list?'

'Sorry, Jimmy,' Big Al replied sheepishly. 'You know I kept that list up to date back when all I needed was pen and paper, but when Twelvis went online, well, you know computers aren't my thing. I got a bit muddled and names and addresses became confused.'

Helen could feel tensions rising, so she jumped in and carried on where she'd left off. 'On the day you all first arrived in Scarborough, Mr Solway overheard Brian arguing with the landlady of the hotel next door, and discovered that Brian had a secret daughter he'd not paid a penny towards. He also learned that Brian had used fake addresses to keep one step ahead of the law when his ex-wife chased him for child maintenance.' She saw Ginger drop his gaze to the table and shake his head. 'Solway tried to blackmail Brian over what he'd learned, hoping he could put the squeeze on him to persuade him to get him another audition for the band. So when he found Brian waiting for his cab on the night of the gig, it was too good an opportunity to miss.

'It seems Brian got into Solway's car of his own free will. He must have been furious at being blackmailed and wanted to try to talk some sense into the man. However, instead of driving him straight to the gig, Solway drove to Peasholm Park, hoping to have another go at demanding a second audition. The park was deserted the night of the gig,' she continued. 'It was dark in there too. And that was where it turned nasty. The pair of them ended up fighting, and as we know, Brian was strangled with his scarf and his body dumped in the lake. Then the killer drove to the gig to join his wife and child and carried on as if nothing had happened.'

She watched Sam place his arm gently around Bob's shoulders and noticed Colin stifle his tears.

'But why didn't he leave Scarborough after murdering Brian?' Kev asked. 'And why did he take Brian's shoes?'

'He stayed on because he wanted to look every inch the innocent family man, on holiday with his adoring wife and child. It also gave him more time to cover his tracks and hide the shoes, and allowed him to stay close to the scene of the crime.'

'He was hiding in plain sight,' Jimmy said.

Helen nodded. 'Exactly right. DS Hutchinson said that he visited the scene of the crime every single morning while the park was cordoned off, and quizzed the policeman guarding the entrance. The copper on duty thought he was a local, just a nosy parker wanting to know what was going on. He had no idea he was the killer.'

'That's shocking,' Ginger said.

'As for the shoes, well . . .' She looked around at the men. 'Solway was obsessed with Twelvis. At least that's what he told DS Hutchinson. He took Brian's blue suede shoes as a good-luck charm. But they ended up being far too big for his size seven feet, so he hid them under the floor in his hotel room.'

'That's just weird,' Davey said, shaking his head.

'You'd be surprised at the strange things people leave behind in their hotel rooms,' Helen said sagely.

'How did he overpower Brian when he was such a little guy?' Colin asked.

'Yeah, and he had a limp, too,' Big Al chipped in.

'He was little and wiry, quick, where Brian was overweight and slow. DS Hutchinson said they're investigating Solway's past. It seems he's been involved in violence before, and his leg injury was caused when he was stabbed in a fight.'

'What'll happen to his lady wife and his daughter?' Alan asked.

'Well, the daughter is being looked after by her aunt, who's arriving today to take care of her. She's innocent in all of this, caught up in her father's deadly obsession. As for his wife, she's demanding a solicitor before she says a word. My suspicion is that she knew something was going on. She seemed too calm this morning; she even helped him try to escape. Anyway, DS Hutchinson said he'll keep us updated.'

'Thanks, Helen,' Jimmy said. 'We appreciate all you've done.'

'We surely do,' Alan added.

Just then, a scraping noise started up at Helen's side. She knew immediately what it was, and turned to see the dumb-waiter rumbling into action, bringing up the first tray of bacon sandwiches.

Much later, Helen was downstairs in her kitchen with Jean when her phone rang. It was Jimmy.

'Me and the boys, we're not in good spirits today,' he said. 'DS Hutchinson called and invited us in for a word. I think he'll probably just repeat what he's already told you. Helen, I . . . I was hoping we could talk today, maybe have a drink together. I've got some news to share. But the boys need me, and I hope you understand.'

'Of course I do,' Helen said.

'After we've been to the police station, we're going to take a walk to the Spa and have a drink in the bar there, to say our goodbyes to Brian. DS Hutchinson said his body can be released now, so there's his funeral to think about when we get home. We're going to sing at the church, and we need to plan which Elvis song to sing.'

'Sure,' Helen said.

'And I'd like to see Jodie too. She's moving out of the hostel into her own flat.'

'That sounds promising.'

'It is,' Jimmy said. 'So what I'm saying is that I guess I might not see you before the party tomorrow night.'

Despite everything, Helen couldn't help feeling a twinge of disappointment. 'It's no problem,' she said brightly. 'I know you've got things to do and of course you must see your daughter. Anyway, I've got decorations to put up and the buffet to help with. I'll see you at the party, Jimmy. It's going to be a great night.'

There was a beat of silence before Jimmy spoke again. 'You're a good woman, Helen Dexter,' he said. And with that, he hung up.

Helen placed her phone on the table and sighed deeply.

'Everything all right, love?' Jean asked.

Helen opened her mouth to reply just as one of the security cameras flashed into action on the display screen, triggered by a motion sensor outside. It was the third camera, the one by the patio doors. On the display, she could see a figure, a man, as clear as day. Suki padded across the carpet to the doors and gave a half-hearted bark.

'Jean, look!' Helen whispered.

'Call Jimmy, get him down here,' Jean said.

'No,' Helen said firmly. 'I've got to handle this on my own.'

She looked around for a weapon, something to protect herself with. The only thing to hand was the porridge spurtle, and she grabbed it from the kitchen counter.

'Jean, get behind me in case I need backup.'

'Should I ring the police?'

'No,' Helen said firmly. 'I'm going to sort this out once and for all.'

She made her way to the doors with the spurtle in one hand. She peered through the glass and spied a man wearing an old-fashioned duffel coat fastened with wooden toggles, black wellington boots and a black bobble hat. His face was beaten and weathered. She gripped the spurtle tight, raised it in the air and yanked the door open.

'Gotcha!' she screamed.

The man stumbled backwards and fell. Helen advanced towards him, standing over him with Suki at her side.

'Don't hit me! Don't hit me!' he cried.

'What are you doing on my property?' she demanded. 'Thought you'd try to break in again, did you? Well, you can think again.'

Suki began licking the man's boots.

'Get the dog off me! Please!' he cried. 'I'm allergic!'

'Get up,' Helen ordered, keeping tight hold of the spurtle.

The man scrambled to his feet.

'What do you think you're playing at?' she asked.

'It's Fluffy,' he said.

'What is?'

'My cat. She's called Fluffy,' he explained. 'She keeps escaping, and the last time she ran away, she ended up in here, so I thought I'd come and look for her.'

Helen eyed him carefully. There was a vulnerable look about him that made her heart soften. 'You've been in here before?' she said, lowering the spurtle.

'Yes, Fluffy jumped in and I had to get her out; she couldn't climb out on her own. She's only got three legs.'

Her heart melted.

'And she's blind in one eye.'

Helen choked back a tear. 'Did you happen to break a plant pot in here when you rescued her last time?'

He hung his head. 'I'm sorry. I'll pay for it. I will.'

From the look of him, she doubted very much if he had enough money to pay for food for himself and his cat, never mind a plant pot.

'There's no need, it's all right.'

'Please, the dog . . .' the man said, backing away.

Helen grabbed hold of Suki's collar. 'Jean, take Suki inside,' she said.

Jean did as she was told, leaving Helen alone with the intruder.

'I'm really sorry,' the man cried. 'I found Fluffy at the back of your hotel one day too; she'd managed to fall in your bin. She'd crawled up some boxes and bags that were piled up at the side and—'

'That was you, by the bins?'

He nodded and Helen's heart sank. If Gav's cameras had worked properly when he'd first installed them, she wouldn't have accused Miriam of dumping rubbish. She knew she owed her neighbour an apology. She looked around the patio.

'Well, Fluffy's not here now, is she?'

'I'll go. I'm sorry,' the man said again. 'If you ever see her – and she's hard to miss – she likes a saucer of milk, and all you need do is lift her up and put her back on the street.'

And with that, he scrambled over the wall and away, calling out for his lost cat.

Chapter 45

On Saturday evening, with half an hour to go before the party, Helen and Jean took one last look at the buffet table laden with food.

'Do you think I've done enough sandwiches and sausage rolls?' Jean asked anxiously. 'There's still time to rustle up more. And what about those vol-au-vents? Does anyone eat vol-au-vents any more? I shouldn't have made them, should I? I knew I should have made more pork pies instead.'

'Jean, calm down,' Helen said. She pulled the older woman towards her and put her arm around her shoulders. 'You've done the Seaview proud.'

At five to six, Jimmy led his men into the lounge and dining room. Helen was relieved to see they all seemed to be in high spirits.

'I sure am ready to have a party, little lady,' Alan said.

'You and me both,' Helen replied.

The Seaview's doorbell rang, announcing the arrival of the first guests, and Jean took up position behind the bar, offering everyone a glass of sherry on the house. The jukebox was switched on, and Elvis tunes floated out. Sally arrived holding hands with Gracie, who was dressed in a frothy pink dress and sparkly shoes.

'Look, Auntie Helen, my shoes light up!' she cried.

Bev and Sue arrived hand in hand, followed by Rosie Hyde, the journalist from the *Scarborough Times*.

'I'm pleased you came,' Helen told her. She'd expected a frosty reception, but Rosie didn't seem in the least bit fazed. Helen directed her towards Jimmy for some quotes.

Marie and Gav arrived together in a bright yellow cab driven by one of Gav's employees.

'You look stunning, Helen,' Marie said when she stepped into the Seaview in her stiletto-heeled scarlet peep-toed sandals and tight-fitting ruby-red trouser suit.

Helen was wearing Tom's white Elvis suit with the legs turned up and the waist nipped in with a turquoise sash that she'd bought in town.

'Paulo's done wonders with your hair,' Marie added, admiring Helen's sleek and shiny short bob.

'Well, that's where you're wrong,' Helen said.

Marie gave her a puzzled look.

'Paulo was double-booked when I turned up for the appointment you made, and I didn't have time to hang around. I called Chez Margery, and fortunately one of their stylists was free, so I went there instead and had my hair done for a fraction of what Paulo would have charged.'

Marie gave a wry smile, then looked around at the men dressed as Elvis. 'Now, which one's Sam? I want to thank him for everything he's done for me with my divorce settlement.'

Helen led Marie into the dining room, where the conversation was flowing, and introduced her to Sam and his husband. Then the doorbell rang again, and she went to answer it. On the doorstep stood DS Hutchinson, and next to him, looking every inch the 1950s rock-and-roll glamour queen in an electric-blue prom dress and matching shoes, was black-haired Sandra DeVine.

'Come on in,' Helen said, holding the door wide.

'Ah, there's Ginger. I just need to have a word with him, dear,' DS Hutchinson told Sandra.

Left alone, Helen turned to her old schoolfriend.

'Did he just call you *dear*? Are you two a couple? You're not actually working here tonight, are you? Because you know what I told you about using the Seaview for that kind of thing.'

'Keep your wig on,' Sandra said. 'No, I'm not working. He's single and I like him. We've started dating; where's the harm in that?'

Helen looked at the side of Sandra's mouth, waiting for the telltale twitch, but it didn't appear. She held her hands up in mock surrender.

'It's none of my business, I know. Go through and get a drink.'

She was about to close the door when Miriam came bustling up the path. Helen pushed her shoulders back and pressed her boots into the carpet.

'Miriam? Are you coming in?'

'Well, I'm not going to get any peace next door when the music's so loud I can't hear myself think.'

'It's not that loud and you know it,' Helen said.

Miriam stepped into the lobby. 'I'm here now, so I might as well stay,' she bristled.

'Miriam, before you go in, I owe you an apology.'

'For listening in on my personal conversations through the wall?'

'No. I mean yes. I'm sorry about that, of course, but I want to apologise for accusing you of dumping rubbish in my bin. I now know it wasn't you.'

'And all that dreadful carry-on with the police and those shoes and the man who killed Brian. It's all been too much. My Durham ladies were so shocked, they left a day early to head home.'

'I'm sorry to hear you've lost business because of it,' Helen said. 'It happened to me, too.'

Miriam waved her hand dismissively. 'Ah, not all the publicity's been bad. I've just had a crime-writing group book in and they've taken all the rooms.'

Helen noticed that as Miriam was speaking, she was looking past her into the dining room, as if she was searching for someone.

'Anyway, you can make amends by doing two things for me,' she said. 'One, you can get me a whisky and Coke, on the house. And two, you can introduce me to that fella over there.'

Helen spun around and saw Twelvis youngsters Trevor and Colin talking excitedly together, behind them Alan and his brother Stuart.

'Which one?'

'The tall one with dark hair. He's just my type.'

'Alan?' Helen said. 'Well, if you're sure.'

Miriam licked her lips. 'Oh, I'm sure.'

Helen made the introductions, then asked Jean for a whisky and Coke. When she headed back to Miriam with her drink, Alan raised his eyebrows at her.

'You never told me you had such a pretty little lady friend living right next door.'

She left them to it and returned to the lounge. She found Gav deep in conversation with Jean, trying to butter her up into agreeing to make cakes and trifles to sell at Tom's Teas. She poured herself a glass of dry white wine and picked up the tiny Elvis figurine that Twelvis had presented her with. She pressed its black head, and little Elvis shimmied his plastic hips.

She mingled with her guests from the council and the charity until it was time for Twelvis to perform. The jukebox was turned off and a hush descended. Jimmy gave a short speech about their friend Brian, and then the twelve men launched into an a cappella version of one of the King's famous ballads. The sound soared up to the ceiling, filling the Seaview, and when the final note died away, there wasn't a dry eye left in the house.

They followed it with a livelier song that everyone danced to. DS Hutchinson and Sandra DeVine smooched in a corner. Bev and Sue jived, skirts flying. Gav and Sally danced with Gracie, the three of them in a circle, holding hands. Miriam downed her second whisky and Coke. And from his spot on the wall behind the bar, Tom looked out, watching the party unfold. Helen was dancing too, with a portly chap from the council, until something caught her eye and she made her excuses, saying she'd be right back. She slipped out of the Seaview unseen and headed across the road to where a figure in a black hooded anorak, black jeans and dirty plimsolls sat alone.

'It's Jodie, right?' she said, sitting down next to her.

Jodie nodded. Helen looked up at the hotel, saw the party going on inside.

'Would you like to come in? You don't need to sit out here; it's getting cold. There's plenty of food and drink.'

'Nah, I'm all right here.'

'Have you come to see your dad? Do you want me to let him know you're here?'

Jodie shrugged. 'I saw him already today.'

Helen wondered what Jodie had turned up for, if not to see Jimmy.

'Your dad says you've moved into a flat.'

Jodie stuffed her hands into her pockets. 'Yeah.'

There was silence between them for a few moments until Jodie spoke again. 'He likes you. Dad likes you.'

Helen smiled. 'I like him too.'

Jodie turned to look at her, and it was only then that Helen noticed how fragile and thin she was.

'I remember you,' Jodie said.

'Yes, we met in the rose garden,' Helen said, puzzled.

'I'm sorry I was rude to you there. I didn't know who you were and I'm not good with people I don't know. But that's not what I mean. I didn't know who you were until Dad told me later. I remember you from years ago, when I was little.' Jodie nodded towards the Seaview. 'I remember being in there.'

'You do?'

She kicked at the ground with her torn shoes. 'They're good memories. It's what brought me back to Scarborough. I feel safe here. I remember the Elvis parties, dancing with Mum and Dad.' Her face clouded over. 'That was before everything went wrong in our family. Before *I* went wrong. Before Mum left me and Dad. I remember the view out over the sea and up to the castle. I remember your husband, and dancing with him in the lounge.

He used to say I was the best dancer in the world and . . .' She stopped and took a moment before carrying on. 'Dad told me he died. I'm sorry.'

Helen bit her lip.

'I remember the dining room,' Jodie continued. 'And the biggest breakfast I ever ate. So much food, and that lady who cooked breakfast, I remember her, she was nice.'

'Jean? She still works for me. She's inside right now. Would you like to come in and say hello?'

Jodie raised her gaze to the Seaview and shook her head. 'I can't handle being close to lots of people. I get claustrophobic. Anyway, Dad's working. He'll not want to see me.'

'I think he might, you know,' Helen said softly.

'No,' Jodie said firmly. She stood and crossed her arms. 'I need to go. Will you tell him I was here?'

'Do you want me to?'

'Yes.'

'Then I will. And Jodie?'

'What?'

'If you need anything, you know, for your flat, or if you need food, just come and let me know.'

Jodie nodded. 'Yeah. Thanks.' She walked away with her shoulders bent, head down.

Helen stood for a few moments looking out over the sea, breathing in the night air. She heard footsteps and turned to see Jimmy.

'Found you,' he said. 'We're having a quick break before singing again. I looked all over but couldn't see you, and then I spotted you standing out here. Everything all right?'

'Jodie was here.'

'Jodie? My Jodie?'

'She's not a bad kid, Jimmy. I think it's great that the two of you are working things out.'

'I'm going to do all I can to help her before I have to leave.'

Helen shot him a look. 'Leave? I rather hoped you might be planning on sticking around.'

Jimmy gazed ahead, where a perfect round moon was reflected in the sea. 'You know I mentioned to you that Twelvis have been given a new singing contract?'

'Yes?'

'Well, that's what I wanted to talk to you about today. Because it's work on a cruise ship, and if I take it, it means I'll be away for six months.'

Helen's heart dropped to the floor. 'Oh.'

'Oh, indeed. I can't turn it down, Helen. It's a dream come true for someone like me. It'll be the trip of a lifetime.'

'Then you must go,' she said, choking back a tear.

'Not all of Twelvis can make it; some of the lads have got work commitments they can't get out of or family they don't want to leave. Those of us who can go, well, we won't perform as Twelvis, just an Elvis singing group.'

'I see,' Helen whispered.

'And I was wondering . . .' Jimmy hesitated. 'I wondered how you might feel about joining me. I mean, joining the group. You could be Helvis again, perform with us as a female Elvis singer. The punters will love it. You look a knockout in that suit. You'd have your own accommodation on the ship, your own space.' He turned to her and took her hands in his. 'And it means that you and I could get to know one another.'

Helen looked into his dark eyes. 'I can't, Jimmy. I can't leave the Seaview, it's my life.' She buried her face against his broad chest and breathed in the scent of his lemon spice aftershave. 'I'm sorry,' she said softly. 'I need to stay where I am.'

'Because the Seaview needs you?'

She shook her head. 'Because I need the Seaview.'

Jimmy wrapped his arms around her and brought her towards him. Under the moonlight, with the sea rippling gently, they shared a long, lingering kiss.

'Will I see you when I get back from the cruise?' he asked at last.

'You'll know where to find me,' she replied.

With their arms wrapped around each other, they walked back into the party.

One week later, Helen was sitting on the window seat at the Seaview, drinking hot coffee and gazing out at a stormy sea. Suki lay on the floor, snuggled against Tom's old woollen jumper. Jimmy had just messaged her with a picture of the cruise ship, the first one he'd ever been on.

Jean and Sally were due to return to work the following morning, when the Seaview's first guests of the season would arrive. Helen's bookings had shot up after the good publicity raised by the party, and she was looking forward to a busy season.

Outside on Windsor Terrace, Miriam walked past. Helen knocked on the window and waved. Then she raised her cup of coffee to the picture of Tom behind the bar. His photograph was no longer stuck to the wall but was now enclosed in a smart silver frame.

Just then, the Seaview's landline rang.

'Good morning, Seaview Hotel.'

'Susan Kennedy here,' a rather posh woman announced. 'I'm executive personal assistant to Richard Dawley, Esquire.'

She paused, and Helen wondered if she was supposed to know who Richard Dawley was. When she didn't respond, the woman carried on.

'Mr Dawley is seeking accommodation for the cast of his new play, who will be rehearsing in Scarborough before the production is staged in the town. Might you have rooms available at the Seaview? We'd require exclusive use. Mr Dawley's artistes can be quite . . . well, let's just say they're a little temperamental. Creative types can be quite a handful at times.'

'Just a moment, please,' Helen said, quickly opening the new booking app on her phone. She smiled to herself, feeling good about where the Seaview was going and positive about what life might bring. 'Yes, I have rooms free. What date would they like to come?'